The Jesters: Volume One

RJ Sansoucy

Contents

Dedication

This book is dedicated to my family, who helped me foster a love of literature, and the Navigation Crew of the USS Ronald Reagan for being the first to support my dream of being an author.

About the Author

Former sailor and world traveler, RJ Sansoucy brings his unique view on the world to light in an exciting and passionate way. He lives in New England after spending his early adult life travelling around the Pacific Ocean on an Aircraft Carrier.

Story 1: Opening Night

Prologue

'If you could have any superpower, what would it be?'

I know you've heard that question before. It can start incredible conversations and intelligent discussions. Flight or super strength? Invisibility or telekinesis? Would you use your powers for good, or would you screw over the world?

I've always hated that question. As if you needed superpowers to be a superhero. These days, all you see is stories about a world chock full of 'enhanced individuals', or whether or not it's right for a superhero to act without some organization backing them up.

What a load of crap.

The operative word in 'superhero' isn't 'super'. It's 'hero'. What makes someone a superhero isn't how flashy their costume is, how mighty their powers are, or how tragic their origin story is. It's about standing up to what's wrong in the world. It's about being there when the weak and helpless need you. It doesn't matter if you get around by swinging on a grappling hook, driving a nuclear-powered car, or flying with your arms outstretched. What matters is 'Are you there when they need you?'

If you're like me, you got tired of bad guys getting away with evil. You saw the good people of the world have their lives ruined by jackasses with more money and power. And if you're like me, then you decided to do something about it.

My friends don't want me to write this stuff down. I could bring a lot of heat down on our heads if our secrets got out. We're not exactly popular in official circles, but our work is done best informally. I've been cataloguing some of our adventures in an attempt to help more people like us do our job correctly. The Jesters were founded on the idea that a group of people with the desire to do right would be more effective than a single hero. And despite our success, we need more good people out there. So, read carefully and with caution, and maybe you'll learn something.

Chapter 1: Reptile Dysfunction

I was lurking behind a dark van with tinted windows, watching a crowd of people rubbernecking around a crime scene. I dialed a number on my phone and pressed it to my ear, watching the crowd. Inside the police tape, one of the FBI agents separated herself from the rest to answer her phone.

"Agent Kane." She answered.

"Good morning, Agent," I said jovially. "How's tricks?"

"Silverbolt…" she said nervously.

"In the flesh," I replied. I could see her looking around frantically.

"What do you want?" She asked.

"To tell you and your task force to back down," I said. "You won't be able to handle this one."

"And you can?" she asked with a huff.

"We hope so," I said.

"Why do you…" she started. "Wait, you know who this is."

"We have an idea," I said.

"Bullshit," Kane snapped. "If you know who the killer is, you should come forward with information."

"If I told you who killed John Decker, would you follow up and arrest them?" I asked.

"Of course." She said without hesitation.

"Then we have a problem," I said. "Because the killer would cut through your best agents and soldiers like a lawnmower."

"Silverbolt, this is an FBI matter, and it will be handled by the FBI." Agent Kane said.

"That's where you're wrong," I said, before hanging up. "This is a superhero matter."

I made my way back to our rendezvous point, a back alley where we parked the Van. It's not a real superhero vehicle like the Batmobile or the Quinjet. It's a cheap van we salvaged from a junkyard a few years ago and refitted. Sitting in the back seat with the sliding door open was Lab Rat, our techie.

Lab Rat was Batman, Ironman and Jimmy Neutron all rolled into one. Without going too deep into his origin story, Lab Rat was the unfortunate recipient of dangerous experimentation after he signed a contract with Alley Cat

Industries without reading all the fine print. He was used to test disease, bio weapons and all sorts of other horrors a person could face. Unfortunately for them, Lab Rat was a genius. He was able to escape and tell his story to a media outlet, but the company shut it down and sent hitmen after him. He survived, and swore revenge against Alley Cat. He broke into facilities and stole their technology, using it to create his arsenal of gadgets to wage his one-man war against the corporate giant. Alley Cat stocks have plummeted ever since he started. Any tech he recovers that he can't use or wouldn't help him, he sold to Alley Cat's competition for profit. His suit can withstand bullets, fire, high pressure, radiation, and electricity. It has a built-in force field, rocket boots, grappling hook, shoulder-mounted laser cannon, cloaking device, reinforced exoskeleton, scanner, hacking module, sleeping gas, and honestly who knows what else. Not to mention Lab Rat himself. All those experiments made him extremely tough. He can survive just about anything. Extreme temperatures, pressures, high altitudes, radioactive areas, disease, nothing seems to faze him. He only needs one hour of sleep, and can go weeks without food or water. He can also digest just about anything as well.

However, his greatest power has nothing to do with the chemicals in his body or the technology he stole. It's his brain. Lab Rat is probably one of the smartest people in the world, and it shows. He speaks dozens of languages, can code and decode just about anything, and memorizes everything.

"Hey, Rat," I said as I approached the van. Lab Rat didn't look up from what he was doing. His arms were outstretched in front of him, typing in the air. If you didn't know him, it would look like he was a crazy person, and for good reason. But I knew he was in the middle of something important. His helmet has a heads-up display that shows him whatever data he needs. Haptic feedback in his gloves and an augmented reality display in his helmet made it look like he was typing on a holographic computer and feel like it too. But for us mere mortals, he just looked insane.

"Silverbolt." He said dully, not taking his eyes off his screen. "What did Kane have to say?"

"She says hello, and wants to know what you're doing this Friday night," I said sarcastically.

"I doubt that, she knows I would never tell," Lab Rat said in a monotone.

"That was a joke, Lab Rat."

"Oh," he said sheepishly. For a man as brilliant as him, he was incredibly awkward at times. I think he's on the spectrum somewhere, be it autism or Asperger's, I have no idea. He once tried to speak Mandarin with a cashier who was Chinese in an attempt to impress her, only to find out that she had lived in the U.S her entire life.

"Kane told us to stay out of it, that this is an FBI matter, blah blah blah," I said.

"The usual?"

"The usual," I confirmed. I pulled the large dark hoodie off to reveal my full costume underneath.

I wore a green hood and facemask, goggles with amber tints over my eyes, a tough armored breastplate, shoulder pads, flexible armored bands over my stomach, a knee-length skirt of Kevlar plates, knee-high boots with steel toes and textured soles. I had a thick belt on with a circular belt buckle, a holster for my grappling gun and boomerang, and five quivers. Two of them hung on my belt like guns and three were on my back. My whole costume was a dark forest green, with two locks of my blonde hair hanging down out from my hood.

Lab Rat was dressed in his costume as well, all white with silver plating on his forearms, thighs, shins, feet, shoulders, chest and back. His helmet was a semitransparent half-dome over his face with backwards symbols and text flickering across it. He had his grappling hook attached to his left forearm, his sleeping gas dispenser on his right. He had a pair of taser guns holstered onto his thighs, rockets on his calves, a folding acetylene torch on the inside of his right wrist, concussive explosives and flashbangs on his belt, a mini rocket launcher on his left shoulder, mini laser cannon on his right. I have no idea what he was expecting, but he was ready for it.

"I don't know why you bother with calling her," Lab Rat said, standing up from his seat and stepping out of the van.

"It's polite. Like how medieval kings would send a herald to announce their presence and demand surrender." I said.

"How many of those heralds got killed doing that, I wonder?" Lab Rat said.

"Who knows," I said. "At least it looks like we're trying to work with them." Lab Rat looked away from his calculations to look me right in the face.

"No, it doesn't."

"Well screw you, you big silvery bastard," I replied. "You get anything on the building?"

"Of course." Lab Rat answered. "Minimal security, a few CCTV cameras, and a lazy cleaning service. Only thing we have to worry about are the FBI agents crawling all over the place."

"How armed are they?" I asked.

"Most of them aren't, and the few that are armed are only packing hand guns. Nothing I can't handle." Lab Rat said.

"You know my suit's not bulletproof, right?" I pointed out.

"Don't you have a collapsible shield on your left arm?" Lab Rat asked.

"Yeah, but I have to activate it. I don't have a force field like you do."

"Hmm. Might have to work on getting you one," he muttered.

"So, we ready to enter?" I asked. "What's the plan for entry?"

"We go in through the back and take the stairs to the crime scene," Lab Rat said. I blinked in surprise.

"That's it?" I asked. "No grappling in through the window, no crawling through vents or using disguises?"

"Nope." Lab Rat said. "We're just going to walk right in when I jam their comms."

"Well, at least we have that part figured out," I grumbled.

"Come on." Rat said, turning towards the building. "They're not prepared to deal with us right now."

"Rat, it's 52," I pointed out. "Their job is to put us behind bars." He turned to face me, and his force field, normally invisible, flashed pale blue.

"And it's our job to catch the bad guys they can't."

Chapter 2: Investigation

We crept through the back alleys towards the back of the building where the dumpsters were. Ahead of us, two members of the kitchen staff were standing around having a smoke. Behind them, the door to the building was left open.

"Shit," I said. I looked over to ask Lab Rat what we should do, but he wasn't there. I looked back towards the smoking cooks to see a faint shimmer in the air, then one of the cooks spun around like he'd been hit. The other looked around frantically, before twitching and falling unconscious. Between the now unconscious cooks, Lab Rat shimmered into existence, holstering a taser gun.

"Holy shit man," I said as I ran up to him. "That was a bit much, wasn't it?"

"They'll live." Lab Rat said casually. "I merely knocked them out."

"Yeah, but still," I said, looking down. "They might need a hospital…"

"Their supervisors will come looking for them soon." Lab Rat answered as he turned towards the open door. "They will be roused and given ice packs for their throbbing swollen heads, then they will go back to work once they feel better."

"But…"

"They weren't going to let us in." Lab Rat interrupted sternly, turning to face me. "And what I did isn't permanent, they will recover. Now please hurry inside before they get up." He turned back towards the door and entered. I sighed and followed him in.

We entered the hotel, and crept through the hallways. The floors were covered in beige carpeting that matched the equally dull cream-colored walls. Every couple of feet, a painting of some landscape was hanging. We snuck past a loud kitchen, the loud cursing of the chefs blocking out our footsteps. We reached the stairs and made our way up towards the crime scene on the 9th floor.

"Where is everyone?" I whispered to Lab Rat.

"The FBI told all residents to remain in their rooms until the scene is cleared." Lab Rat replied. I grunted in assent. As we neared the 8th floor, an FBI agent stepped out into the stairwell, texting on his phone. Without waiting for him to see us, I raised my arm up and tapped a switch on the side of my glove with my thumb. A small dart whistled out of a slot on my forearm, hitting the agent right in the jugular. He had a moment to look down at the dart sticking out of his neck, then he collapsed onto the floor.

"Nice shot," Lab Rat said.

"Thanks." I replied, glowing with pride. The darts have a small dose of a knockout fluid that can put a grown man on his ass in a second. We dragged him away from the door and I recovered my dart. After that, we continued up to the 9th. Once there, we crept into the hall.

"What was the room again?" I asked.

"907," Lab Rat replied. "This way," I followed him down a bend, right into the pair of agents standing outside the door to 907.

"What the…" One of the agents said before Lab Rat doused him with a blast of knockout gas from his wrist. I nocked an arrow to my bow and fired. The arrow struck the second agent in the right shoulder and made a sharp buzzing sound. The agent's body writhed for a second and then he collapsed. Lab Rat turned to face me. Through his frosted helmet, I could barely make out his face. But from what I could see, he looked impressed.

"Taser arrow?" he asked.

"Yep," I replied.

"Nice." He said. He flicked his arm out and a cartridge popped out from his knockout gas dispenser. He caught it in his other hand and put it in a pouch on his belt. He pulled another one out and popped it in the dispenser. As I strode over to the guard I tasered and retrieved the arrow.

"Ready?" I asked. Lab Rat responded by waving a hand over the key reader. The light turned green and Lab Rat opened the door, gallantly gesturing me in first.

"Ladies first," he said.

"Why thank you, good sir." I replied in my worst British accent, curtseying. We entered the room.

The room was a modest one-bedroom suite with two beds. To the left was a small kitchenette, with a small tray of unopened water bottles on the counter. The large windows had the shades pulled closed, leaving us in the yellow tinted interior lighting. Between the beds was the corpse.

"Jesus," I swore.

"Don't let Dragonman hear you say that." Lab Rat teased.

"Oh shut up," I replied. The body was sprawled out, the only wound was a single hole in his head, right between his eyebrows. He was dressed business casual, a white dress shirt, gray jacket and khaki pants. His shoes were off, showing his argyle clad feet. The victim had dark brown skin, a clean military fade haircut and a stylish goatee.

"John Decker," Lab Rat said, reading off a file on his HUD. "Banker and amateur guitarist. Divorced wife, no children, and loved seafood."

"Where are you getting this info?" I asked.

"Facebook. No one realizes how much info they put out on social media." Lab Rat replied. I looked up from the corpse to see the wall behind him painted red and chunky with the back of his skull all over it.

"I take it this is how he died?" I asked.

"Very good," Lab Rat said sarcastically. "What tipped you off?"

"Shut up," I snapped. "I just don't know what we're looking for."

"Good thing I'm here." Lab Rat said. I watched him turn towards the side of the bed on the far side of the room and lift up a suitcase. I peered around to see a small yellow plastic placard labeled 'A'.

"Does this count as tampering with investigation?" I asked.

"Technically, yes." Lab Rat replied. He opened the suitcase and started looking through it. I watched him with mild confusion. Just as I was about to ask him what he was looking for, he sighed in disappointment.

"What's wrong?" I asked.

"This." He answered as he pulled out a large green outfit and laid it out on the bed. It was a full-body suit made from green cloth. It looked somewhat stiff, as if it had something else sewn into it. The top of the suit had a hood with cameras attached. Around the waist was a dark green utility belt similar to the one Lab Rat wore. Lab Rat reached into the suitcase and pulled out a coiled green whip the same color as the belt and tossed it unceremoniously onto the suit.

"No way," I said, an idea forming in my head. Stenciled on the chest of the suit was a black profile of a chameleon.

"Yep," Lab Rat said.

"He was a superhero?" I asked incredulously.

"Chameleon Man," Lab Rat said. "Decker was an MIT graduate who had invented a cloaking device so sophisticated that he could blend in anywhere. Rather than profit off his invention, he took to the streets to fight crime."

"You knew him?" I asked.

"No, but he was a small timer we kept an eye on," Lab Rat said sadly. "He was considered for a position in the team."

"Oh," I said. "You mean…"

"We could have recruited him instead of you," Lab Rat finished.

"Who killed him?" I asked. "If he was a crime fighter, how did they get the drop on him?" Lab Rat pointed at the bullet hole.

"Look at that wound and tell me what you think." He said. I squatted over the corpse and looked closer at the hole.

"It's a perfect shot," I said. "Right through the brain. His face has a look of shock on it, like he was surprised."

"What else?" Lab Rat asked. I looked around the room.

"Unless someone came in and tidied up, there wasn't a fight. The killer just walked in and shot him in the face point-blank, then left." I said. I thought for a moment. "It looks like a 9mm round, standard issue for military, right?" I asked. Lab Rat see-sawed a hand. "Umm, the killer caught him by surprise. He didn't fight him, or monologue with him. Just *blam!* Dead."

"Meaning the killer didn't get emotional." Lab Rat said. "He killed Decker in cold blood then left. Not to mention one other important thing."

"What?" I asked.

"Decker isn't in his suit. He's in civilian attire."

"Meaning either he had some enemy in his civilian life, or someone guessed his secret identity," I said with growing understanding.

"I don't know about you, but I seriously doubt that a banker who goes kayaking in the summer with his friends and plays acoustic guitar for fun would have many enemies willing to kill him like this," Lab Rat said.

"You think someone put a hit on Chameleon Man?" I asked.

"Looks possible," Lab Rat said.

"And they figured out his secret identity?"

"Or the killer did." Lab Rat said. "Did all they could to figure out who this guy was, when and where he was most vulnerable, and killed him."

"Damn," I said. "That's a chilling thought."

"I know," Lab Rat said. I turned to face the wall with my hands on my hips, my mind racing.

"Wait a minute," I said, turning to look at him. "Do you think this killer could come after us?" I asked.

"Possible," Lab Rat said. He kept staring at the costume.

"What's on your mind?" I asked.

"Us leaving," he said.

"Already?" I asked. "There could be more clues here to…"

"We're leaving," Lab Rat repeated, and pointed at the door. Outside, I could hear shouting and footsteps.

"Shit," I said, readying my bow.

"Here," Lab Rat said, opening the window. "We'll grapple down and out towards the van."

"Hang on, shouldn't we take some pictures for the team to look at?"

"I've seen enough," Lab Rat said, firing his hook at a nearby balcony. I paused as I drew my grappling gun.

"So you *do* know who did this."

"I'll tell you more at the Fortress," he said. "But right now, let's focus on not getting arrested."

"Stop!" A voice called. I looked over my shoulder to see Agent Molly Kane burst into the room, pointing a gun at me. Two more agents flanked her.

"Sorry about this Kane, figured you needed a hand!" I called, tossing two small silver balls onto the carpet before leaping out the window. The balls burst into white smoke that filled the room. I could hear coughing and retching inside. I fired my hook at a different balcony than Lab Rat. It wouldn't do to get tangled this high up. I swung around the side of the building and retracted my cable. As I fell, I pulled a cord just under my arm. A pair of wings sprung out from under my quivers, turning my fall into a glide. I grabbed the handles of the wings and steered towards the Van. I could hear shouting and gunshots from the other side of the building, meaning that Lab Rat had surprisingly taken all the heat for me.

And they say chivalry is dead.

Chapter 3: The Jesters

The Fortress of Destiny isn't so much a 'fortress' as it is a really bad joke. It's a humble two-story house in the middle of the woods somewhere in the North. That's all I'm saying, because that's all I know. I grew up in the woods and even I can't tell what state we live in.

The house is painted baby blue and has a two-car garage on the side. The front port has exposed brick around it, and the lawn is overgrown. In the back is a small hill that's great for sledding in the winter. The long driveway is seldom used, as we normally teleport the Van anywhere we wanted to go. The only time we use it is to pick up Amazon packages that get dropped off at the mailbox.

By the time we returned home, the Jesters had already gathered in the Garage for a meeting. The Justice League had the Hall of Justice, with marble tables and overhead lights that didn't flicker if you slammed the door. The Avengers had Stark Tower, with clean, unbroken windows looking at the New York Skyline.

The Jesters have a broken air hockey table with mismatched chairs around it that we got at a yard sale two years ago sitting in a dusty garage that reeks of motor oil and energy drinks. The yellowed lights, once clean white, would flicker at the slightest disturbance. Dragonman and I once had a shouting match, trying to make them turn off until Lab Rat made us stop. The whole house creaks and groans in storms, and the walls have so little insulation that you can hear everything, like Lab Rat playing video games at three in the morning, Dragonman watching a black and white film, or Blue Fox chatting with her friends in rapid-fire Japanese because it's lunchtime in Tokyo.

Or when Professor Magic brings his girlfriend over to spend the night. The lungs on that woman, I swear.

Still, despite all its faults, I love the place. It has character, and you can tell there's love in the walls. Along with roaches, spiders and maybe a ghost, but still.

I was sitting in the garage with the rest of the team. They had ordered pizza, and in true Jester fashion, it was a mess. I had my face stuffed with cheesy, greasy delight as Lab Rat and I gave our report. I had my hood, goggles and mask down, letting my shoulder-length blonde hair loose. I'm a Norwegian blonde, with pale skin and pale blue eyes. Mom said I looked like an angel, Dad said I looked like Legolas. Well, back when they still spoke to me.

On my left was Lab Rat, who had taken off his helmet so he could eat. He had dark brown skin and was shaved bald, and he waxed his scalp so it would shine. He had a short chinstrap beard and a small gap in his front teeth. He was surprisingly handsome, all things considered. His dark skin helped hide all the scars from incisions and surgeries performed on him, which is a small blessing.

To my right was Blue Fox, the Fox Witch of the East. She was a gorgeous living rendition of a classic Japanese geisha. She had porcelain white skin, dark black hair down to her hips, cherry red lips, sunset purple eye shadow, sharp vulpine features, and eyes so dark they were almost black. She wasn't always like this. She used to be a scrawny nerdy college girl trying to get a degree in medicine. Her boyfriend was a yakuza thug who guilted her into stitching him and his boys back up after a fight. The rival gang showed up for round 2, and Blue Fox took the worst of it. That would have been the end of her, but she was rescued by a spirit fox. The fox offered her a deal. She would repair the damage done to her and help her get revenge in return for giving her body over to the spirit. She was desperate, and agreed. The fox possessed her and made her do horrible things. While the fox made her beautiful, it also had her kill people. The two eventually agreed to work together for the greater good. The Fox taught her all sorts of magic. Illusions, potion-making, weather control, even mild mind control. Plus, Blue Fox had a few skills of her own. She's a brilliant doctor, and had some ninja moves she never explained where she learned them from.

Across from her was Dragonman. Dragonman was born in 18th century Italy as the result of a madman working for the Vatican to make a supernatural supersoldier. Dubbed a 'gargoyle', he was the mix of a dragon, troll, vampire, goblin and werewolf. He was seven and a half feet tall with cement gray skin, thick glossy black hair, boar-like tusks, completely blue eyes with slitted pupils, large batlike ears, a pair of black horns on his head, a long beard braided Viking style, and blue markings all over his body. His body is covered with muscle, and not the glamorous body builder kind either, but tough functional muscle with a bit of fat. I've seen men built like him before, and they are deceptively fast. The craziest thing about him is that he's eerily quiet, and you somehow forget he's even there. Apparently, it's a result of his goblin heritage, but I've seen him brazenly walk past guards and get ignored. He can also regenerate, his senses are way stronger than a regular human's is, and he's incredibly strong.

Between them was Thundergirl. Like Dragonman, she was a super soldier as well. She had joined up with a cult determined to rid the world of evil, but she was enhanced *before* they explained that their method of fighting evil involved wholesale murder. She dipped out and raised some hell on the way out. She's faster, stronger and tougher than any human. Her bones are as tough as titanium, and her skin as tough as steel. She has hawk-like vision, reflexes fast enough to snatch a bullet from the air, and a whole host of psychic powers. I'm talking telekinesis, levitation, and telepathy. While Blue Fox has engineered beauty, all sharp edges and supermodel height, Thundergirl had natural good looks. She had caramel colored skin that could have come from any part of the world, jet black hair that hung around her head like a lion's mane, violet eyes, a great smile and killer dimples.

Sitting at the head of the table was Professor Magic, our leader. We call him that because he hates it, but the Jesters were his idea to begin with. Professor Magic is probably the most well-known superhero of our time. Well, the most well-known that isn't a comic book character. You know the look. Long white beard, close-cropped hair, hawk-like nose, and brilliant green eyes. But what if I told you that was an illusion? That the Professor Magic you see on the news today isn't the same as the one your parents knew?

I'll let you in on a secret. Remember when everyone thought Professor Magic died a few years back? He really did die. But his powers passed on to another person. See, there's only Seven real Wizards at a time. When one dies, their powers, memories and experiences get passed on to a like-minded individual. The new Professor Magic simply used a metamorph spell to make himself look like the old wizard to protect his identity. Smart, right?

Everyone else had clearly been enjoying some off time. Dragonman was dressed in sweatpants and an extra-large Boston Bruins jersey, Thundergirl was wearing a black Superman tee and yoga pants, Blue Fox in a loose shirt, sports bra and running shorts. The Professor was in jeans and a hoodie, and didn't have his old man face on. He has curly brown hair tied in a man bun, clean shaven face, and mismatched eyes. His right one blue, the left green.

"You're sure it was him?" Dragonman rumbled. His voice is so deep, you feel it more than you hear it.

"Positive," Lab Rat replied. "No one else is that good."

"Bit much though, innit?" Professor Magic asked. He grew up in the slums of London, and had a Cockney accent.

"What do you mean?" I asked.

"There are other assassins out there. Killin' ain't that complicated," Professor Magic replied.

"You weren't there," Lab Rat argued. "This wasn't just accurate. It was surgical."

"I believe him," Thundergirl chimed in. She was lounging in mid-air, flaunting her levitation powers (the bitch) and splashing hot sauce into a bag of Doritos. "I don't want to, but I believe him."

"I'm sorry, but am I the only one who doesn't know who we're talking about?" I asked.

"The Nocturnal," Lab Rat said. The whole room got quiet.

"Oh," I said. "Him."

The Nocturnal is probably the Jesters' biggest skeleton in their closet. He was a founding member of the team, along with Dragonman and Professor Magic. The Nocturnal was like a combination of Spawn and Robocop. From what I heard, he was a black ops agent who was cybernetically rebuilt after getting blown up. He was the best in the business, and wanted more. He turned on his creators and went rogue. He was a contract killer for a bit, before joining the Jesters. He stuck around for a while, but was way too willing to kill. The team clashed with that mentality for a long time before he got voted off the island. I'm the only member who hasn't met him.

"There's no proof it was him," Dragonman said finally.

"That alone can be proof it was," Lab Rat said.

"Come again?" Professor Magic asked. Lab Rat sighed.

"He's a cyborg. He doesn't leave fingerprints, barely has any DNA, and can fire a perfect shot. He always killed in cold blood without causing pain," Lab Rat said. "It was his idea of mercy."

"Twisted bastard," Thundergirl said idly through a mouthful of Doritos.

"Why did he kill Chameleon Man?" I asked. "If he was a Jester, he should have been after serial killers, rapists and such, right?"

"He was probably paid to," Thundergirl said. "He had this weird sense of honor, doing whatever job came his way. He didn't care about fighting evil, he cared about getting paid."

"I thought he helped form the team. Didn't he save Lab Rat in South America?" I asked. Lab Rat winced at that.

"He did, but he wasn't as idealist as the rest of us," Professor Magic explained. "He never went on patrol; he just took commissions. The only jobs he didn't get paid for were group missions."

"The question we should be asking is this: Who paid the Nocturnal to nix Chameleon Man?" Thundergirl asked, popping another chip into her mouth.

"Assuming it was Nocturnal," Professor Magic said.

"Even if it wasn't, it was still a hit," Thundergirl said. "How many enemies did Decker have? He mostly dealt with small time criminals. Purse snatchers, muggers, car thieves. I've never heard of him going after gangs or the mafia."

"Lab Rat, what do we know about John Decker?" Professor Magic asked. Lab Rat put his helmet back on and typed in the air for a bit.

"Not much. Chameleon Man wasn't a well-known superhero, but had the makings of being a proper vigilante. Has a small fan club behind him in Baltimore, a couple reptile enthusiasts…" Lab Rat said, trailing off as he searched.

"Who was the last bad guy he caught?" Thundergirl asked.

"Let's see," Lab Rat said, typing something else. "Some pedophile in Baltimore. Which doesn't explain why he was in Miami."

"Feds release anything yet?" Dragonman asked.

"Just did. Apparently, our intervention shed some light on Decker's superhero life," Lab Rat said.

"That should help, right?" I asked, nudging Blue Fox. She said nothing. I looked over to see her reaction and Holy Shit, did she look pissed. Her dark eyes were glaring daggers down at her hands, which were clenched around the edge of the hockey table, her wine-colored nails digging into the plastic rink, leaving gouges.

"Blue?" I asked nervously. "You okay?"

"Leave her alone, Silver," Professor Magic said. "She just gets a little upset whenever Nocturnal gets mentioned."

"Why?" I asked.

"Silver. Drop it," Dragonman growled.

"It's fine," Blue Fox finally said. She had a thick Japanese accent. "She deserves to know."

"Know what?" I asked, taking a sip of my drink.

"We slept together a couple times," Blue Fox admitted. I coughed on my drink, spraying Mountain Dew across the table. Dragonman swore loudly in Italian and swatted at his shirt. Lab Rat clapped me on the back.

"You what?" I asked, my eyes watering.

"We weren't a couple or anything," She said, as if I hadn't doused the table in soda. "We just fooled around a bit. When he left, he asked me to come with him. We argued about it, and we both ended up saying the wrong things to each other."

"Oh," I said. I coughed some more and pushed Lab Rat's arm away. "Good to know."

"Right." Professor Magic said sheepishly. "Back to business. What was Chameleon Man doing in Miami? I thought he operated in Baltimore."

"Good question. It's kinda hard to track someone whose whole gimmick was not being seen," Lab Rat said. He typed some more. "Hang on," he said gravely.

"What's up?" Thundergirl asked.

"There's been another murder," he said. He pulled out his phone, pulled up his news app and selected a video.

"This just in," the anchorwoman announced. "The body of Tobias White has been found on Daytona Beach. The victim was killed by a bullet wound to the head; police say he died instantly. Tobias White was known for his work at Grace Hospital in Chicago, and moonlighted as the vigilante Screaming Eagle, considered by many to be a 'superhero', similar to Stinger, Blue Jacket, the late Chameleon Man, and the Jesters. Due to the nature of the victim, the FBI's Task Force 52 has been dispatched…" Lab Rat paused the video. No one said a word for a good while.

"Damn," Thundergirl said finally. "Screaming Eagle…"

"You knew him?" I asked.

"Yeah. He was at the reactor meltdown in Iowa 10 years ago. The radiation mutated him, giving him a sonic scream. He made his own wingsuit, powered by his voice to fly and fight crime," Thundergirl said. "Had this whole patriotic theme to his costume too."

"I'm sorry," I said. She looked down at her hands.

"He was a vet who was dealt a bad hand. Still wanted to serve, still wanted to fight. He said that fighting crime and saving lives was the best way to keep the screaming out of his head," Thundergirl said. She wiped an eye, "He had a wife and a baby girl."

"Another superhero," Lab Rat said. "Killed the same way. In Florida."

"You think Nocturnal is nixing superheroes?" I asked.

"Looks like it," Lab Rat said.

"We can't know for sure until we see the body," Professor Magic said. "But the timing is way too close to be isolated events. If anyone could get close to them, it would be the Nocturnal."

"Shit," I said. "You think he's going to come after us?"

"Not likely," Dragonman said. "We operate as a group. We're the only superhero team in the world. These are small timers. Lone heroes who stepped up on their own."

"If the Nocturnal is killing superheroes, we need to figure out who his next target is," Blue Fox said. "Who else is out there?"

"Not a lot," Lab Rat said. "There's Stinger, the bee-themed hero in L.A, Blue Jacket, the Navy's supersoldier, and Captain Chernobyl."

"That asshole," Thundergirl muttered.

"Who do you think he's after next?" I asked.

"Good question," Professor Magic replied, rubbing the bridge of his nose. "Where's Blue Jacket stationed?"

"Yokosuka, Japan," Lab Rat said. "Stinger has always worked out of L.A, and Captain Chernobyl was last seen in Pripyat, Ukraine."

"Alright. We'll split this up into teams of two. Lab Rat, you go after the Captain. His radiation won't affect you. I'll go with you, after I brew the right potions. Dragonman and Thundergirl, you two head to L.A and find Stinger. Silverbolt and Blue Fox go to Japan," Professor Magic said.

"Why am I going to Japan?" I asked. "Dragonman speaks Japanese."

"Because you have the most experience breaking into military bases," Professor Magic said. "Besides, I hear Blue Jacket is a big time Silverbolt fan."

"Seriously?" I said. "I didn't think I had any fans."

"Kid, you ride with us now. We all have fan clubs," Thundergirl said with a laugh. I thought it was a bit much for Thundergirl to be calling me 'kid' as I am a few years older than her. None of us knew the exact ages of each other, but I knew she was too young to drink. Legally, that is.

"Any other questions?" Professor Magic asked. No one said a word. "Alright then. Move out!"

Chapter 4: Yokosuka

"Never been to Japan before," I said, looking around the city. Yokosuka wasn't a very large city, only a handful of areas were densely populated.

"Have you not been outside of America?" Blue Fox asked me.

"Well, I went to Niflheim once when Professor Magic mucked up a portal."

"That doesn't count."

"Then no, I haven't." I replied. Blue Fox sighed and shook her head. We strode down the street towards the Navy base. It's street entrance was guarded with a large white gate and a ramp leading up to a pedestrian entrance.

Blue Fox and I were dressed for action. I was in my usual get-up, quivers and all, while Blue Fox was in full fox-witch mode. She wore a skintight blue leotard with the chest part designed like the front of a kimono. Over that, she wore a short blue leather jacket with a high collar. The bottom barely reached below her ribcage and had rows of kanji written on the sleeves. She wore blue fingerless gloves that reached her elbows, thigh-high boots that loosely resembled samurai greaves, and had a small sword hanging from her hips. Her body had also changed. Her dark hair was now reddish-orange like the pelt of a fox, and her ears now resembled a fox's and poked out the side of her head, giving her an elfish appearance. Behind her she had nine fox tails that waved back and forth, like a giant orange peacock. Over her eyes she wore a blue chevron-shaped mask with white lens over her eyeballs, like a comic book character. She carried a sword on her hips and a large bag slung over her shoulder.

Knowing Blue Fox, I had no idea what she was actually wearing. Her entire outfit could be an illusion. She could be out here fully nude, no one would know and anyone who knows her wouldn't put it past her. Sharing a body with a spirit fox can have some undesirable side effects.

Blue Fox and I made our way up the ramp and into the base. We reached a small guard shack where a Japanese man was standing. He held out a small handheld scanner and smiled at us, then he realized who we were. Before he could radio for help, Blue Fox grabbed him by the collar and forcefully pulled him towards her. She pressed her lips to his and held it there. The man's eyes widened in shock, then slowly glazed over his body slumped. I looked away, blushing under my mask. Blue Fox held it there long enough to be awkward, then dropped the guard. He staggered back as if he were drunk, then slumped to the ground. Blue Fox gagged and spat.

"Ugh," she said. "Nasty."

"What was?"

"His breath," Blue Fox said, her nose wrinkling in disgust. And this, kids, is why you don't go around kissing random people you just met.

"He gonna be okay?" I asked, pointing at the crumpled guard.

"He'll be fine. I just took some of his life force," she said with a shrug. "You have a mint at all?"

"Sorry, left them in my other costume," I said sarcastically. "Maybe next time you don't stick your tongue all the way down to his stomach."

"Ha ha," Blue Fox said, rolling her eyes. We walked further down the sidewalk into the base. As we got further in, a small vehicle pulled up next to us.

"Excuse me," a voice called. The window was rolled down and a heavily armed guard leaned his head out.

"**Hey there, sailor**," Blue Fox said, smiling and brushing her hair back seductively. I could feel the magic kicking in, making the back of my neck tingle and my body squirm. I've been around Blue Fox long enough to figure out that when my body starts, ah, 'acting up', it's usually her fault. I was only feeling the side effects, and this poor sap was getting the full blast.

"Umm, hi," he said, his voice losing all bravado as his face turned red. "I.. umm…"

"Could you help me?" Blue Fox asked, still smiling and fidgeting with her hair. She leaned forward and gave the guard a small peek at her chest.

"Uhh, yeah sure," the guard said, a little too fast. "What did you need?"

"I was hoping a big strong man like you could help me find someone," Blue Fox said. I rolled my eyes. She was laying it on pretty thick, as if someone as good looking as her hardly needed magic to get a guy to help her.

"Simmons, what the fuck?" I heard someone say. The driver's side door opened up and a short girl in a matching uniform got out of the car to approach Blue Fox. "Listen here, I don't know what you did…"

"Shhhhh…" Blue Fox said, placing a hand on the girl's forehead, pushing her hat back. Her eyes rolled to the back of her head and she slumped backwards. I ran forward to catch her before she hit the pavement.

"What did you…" the guy asked.

"It's okay, baby," Blue Fox said, reaching up to stroke his ear. I saw his eyes flutter a bit when she did that. **"We just need to find Blue Jacket. If you help us, I would be sooo grateful."**

"Oh, yeah," the guy said sleepily. "He's down at the NEX doing a meet and greet."

"Could you give us a ride there?" Blue Fox asked. She leaned in further and gave him a small peck on the lips. **"If you do, I might give you a ride later."**

"Oh my God…" I said, struggling to drag the girl into a hiding place behind the bushes. She was snoring like a belt sander. Simmons opened the door so fast he almost hit Blue. She only giggled and hopped in. I jogged over to get in before he pulled away, seeing how he forgot I existed. I squeezed in the back and was barely sitting down when he pulled off. Blue was leaning on his shoulder and was lazily tracing her fingernails up and down his thigh.

"What did you do to him?" I asked, keeping my voice down to not break the spell.

"Just made him focus more on his hormones and libido more than his reasoning. It's not that hard with some guys. Especially the military."

"And the girl?"

"Had her brain focus more on how tired she was more than how suspicious we were."

"How did you know she was tired?" I asked.

"The American military runs these poor *baka* ragged. They're always tired," Blue Fox replied. We were quiet for a bit.

"Think the Nocturnal is here?" I asked, breaking the silence

"Perhaps," Blue Fox replied, pausing to nibble on the guard's ear. "If Blue Jacket is here, he might be."

"Yeah, who is the Blue Jacket?" I asked.

"He's sort of an aquatic Iron Man," Blue Fox replied. "The American Navy built the armor back in the Second World War, during the war with Japan. They needed someone to infiltrate the Japanese bases and sabotage their ships. Once the old Blue Jacket retires or quits, your Navy selects a new champion to don the suit."

"Huh. What kind of features does the armor have?" I asked.

"Obviously it lets you breathe underwater, it had shoulder-mounted cannons, mini drones deployed off the back, a collapsible trident, a pair of grappling hooks shaped like anchors, underwater thrusters, radar and sonar sensors, and a wrist-mounted machine gun," Blue Fox said.

"Wow," I said. "Impressive."

"It is. Almost every Blue Jacket is American Special Forces," Blue Fox replied.

"Like Navy SEALs?" I asked.

"Maybe. I don't know a whole lot about the American Military," Blue Fox admitted. As we drove deeper into the base, there was an explosion further ahead, followed by the drone of an alarm.

"Think we're going to learn a bit more about them," I said. "Let's go!"

Blue Fox had the guard floor it towards the explosion, dashing past gaping pedestrians and armed guards. We passed by what looked like barracks and a McDonalds (How American) and reached a large building with a glowing sign saying NEX. In the parking lot in front it a super fight was going down.

To the left was a large man dressed in white power armor. He had one of those white sailor hats you see in cartoons on his head, a green LED on his right shoulder, a red one on his left, and a fancy blue admiral's jacket hanging off his shoulders like a cape. He was holding a large golden trident in one hand as he circled his opponent, his feet thudding with every step.

Blue Jacket's opponent was dressed in all black. Black Kevlar, trench coat, and body armor. His legs and hands looked mechanical, but it was hard to tell. I've never seen a shade so dark before, like a living shadow was facing off against robot Pop-Eye. The only color on him was a white crescent moon on his chest and white fang decals on his mask, along with white eyes. In his hands were a pair of black SMGs. Surrounding the two fighters were a loose ring of sailors and marines armed with assault rifles and shotguns, taking cover behind whatever they could. The parking lot was a wreck of craters and busted cars.

"C'mon Blue, don't make this difficult," The dark figure said coyly, his voice buzzing slightly.

"You're trying to kill me!" Blue Jacket protested, gripping his trident with both hands.

"You're a supersoldier. This really shouldn't bother you," Nocturnal said. "I told you it wasn't personal," Blue Jacket replied by charging the assassin with a cry, raising his trident to impale him. Nocturnal turned out of the way at the last minute and fired a volley of bullets at point blank range.

Blue Jacket cried out as he turned to stab again. Nocturnal dodged again and dropped a small black object from his coat onto the ground.

"Grenade!" one of the guards cried out. Everyone ducked, except Nocturnal and Blue Jacket. Nocturnal leaped out of the way, a good thirty feet back. Blue Jacket didn't get a chance. The grenade went off, shredding his iconic jacket and launching him forward onto his face. Nocturnal leapt back to his original position as if nothing happened. He bent to pick up Blue Jacket's fallen trident and raised it up to spear the super-sailor.

"Any last words, Cap'n?" Nocturnal asked.

"NOCTURNAL!" Blue Fox cried out, drawing her sword. The assassin looked up sharply, his movement way too rigid to be human.

"Blue Fox!" He said warmly. "What a pleasant surprise! You here visiting family?"

"Let him go, *baka*," Blue Fox said, pointing her sword at him. "I won't ask again."

"I have a better idea," Nocturnal said, raising the trident slightly. I quickly nocked an arrow, drew the bow and fired right at the trident as he brought it down, knocking it away from the fallen Blue Jacket. The trident sank into the ground harmlessly. Nocturnal looked down at the silver arrow slowly rolling across the pavement.

"Nice shot. Is that Silverbolt?" He asked, looking up at me. "Holy shit! It really is her!" He laughed. "Is she supposed to be my replacement?"

"Trust me pal, I'm an upgrade," I called back. Nocturnal laughed, a deep belly laugh.

"Oh, I *like* this one!" he said, still chuckling. Blue Fox growled at him, her ears flattening against the side of her head.

"Oh relax, Blue! Is that any way to treat an old friend? Granted, we used to be a bit closer than just friends..." Nocturnal said. Blue Fox yelped like, well, a fox and charged Nocturnal, swinging her sword at his neck. Nocturnal blocked with an upraised arm. Sparks few as Blue Fox pressed on him, her sword a silvery blur against Nocturnal's arms. I tried to aim a shot at him, but the two were moving too fast. I muttered a curse and lowered my bow. I pressed a finger to the communicator in my ear to contact the rest of the team.

"Calling all Jesters! This is Silverbolt! We have the Nocturnal in Japan! Repeat! All Jesters come to Japan!" I called. I heard a large clang and looked back up to the fight. Blue Fox and Nocturnal had moved further apart. Blue Fox's sword was lowered and she was panting. Nocturnal idly looked down at the scratches on his forearms.

"Oh God damn it, babe," he said. "Look what you did to my paint job! You know how expensive this color is?" I took the chance to fire an arrow at him. Without even looking, his arm shot up to catch it midair. Dammit.

"I'm serious. They don't make paint this dark cheaply," Blue Fox snarled at him, and raised her left hand up and made a sign with her palm facing forward and her ring finger down. Below us, the ground rippled like something was moving below us. The ground shook, and erupted beneath Nocturnal. He jumped out of the way as an enormous white snake burst from the ground. Its eyes were completely red as it glared down at Nocturnal. It hissed once, then struck down at the assassin like a lightning bolt. There was a gunshot and Blue Fox yelped in pain, clutching her shoulder. Suddenly, the snake vanished. The ground was exactly the same from before the snake appeared. Almost as if…

"… There was no snake," I muttered to myself in awe.

"Sometimes I forget how good you are at those," Nocturnal said. "You had me for a second. But I know you too well. You don't kill anymore, and you wouldn't let me get eaten by a giant snake." Blue Fox slumped down against a broken overturned car, wincing in pain. Red seeped from her shoulder, bright red against her blue costume. She gasped in pain and tried to stem the bleeding. She dropped her sword and started digging around inside her bag. Nocturnal raised a gun and leveled it at her head.

"Sorry it has to end this way, beautiful."

"No!" I yelled, shooting another arrow at him, this one with a little surprise in the arrowhead. As soon as the arrow left my bow, the Nocturnal's form blurred, and the arrow flew away from him, spinning around before exploding into pink foam that quickly hardened, falling to the pavement like a boulder. I stared in confusion before I realized he had spun around completely and knocked the arrow away with his gun.

"You've gotta be kidding me," I growled. The cyborg wasn't even looking at me or Blue Fox anymore. His eyes were fixated on the sky, where a golden circle appeared. Inside, sunlight streamed out into the dusk. Two figures dropped out and landed on either side of Nocturnal.

Landing between Nocturnal and Blue Fox was Dragonman, dressed in his own black trench coat, silver gauntlets, armored boots and black and white camo pants. He snarled, smoke curling from his fanged mouth. On the other side of Nocturnal was Thundergirl.

Thundergirl has got to have the most impressive set of armor in the world. She wears a dark purple body suit decorated with tiny gleaming white stars like the night sky, a golden breastplate, gauntlets, lioness shaped pauldrons, and golden thigh-high boots. Her cape was an iridescent show of light that shimmered as it moved, shifting in rainbow colors. Her helmet was golden to match her armor, a half mask decorated with wings with purple lenses. Her hair was tied into dreads and hung out the back of the helmet in a ponytail.

The Nocturnal was clearly a black belt in something, because Thundergirl couldn't land a hit on him. She swung and swung hard; you could hear it from ten feet away. Finally, he got a grip around her wrist and flipped her over his head and slammed her into the pavement hard enough to shatter it. It took him 5 seconds to do that.

"Thundergirl. So happy to see you too. You still drawing that web comic? I've been *dying* for the next chapter," Nocturnal teased. Dragonman roared and dove at him. Dragonman swung his clawed hands at him, forcing the cyborg away from the downed Thundergirl. Nocturnal leaped over Dragonman with a flip worthy of an Olympic gymnast and drew a pistol. Before he could shoot, Dragonman flung a silver thread at him. It wrapped around Nocturnal's gun and fingers. Dragonman tugged hard, crushing the weapon and drawing a groan from Nocturnal's fingers.

"Shit!" Nocturnal said, tugging in vain at the thread.

"End of the line, Nocturnal," Dragonman snarled. He started reeling the thin line in, dragging the assassin in. "You have a lot to answer for," Nocturnal responded by lifting his other arm and blasting a bluish mist at Dragonman. He cried out in pain and staggered back. Frost was forming on his armor as he swatted the icy mist away. Nocturnal managed to wrench the silver thread off of his hand. He flexed his fingers to see if they still worked, then looked up at the gargoyle.

"Dragonman! Tell me, old man, how long did it take the World's Greatest Tracker to find me?" Nocturnal asked. Dragonman responded by blasting the cybernetic dickhead with a column of fire from his mouth. I thought that was the end of the Nocturnal, but then I heard a loud wet smack and the flames died as Dragonman toppled to the side, clutching his cheek.

"Good effort. Unfortunately, I had some recent upgrades that help with heat regulation and flame resistance. It's this really cool chemical coating with..." Nocturnal started before Dragonman swung his hand up. Nocturnal's hand blurred up and caught his hand, the claws inches away from his throat.

"… a very high flash point," Nocturnal finished without missing a beat. "Now that was very rude. Interrupting me in the middle of a cool science fact," Dragonman tried to pull his hand back, but Nocturnal held tight, idly swatting another of my arrows away.

"Dammit!" I shouted. Nocturnal ignored me again as he pulled a garotte from his jacket and wrapped it around Dragonman's neck and started to choke the hunter out. Thundergirl groaned as she raised her head from the crater it made. She glared at the assassin as she raised her hand. Blue light streamed from her palm towards the cyborg, making smoke rise from Nocturnal's vest from where it hit. He looked down to see it, then flipped over Dragonman and slammed him into Thundergirl with a grunt of effort. There was a loud crunch as the two heroes collided.

"Anyone else?" Nocturnal asked, raising his hands up in a challenge. Suddenly, something hit Nocturnal right in the stomach, making him suck wind. Lab Rat suddenly materialized right in front of the Nocturnal, his fist wrist deep in Nocturnal's diaphragm.

"Hello, bitch," Lab Rat said. "Got enough for another?"

"Lab Rat," Nocturnal wheezed. "Good to see you too." He moved back and raised his fists into a fighting stance, breathing deeply. Lab Rat did as well. The two leapt towards each other and started trading punches. Unlike Thundergirl and Dragonman, Lab Rat actually got a couple hits in, knocking Nocturnal around a bit.

"Not bad, Ratty!" Nocturnal said. "You've been practicing."

"You can't beat me," Lab Rat said. "I know all your moves and programmed them into the suit. You have nothing that I can't see coming a mile away."

"Really?" Nocturnal said, ducking a right hook. "Does it know this one?" He asked as he spun Lab Rat around and yanked a cable out the back of his helmet. Lab Rat slowed to a stop, his suit locking up.

"Oh, son of a bitch," Lab Rat said, frozen in place.

"Yeah, not so tough now, you little nerd," Nocturnal said, gently nudging Lab Rat off balance and onto the ground. "All that's left is…"

"**PYROS MAXI-**" a voice thundered. Nocturnal spun around and fired something black and thin from his arm. The black thing wrapped itself around Professor Magic's mouth, stifling the spell before it could be cast. The force of it knocked the Wizard flat on his ass, his staff clattering to the ground. He was dressed in all black with a black wizard hat and a white pentacle on his chest and a black cape. His gloves and boots were black with red trim. He had his old man face on with a long white beard and a monocle over his right eye.

"Damn, that was close!" Nocturnal said. "You almost got me with that spell!"

"Mmmf!" Professor Magic cried out, clawing desperately at the metal gag.

"You like it?" Nocturnal asked. "Whipped it up myself in case I needed to silence a Wizard. Who would have thought the most powerful man in the world could be laid low by covering his mouth?" He cracked his knuckles (I still don't get that, they're mechanical!) and started walking towards the Professor.

"This is for turning my favorite gun into a hedgehog, you fraud," he said venomously. "I'm going to enjoy this." He kicked Professor Magic in the ribs, making him fold up like a lawn chair. "And there's no one here who can stop me."

"You still have me to deal with, murderer!" I cried out, firing another arrow at the cyborg assassin. He caught it again without even looking up from kicking the Wizard.

"Okay, can you stop that?" he said, finally looking up at me. "We both know you can't hit me."

"Yeah, but I can try!" I said. Nocturnal sighed, and kicked Professor Magic again before stalking over towards me.

"Look kid, I respect your energy. Truly I do," He said. "But you're nothing. You're just a small-time vigilante the Jesters hired because they needed a marksman. You don't belong here. You can't fly, turn invisible, lift a car, or shoot lasers. You just have a handful of arrows that do party tricks. That's it. Do you honestly think you can beat me?" I think it's worth noting I didn't stop shooting arrows at him for the entirety of that speech. He just kept knocking them out of the air. I reached back for another arrow when I felt something. It was an arrow, but heavier than the others. I forgot about this one. It was an experimental one, and a failure at that. I didn't realize I had packed it. I pulled it out of the quiver and nocked it. Sure, it failed its trial run, but maybe it would work this time. I drew the arrow back and released. Nocturnal didn't get a chance to deflect it, because it flew maybe six feet before hitting the ground and impaling itself there. He looked down and stared at it before looking up at me.

"Are you kidding me?" He asked with a laugh. "What was that? A lead arrow?"

"Nope. That was the Tesla Arrow," I replied, hitting a switch on the handle of my bow. A loud popping filled the air as lightning arced from the arrow and into the Nocturnal, the bolt flickering like the machines in Dr. Frankenstein's laboratory. Nocturnal let out a loud, high-pitched scream, his body convulsing like a rag doll in an earthquake, before collapsing onto the ground as the arrow ran out of juice.

"Told you someone was still around to stop you," I said smugly. I heard the click of weapons as the remaining marines closed in around me. I turned to see Blue Jacket limp over to me.

"Silverbolt," he said firmly. I stared up at him nervously, and he held out a hand.

"It's an honor to meet you," he said warmly.

"Uhh, you too," I replied. He was shaking my whole arm, and it took some effort to stay stable.

"You really saved my bacon back there," he said. "Are you alright?"

"I'm fine," I replied. I looked over to see Thundergirl had recovered enough to help Blue Fox with her shoulder. Lab Rat was thawing out Dragonman. I relaxed. Nocturnal had soundly beaten them all, but everyone was okay.

"Sir!" one of the guards called. He had a gun trained on the Nocturnal's unconscious form. "What should we do with this one?" Blue Jacket looked down at me, then at the guard.

"We have civilians and sailors injured from his entrance," Blue Jacket said in a commanding voice. "Focus your efforts on helping them."

"But sir, shouldn't we inform the FBI about the Jesters?" another one asked.

"I'll handle them," Blue Jacket replied. "Go help our brothers and sisters." I looked over to see Professor Magic managed to wrench the mouth covering off and start securing the Nocturnal.

"So, the Jesters aren't the type to 'come quietly'," I said.

"I am aware," Blue Jacket said. "It's a shame that the injuries I sustained from my fight with the Nocturnal prevented me from stopping you." I grinned at him under my mask and held out a hand towards him.

"It's been a pleasure working with you," I said.

"The pleasure's all mine," Blue Jacket said. "Before you go, could I get a photo with you? My niece is a huge Silverbolt fan."

"Oh? Yeah, okay," I said. Blue Jacket opened a compartment on his hip and pulled out a smartphone. He held it up we leaned in for a selfie. After taking three photos, he finally put his phone away and shook my hand before limping off to report that he couldn't stop us. I watched him go, wondering what it was like having to make reports like that to people.

"You good Silver?" Thundergirl asked.

"Fine, just thinking," I said.

"Hey, told you he was a fan," she said. I laughed and followed her through the portal.

Chapter 5: What We Hide Under Our Masks

Back at the Fortress, Professor Magic had Nocturnal chained up in the backyard with magical chains made of golden sparks. We all stood in a semicircle around him as he started to wake up.

"Ugh," he groaned, looking up blearily. Lab Rat tore his mask off, showing off a shock of orange hair, scars and completely black eyes. Like a shark's.

"Hello, Nocturnal," Professor Magic said coldly. "Glad to see you're awake."

"Professor," Nocturnal said, looking around at all of us. I had an arrow nocked just in case. Dragonman snarled and blew a plume of white smoke from his nostrils. "Gang's all here by the looks of it."

"Indeed," the Professor said, leaning on his staff. "We need to talk."

"Do we? Well, had you said that before, maybe I would've just came with you, instead of thrashing you in front of the military," Nocturnal said smugly.

"Last I saw, you were the only one thrashing," I said. "On the ground. Like a worm. Plus, I think you pissed yourself a bit." Nocturnal only chuckled at me. Bastard.

"Drop the act, Noc," Blue Fox snarled; her ears pressed back. "Tell us who ordered the hit on Chameleon Man."

"And Screaming Eagle," Thundergirl added. Nocturnal laughed.

"Is that what this is about?" he said. "Well, congrats on figuring out who dunnit. Bet that was Lab Rat who pieced it together, huh?"

"Answer the question, cyborg," Lab Rat said.

"Afraid I can't do that for you. Not even for you, foxy," he said, winking at Blue Fox. She snarled at him in reply.

"And why not?" Professor Magic asked.

"Trade secret," Nocturnal replied. "My client paid for my discretion, and my rep would tank if word got out that I snitched." Dragonman growled, a low rumble like thunder.

"Talk, Nocturnal," he snarled. "Or…"

"Or what? You'll torture the info out of me? Full Inquisition style?" Nocturnal spat. "I'm not one of your witches pal. No offence, babe," Nocturnal said, ending the last part with a smirk towards Blue Fox.

That was the last straw for Blue Fox. She howled and pounced on the assassin; her nails lengthened to claw-like proportions. She raised her right arm, ready to claw his face off while squeezing his throat with the other.

"Tell us who paid you off, you shitty little creep, or I'll tear your throat out!" She screamed.

"There she is!" Nocturnal choked. "There's the little psychopath I fell in love with!"

"Blue Fox!" Professor Magic said sternly. She glared down at Nocturnal, her eyes burning with blue flame.

"Stay out of this, mage," she growled.

"Don't kill him," Professor Magic warned. "We need him to talk."

"Don't listen to him," Nocturnal said, his pale face turning blue. "Kill me. Kill me like all the others you've murdered before you joined this little country club."

"Easy," Thundergirl said gently. "Easy there, princess." She gently, but firmly, pulled her off of the Nocturnal, who gasped as his throat was released.

"Pity," he said, coughing. "That could've gotten interesting."

"Enough games," Professor Magic said. "Tell us what you know."

"Oh spare me, Professor Magic," Nocturnal said. "Either you kill me or let me go, because I'm not telling you a damn thing."

"You willing to die for this?" Lab Rat asked. "Willing to die over some cash?"

"You bet I am," Nocturnal said. "I'm a businessman. Your word is your life. If I squeal to you weirdos just because you smacked me around a bit, my word doesn't mean shit. That means I get less business and less moolah because I can't be trusted to carry out my end of the bargain. Oh, and for the record, I know from personal experience that you can choke *way* harder than that, sweetheart." Blue Fox lunged at him again, but Thundergirl held her back.

"So, either you cut your losses and let me go, or one of you needs to man up and kill me," Nocturnal said.

"We're not killers," Lab Rat said. "But we can make this difficult." Nocturnal laughed again, this time a deep belly laugh. One of actual, genuine amusement.

"Not killers? Who released a bioweapon in Panama that wiped out an entire hotel?" Nocturnal asked. Lab Rat glanced down and balled up his fists.

"That was an accident," he muttered.

"Really? Well, I'm sure all those dead families will understand that," Nocturnal said. "How about you, flame-breath?" He asked, looking up at Dragonman. "You gonna do it, or should I get out an Ouija board and ask who has a crush on me first?" Dragonman snarled at him, smoke leaking out of his clenched jaw.

"You don't know what you're talking about," Dragonman growled.

"Really? Well, I'm sure you had a compelling reason to burn down that house without checking to see if that little girl got out first. Not to mention all those Native American shamans trying to protect their tribes and territory. But that was a long time ago, wasn't it?"

"Don't listen to him, Dragonman," Professor Magic said. "He's just trying to get under your skin."

"And you, Professor Magic. Or more like Professor Hypocrite. Didn't you kill a man called Bartholomew Page?" Nocturnal asked with mock innocence. Professor Magic froze at that name.

"I didn't want to kill him. He was the one who conjured that spear, not me," Professor Magic said coldly.

"Right, did he plant it six inches deep in his own heart, too?" Nocturnal asked. Professor Magic said nothing. "Didn't think so," he looked over at Blue Fox and smiled.

"And you! The woman who dominated the news in Japan for tearing bigwig executives and politicians to shreds with her bare hands for weeks is now on a team that has a problem with murderers. You'd better be careful tossing those stones around your glass house," Nocturnal said. He turned his gaze towards Thundergirl, who glared at him defiantly.

"And Thundergirl!" He said. "You were part of a big time murder cult led by a maniac with a god complex and a gold fetish. How many killings have you been a part of?" He laughed. Thundergirl glared at him but said nothing. "I don't know about Little Miss Arrow Girl here, but I'm sure there's some skeletons in that quiver," he said with a shrug. "So, who's gonna do it? Who's gonna pull the trigger and save all those poor little vigilantes from the big bad hitman?" No one said anything.

"I'll do it," Blue Fox said finally. "I'll tear this creep's head clean off."

"No you won't," Thundergirl said, holding Blue Fox in place. "You're not a killer. Not anymore."

"How much?" I blurted out. Everyone looked right at me.

"I'm sorry?" Blue Fox asked.

"You said you're a businessman," I said, looking straight at Nocturnal. "How much do you want for the info we need?" Nocturnal stared at me in surprise, then broke out into a broad grin.

"I knew I liked you," he said jovially.

"Silver, what are you doing?" Lab Rat asked. "Trust me, you can't afford him."

"He's right," Nocturnal said. "I am expensive. But you are willing to negotiate, rather than offer bodily harm. Let me think. What do I want…" he said, humming dramatically.

"I know," he said finally. "Your name."

"My what?" I asked.

"Your name. Not your full name, just your first name will do," he said.

"What do you want with my name?" I asked.

"Consider it a collector's item," he said with a smile. "I know all their names; Berengar, Roman, Soren, Athena, Tomoko. But we've never met before. It would be nice to have the whole set, wouldn't you agree?"

"Don't do this, Silver," Thundergirl said. "This snake will sell it out for a small fortune."

"You know I wouldn't do that, Athena," Nocturnal said. "You can tell because the mafia hasn't shot up your uncle's little barbershop in retaliation for ruining their meth labs." He looked back at me.

"There may not be any honor among thieves, but there is among assassins," he said. "Rest assured, I won't tell a soul who you are," he smirked evilly. "Besides, I'm curious if they know."

"Who? The Jesters?" I asked. "I've never told them my name. It's a policy we keep," I replied.

"Not your name," Nocturnal said, his voice low. His eyes flicked down towards my groin and back at my face. "I want to know if they know what you are."

Under my mask, my face burned red. I clenched my bow until my knuckles turned white.

"How…?" I stammered.

"Omni-Vision," he answered. "Infrared, Ultraviolet, radio. Even auditory and olfactory information is used to let me see everything. I can see right through your mask and your armor. You've got a secret, and it's more than just your mild-mannered alter ego. Tell me your name, what you are, and I will tell you everything I know about my client," he said with a playful smirk on his face. I glared at him.

"You bastard…" I whispered, my voice shaking.

"Silverbolt," Professor Magic said gently. I felt a hand on my shoulder. "It's okay. You don't have to do this. No one would think less of you for not wanting to…"

"Aiden Rose," I spat. "My name is Aiden Patrick Rose. I'm transgender," my voice was shaking with emotion now. I could barely hold my bow. I felt the Professor's hand leave my shoulder.

"You're…?"

"I was born male," I said, tears forming in my eyes. "It never felt right. I was aiming for the Olympics. I was the best archer in my high school. No one could beat me. My parents were so proud of me. Then I told them. Told them I wanted to be female. They hated me for it. Kicked me out, forbid me from getting the surgery. My father called me a sick pervert, my mom cried and asked where she went wrong with me. I left. I almost killed myself twice. I still have the scars on my arm from where the razor cut me." The words just came flowing out after years of being pent up. "Everywhere I went, people called me a freak, a monster. I was hounded by the Church of the Holy Hand of God, a hate group that wanted to purge the world of sinful people like me. They lynched atheists, gay people, transgenders, Muslims, anyone they thought offended God. I couldn't bear it. I fought back, using the technology I salvaged from the wreck off a spaceship I found in the woods. I was good, people loved me again, because they didn't know what was behind my mask," I felt my throat tighten up. "I…"

"Enough," I heard Nocturnal say. I couldn't look up from the ground. "That's more than I wanted." His voice was gentle, sad even. "I'll tell you what you want to know."

"You fucking monster," I heard Thundergirl say, her voice dripping with hatred. I winced as if she had punched me.

"We'll deal with this in a second," Dragonman growled. "But first, talk. Tell us everything."

Oh God, not again. Dragonman used to work for the Vatican before he started hunting criminals instead of monsters. Every other word out of his mouth was about his religion. How could he work with someone like me?

"I don't know his name," Nocturnal said evenly. "His bank accounts are under a false name. But he hates superheroes. Any costumed vigilante, he put a bounty on. 500 grand per mask." I heard Lab Rat whistle in appreciation.

"I know," Nocturnal said. "He's good for it too. Got paid for both hits on my way to Japan."

"You keep saying 'he'," Thundergirl said. "How do you know their gender?"

"I don't. Could be female, but I doubt it. The tone in their messages just seemed male to me," Nocturnal answered.

"Why the bounty on capes?" Dragonman asked. "They a part of 52?"

"No, they're private. Some billionaire by my guess," Nocturnal said. "Something about 'not taking any risks.'"

"The hell does that mean?" Lab Rat asked.

"No clue. Check the dark web. The bounty's posted on there," Nocturnal said. "Maybe you can get more out of it than I did. I wasn't really trying too hard to find them."

"Anything else?" Dragonman asked. Good lord, he sounded pissed.

"Afraid not," Nocturnal said. "That's all I have."

"So be it," Professor Magic said. He snapped his fingers, and I could see Nocturnal get up from the ground.

"Thank you," Nocturnal said. I could hear him brush the dirt off his shoulders. "Now that our business is concluded, perhaps you could summon a portal for me, Professor? I mean, I could walk, but I'm sure you all want me gone as quick as possible."

"Of course," Professor Magic said icily. "Got everything you need?"

"Always," Nocturnal said.

"Perfect," Professor Magic said. He slammed his staff on the ground and a golden circle with an icy tunnel inside opened up beneath Nocturnal.

"What the fuuuuu…" Nocturnal called as he fell down the frozen chute. Professor Magic tapped the ground again with his staff and the portal closed.

"See you in Hel, bloody metal wanker," he said, flipping the Vs.

"Professor, where did you send him?" Dragonman asked.

"Helheim," he replied nonchalantly. "Realm of the Dishonored Dead."

"Nice," Lab Rat said.

"Now, onto more pressing matters," Professor Magic said turning to face me.

"Look, I get it. I'm a freak, and if you don't want me around…" I started to say before something hit me full in the chest. It took me a second to realize it was Thundergirl wrapping her arms around me in a tight bear hug.

"You poor thing!" she wept into my shoulder. "Are you okay!?" I could feel tears dripping onto my neck

"Thunder…" I managed to gasp. "Need… air…"

"Oh my God!" She said and released me and held me at an arm's distance. I could see the distress on her face. Hell, I could see it on all their faces.

What the hell is going on?

"How could he do that to you?" Thundergirl asked. "Make you give your name like that?"

"And he calls himself a professional," Lab Rat growled. "I'm glad you kicked him into a pit."

"That might be a problem later on," Dragonman warned. "The Lands of the Dead can't contain the Living. Not for long."

"He deserves it," Blue Fox spat. "Bastard wants to humiliate Silverbolt because she beat him. Petty, little, small dick having, arrogant…"

"You don't hate me?" I asked, sniffling. Everyone turned to face me in shock.

"Hate you?" Lab Rat asked. "Why would we hate you?"

"Because I'm…" I tried to say, waving my hands down at myself. "You know… different."

"You think we care about different?" Thundergirl asked. "I break every chair I sit in because my body is mostly metal. Dragonman can set the house on fire with a sneeze. Professor Magic is British. Blue Fox is possessed by a horny demon fox, and Lab Rat is well... You know… Lab Rat."

"Hey!" Lab Rat said.

"Bloody Yanks. What's wrong with bein' English?" Professor Magic demanded.

"Everything," Dragonman said seriously.

"At least I don't use up all the hot water in the shower every morning!" Professor Magic said.

"Yeah? Well we don't overtax our colonies without asking them!" Dragonman shot back.

"That was 200 years ago, ye great gray twat! How are you still mad about the Tea Tax!?"

"See?" Thundergirl asked with a smile. "That's what different is. None of us fit in with regular society. We use what made us outcasts to help others. To save lives. To make the world a better place. There's no shame in being different."

"You really mean that?" I asked. Thundergirl beamed at me.

"Of course I do! Besides, Blue Fox and I need another girl in the team, otherwise we'd be outnumbered by guys," she said. I could barely find the words for what I wanted to say.

"You mean, you really see me as a girl?" I asked, my voice choking up.

"Sweetie, you are the girliest person I've ever met. And I mean that in the most wholesome and complimentary way possible," Thundergirl said.

I didn't know what to say. Ever since I joined, I dreaded the day they found out what I was. That they would see me as some sort of aberrant. Like a tumor that had to be removed. That the guys would see me as some weakling, or the girls would call me a disgusting pervert.

No part of me expected this to happen. Sure, I hoped it would. And if I believed in God more, maybe I would've prayed. But I honestly prepared for them to kick me out.

But be accepted for who I am?

Damn.

I didn't think that was going to happen.

We all walked back into the house together. Dragonman and Professor Magic were arguing back and forth about colonizing, tea, taxes, and imperial laws. Lab Rat was bragging that he had always known that I was transgender, but didn't want to spread rumors. Blue Fox insisted she believed him, despite her eye rolls. Thundergirl smiled at me and walked inside with me.

I had always been deeply ashamed of what I was under my mask. But for the first time in my life, the only thing my mask was hiding was the biggest smile I had ever had.

Chapter 6: Always Room for Cookies

"You know what's bullshit?" Dragonman asked through a mouthful of cookie.

"No, but I feel like you're going to tell us," Blue Fox said evenly.

"*Nosferatu*," Dragonman said. "That damn rip off of *Dracula*."

"The black and white film?" Thundergirl asked.

"Why?" Blue Fox asked.

"It was the first ever story of a vampire dying in the sunlight. All it does is scare them off." Dragonman said. "Now everyone thinks that if they run into the sunshine, they're safe from the bloodsuckers."

"That's a problem?" Blue Fox asked.

"It is when they let their guard down and the vampire in question just walks up to them and stabs them," Dragonman said.

"So vampires don't burn up in the sun?" Thundergirl asked.

"Nope. Just Hollywood ruining it for everyone." Dragonman said stubbornly.

"So, how come you hate the sun?" Blue Fox asked.

"My troll heritage. I can just feel my skin calcifying in the sun," Dragonman replied.

"Maybe if you wore a shirt more often, you could avoid that?" Thundergirl suggested.

"Who wants more?" I said in a sing-song voice, pulling another tray out from the oven.

"Please Silver, that's enough," Blue Fox begged. "Some of us are trying to watch their figure."

"I'm not, bring that over here!" Thundergirl said. Blue Fox glared at her. Blue Fox was a bit of a health nut. Before her accident, she wasn't very pretty or healthy. Now that she had a killer body, she was determined to keep it that way.

"This is really unfair," Blue Fox said sourly. "You two can eat whatever you want and not get fat."

"Not true," Thundergirl said. "I still gain weight."

"Yeah, but it never goes to your belly, just straight to your ass," Blue Fox said. "Totally unfair."

"So?"

"So you eat candy and cake all day and just get… what's the term called?" Blue Fox asked.

"Thick?" I prompted.

"That's it. Thick," Blue Fox said. "It's probably your best superpower. Having a perfect ass."

"Pervert," Thundergirl snorted. Blue Fox sighed.

"And you, Dragon-*san*," she said, batting her eyes at Dragonman. "All beard and muscles. Yum." Dragonman rolled his eyes.

"Blue," He chided. "Relax." Blue Fox blinked and took a steadying breath.

"Sorry," she said quietly, looking down.

"It's alright," Dragonman said reassuringly.

"What's wrong?" I asked.

"Nocturnal was starting to get to me. When I get stressed or emotional, I get…" Blue Fox started to say. "You know… Pent up." I stared at her for a second, then understood. I blushed slightly.

"Oh," I said. "Because of the fox?"

"Sort of," Blue Fox said. "He was right, you know."

"No he wasn't," Thundergirl said seriously. "You belong here."

"I'm a killer, Thunder-chan," Blue Fox said. "I've killed more people than most of the murderers we face."

"That wasn't you, though," I said. "It was that fox that possessed you, right?" Blue Fox shook her head.

"No one can force you to do anything. We all have the power to make choices," Blue Fox said. "You can't control someone with magic. You can influence them, accelerate emotions that are already there, but you can't make choices for them. Like those guards back in Japan."

"You mean…"

"I mean that even though the fox was ramping up my aggression, there was a part of me that wanted to kill all those people," Blue Fox said quietly.

"There's always redemption," Dragonman said. "No matter what. You chose to fight the fox and your demons. You rose above them, and made the choice to stop. There is power in that."

"He's right," Thundergirl said. "You may have been a monster before, but you beat it. And I think you have more than paid for your crimes by now."

"Maybe," Blue Fox said. "But it's hard. It still wants me to kill you all."

"But you don't, and that's what matters," Dragonman said. "It's still your choice."

"Why is it so evil?" I asked. "I mean, I don't know much about this mumbo-jumbo stuff, but it has to have a reason, right?" Blue Fox only looked at me sadly.

"It loves carnage and death. It's a sadist in the truest sense of the word," Blue Fox admitted. "It once drove a woman insane back in China. You might have heard of her before. Her name was Da Ji." Dragonman furrowed his brow at that.

"You never told me that before," he said, his voice filled with concern.

"You never asked," Blue Fox said.

"I'm sorry, who's Da Ji?" Thundergirl asked, making me feel better about not knowing.

"Da Ji was the favorite concubine of the Emperor of China. She was a psychopath who would get off to the sounds of people being tortured," Blue Fox said.

"Jesus," I swore. Dragonman's eyes flicked towards me with disappointment.

"The fox that drove her mad fled when she was captured and killed by the rioting citizens. The fox fled to Japan, where it was found and imprisoned by Inari Okami, the Shinto goddess of Foxes."

"There's a goddess of foxes?" I asked.

"She's also the goddess of rice, blacksmiths and agriculture," Blue Fox explained.

"Huh."

"Anyways, the fox was imprisoned so it wouldn't cause any more harm. Until I let it out." Blue Fox said with a grimace.

"Yikes," I said.

"Yeah," Blue Fox said. "It got worse when I found out I was meant to imprison it inside me."

"Hold up, what?" I asked. "How were you meant to?"

"My father was the descendent of a clan of Fox Witches from ancient Japan," Blue Fox said. "His ancestors had good relations with foxes, and had developed a natural skill in fox magic. My mother was a 500-year-old spirit fox from Korea who had Become Human," Dragonman whistled in appreciation.

"That's some serious magic," he said.

"Is it?" I asked. "Blue Fox changes forms all the time. Is a fox turning into a human really that impressive?"

"Silver, when someone shapeshifts, they aren't actually turning themselves into that thing," Dragonman said slowly. "They just reconfigure their body to that form. They are literally shifting their shape."

"So?" I asked.

"Hang on, you mean they are just altering their cellular structure?" Thundergirl asked. "Not their DNA?" Blue Fox and Dragonman looked at each other.

"You know what? I think she's right," Blue Fox said. "I never thought of it that way."

"Would explain a lot," Dragonman muttered.

"So you're half spirit fox?" I asked.

"Not really. My mother didn't just look human. She Became Human. She altered her DNA to truly become human," Blue Fox said.

"It's how she was conceived," Thundergirl explained. We all looked at her in confusion.

"What? Human DNA is all practically the same, it's why humans can't interbreed with other species, the way a horse and a donkey make a mule. If your mom was still a fox in the shape of a human, the DNA wouldn't blend, and she couldn't get pregnant," Thundergirl said. "Don't tell me I'm the only one who got that."

You know those kids in school that are crazy smart, yet don't apply themselves to academics? That's Thundergirl. She could have gotten a scholarship to Harvard if she actually tried. Instead, she makes amazing cosplay and writes a webcomic online. Oh, and solves crimes in her head.

"Where did you learn all that?" Dragonman asked.

"Snapple cap," Thundergirl said simply.

"Okay," Blue Fox said slowly, still processing the fact that Thundergirl knew more about her biology than she did. "Anyways, my body was more attuned to fox magic than the average human. Inari had been grooming me my entire life to have my body be a living prison to contain Da Ji's fox."

She looked really depressed right now. I can't say I blame her. Sure, we all want to know out purpose in life. Who wouldn't? But if your purpose turned out to just be a living cage for a demon, what then?

I realized that the team all didn't really have a choice. They all had this incredible power, and not a single one of them asked for it. Except me. I worked hard for my skills and gear. The others just got blessed with it and had to try their best. I really couldn't imagine what that was like. I could always put down the bow, hang up my mask and walk away. But Thundergirl would always be that strong, Dragonman would always breath fire, and Blue Fox would always have a demon inside driving her to sex and violence.

Just when we fell into an awkward silence, Professor Magic poked his head into the kitchen.

"Oi! Lab Rat thinks he found him!"

Moments later, we were all clustered around Lab Rat's computer in the Basement. It was a massive block with three servers, an enormous monitor, and a handful of keyboards. There was a key for just about every character in any language, including Chinese script, Cyrillic, and some Egyptian hieroglyphs. The Basement was a mess of hand-made technology and ancient alchemists tools. The mystics had taken over one side of the Basement, filling it with cauldrons, magical circles and all sorts of stuff that would get you burned at the stake 200 years ago. On the technology side, we had Lab Rat's computer, Thundergirl's costume maker, and my arrow workshop. The costume maker looks like the unholy offspring of a sewing machine and a 3D printer. It made most of our costumes, and can print/sew a costume that's tough and breathable. Also really comfy and doesn't chafe, which is a must for any supersuit.

"What did you find?" Dragonman rumbled.

"Not a whole lot, but I have an idea," Lab Rat said. "I took Nocturnal's advice and started scouring the deep web, which is not something I would recommend."

"Preaching to the choir," Thundergirl muttered.

"Anyway, I was able to find the bounties on capes," Lab Rat continued, pulling up the site. It was a bland, undecorated page with simple text and a price.

"Here's the kicker," Lab Rat said. "Turns out the client pays upon seeing photographic confirmation. Meaning he needs a photo of the corpse sent to him."

"So?" Professor Magic asked.

"So, he needs to be contacted, and left a way to be contacted," Lab Rat explained. "I was able to trace that to an IP address, and find out who owns it."

"Well?" I asked. "Don't keep us in suspense," Lab Rat typed a few commands into a program, and pulled up a string of code.

"Boom," He said triumphantly.

"Lab Rat, we can't read code like it's our first language," Blue Fox said shortly. "Who owns it?"

"Pastor David Sawyer," Lab Rat said, looking a little deflated.

"Wait, Pastor?" I asked.

"This asshole," Dragonman growled.

"You know him?" I asked.

"Pastor Sawyer is a famous televangelist who spews bullshit online and makes millions off his sermons. He owns a massive church the size of a stadium for his preaching," Dragonman said.

"Is he a bigot or something?" Thundergirl asked. "You know, like those maniacs who protest gay weddings?"

"No, his stuff is fairly tame, but he just talks nonsense," Dragonman said. "Worse, he lives like a movie star. He has his own private island, a bunch of fancy cars, three mansions and his own clothing line."

"Doesn't the Catholic Church have its own city?" Professor Magic asked.

"It's not like that!" Dragonman snarled. "The Church donates it's money to charities, feeding the homeless, treating lepers, and keeping the population safe from supernatural threats!"

"Alright, alright, let's not get our religious panties in a bunch," I said, stepping between the Wizard and Hunter. "Rat, you sure it's this Pastor dude?"

"Well, it's either that or someone who works for him," he said thoughtfully. "The IP leads straight to Miami, which is where both of the murders were."

"Not taking any chances," Thundergirl mused. We all looked at her. "It's what Nocturnal said earlier, the reason this mystery client wanted these guys dead."

"And?" I asked.

"Think about it. What were Screaming Eagle and Chameleon Man doing in Miami? Eagle worked in the Midwest, and C.M in Baltimore," she said. "I think that they got too close to something in Miami, and the client got spooked, and had them dealt with."

"Hmm," Professor Magic said thoughtfully, tapping his chin in thought. "It's not a bad theory. Think you could retrace their steps, find out what brought them to Miami?"

"Sure. Can't be too hard," she said.

"Awesome. Rat, keep up the hacker shite, find out more about this Mystery Client. Blue Fox, you still remember that divination spell?"

"Yes, you thinking we should put it to use?" she asked.

"I do. Between the two of us, we should be able to conjure up something."

"What about me?" I asked.

"You and Dragonman investigate Pastor Sawyer. Try and find out why the contact info leads back to him. Check for anything magical or mundane. You're both experts in those fields."

"Sure," I said. "Up for some detective work, Flame Breath?"

"Always," Dragonman said.

Chapter 7: Miami

In less than an hour, Dragonman and I were strolling down the streets of Miami.

Dragonman was by far the oldest superhero ever, old enough that a lot of people doubted his existence. He had come to America back when it was just a handful of colonists and tribesmen. He fought in the revolutionary war, when a satanic warlock from England had tried to use the colonists as his personal guinea pigs. The Warlock, Lord Nathaniel Pendleton, Duke of Estershire (yes, that's his real name) had done enough dark magic that he was able to rise from the dead as some sort of demi-vampire. He was called the Redcoat for a while, and was Dragonman's archnemesis ever since.

"So," I said, trying to break the silence. "You know a lot about his Sawyer character?"

"A bit. He's not part of any religious organization other than his own. He doesn't preach that much controversial stuff." Dragonman rumbled in response.

"Example?" I prompted.

"He says you should wait for marriage before having sex, religion should be taught in schools, that sort of stuff," Dragonman said.

"Why don't you like him?" I asked.

"There's something off about him," Dragonman said. "He does 'faith healing', where he cures someone of having their arms of different lengths by slightly pulling on one arm. It's a stupid parlor trick, but people eat it up."

"Is that it?" I asked. "I mean, it's sad that he's fleecing people out of their money like that, but he doesn't sound like the Anti-Christ."

"I'm not saying he is. I just think people need to ask more questions about their faith, rather than just follow blindly," Dragonman replied. "Otherwise, people like Sawyer can con them out of everything they have."

"Don't take this the wrong way," I said. "But that sounds a little odd coming from you."

"Does it? Jesus questioned the local elders and scribes all the time. God wants us to be happy and love one another," Dragonman said. "You can learn a lot from the gospels if you put some thought into it."

"I'm still not coming to church with you," I said hastily. Dragonman chuckled.

"I wasn't going to ask," Dragonman said. "Well, not this time. But the offer still stands."

We eventually made it to Pastor Sawyer's Megachurch. I almost didn't recognize it; the thing was so big. It looked like a bank or a government building with white roman pillars, red brick walls and a gently sloping roof. The building was surrounded by a large wrought iron fence with a gate and a guard shack. Hell, the only church-like part of it was the enormous sign saying 'Hopeful Wish Church'. But it was huge. Big enough to be a stadium.

"Holy shit," I muttered. "That's a church?"

"Not really," Dragonman said. "This place isn't even hallowed ground."

"How can you tell?" I asked, looking up at him. His eyes were narrowed as he scanned the premises.

"There are certain energies surrounding holy places that the magically gifted can pick up on," Dragonman said. "Some places that just bring you peace as soon as you get near. Cathedrals, missions, and baptismal rivers have that quality."

"But not here?" I asked.

"No. I don't think God visits this place much," Dragonman said confidently.

We approached the gate. The damn thing was ten feet tall.

"I take it you're gonna jump over?" I asked.

"Yep. So are you," he said. I blinked.

"What, you have some fairy dust-like Tinkerbell or…" I asked before he grabbed me by the shoulders and flung me over the gate.

I didn't scream, or cry out. Definitely not. What some of you may have heard was a battle cry. That's it.

I landed roughly, bouncing slightly on the manicured lawn. I pushed myself up as Dragonman leapt over the gate.

"Jackass," I growled, dusting myself off. "I have a grappling hook."

"I know," Dragonman said smugly. I glared at him under my mask. We walked up to the building and past the sign.

"Is anyone here?" I asked.

"It's Wednesday," Dragonman said. "Not many Christians going to church on Wednesday."

"Fair enough," I said. Then something clicked with me.

"Hang on, this is a church. Not a government building or a military base. Why is there a locked gate and a guardhouse outside a house of God?" I asked.

"Good point," Dragonman said. "You'd think he would want this to be an easy place to get into."

"Hey!" a voice called. "This is private property! Vacate the premises or I will be forced to…"

I never heard what he would be forced to do, as I had whirled around to the source of the voice and fired a sleep dart into the guard's neck before he could reach for his walkie-talkie. He stumbled and collapsed into a uniformed snoring pile.

"Anyway," I said. "Never heard of a church being this well guarded."

"Yeah," Dragonman said, thoughtfully stroking his beard. "We should be quick about this. I'm sure a security camera saw us already, and we don't have Lab Rat disabling the system for us."

I muttered a curse. I had gotten so used to the little maniac turning the security systems against its owners, I had forgotten what it was like to get passed one on my own.

Man, running with superheroes can make you soft.

"You have a plan?" I asked.

"Sort of," Dragonman said. He walked up to the glass door leading into a lavish lobby and tore it off entirely. It was eerily quiet, as if someone had turned the volume of the crash down.

"Wow. And here I thought you had some crazy vampire or fairy power to pick locks or something."

"Do I look like Lab Rat or the Professor to you?" Dragonman said as he stepped through the pile of broken glass. I gingerly stepped through, my cautious steps somehow sounding louder than his blatant stomping. Which was totally unfair.

The lobby was decorated nicely, with a reception desk made from stacks of gray stone with a polished hardwood top. It looked more like something you would find at a hotel or resort than a church. The lights were all dimmed, but there was enough light to make out the pamphlets on the desk. Out of curiosity, I checked one out.

I could kind of see what Dragonman meant about Pastor Sawyer. His teachings were like Chinese takeout. Quick and easy, but not very filling.

"Come on, before someone sees the wreckage," Dragonman whispered. Flanking the reception desk was a pair of dark wooden doors with brass push handles. We entered one, and saw the main church.

Holy. Shit.

It was huge. Rows upon rows of pews, staggered in lairs like a theater, covered the floor. There were even box seats above us, for upper-class Christians I assume. Down at the back of the massive room was the altar, although it looked more like a stage. Massive TV screens hung from either side of the altar; making it easier for the people in the back to see the Pastor. We walked through the aisles of pews towards the altar.

"This is wrong," Dragonman growled. "So wrong."

"What is?" I asked.

"This isn't preaching. It's a damn show. This place is just…" he rolled his wrist around, looking for the right word.

"Magnanimous?" I suggested.

"It is. Not even a Cathedral is this excessive," Dragonman said.

"I don't know," I said. "I think stained glass is still a bit much." Dragonman glared at me.

"But hey, what do I know?" I said, holding my hands up in surrender. He rolled his eyes and strode forward. That's when I noticed something odd about the place.

"Dragonman?" I asked.

"Yeah?"

"I don't spend a lot of time in churches," I said, looking around. "But isn't there supposed to be a big cross on the altar?" Dragonman furrowed his brow, then looked up at the altar. Sure enough, no cross. Just a large podium, an impressive set of speakers, and a purple curtain.

"Son of a bitch," Dragonman growled.

"So we have a guarded church, excessive interior design, a theater layout, and no actual Christian imagery," I said, counting each item off on my fingers. "Bet there isn't even a bible in the pews." I checked. "Nope."

"But there is this," Dragonman said, picking up a small slip of paper off the carpet. I stepped closer to get a better look.

"It says '9:30 Showing. Seat 11A12'," I said. "Wait, is this a…"

"Ticket stub," Dragonman finished.

"Hang on, he's *charging* people for admission?" I said incredulously. "That's insane!"

"Yeah. This guy doesn't add up," Dragonman said hotly.

"Well, this is weird and super shady, but it doesn't explain why his IP is on the deep web," I said. Dragonman grunted in agreement. We both turned towards the curtains behind the stage- ah, "altar." Then looked back at each other.

We looked behind the curtain to find a plain-looking hallway lit with fluorescent lights. To our right was a dressing room. Yes, it even had a little golden star on it with 'Sawyer' stenciled around it.

"Ugh," I said. "I bet there's a mirror back there with light bulbs all around it," Dragonman snorted in amusement, blowing a small cloud of white smoke out his nostrils.

To our right was a simple wooden door, not unlike one you would find in a corporate office building. There was no sign on the door to indicate what was behind it.

Very mysterious.

Dragonman tried to open it, only to find it was locked. He grabbed the door knob in one hand, braced his other one around the door, then pulled the door knob out of the door entirely.

"Dude," I said, shaking my head. "Is this how you investigated monster killings? Just smash your way through everything?"

"Yep," he said, casually tossing the doorknob behind him. "Works better than you would think." I sighed and shook my head. The room was pitch black inside, but revealed itself to be a small office with a modest computer inside.

"Damn," Dragonman said. "We should've brought Lab Rat with us."

"Nah, I got this," I said, cracking my knuckles as I sat down and typed in the login info. I looked up to see him scowl at the computer screen.

"How did you do that?" he asked. I smiled at pointed at a small post-it note with the username and password written on it.

"You've got to be kidding me," he said with a sigh. I chuckled and started digging.

"Let's see, email is still logged in," I said. "Let's start with that."

There wasn't much to look at. Most of it was invitations to preach at a variety of places, publishers asking about his newest books, and a few tech questions regarding his podcasts, radio shows, and the actual running of his business.

"Blah blah blah," I said. "This is getting nowhere." I was about to click out, when Dragonman said, "Wait." He pointed out another email labeled 'Entertainment.'

"Ooh," I said. "Bet we find something juicy in here," I said jokingly. I opened the email.

"Sawyer. Gotta hand it to you. You said she was the perfect one for me, and you son of a bitch, you were right," I read aloud. "Jessica is the sweetest thing ever, literally the perfect girl."

"Ugh, what is this?" Dragonman said with disgust.

"Sounds like he recommended a girl to someone?" I said. "Doesn't sound too bad," I kept reading.

"No one else can please me like she does. She's the cutest little thing ever," I said. "It's so sad that she's going to grow up one day…" I froze.

"What?" Dragonman said, his tone icy.

"… going to grow up one day like all the others. Why can't they just stay…" I said, feeling bile rise up in my throat.

"Twelve," Dragonman read, his voice seething. I felt sick.

"This guy's a pedophile," I said, my voice shaking. I could smell smoke coming from Dragonman's mouth. He always does that when he's furious. Can't say I blame him.

"He's not just a pedophile," Dragonman snarled. "He's a damn pimp. He's selling kids to these perverts."

"Why?" I asked. "He's clearly got enough money doing his Jesus shows. So what the hell?"

"I don't know," Dragonman growled. "But we need to tell the team."

"Hey!" a voice called. "What the hell do you think you're doing?" a voice called behind us. We both whirled around to see another guard in the doorway, holding a paper cup of coffee. His eyes widened when he saw two masked vigilantes, one huge, horned and covered in studded leather, the other armed with a massive silver bow. Oh, and we were both very, VERY angry.

"Dispatch, I have two…" he said into his walkie-talkie before Dragonman flew out of the office and pinned him to the wall.

"Where's Sawyer!?" He demanded, the smoke coming from his mouth darkening to black.

"Ack… gack…" he managed to say.

"Dragonman!" I yelled. "We need to go!"

"Talk!" Dragonman yelled. The guard only choked and coughed.

"Dammit," I said. I reached into a pouch on my belt and pulled out a flash drive and stuck it into the modem. I quickly searched through the computer for relevant files, transferring as much as I could. The drive was made by Lab Rat, and could store a whole lot. I saved as much as I could and yanked it out, stuffing it back into my belt as I walked out.

"Dragonman!" I yelled again. He whirled around to look at me, much too fast for a human. His eyes were glowing with rage. Literally glowing. There was almost a glare.

"I know you're pissed," I said. "Who wouldn't be? But we have to go."

He snarled, then released the guard. He slumped down onto the floor, his face slightly blue. We turned down the hall and through the curtain to the showroom and onto the stage. Among the pews, a small detachment of dark figures crouched in the semi-darkness.

"Freeze!" a voice called. Dragonman stomped a foot, threw his head back and roared like a lion.

Fun fact about auditoriums: they are built to reflect sound from the stage to the seats, even without a speaker system. A lion's roar is one of the loudest sounds a mammal can make. It can be heard from miles. (Thundergirl's not the only one who drinks Snapple.)

My point is, even without the sound system set up, Dragonman's roar sounded like a jet engine. I heard the initial blast of sound before my ears started ringing like church bells. I yelped and clapped my hands over my ears. I was able to look up to see Dragonman dashing between pews, swinging his massive iron shod club. I groggily stood up and nocked an arrow to my bow. I picked out a guard a good distance away and shot. The arrow struck him right in the shoulder and started leaking pink foam rapidly. Before the guard could realize what hit him, the foam covered his upper body and solidified. He stumbled from the sudden weight and staggered to the ground; his gun having fallen to the ground by his feet. I picked out another target and hit him with a taser arrow, another with a net arrow. More guards were coming in through the doors, all firing at Dragonman. He roared in pain, staggering back. He flew up to the upper levels, away from the gunmen and ran along the banister. The guards tried to track his movement, but he was too fast for them. He dove down like a cat and swung like a demon at them, his club whirling around, striking one guard after another. I tried to target one, but a gunshot rang out and my shoulder exploded with pain. I yelped and fell back.

I'm not that good with pain. It's part of the reason I prefer to fight from a distance and surprise my target. On the stage, I was a sitting duck. Plus, the guards all had the high ground. I tried to crawl into cover and managed to activate my shield, which only made my gunshot wound scream out again. I managed to get the rational part of my brain in front of my gibbering crying one. My left shoulder had been shot, and I could barely move it, much less lift my bow. I clamped my right hand over the wound, putting pressure on it to help stop the bleeding.

"Dragonman!" I yelled hoarsely. Thankfully his hearing was good enough to hear me, or it was just *that* good of an auditorium. He whipped his head around to see me crouching behind my shield. Another shot hammered against it, making my arm rock back. I let out an involuntary yell as the force of the shot made the pain in my shoulder spike. I peeked over my shield to see a gunman crouching in the shadows. For a brief moment, I thought it was Nocturnal, but then I saw Dragonman pounce on him and slam him into a pew, knocking him out cold. He leapt up to me on the stage, and looked me over.

"You're bleeding. What happened?" he asked, his voice full of concern.

"What do you think?" I snarled. "Bastard caught me in the shoulder."

"Dammit," he replied. He knelt down to pick me up with the doors burst open and even *more* guards poured out.

"Oh, come *on*!" I complained. "How many guys does this maniac have?"

"Those aren't guards. It's the police," Dragonman said. "Heard the sirens while I was up by the doors." He pressed a finger to his earpiece. "Professor, we need evac. Silver's been shot." I looked over his shoulder to see the police advancing on us.

"Dragon…" I muttered. I was beginning to feel faint. Behind us, a portal opened, showing beautiful golden sunlight and verdant green grass. He scooped me up like a child and carefully, but quickly, advanced through the portal.

Chapter 8: European Medicine

"One job!" Blue Fox said as she wrapped more gauze around my arm. "You had one job, Dragonman!"

"Give me a break!" Dragonman replied, throwing his arms up. "My job was to get information!"

"And you can't keep her safe at the same time??" Blue Fox snarled.

"I can keep *myself* safe, thanks," I said. I was sitting in a chair in the kitchen like a two-year-old who skinned their knee as Blue Fox worked the bullet out of my shoulder.

"Clearly," Blue Fox said sarcastically. She poured a foul-smelling concoction from the kettle on the stove into a stone cup and shoved it into my hand.

"What's this?" I asked.

"Drink," she demanded.

"But what is it?" I asked.

"Powdered oni horn, kappa spleen and green tea brewed in a shark's stomach," Blue Fox said as I took a sip. I gagged and was about to spit it out. Quick as a viper, she clapped a hand over mouth.

"Swallow. It." She said harshly.

"Love hearing that right when I come into the kitchen." I heard Thundergirl say. She was still in costume, but had changed her boots out for bright orange crocs. She was holding a bottle of Snapple and an unopened granola bar.

"How was Miami?" he asked, setting down her Snapple to open her granola bar.

"Silverbolt got shot," Blue Fox said shortly.

"Oh good job, Dragonman. Can't keep the new kid safe," Thundergirl said through a mouthful of granola bar.

"Hey!" I protested. "I don't need a baby sitter! I got myself shot. And quit calling me 'kid'. I'm older than you!" Thundergirl smirked at me, then looked at Dragonman.

"What happened?" she asked. Dragonman scowled and crossed his arms.

"I'll tell you at the debrief. You're not gonna like it," he said. Thundergirl frowned.

"Yeah, I found out something bad as well," she said sadly. "How did the divination spell go?"

"Not good," Blue Fox said. "We kept getting visions of him, but that was it. Nothing incriminating or suspicious."

"What was he doing?" Dragonman asked.

"Sitting on his arse and typing on a laptop," Professor Magic said, coming in from the hall. Dragonman and I shared a look.

"That might be a problem," I said nervously. Professor Magic cocked an eyebrow dramatically.

"Oh?" he asked.

"Aw hell, you guys found the same thing I did?" Thundergirl said disappointedly.

"What did you find?" Blue Fox asked.

"Let's wait for Lab Rat," Dragonman said. "I really don't want to tell this twice." Professor Magic nodded and opened the door to the basement.

"Oi! Rat! Get up here, we're havin' a chin-wag!" He yelled.

"Ugh. So British," Thundergirl complained. Dragonman grunted in assent. Lab Rat came up into the kitchen, still in his costume.

"Do you ever take that thing off?" I asked, pointing with my good arm.

"It's self-cleaning," Lab Rat replied, which didn't exactly answer my question.

"So. What did everyone get?" Professor Magic asked. "Because that divination didn't do fuck-all."

"I contacted some friends of Screaming Eagle. Private investigators, close friends, and his engineer buddy that helped design the suit." Thundergirl explained. "Eagle was after Sawyer, kept dogging his footsteps, but never said why. Chameleon Man was a bit harder, but his ex-wife had similar information about her husband's activities."

"Surprised they were willing to talk to you," Lab Rat said.

"They wanted their friend avenged," Thundergirl replied simply. "But here's the kicker. Sawyer isn't the saint he portrays himself as. Because when I investigated the Navy's actions, I found something interesting."

"The Navy knew Sawyer was selling kids?" I blurted out. Thundergirl looked at me, disappointed.

"Way to ruin the surprise…" she said. Lab Rat's eyes widened. Blue Fox let out a stream of Japanese, which had to be swear words, because she got a look of amazement from Dragonman.

"Bloody hell," Professor Magic said.

"Sorry," I said sheepishly. "Couldn't help myself. How did the Navy factor in?"

"Because Blue Jacket recently crashed a human trafficking ring in the Philippines," Lab Rat said.

"Hey!" Thundergirl protested. "I was getting there!"

"Blue Jacket, Screaming Eagle and Chameleon Man were the closest to figuring him out," Lab Rat continued, ignoring Thundergirl entirely.

"How do you know?" Professor Magic asked.

"Because they had the highest bounties," Lab Rat explained. "I was able to do some digging, and found that Sawyer was paying a higher fee for those three. It explains why Nocturnal was in Japan. He always went after the highest rewards."

"Wish we knew that before," Dragonman growled. "Could've saved us a trip."

"Hey, Stinger was nice!" Thundergirl said.

"What was he like?" I asked eagerly. Stinger was a legend among superheroes. He took down an entire cartel on his own using bee-themed gadgets back in the 80s. He was the first costumed vigilante that wasn't acting out some sort of comic-book power fantasy.

"He's old and retired. Looked like one of those old school Latino lovers," Thundergirl said. "Had his leg in this weird brace. He showed us his wings, suit and stinger blades."

"That's so cool," I said enviously.

"Let's stay focused." Professor Magic said. "Dragonman, what did you and Silverbolt find?"

We took turns explaining what happened in the 'church', and how I was able to download most of Sawyer's hard drive.

"Give," Lab Rat commanded, holding out his hand. I passed the drive to the Professor, who handed it to Lab Rat.

"This should come in handy," he said, turning the drive over in his hands. I'm not saying he was hunched over it and calling himself 'Precious', but he was getting close.

"So what now?" Blue Fox asked. "We have to do something."

"Oh, we will." Professor Magic said, stroking his chin in thought. "We need to find out where these kids are being kept and get them free."

"What about the kids from the Philippines?" I asked.

"I'll make a portal for them," Professor Magic said. "From there, we can let the authorities handle it."

"Tell me you aren't going to just hand this to the police," Thundergirl said.

"Of course not," Professor Magic said crossly. "The evidence was stolen and can't be used in court. Not to mention the battery of lawyers he has to have in case he got found out."

"So, what's the play?" I asked, taking a tentative sip of the healing potion. Ick.

"We find out who's been nabbing kids," Professor Magic said. "Blue Fox, you head for the Philippines and start finding out where the kids are being snatched from."

"Got it," Blue Fox said.

"Dragonman and Thundergirl, you two head for the Midwest, where Screaming Eagle worked out of."

"On it," Dragonman said.

"Aye, sir!" Thundergirl said loudly. I didn't get it, but Blue Fox smirked at that.

"Lab Rat, find out everything you can about Pastor Sawyer. Legal troubles, net worth, who he's investing in, how his company works, everything."

"Easy," Lab Rat said.

"Silverbolt. You're with me," Professor Magic said. "We're heading for Baltimore, picking up the trail that Chameleon Man was on."

"Awesome," I said.

"Hey! Her arm still needs to be healed," Blue Fox said. Professor Magic frowned at me.

"Silver, what happened to your arm?" he asked, his voice filled with concern.

"I got shot," I said simply.

"I gave her a healing tea," Blue Fox explained. "Oni horn and kappa spleen." Professor Magic nodded sagely.

"Brewed?"

"Shark stomach."

"Hmm," he said, frowning. "That might take too long."

"Oh, what do you know about healing?" Blue Fox said defensively. "You Europeans thought sticking leeches would help plague victims."

"First off, I'm not European, I'm English," the Professor said calmly. "Second, I have something better than a leech." He reached up to one of the cabinets and unlocked the padlock, chaining it shut.

Despite constant complaints, Blue Fox and Professor Magic store some of their potion ingredients in the kitchen. It's creepy and gross, and once Thundergirl accidentally opened the wrong cabinet and almost ate a bag of dried eel skin, thinking it was European potato chips (her excuse). He pulled out a gray ceramic jar and popped the cork lid off it.

"What is that, Pooh Bear's honey?" I asked sarcastically.

"Not exactly," he said. He reached into it and pulled out a black snail shell. "Black Forest Healing Snails." Dragonman backed up instantly upon seeing the shell.

"Are you insane?" he demanded, his eyes wide with fear. "Those things were put to death centuries ago!"

"They almost were, but I was able to save the species," Professor Magic replied.

"Those things are parasites!" Dragonman said. "Their saliva triggers cellular regeneration, which they use to grow tumors and eat them!"

"They do *what*?" Thundergirl asked in horror.

"Oh, don't be ridiculous," Professor Magic said. "They're harmless!"

Just as he said that, a long black stalk shot out from the shell. It was three inches long and ended with black tendrils around a toothy red maw. The snail started making shrill shrieking sounds and snapped the tendrils at Professor Magic's face. He had to lean back to avoid the thing grabbing him. Just as sudden it appeared, the stalk shrank back inside the shell, leaving us all staring at it in fear.

"Yeah, I'll just stick with the tea," I said, my voice a little higher than usual. "Mmm, yummy spleen tea!"

"Your call," Professor Magic said casually. He dropped the shell into the jar, closed it, placed it back on the shelf and locked the cabinet back up.

"What?" he asked when he saw us all staring at him.

"Nothing," Thundergirl said quickly. "I'll start getting ready for Chicago. Coming, Dragon?"

"Right behind you," Dragonman said, eager to leave. "We can swing by a Dunkin' Donuts on the way."

"That sounds awesome," Thundergirl replied.

"I'm gonna get the teleporter ready," Lab Rat said, sounding shaken.

"I'll come help you!" Blue Fox said eagerly and followed him down into the basement. Soon, it was just Professor Magic and I in the kitchen. He looked at me perplexed.

"What's their problem?" he asked. I sighed.

"Who knows. Maybe they're just not fans of escargot remedies."

Chapter 9: Suburban Nightmare

Professor Magic and I followed Chameleon Man's path all the way from Baltimore, down into Georgia, back up north to Tennessee, then up to Ohio, and into Kentucky. We had been after Sawyer for three days. The other members had similar luck. Lab Rat had dug up all he could about Sawyer. He was once a small-time crook who got his start working for big time criminals in human trafficking. He didn't just sell children, but young women as well. Girls who wanted to be big time movie stars who had trusted the wrong people were now working on street corners in red light districts, kept loyal to their pimps through drug addiction.

It was sickening. Sawyer had turned to God later on, but still bought and sold human lives on the side. Lab Rat couldn't figure out why, but his theory was that Sawyer did it to protect himself. If the kiddies stopped coming in, it might upset the wrong people. People who could afford hitmen.

Dragonman and Thundergirl had last reported from Kansas, with similar results as ours. No real connection between the abductions and Sawyer. The only connection we had was that one email we found in his office. Blue Fox was still in the Philippines, but had requested backup from Lab Rat. She said she had a hunch, but wasn't certain. That was the last thing she had said, which was almost a full day ago. She hadn't reported anything since.

For the record, we have a group chat on a social media site that Lab Rat made. We use it to communicate during missions like this, but Thundergirl still posts stupid memes on it.

Professor Magic and I were riding through a fancy neighborhood in northern Kentucky, just south of Cincinnati. I was driving, as the Professor wasn't used to driving on the right side of the road.

"I still don't get it," I said hotly. "We've been up and down the country for half a week and have nothing to show for it. Just dead ends and half-remembered rumors."

"Relax," Professor Magic said as he watched the houses pass by. "I'm sure we'll find something soon."

"You sure?" I asked. "Because I'm starting to agree with what Thundergirl was saying last night."

"Which was?"

"Storming Sawyer's Mansion," I said. "Or his private island. Or his summer home."

"And what makes you think that will solve this?" he asked.

"Because we can beat the shit out of him?" I suggested, turning right onto another street. Screaming children ran through yards, chasing each other past houses with toy swords and Nerf guns.

"If we did that, there's no guarantee that we stop this," Professor Magic said. "There is an entire system at play here. We need to stop this at the root of the problem."

"Which is?"

"How he's nabbing kids in the first place," Professor Magic asked. "Not to mention our first concern is finding out where he's keeping the children he's abducted."

"I get that we need to save the children," I said, stopping to let a kid pass to catch a runaway soccer ball. "But what if we just grab Sawyer and beat the info out of him?"

"We could," Professor Magic said. "But what does that look like to the public?"

"Who cares what the public thinks?" I asked. "We do what's right regardless of what people say."

"True. And if you turned on the news and saw that a group of people with super powers had burst into someone's home and beat them within an inch of their life based on one email, what would you think?" Professor Magic asked. I frowned under my mask.

"I'd be worried," I said reluctantly. "I'd be afraid that they might come after me off of a rumor."

"Spot on," Professor Magic said. "I appreciate your enthusiasm, but we need to stay focused. I'd like nothing more than to hex that twat into a hundred pieces, or turn him into a goldfish and flush him down the loo, but we need more information. We nip this now; we could miss out on more information. Not to mention that our priority is the preservation of innocent lives, not beating up bad guys. Savy?"

"I guess," I said glumly. Once again, the Cockney bastard was right. Heroes save lives, thugs bash people's teeth in. It was important to maintain our image of heroes, otherwise we'd become part of the problem we were trying to fix. We rode in silence for a bit when the Professor suddenly became excited.

"Oi!" He said, holding up his phone. "Look here!"

"Professor, I'm driving. What did you find?"

"Police report. Kids have gone missing from this neighborhood."

"No shit. That's why we came here," I replied.

"But listen. Last abduction was last night," he said.

"Really?" I asked.

"Yeah. Hang on, I'll call the girl's mum, see if we can't score a meeting."

"Cool," I said. Finally, maybe we found a lead. Professor Magic put the phone on speaker so I could hear the conversation as well.

"Hello?" a woman's voice asked after the ringing.

"Hello, is this the Bennet household?" Professor Magic asked.

"Yes, who is this?" the woman asked.

"I'm calling about your daughter," Professor Magic asked.

"Bethany!?" the woman asked desperately. "Have you seen her?"

"We're not sure. We just had some questions concerning her abduction," Professor Magic asked.

"Oh," the woman said, sounding deflated. "I told the police everything I knew."

"We're not the police," Professor Magic replied.

"Then who are you?"

"We're just a handful of good Samaritans who want your daughter returned to you. That's all," Professor Magic answered, winking at me.

"I don't understand."

"Perhaps we could meet in person?" the Professor asked. "Maybe you could tell us more about the disappearance of your daughter.

"Oh, okay," the woman said. "Sure, we could do that." I cocked an eyebrow at the Professor as she gave us her address.

"That was easy," I said after Mrs. Bennet hung up.

"Yeah," Professor Magic said, staring down at his phone thoughtfully. "Normally they pry a bit more."

"Maybe she's just desperate," I suggested.

"Perhaps," he said. "But I've got a bad feeling about this," I frowned. One of the Professor's abilities was foresight, meaning often times he knew was coming next. If he was worried about something, then a smart person would be worried too.

We drove to the address of the Bennet house and pulled into the driveway. We stepped out and walked up to the front door. Unlike the rest of the neighborhood, there were no children running around. I drew my bow as we got out.

"Easy," Professor Magic said.

"Don't tell me you think this is legit."

"I don't. But you go in with your bow ready, you'll set them off."

"Who's them?" I asked.

"Not sure," Professor Magic said. "But for now, just act relaxed. We don't want them to know we're onto them."

He strode up to the front door and rang the doorbell. I scanned the neighboring houses. The whole street seemed deserted. Too late I realized that almost every house had a dark van with tinted windows parked either on the street or in the driveway.

"Professor…" I said nervously. I looked back at him to warn him when the door opened.

"Hello, Profethor," a nasally male voice said. Standing in the doorway was a strange looking man holding a gun to the Professor. He was overweight, with a double chin and a round egg-shaped belly. He wore all black, black jeans, a black canvas trench coat and a trilby. His shirt was black with a six-pointed star, like the Star of David. He had small brown eyes that seemed to be too far apart, and a round babyish face. He carried a black messenger bag over his shoulder with pink and purple pins decorating it. His shoes were old dirty white sneakers with Velcro straps.

"Sigil," Professor Magic replied icily. I quickly drew an arrow and aimed it at the man.

"Drop it, doughboy," I demanded. "Or I drop you." The man laughed, then snapped his fingers. Suddenly, the yard was filled with armed men. They were dressed in American flag styled robes and armed with AR-15s, all pointed at me.

"What the…" I muttered, recognizing the robes. I hadn't seen them since my first time as Silverbolt, back in Mississippi. Behind the man called Sigil, a tall man in matching robes stepped out. Unlike the men outside, his hood was down, and I could see his red-blonde hair and beard, as well has the cane he leaned on.

"Erik Lynch," I growled. "The Hangman." He smiled at me.

"Mornin'," He said in a smooth southern drawl. "Why don't y'all come on in and get yourselves somethan' to drink?" I glared daggers at the Hangman.

"Thilverbolt," Sigil called out in. "Put down your bow, before I have these men gun you down now," I held my bow on him still.

"Please, Silverbolt," the Hangman asked. "No need for this to get violent. At least not out here in public." The men surrounding me switched their safeties off.

"Silver," Professor Magic called. "Lower your bow. It's alright." I glared at the Hangman one last time before lowering it. The Hangman smiled and nodded at the robed men. One of them punched me in the side of the head and another took my bow as I fell.

"Tie her up good!" The Hangman ordered. "Don't take no chances with her!"

"Ith this really nethethary?" Sigil asked as they tied zip ties around my wrists

Okay, you know what? I really hate writing this asshole's lisp. He had one, and it's terrible. From here on out, just do it in your head. It's making my story look awful.

"Is this really necessary?" Sigil asked, looking up at the Hangman.

"Trust me, this is," Hangman said. "She's escaped worse situations before."

"But I'm here," Sigil replied. "She can't escape me."

"You handle the Wizard, witch," Hangman said. "Silverbolt is all mine."

"I'm a warlock, not a witch," Sigil replied stubbornly.

"To be fair, they both mean the same thing. You know, a spellcaster who sold out," Professor Magic said.

"You shut up!" Sigil yelled, spraying Professor Magic with spit. "You try any spellcasting here, you pompous British swine, and we kill the girl!"

"Understood," Professor Magic said coolly, wiping his monocle clean on his cape. Two guards grabbed me by the shoulder while the others kept their guns trained on me. The guard on my left carried my bow while we all trudged inside. As we passed Hangman, I glared evilly at him as the guard handed him my bow.

"Beautiful," he said, holding it up to the light to examine it. "Beautiful craftsmanship."

"Get a good look while you can," I snarled. "You'll never get another chance."

"Oh Silverbolt," He said, limping along with us as I was guided to the kitchen. "How long I've waited to see you in binds."

"Pervert," I spat.

"Please. My wife is the only woman for me," Hangman said, placing a hand on his heart. "My only wish is to make this country great again."

"Yeah, I remember," I said. "Back when white people were in charge, black people couldn't vote, and women stayed home, barefoot and pregnant? Or has the pamphlet changed?"

"You know me so well," he said. "What a pity a beauty like you doesn't see eye to eye with our goals."

"Probably because my black Muslim girlfriend would want me out of the kitchen so we could have premarital sex on a burning flag?" I teased. I could see a vein bulging in his temple as his face reddened.

"You sicken me," he growled. "You've been poisoned by the deviants that our blessed nation has allowed to exist. But not for much longer."

"Hangman!" Sigil called. "Enough with the hate speech. Bring her over here." Professor Magic and I were seated at the kitchen table, side by side. Sigil sat opposite from him, while the Hangman sat across from me. I noted with pride that struggled to sit down.

"Alright," Professor Magic said. "You've got us. What do you want?"

"What do I want?" Sigil said, smiling like a little kid holding a magnifying glass over an anthill. "Well, for starters, I want you to pass your powers over to me. Or resurrect my Master, whom you've killed. But other than that…"

"There's a bounty out for superheroes," Hangman answered. "50 grand for dead capes. But recently, there's been an update."

"Yes," Sigil said, rubbing his hands greedily. "Double for taking you alive. Jesters only."

"Really?" I asked. "Why us?"

"Does it matter?" Hangman asked. "What does matter is that we can get both vengeance and capital. This is an offer we can't pass up."

"How did you catch us?" Professor Magic asked. "Where's the Bennet family?"

"You mean me?" Sigil said, his voice changed to a female's. His voice sounded exactly Mrs. Bennet's from the phone.

"That's unsettling," I said. I looked over at Professor Magic. "Who is this clown anyway?"

"You don't know who I am?" Sigil asked. "I am his nemesis. His greatest opponent! The very opposite to everything about him!"

"No you're not," Professor Magic growled. "You're nothing but an overweight fanboy." He looked over at me. "His real name is Jacob Baron. He was an acolyte of the late Black Wizard, Bartholomew Page. When I killed him, he held a grudge."

"I swore vengeance!" Sigil yelled.

"Right," I said. "Is he a threat?"

"Not really. He's a decent sorcerer, and has a few contracts with various beings, but he's no Wizard. He's been jealous of the Seven and their abilities ever since he met Page," Professor Magic said. "Most dangerous thing about him is his body odor."

"Hey!" he protested.

"So who's this Hangman?" Professor Magic asked.

"He's actually my nemesis," I replied. "He's the leader of the Holy Hand of God, a hate group that wants to repeal civil rights."

"Hardly accurate," Hangman replied. "We're an organization dedicated to removing the deviants that weaken and degrade our blessed nation."

"Yeah. These 'deviants' include anyone who isn't white, Christian, straight, and any female who isn't a housewife or a nurse," I replied. "Anyone he doesn't agree with or gets in his way, he kills. He's lynched hundreds. Just for the crime of being black or gay or whatever."

"Bloody hell," Professor Magic said. "Sounds like a real charmer."

"Yeah. He's more than earned the title of 'Hangman'," I said. "How about doughboy? How'd he get the name Sigil?"

"He picked it himself," Professor Magic said with a sour look on his face. I grimaced.

Here's a little tip for all you would be superheroes: let the media pick your name for you. Giving yourself a superhero name is just pretentious and it's just telling the world you're doing this for attention. No one in the Jesters picked their name. Blue Fox got hers from the Japanese police during her first killing spree, based on her shapeshifting and choice of clothing. Dragonman got his from the colonists who saw him charging into battle and breathing fire. Lab Rat got his from the guards at Alley Cat, based on his story he gave the media when he called himself a 'human lab rat.' Thundergirl is named after her thunderous yell and the blast of air that surrounds her as she flies. Professor Magic got his from his predecessor, who was an actual professor. I think it was the Queen herself who actually named him. I got my name from all the silver arrows left behind at crime scenes where I stopped bad guys.

"Oof," I said. "Edgy much?" I asked. Professor Magic snickered.

"Listen here, bitch," Sigil growled. "You won't be talking shit when we sell you to our client."

"Yeah, who is that, anyway?" I asked.

"Don't worry about that," Hangman answered. "All that matters is that I've finally beat you. You finally lost." I glared at him.

"What are you doing this far up north? I thought you operated further south," I asked.

"Our brothers in Kentucky have always been eager to assist our cause," Hangman said proudly. "Which reminds me." He pointed at one of the guards. "You. Contact the client. Tell them we have Silverbolt and Professor Magic."

"Glory to the New America!" the guard cried out before leaving into another room. I cocked an eyebrow at Hangman, who sighed and rubbed his temple.

"New guy?" I asked.

"New guy," he answered.

"How did you know we were here anyway?" I asked.

"Divination spell," Sigil said proudly. "We've been following you for quite some time. When we found out you were heading to Kentucky…"

"How?" Professor Magic asked. "How did you know?"

"Sigil," Hangman growled. "Mind your tongue. Don't tell them anything else."

"Oh please, it hardly matter as this point!" Sigil said casually. "We've caught them and have them dead to rights! All that matters is shipping them to Firefly Island…"

"Sigil!" Hangman cried.

"Firefly Island, huh?" I muttered to the Professor while the two villains argued. "Worth checking out," he only grunted in response.

"Oh this is so boring!" I declared, interrupting our captors. "How long until you take us to this client of yours?" I asked while stretching my arms over my head, my wrists still bound.

"Until we receive confirmation," Hangman growled.

"Ugh," I complained. "You guys have any food? The last villains who held us prisoner had snacks." I looked over at Professor Magic. "Remember them? The Bayou Brothers?"

"Ah, I remember," Professor Magic said knowingly. "Those were the crocodile blokes, eh?"

"Alligator, actually," I said. "But yeah. Proper villains too. Knew how to treat a guest."

"What are you two blabbering about?" Hangman asked.

"The Bayou Brothers. Two brothers in the swamps of Louisiana who were mutated with alligator DNA. They were a pair of eco-terrorists that captured me when I had just joined up with the Jesters. Oh wait, were they alligators with human DNA…?"

"I've heard of them," Sigil said. "They had alligator heads, right?"

"Yep," I replied. "You wouldn't believe how I escaped."

"Do tell," Sigil said. I grinned at him like the Cheshire Cat.

"Well, when they captured me, they confiscated all my gear. My bow, grappling gun, quivers and boomerang. Along with my tear gas pellets, which I don't know how they found. But they forgot to take my dart launchers," I said, holding up mine. Hangman's eyes widened in fear.

"You fools!" He cried as I hit the switch on my gloves. A dart flew out, cutting through the zip-tie. I rolled back in my chair as I pulled my wrists free. The guards tried to stop me, but Professor Magic stood and shouted, "AVOS MAXIMA!"

Wind roared around us, scattering debris and knocking the table away from us. Sigil managed to dodge at the last moment, but Hangman wasn't able to get up fast enough with his bum knee. The table knocked him back into the refrigerator behind him.

"Kill them!" he wheezed. I quickly righted myself and fired two more darts at the approaching guards. At this distance, my bow would be useless. I had to rely on other methods.

Sigil got to his feet and raised a hand to Professor Magic.

"DRAKAS!" he cried, lightning flashing from his palm.

"NINI!" Professor Magic cried at almost the same time. The lightning vanished instantly.

"Smart move, Professor," Sigil snarled. "Try this on for size!" He raised both hands to the Wizard and cried "PYROS MAXIMA!"

A column of flames shot from his outstretched hands, threatening to engulf the Professor. He raised his hands and cried "CRYOS AEGIS!" A round shield appeared made entirely of ice. The flames splashed against the shield like waves crashing against rock. I expected the shield to melt, but to my surprise it held.

One of the guards took advantage of the distracting battle of magic and hit me in the face with the butt of his gun. I fell back, slightly dazed from the blow. He aimed it at me, and I barely had enough time to dodge the oncoming gunfire. I fumbled around my belt and retrieved my boomerang. I threw it at him, catching him right in the nose, knocking flat on his ass. The boomerang curved its flight and returned to my outstretched hand. Another guard came down the stairs, toting a shotgun. I tossed the boomerang at him, taking time to duck behind the toppled table. I heard the shotgun go off once, then the satisfying thwack of the boomerang hitting his chest. I reached up and caught it as it returned.

"You bitch," I heard a voice snarl. I turned to see the Hangman curled up behind me, clutching his bad knee.

"Still here?" I asked.

"You can't beat us," he growled. "We're an idea. A light that can't be extinguished. And we will never yield to…"

I cut him off by hitting him in the knee with my boomerang, swinging it down like a club. He howled in pain, desperately clinging to it. I took the time to retrieve my bow from him.

"Heard that speech far too many times," I said. "And I will stop you and your fake church. One day." He only gasped in pain, his mouth sucking in air like a fish out of water. I peeked over the table to see the spellcasters battling like demons. Sigil had conjured a sword of flame, while Professor Magic whirled around him, wielding a pair of hatchets that looked like he carved them out of waves. Picture a raging ocean, then condense it into a small axe. Still, Sigil wielded his sword proficiently, and where the weapons met, steam hissed out, sizzling like oil.

"You're getting soft, old man!" Sigil cried out. "You can't beat me!"

"Oh shut up, you winy little git!" Professor Magic retaliated. "I've fought worse than you before breakfast!"

"Oh yeah?" Sigil asked, parrying another blow. "Prove it!"

He did, by catching the sword under one axe and sinking the other into his shoulder. It bit down, and the churning waves cut deeper, slowly pulling the axe deeper into his shoulder. With a bit of effort, Professor Magic pulled the axe out. Sigil gasped in agony, blood pouring from the wound. He sank to his knees, trying in vain to stem the flow of blood. His sword vanished with a faint whuf. Professor Magic stood over the warlock; one axe slightly pink. At first, I thought he was going to execute him, but his axes melted into puddles of seawater. He raised his right hand over Sigil's shoulder and said "Cryos." Ice formed over the cut, crackling into existence. Sigil moaned in pain, but the blood stopped.

"That should stop the bleeding," Professor Magic said, his voice darker than usual. "Get yourself a healing potion or go to a hospital. I don't care which. Either way, we're never going to cross paths again. Understood?"

"Damn you," Sigil moaned. "My vengeance isn't satisfied."

"Leave it. Leave your magic behind. Get a real job, a real life. This won't end well for you," Professor Magic said sternly. As he turned to walk out, Sigil traced a symbol in his blood on the floor.

"Professor!" I yelled. Professor Magic whirled around, but it was too late. The symbol began to smoke, and flames rose from the spilled blood. Sigil started laughing, then staggered out the room, still clutching his now frozen shoulder. The flames grew rapidly, taking the form of a massive flaming figure.

"Oh bollocks," Professor Magic said.

"Professor!" I called. "What the hell is that?"

"A wrath demon," he replied. "Probably one of his familiars. The thing burst out of the flames, a massive red-skinned giant with a goat's head. It had horns made from fire, and a trail of flames ran down it's back. It had goat legs and a long scorpion tail. The beast roared, and conjured a whip of flames out of nowhere. The fire spread through the house as it closed in on Professor Magic.

"Shit!" I yelled, grabbing the Hangman by the robes. "Shit shit shit!" I dragged him out the back door onto the lawn and dropped him on the ground far enough away from the burning house. I ran back inside and grabbed another guard. I helped him to his feet as the house started to fill with smoke. Professor Magic surrounded himself in a large bubble of icy water, and was firing blasts of prismatic light from inside it at the demon. The monster howled and whaled on the shield, making it waver and shake like a mound of gelatin. I supported the guard as we left the house. I ran in and out, making sure all the guards escaped. As I got the third one outside, I heard an explosion of flames, all the glass shattering at once.

"Professor!" I called. I stared at the inferno. It was no longer safe to go back inside. I could feel the heat from the yard. The neighboring trees and bushes around the house started to smolder. I could hear yelling and sirens from a distance. Finally, I saw a figure stumble out, half carrying half dragging the last guard. Professor Magic stumbled out and dropped the guard next to the others.

"Professor!" I said as I ran up to him. "What happened? Was that the last one?" He coughed and nodded.

"Yeah," he finally said, his voice scratchy from the smoke. "There was only four guards. Did you see where Sigil went?"

"No, he was long gone by the time I got everyone out. What about the demon?"

"Banished it," he said. "Got that light spell to work and trapped him in a circle. Could barely work the incantation with all the smoke."

"Thank God," I said. "I was afraid we were gonna need Dragonman or a priest to get rid of that thing."

"Hunting demons and witches was the prerogative of Wizards long before the Church or the Silent Prayer," Professor Magic said. "Especially my Line."

I was about to ask what he meant by 'Line' when one of the guards got to his feet and approached us.

"You saved us," he said.

"We did," I replied.

"Why? We tried to kill you," he said plainly. Professor Magic and I exchanged a look.

"Well, we couldn't just leave you in there with that thing," I said. "That would be the same as just shooting you in the head."

"But we're enemies," he said, still in shock. "We were going to sell you to a crime boss. I hit you in the face and tried to shoot you."

"You're misguided," I said. "Not evil. I don't want to hurt you, but I have to so you stop hurting others." He blinked at me in confusion, then looked down at his robes. He looked disgusted by them.

"My wife…" he said, struggling to find the words. "There was a riot. She was out shopping, and the store got looted. The rioters were nig… I mean, black people. She was white. They were angry, and they beat her to death." Tears ran down his face. "I joined because I thought that maybe we could prevent that from happening. But all I did was spread more hate." He looked up at me in despair.

"I'm sorry your wife was killed," I said. "But hatred doesn't cancel out hatred."

"I think I'm starting to see that," he said. He looked down at his hands in anguish. "I've done so much wrong. Killed so many…"

"Then pay for it," I said. "Turn yourself in, and plead guilty. After your time in prison, make it up to them. Spread love and acceptance, not hatred and bigotry. It won't bring your wife back, but maybe it can save someone else's." I put my hand on his shoulder. "Think about what I said."

"Silver," Professor Magic said. "Cops are coming."

"Shit," I said. "We need to leave."

"Wait!" the guard said. I stopped to look back at him. "The person you're looking for is Pastor David Sawyer. He has an island called Firefly Island."

"We know!" I said, starting to leave again.

"Hang on! There's more. The island is guarded. He keeps people there, kids, teenagers, even the elderly to sell as sex slaves. He's the one who hired us. He has more hitmen guarding his house. He wanted you alive to pay for what you did to his church," he said in a rush. "You have to stop him. There's a rumor his home is guarded by a superhuman."

"Thanks!" I said, turning to run. I could hear firetrucks just down the street from us, as well as see flashing red and blue lights. "I won't forget!"

Chapter 10: Dinner Antics

We reconvened at a restaurant in Cincinnati to discuss our options. After telling the others what the grateful guard said, we all discussed ways of breaking in.

"Firefly Island," Lab Rat said, looking it up online. He was doing his air typing thing again, drawing a lot of stares from the other patrons. To be fair, we all were drawing a lot of stares, as we were all in costume. I had pulled down my mask so I could eat, but I left my goggles on to protect my identity. The others didn't have their mouth covered, so they were free to eat. Lab Rat kept his helmet on, claiming he wasn't hungry.

"Find anything?" Dragonman asked through a mouthful of steak. Everyone else ate in silence. Thundergirl had demolished her burger and was half-way through her fries and eyeing everyone else's food hungrily. Professor Magic had a plate of pasta and meatballs. Dragonman had ordered a raw steak and a side of mushrooms, much to the waitress' confusion. Blue Fox had a plate of chicken and waffles she was eyeing with suspicion. I had myself a nice platter of fried chicken and a pickle. Lab Rat simply ordered a glass of pink lemonade that he barely touched.

"Got it," Lab Rat said finally. "Firefly Island was a small island that was used by the Russians in the Cold War as a base of operations for their spies in the US."

"Interesting," Blue Fox said, tentatively trying a bite of chicken. "Why does Sawyer have it?"

"No idea," Lab Rat said. "But the place was built like a fortress. Sawyer already has a summer home. Or homes, I should say. One in California, another in Hawaii."

"Rich asshole," I muttered through my chicken. "Why does he need this?"

"So he can keep his 'cargo' safe, obviously," Thundergirl said. "You gonna eat that pickle?"

"Yes, so stop asking me," I said defensively.

"I'm a bit concerned about this 'superhuman' guarding the island," Professor Magic said. "What else can you find?"

"Well, Wikipedia isn't being very useful in that regard. There's rumors of it being haunted naturally, but what old place isn't?" Lab Rat said.

"What about all the supersoldier experiments the Soviets did?" Dragonman asked.

"Like Imperial Japan did in WW2?" Thundergirl asked with a smile. Blue Fox covered her face in embarrassment.

"I get it! My country made Patient Zero! Stop bringing him up!" she wailed.

"Hmm, not much. There is something interesting though," Lab Rat said. "Apparently, Stalin had a plan for a monkey army."

"I'm sorry?" I asked.

"Okay, technically, it's a chimpanzee army, but still," Lab Rat said. "The idea was to breed humans with chimps in order to produce super strong and durable soldiers during the Second World War."

"Did it work?" Professor Magic asked.

"Of course not," I said. "Human DNA is all practically the same, it's why humans can't interbreed with other species, the way a horse and a donkey make a mule."

"That's… correct," Lab Rat said slowly. "How did you know that?"

"Snapple Cap," I said simply, looking smugly at Thundergirl.

"Bitch," she muttered, but I could see her smile.

"Excuse me?" a voice said. We looked up to see our waitress looking at us. "I just want to say that I don't support what you do, and that the police have been notified. They said the FBI is on their way to arrest you."

"Cool," I said. "Can we get more rolls?" I asked, holding the empty plastic basket towards her.

"Of course," she said, her teeth clenched together as she left.

"Anyways, that was back in WW2," Professor Magic said. "Anything about the Cold War?"

"Hmm, let me see. There is something about a possible Area 51 raid," he said.

"I thought no one showed up to that," I said as I bit into my pickle. Thundergirl looked at me from her empty plate sadly.

"Not that one," Lab Rat said irritably. "Back in '56, there was a supposed raid of Area 51. The entire state was locked down, and MIBs were seen all over the place, asking about Soviet connections.

"MIBs?" Blue Fox asked.

"Men in Black," we all replied.

"Well, damn. Okay then," she said softly, her hands up in surrender.

"That's not much to go off of," Professor Magic said.

"There's not a lot to begin with," Lab Rat said simply. "Plenty of people deny that Firefly Island even exists."

"Brilliant," I said as the waitress returned with a fresh stack of rolls that Thundergirl all but pounced on.

"We should plan our attack based on what we do know. This island may have a superhuman on it, but we have 5," Dragonman said.

"6," I corrected.

"Silver, you are a good shot, but you're only human," Lab Rat contradicted. I folded my arms and frowned at them.

"Snobs," I said.

"Dragonman's right," Blue Fox said. "What other sort of defenses does this island have?"

"Walls, armed guards, towers," Lab Rat said. I could see pictures reflected from the inside of his helmet. "Looks pretty standard to me."

"So it's the usual then," Professor Magic said. "We get in, get the prisoners, and get out."

"Oh yeah," Thundergirl said sarcastically. "This is going to be sooooo easy."

Outside, we heard tires screech. We looked up to see FBI agents rushing out from a dark truck.

"Ah, crap," I said. Agent Kane strode into the building.

"Jesters!" she declared. "We have the building surrounded! Come quietly and no one has to get hurt."

"Alright, how much was everyone's meal?" Dragonman said, casually pulling out his wallet. Lab Rat started rattling off prices as we started pulling out money. Kane watched us with growing resentment.

"I said…!" she started to yell.

"We heard you the first time, Kane!" Professor Magic called out. "We still have to pay for our meal," he looked into his wallet and frowned. "Ah, bollocks. I don't have any American bills. Can anyone cover me?"

"I got you," Lab Rat said. "You owe me though."

"16.89 for an uncooked steak," Dragonman sighed. "All they had to do was take it out of the freezer and put it on a plate."

"In Nippon, you pay for your meal as you leave, rather than wait for the server to bring you the check," Blue Fox said.

"Really?" Thundergirl said. "Sounds useful."

"Everyone pay?" I asked as I stood up from the booth and grabbed my bow. Everyone nodded or answered simply.

"Good," Kane called. "Now, just place your hands where I can see them…"

"What realm should we cut through?" Professor Magic asked, ignoring Kane entirely.

"Not Niflheim again," I said with a shiver.

"Or Muspelheim," Lab Rat said. "We don't want to repeat the Wal-Mart Incident."

"How about Vanaheim?" Blue Fox suggested.

"Ugh. Pass," Dragonman said. "Too bright."

"Alfheim?" Thundergirl suggested.

"That's even worse," he said.

"Hey! I said you're under arrest!" Kane yelled, stomping her foot.

"Could you keep it down?" Thundergirl asked. "We're trying to plan our escape."

"I know!" I said. "Asgard! We haven't been there in ages!"

"Asgard sounds nice," Lab Rat said. Everyone else nodded in agreement."

"Asgard it is," Professor Magic said.

"Oh no, you don't!" Kane yelled. She grabbed her walkie talkie and shouted "Take them!" into it. Armed FBI agents clad in black armor crashed through the windows.

"Freeze!" one agent yelled. "Get down on the ground now!" We ignored them as Professor Magic opened a portal to Asgard. I could see ruins and a starry sky through the golden circle.

"Stop, or I will be forced to use deadly force!" the agent yelled.

"Don't!" Kane shouted. "There are civilians present!" We all waved goodbye as we stepped through the portal. I made sure to salute Kane before the portal closed.

Chapter 11: Firefly Island

"Lab Rat, I hate you," Thundergirl said.

"Why?" he asked, sounding hurt.

"You never mentioned Firefly Island was in the middle of a damn swamp!" she said angrily.

"You never asked! Besides, Kane showed up and ruined dinner."

"You didn't even eat anything!" Thundergirl yelled.

"Keep your voices down, children," Dragonman rumbled. We were hiking through the swamp, heading for Firefly Island. After a brief shortcut through Asgard, we ended up as close as we could to Firefly Island, which was surrounded by bog and mud.

"I know *damn* well you did not just call me a child," Thundergirl said hotly.

"Thundergirl, you're barely old enough to vote," Dragonman said. "So shut up so we can get the drop on these idiots." Thundergirl glared at him, but stopped shouting. She settled for crossing her arms and floated angrily.

Unlike Thundergirl, I was thrilled to be in a swamp. Finally, I was in my element. No roads, no cars, no hiding behind dumpsters. Just the good ol' outdoors. I took a deep breath and smelled the foul bog air. Sure, it might stink to you, but I felt way surer of myself here. Lab Rat was leading, following a holographic map being projected out of his wrist. I was right behind him, searching for any tracks that might indicate human settlement or dangerous wildlife. Behind me was Professor Magic and Dragonman, Professor Magic using his staff like a cane. Bringing up the rear were the girls. Thundergirl was floating like an angry balloon, not wanting to get her boots dirty. Blue Fox was following in the form of a wolf-sized fox with nine tails, making it easier for her to walk through the rough terrain.

"Hold up," I said. We all paused, except for Thundergirl, who crashed into Dragonman's back.

"Hey!" she protested.

"What's up, Silver?" Professor Magic asked.

"Tracks," I said, kneeling down to get a closer look. Just in front of Lab Rat was a muddy bare footprint, but with a weird big toe that looked more like a thumb.

"Shallow," I muttered. "Means they weren't very heavy, and the toes are pointed towards us." I frowned and looked behind us. The only tracks were ours.

"That's not good," I said.

"What's wrong?" Lab Rat asked.

"There's a trail of tracks leading right towards us," I said. "But they stop right here."

"That doesn't make any sense," Professor Magic asked. "Where did they go?"

"Above us!" Dragonman suddenly cried, readying his club. We all jumped to battle poses. I couldn't see what he was talking about, until a dark shape dove out from the treetops and pounced on me. I barely managed to dodge, and the thing landed right in front of me. I could barely make out a squat, hairy creature with long arms and fangs.

"Cyka Blyat!" It cried, swinging a K-Bar knife at me. I managed to block it, just as Lab Rat grabbed the creature by the hair and spiked its head into the ground like a volleyball.

"Thanks," I said. Before he could respond, another one leapt out at him. This time I was ready. I fired a concussive arrow at it midair, knocking it into a tree. All around us, a small troop of these things were flying out of the treetops, brandishing knives, machetes and screaming in Russian. Dragonman was fighting off three of them, roaring and snarling like a rabid dog. Blue Fox the Fox had one in her mouth and was thrashing it like a chew toy while one was on her back trying to throttle her. Professor Magic was fending them off with a fire sword in one hand, the other blasting bolts of green energy out of the top of his staff. Thundergirl was blasting blue lasers from her palms, calling out special moves from various anime.

"Kamehameha!" she cried, firing a huge blast from both hands, sending five of them toppling like bowling pins. One managed to drop down on her and hit her with his knife. The blade snapped off with an audible pop. She turned around to face it, her face lit up with a brilliant smile.

"Nyet…" it said sadly.

"Falcon… PUNCH!" she cried, punching it in the chest so hard it flew out into the swamp out of sight. The other creatures, upon seeing that, ran back into the forest and disappeared.

"What the hell were those?" Professor Magic asked, panting from the fight.

"No clue, but they were tough," Dragonman said. He was breathing hard too, but not from exertion. His face was lit up like a little kid on his birthday.

"You said it," Thundergirl said, her smile equally manic

"Well, glad you two *baka* had fun," Blue Fox said sourly, returned to human(ish) form. Her suit had small cuts and gashes on it, and her mouth was covered in blood.

"Hey guys?" Lab Rat said, examining the one that attacked me. "Remember the chimp army I mentioned?

"Yeah?" I asked.

"I think this is it," he rolled the creature on its back, and we all got a better look at it. It was roughly human shaped, but much shorter. Its entire body was covered in hair, aside from its face, where this one had a thick bushy beard growing. Its arms were covered in lean tough muscles, and they were much longer than a human's. Its mouth was slightly open, showing off long white canine teeth. It was dressed in dark green camo pants, a bulletproof vest, and wore a green army helmet with night vision goggles attached. Its feet were bare, with the feet looking like a blend of hand and foot.

Just like the tracks I found.

"Son of a bitch," I said.

"I thought you said humans couldn't make hybrids," Blue Fox said accusingly.

"Yeah, what does your Snapple Cap say about this?" Dragonman said. Thundergirl frowned at the creature.

"Well, you two are half-human, you tell me!" she said finally.

"Magic didn't create this thing," Professor Magic said, gently tapping it with the bottom of his staff. "This is a creature born of science."

"Maybe it's a mutant?" I asked. "Like the Bayou Brothers?" Lab Rat scanned the monkey-man, a blue triangle of light coming out from the side of his helmet, running up and down the body.

"Maybe not. It's got human and chimpanzee DNA, but there's also something else. Something I can't determine," Lab Rat said, looking at the data. We all exchanged a nervous look. There wasn't a lot that Lab Rat didn't know, aside from the magical side of things. If this was something even *he* couldn't understand, then we were in for one hell of a fight.

"Well, now what?" I asked.

"Way I see it, this is the superhumans the racist dude mentioned. Only there's an army of them guarding Firefly Island," Thundergirl said, straightening her gloves. "But those kids are still trapped there."

"We need a plan," Professor Magic said, furrowing his brow in thought.

"No," Thundergirl said defiantly. We all looked at her.

"No?" Blue Fox asked.

"No more plans. No more splitting up. Those things already know we're here, and that we can fight them off. They're going to put that whole island on lockdown and get their weapons ready. Stealth isn't going to do this," Thundergirl said. "We charge in, full frontal assault."

"Yeaaah," I said. "I don't do those."

"Then find a vantage point and start dropping chimps," she said. "Dragonman and I lead. Lab Rat, Professor and Blue Fox follow. The two of us soak the bulk of the damage while you three start firing."

"This sounds suspiciously like a plan," I said sarcastically.

"I'm tired of pussyfooting around these a-holes," Thundergirl snapped. "We go in, blow some stuff up and save the day. No more waiting around, no more investigating. And if we find Sawyer, I'm gonna punch him in the dick. Sound good?" she asked. No one said a word. "Perfect. Move out!"

For the record, Lab Rat decided to call the hybrids 'humanzees'. I guess it makes sense, a nice mix of human and chimpanzee. But that is a pain and half to write, so I'll stick to calling them chimps.

Galvanized/terrified by Thundergirl's "plan" we all forged ahead into the swamp, until we came up on Firefly Island. It wasn't much of an island, just a lump of land in the middle of the deepest parts of the swamp. There was a narrow strip of land connecting it to the rest of the land (mainland?) where trucks could go in and out from the island to the airstrip and helicopter landing pad not too far away. I had managed to grapple my way through the trees like a less graceful Spider-Man and get a good view of the compound. The entire place was rusted corrugated steel, and those chimps were *everywhere*. They could walk just fine, but were equally comfortable climbing on rooftops and up trees. I was a bit concerned they would climb up *my* tree, but I saw a patrol enter the treetops through a different one.

"Silverbolt in position," I said through my comms. "How can you hear me?" I asked.

"All clear," Lab Rat said. Despite Thundergirl's 'plan', Lab Rat insisted on stealth. He dove into the water with the plan of entering through the massive pipes. His suit had a rebreather on it, so water transport wasn't an issue for him.

"*Gurgle*," Blue Fox the Octopus answered. Blue Fox had gone with Rat through the water in the form of a bright orange octopus with nine tentacles. Because why not.

"All good here," Thundergirl replied. She was walking across the land bridge like she owned the place. Behind her were Dragonman and Professor Magic walking single file. Dragonman was only slightly less bulletproof than Thundergirl, and Professor Magic wasn't bulletproof at *all*.

"Loud and clear," Dragonman said.

"Same with me," Professor Magic replied.

"I hear you all the same," I said. "Except Blue Fox, but I think that's okay."

"*Burble*," she answered.

"Sure," I said. "You sure this is going to work?"

"I'm positive," Thundergirl said. She looked up at the massive iron door, cracked her knuckles, and tore it open like it was made of wet paper. The thing screamed in protest, that high pitched metal whine. This got the attention of every chimp on the compound. I saw hordes of them pouring out of buildings and shacks, many of them armed. Some started giving orders in Russian, which I then shot with my knockout arrows. Best way to take down a military base.

"HEY!" Thundergirl bellowed, her supersonic yell echoing across the swamp, sending ripples across the water. The chimps closest to her stumbled from the force of it. The ones higher up in the back started to open fire at her. Dragonman tried to block his face and the sensitive areas of his body, while Professor Magic conjured a golden bubble around himself and focused on keeping it up.

Thundergirl ran forwards, the bullets bouncing off her, harmless as rain drops. She flashed through the army, I only caught flickers of her movement. She was punching and kicking them, each hit felling a chimp. Dragonman and Professor Magic followed her, the gunfire no longer keeping them outside. They tried to help, but Thundergirl was too far ahead of them. She whirled through the ranks, like a smiling goddess of war. She blasted two off the roof, and another into what must've been the magazine, as it exploded dramatically. I fired more arrows, picking off stragglers and snipers. A bullet brushed past me, making me flinch and almost lose my footing.

"Shit!" I said. "I think they saw me!" I saw a chimp take aim at me, cursing in Russian.

"Guys?" I asked. Thundergirl suddenly appeared in front of it as he squeezed the trigger. His arm blurred, and I saw her drop the bullet she caught midair. The chimp stared in abject horror as she punted him like a football into the swamp outside.

"Outside, clear!" Thundergirl called.

"Still more inside," Lab Rat whispered. "I think I found where the kids are being kept.

"Finally," I said. "We moving inside?"

"We are. Silverbolt, get down here and head inside with Thundergirl," Professor Magic said. "Dragonman and I will head up into the control room. Blue Fox and Lab Rat, get to the kids."

"Got it," I said, gliding down out of my tree. We were about to enter the building, when I saw a huge dark shape drop down behind Thundergirl.

"Behind you!" I cried. The shadow raised a fist and punched Thundergirl into a wall. She slammed into it with a loud metal clang. The thing turned around, and my blood froze.

If the little ones were half human, half chimp, this thing was half gorilla, half human. The monster beat its chest and roared. It looked more human, but had a long prehensile tail, gray skin under its black hair, with silver covering the back in the shape of a hammer and sickle. And no, I wasn't making that part up.

"Privyet," It said. "Little Americans."

"Uhh, hi?" I said nervously.

"You come to my base, kill my men, and expect to live, da?" it asked. It had a smooth voice with a thick Russian accent. Unlike the chimps, this thing was dressed in sweatpants and no shirt. However, it was carrying a handheld grenade launcher (for its size) holstered on its belt, a minigun strapped on its back next to a rocket launcher.

"Umm, kinda. Yeah. Da," I said.

"Interesting," the beast rumbled. Good lord, it looked like it could eat Dragonman. "Little archer, tell me your name, so I may know who I have the pleasure of killing."

"Umm, I'm called Silverbolt," I replied meekly.

"Silverbolt, eh?" it said, and laughed. "Is funny, I am called Silver*back*!" He laughed some more, then drew the grenade launcher.

"Okay," Silverback said, his laughter dying down. "Time for you to die."

"HOLD IT RIGHT THERE!" Thundergirl called out. She pulled herself out of the dent in the wall and glared up at Silverback.

"Ah, the little gold girl is tougher than she looks, da?" he said with mild amusement.

"*Little gold girl*!?" She bellowed. "I'll show you little gold girl!" She leaned back and punched Silverback right in the gut. I could hear the punch from twenty feet away. Silverback wheezed and dropped the grenade launcher. I took the chance and dashed behind cover in case it went off. It didn't, but the two brawlers didn't seem to notice. The giant looked down at Thundergirl.

"Is that all?" he asked. His fist shot towards like a cannonball, but she dodged and flew to his side and punched him in the side of the knee. Silverback howled in pain as his leg collapsed in on itself. He glared at her, and his tail shot towards her like a snake. It coiled around her neck and started squeezing. She gasped and pulled at it, but was losing oxygen.

"Any last words?" he growled. She raised a hand towards his face and said:

"Excelsior!" A blue blast rocketed out of her palm, right in the gorilla's kisser. Silverback roared in pain and fell down on his ass. His tail unraveled from her neck as he fell, dazed. She wound back her fist to hit him one last time.

"RAAGH!" she screamed and hit the gorilla-man with enough force to send a visible shockwave out. His jaw popped like a giant kernel of popcorn as he flew up into the air and down on his back, landing heavily. Thundergirl tossed her head back and yelled triumphantly.

And I swear, it sounded *exactly* like thunder.

"Wow," I said, striding up to her. "That was dramatic."

"Ahh," she said, rolling her shoulders and bouncing on her heels. "That feels much better."

"I bet," I said, still in awe. I've never seen her cut loose like that. In fact, if I didn't know better, I'd say she was still holding back.

Yikes.

We continued deeper into the compound, where we found a few unconscious chimps. The interior was a mess of rust and cement dripping rust. We eventually found a large cage of people from all over the world. It was mostly kids, but there were a few teenagers among them. Many of them were crying, and Professor Magic was gently shepherding them through a portal to Vanaheim. A nice touch, seeing how Vanaheim is probably the nicest of the Nine Realms. Lab Rat was scanning them and getting names to return them home, Blue Fox was being a total mom and fussing over the kid's hair and wellbeing. Even Dragonman was being helpful, calming down the youngest ones by (get this) singing to them in Italian. He can have a very soothing voice when he wants to.

We got the last of them through the portal. Having Thundergirl around was very helpful, as she was very popular with children. After Vanaheim, we took the kids all over the country, back to their homes and to their parents, who were overjoyed at seeing their children return home.

Chapter 12: Judgement Day

We were all over the news for the next week, the tale of the children's rescue dominating every network. Task Force 52 had to eat crow as someone had filmed us blowing them off during an 'arrest' and then posted it on YouTube. Worse, the entire FBI was ridiculed for not finding out Pastor Sawyer was the culprit.

The six of us were glued to the news, waiting to see Sawyer's arrest. Nothing. There was no call for it. Hell, the media seemed to forget he was involved after the first week.

Not a good sign.

"And so, my brothers and sister, we must rejoice!" Pastor Sawyer called out to his massive crowd. The megachurch thundered in reply. "We must rejoice, for the children that were lost have been found. Can I get an Amen?"

The foundations shook with the cry of 'AMEN!' Just after the amen, one voice called out:

"Pedo!"

My voice.

Everyone whirled around to see me. I stood up and strode down the aisles. I saw Dragonman do the same. Professor Magic, Blue Fox and Thundergirl all walked up to the altar to stand next to Pastor Sawyer. Up close, he didn't look like much. He had mouse-brown hair that had receded to the middle of his head, large glasses with thick lenses and a thinning beard. His gray suit looked expensive.

"Uhh, brothers and sisters. I don't normally allow people to come up onto the altar," he said nervously. He damn near jumped out of his skin when Lab Rat appeared out of nowhere next to him.

"Children of God!" Dragonman called out. Lab Rat had connected our communicators to the speakers earlier.

"You have all been deceived!" Professor Magic called.

"Your 'pastor', if that's what you want to call him, is nothing but a liar and a pedophile!" Blue Fox said.

"Okay, that's enough!" Pastor Sawyer said. "Security!" Thundergirl's arm blurred towards his groin. The Pastor gave a pathetic squeak, then collapsed into the fetal position. Never say that Thundergirl doesn't keep her promises.

"This man has been stealing all your money and spending it on debauchery and child-love!" I called out.

"Roll the footage!" Lab Rat tapped a few imaginary keys, and the screens behind us changed to bodycam footage of a Holy Hand of God guard standing outside of a burning house.

"Hang on! There's more. The island is guarded. He keeps people there, kids, teenagers, even the elderly, to sell as sex slaves. He's the one who hired us. He has more hitmen guarding his house. He wanted you alive to pay for what you did to his church," the guard said.

Murmurs and gasps went up from the crowd.

"You've heard the rumors," Lab Rat said. "All the evidence that points to this 'man' has been swept under the rug by his platoon of lawyers."

"Will you continue to follow this pervert?" Thundergirl thundered (pun *partially* intended). She was the only one not connected to a mic. Trust me, she doesn't need it.

"The Jesters has stood against tyranny and evil since its beginning," Professor Magic said.

"Always has been…" Dragonman said.

"… Always will," I said.

"The system has failed us," Blue Fox said. "They chose to ignore this man and his crimes because he bought them off. Either with your money or your children." The crowd's murmuring started to get more aggressive and angrier.

"We leave it up to you now," Thundergirl said. "The People."

"He's in your hands now," Professor Magic said. "Do what you will."

We all filed out of the church. A good portion simply stormed out. Most of them were families, mothers and fathers keeping their children close and protected. The ones closest to the altar got up and started gathering around him with fists clenched.

"Wait a minute!" I heard him beg. "I never did any of that! It's all lies and slander. T-The Good Book says…"

Whatever the Good Book said, I didn't hear over the roar of the angry mob that had descended on the fallen Pastor.

"You think they're going to kill him?" I asked as we left the building

"Not sure," Professor Magic said, stroking his beard. "I hope not."

"His security detail was coming in," Lab Rat said. "They'll probably stop them from going too far.

"Or join in," Blue Fox said darkly.

"We knew this could happen," Thundergirl said, although she sounded uncomfortable with the prospect.

"We should've just beat his ass ourselves," I said.

"Too late now," Dragonman said. "The truth always comes out. He'll get his due. Be it by man or God, he will pay what he owes."

"You just come up with stuff on the fly?" I asked in amazement.

"I'm just glad you have a camera in your goggles," Professor Magic said. "Didn't know you had that."

"Yeah," I said, looking at Lab Rat. "Me neither." Everyone else looked over at Lab Rat, who had suddenly become very interested in something on his suit.

"Did you guys know that the average gorilla is nine times stronger than a human?" he said. "I guess that makes Silverback one hell of a..."

"Rat," Thundergirl said accusingly.

"Oh, alright! I may have stuck cameras on all of your masks, alright? Just for security reasons," Lab Rat said, throwing his hands in the air.

"You did what?" Dragonman asked.

"I don't even wear a mask!" Professor Magic pointed out.

"It's on your monocle," Lab Rat said.

"Oh my God!" Blue Fox said. "You've been filming everything we see!?"

"Sort of, and I know why *you're* upset…"

"Oh God, I've worn this mask while I've…"

"Trust me, Blue, I know," Lab Rat said. "Not to worry, that data is safely archived."

"You *kept it??*" she asked incredulously.

"Of course! We might need it later! We never know when you might end up sleeping with an important informant or future supervillain," Lab Rat argued. Blue Fox howled in rage and tackled Lab Rat to the ground, clawing at his face and screaming at him in Japanese. Had it not been for his forcefield, Lab Rat would've been torn to shreds.

"Is anyone filming this?" I asked.

"Apparently, he is," Dragonman said, pointing down at the struggling Lab Rat.

We all got a good laugh at that.

Do you understand why I hate that question? You don't need superpowers to be a superhero. You need conviction to stand up and save the innocent. Even more to save the guilty. It doesn't matter if you can breathe fire, turn invisible, shapeshift, cast spells or punch a Soviet gorilla man so hard his kids are born dizzy.

The only power worth having is courage. Courage to admit you're wrong, courage to face your demons, and courage to risk your life to save an enemy.

So hone your skills, iron your cape and shine your mask. Because the truth about superheroes is that anyone can do it.

THE END

Story 2: Bread and Circus

Chapter 1: Welcome to Jester Park!

Being a superhero, you often wake up in strange places. Hotels, warehouses, the backs of vans and trunks of cars. Being in the Jesters, I've woken up in even stranger circumstances. Full-blown fights over the pettiest things, ranging from who ate the last cookie to whether or not Nicholas Cage is a good actor.

Waking up to circus music isn't one of the good ones.

My head was pounding, and my mouth felt like it was full of cotton. I groaned and lifted my head, blearily looking around. Bright lights and warm colors filled my vision and cheap grinder organ music, the kind they used to play to dancing monkeys back in the day, surrounded me.

I blinked and felt the effects of whatever drug I was given slowly fade. I could see that I was on a carousel. Blinking lightbulbs flashed overhead, reflecting off of mirrors placed around the central pillar. I was astride a brown plastic horse, which I didn't mind as much. Horses are my favorite animal. I tried to sit up and felt resistance at my wrists. I looked down and took inventory of what I could see and feel.

I was in costume, and I could feel my mask and goggles on.

My equipment was missing, which really bothered me.

My wrists and ankles were fastened to the carousel with leather straps.

I struggled at the straps, pulling in vain. I muttered a few curse words under my breath. This was just insulting. Any other member of the Jesters could have gotten free of these in a matter of seconds. Dragonman and Thundergirl could snap these things like they were wet cardboard, Professor Magic could cast some sort of unlocking spell, Lab Rat could probably bend his fingers or fold his hand to squeeze through, and I know Blue Fox could shapeshift into something smaller and be free. But no, it only took two pairs of leather straps to hold Silverbolt down.

What made it so much worse was that I could see my bow and quivers poking up from a carriage pulled by two wyverns ahead of me.

"Greetings, Silverbolt!" a voice called from a speaker above me. I jumped like a scared cat, which wasn't doing much to uphold the badass heroine image we superheroes like to portray.

"Who's there?" I asked, mustering as much menace as I could.

"Welcome to Jester Park!" the voice replied. "You have been selected along with five other visitors to test our new attractions!"

Oh great. This was going to work out *perfectly*.

I pulled harder at the straps. "Who's doing this?" I called out again. "And can we get some different music please?"

"You have been chosen for our new Carousel of Adventure!" the voice continued, ignoring my questions and pleas for different tunes. "Our Carousel of Adventure offers an exciting new twist on a timeless classic." Behind me, I heard a chain rattle and a soft growl. I twisted around as best as I could and saw a lion with a chain connecting it to a rail on the ceiling of the carousel.

My eyes widened in fear. The lion growled again and shook his mane, rattling the chain. The chain was attached to a harness around the beast's shoulders and was being tugged along the rail by a small machine.

I froze. The lion was slowly being tugged in my direction. It had some difficulty squeezing between the animals and swatted a massive paw at a plastic horse in frustration. The horse shattered, the pieces crashing onto the floor. I struggled at my bonds more frantically. Whoever had trapped me here was smart about it. My wrist-mounted dart launchers had been removed, which sucked because I had used them to break free of bonds like these in the past. I glanced back at the lion. It had picked up on my frantic movements and was getting interested. It moved closer with earnest, hardly needing the chains tugging.

"You've gotta be shitting me," I hissed. The straps were built like a belt, with a buckle feeding through small holes in the leather. If I could get one hand free, I could easily free the other. I tried to squeeze my hand through the loop in a desperate ploy to escape.

That's when I felt the lion's warm breath right behind me. I froze in fear. I could hear it sniffing me, trying to see if I were a snack or a threat. I gulped. My costume is tough, but lions are strong. That thing could shatter my ribs with one swipe, its claws could easily tear through my armor in a matter of seconds. Not to mention the size of the thing. Lions are huge, and this one looked hungry. I felt its muzzle brush against my back, and I jerked back involuntarily. The lion jumped back as well, startled by the sudden movement.

The lion growled and raised a paw to strike. I could see the tips of its claws poking out from its tawny fur. I jumped up, trying to stand up on the plastic horse as best as I could.

That alone saved me.

The lion brought down his paw, shattering the horse and sending shards of plastic flying. The pole holding the horse up fell from its housing in the ceiling. I quickly scrambled away from the lion. I slid my straps free of the pole. Free of the horse, I managed to curl up and draw my knife from the strap on my leg.

I don't get along well with my Dad now, but one thing he taught me always stuck: always keep a knife on you. You never know when you'll need it.

As the lion snarled and batted at the plastic pieces, I quickly cut through my leather restraints. I jumped back up to my feet and instinctively reached for an arrow. Too late, I remembered my bow and arrow were sitting on the carriage right in front of my horse.

Where the lion was now standing.

He stared me down, lowering himself into a crouch. I'd seen cats crouch down like this before, right before they tackled a laser pointer dot or a toy mouse. I froze again. I knew enough about animals to know that any sudden movement would trigger that thing into a pounce. The only weapon I had on me was a knife. It wasn't a bad knife. It had a serrated edge and was long enough to get you arrested in some states, but it wasn't made for killing lions. For the millionth time, I wished I had some sort of superpower. Flight, super strength, laser eyes, telekinesis. Hell, I'd even settle for Aquaman's fish powers.

That gave me an idea. I started making gentle shushing sounds and put my hand forward. The lion stopped growling, and slowly raised itself up from the crouch. I watched the tension ease out of its muscles as I slowly approached the lion, making sure to not make any sudden movements. The lion slowly stood up as I approached.

"Easy," I murmured. "Easy, big guy."

See, I figured that if someone had chained the lion here, he was used to seeing people. After all, how many wild lions do you see chained to carousels? He was likely brought here from some zoo or circus, and had to be used to trainers or keepers, which meant humans might have shown him affection or brought him food. I was hoping I could convince the lion I was one of the good ones.

I had no bow, no fancy arrows, and no other options. If that lion suddenly decided to eat me, it could, and I had no chance of escape. Soon, I was close enough to touch the big cat. I gently placed a hand on his head, trying not to make eye contact with the beast. He flattened his ears, and I backed off. The lion growled, and my heart felt like it was trying to abandon this plan and escape on its own.

But the lion rumbled again and closed its eyes. I reached out again and scratched his head, right behind the ears. The big cat rumbled deep in its chest and leaned into my hand. The damn thing was purring, like a giant kitten. I scratched more eagerly at the lion's head, and he purred even deeper.

"Aww, who's a big softie?" I said in a voice most people reserve for babies, running my hands through his mane, scratching under his chin and on the back of his head. "You're not a mean lion, aren't you? You're just curious." The lion purred contentedly and slumped down onto the floor, almost knocking me over. I scratched his head some more, and then stood. The lion started to doze, his chain almost taut. I managed to step away and retrieve my bow and quivers. I looked up at the carousel to see a security camera watching me.

"You like that, you sick creeps?" I asked. I flipped off the camera. "Bet you didn't think I would befriend your pet lion, huh?" I stepped off the carousel platform onto the ground and started walking toward the exit. Behind me, I heard a low growl. I looked up to see the lion had gotten up and was watching me leave. The poor thing looked sad that I was leaving.

Maybe this sounds dumb, and I'm sure many of you wouldn't have done this, but I'm a big softie myself where animals are concerned. I love all sorts of animals and I was raised on *Animal Planet* as a kid. I spent most of my time watching Steve Irwin on *Crocodile Hunter* and all sorts of nature documentaries. So maybe I might've made a mistake nocking an arrow and hitting the chain with an incendiary arrow and cutting it. The hot metal fell down around the lion and spooked it. It turned and high tailed it away from me, maybe back to its cage. I shrugged and left the carousel and my new friend behind.

Chapter 2: You are Here

I walked around the open area of this 'Jester Park', trying to get my bearings. My phone wasn't getting any service, and I tried to remember what I was doing before I woke up to circus music on a carousel.

We were investigating something Lab Rat had found, a kidnapped rich girl rumored to be in Ohio. We entered some warehouse to meet an informant, and then…

… Nothing.

I'm not much of a gambler, but I would've put money on that saying that's where these sickos caught us. I furrowed my brow as I walked. Getting the jump on us is not an easy feat. We're all pretty sharp on our own and can usually see an ambush before it happens. Thundergirl is an empath and can read someone's emotions long before she can see them. Dragonman's hearing is strong enough to pick up a person's heartbeat from across the room, and Professor Magic can see a few moments of the future, more if he focuses.

So how did they get the drop on us?

Also, I'm betting it was no accident that I was almost fed to a lion. In my free time, I like to go hunting. I know I just said I'm an animal lover, but hunting is part of who we are as humans. You can claim we've evolved past that but eating deer and small game is an ancient part of humanity. I choose to celebrate that part rather than ignore it.

So, having the only game hunter in the League get killed by big game? Seems like a pretty ironic way to go.

I was willing to bet the others were trapped somewhere in this park on some twisted attraction that played to their weakness. Apparently, mine was just having my bow and arrows out of arm's reach.

That stung.

I rounded a corner and found myself at a wide-open dining area. Dark green tables filled the lot with closed umbrellas topping them. Ringing the pavilion was a slew of famous fast-food places with closed shutters. Sbarro, McDonalds, Taco Bell, Pizza Hut and Panda Express to name a few, along with an Arby's. Yuck.

More interesting was a large map of the place on a board. I stepped up to it and had a look.

Honestly, had this not been some sort of crazy sick death trap, it looked like a lot of fun to visit. There was a haunted mansion, a Hall of Illusions, a corn maze, bumper cars, and even a Christmas village with a train. There was a massive roller coaster called 'Uncanny Valley', which just looked fun to me. I looked them over as best I could, trying to figure out which one might have a superhero trapped in one. The closest one was 'Blackbeard's Cove', which just sounded awesome, fun, and the perfect place to hold the Dragonman.

Dragonman is one of the toughest people I know, but everyone has their weaknesses. Dragonman is an amalgamation of several monsters combined with the goal of making one super monster to hunt other monsters. He has the power of a dragon, the strength of a troll, the magic of a faery, the guile of a vampire, the senses of a werewolf, and the wits of a witch. He can breathe fire, throw cars, mask his presence entirely, regenerate wounds, cast cantrips, and has the senses of a wolf. Despite all his quirky powers, Dragonman also has all their weaknesses. Iron and silver burn his skin, sunlight makes him sluggish, gold attracts his eye, and water can nullify his abilities. That last one is a doozy. He's like Superman, if he were on a planet that was 70% kryptonite and fell from the sky. Not so super now.

If I were some crazy amusement park tycoon trying to imprison and possibly kill the Jesters, trapping Dragonman on a water ride sounded like the most disrespectful way to do it. Plus, having it be a pirate themed one meant gold, and that could distract him from more important issues, like escape and vengeance for instance. I quickly noted the fastest path there and started running.

Upon seeing Blackbeard's Cove, I realized just how unfair all of this was. I had been trapped on a cheap carousel with blinky lights and obnoxious music. Blackbeard's Cove looked like something out of a *Pirates of the Caribbean* movie. The whole ride was dominated by a massive skull-shaped cave with a waterfall coming out the gaping jaws. A heavy blanket of fog sat over the water with flickering tiki torches giving the whole area a haunted jungle look. Ancient ferns and bushes planted thickly along the water's edge, and old Mesoamerican ruins and carvings dotted the landscape. The ride looked fun, spooky and exciting.

"No fair," I muttered to myself. "I get stuck on the cheap county fair ride, and they had rides like this in the park?" I looked around for clues. By the entrance I saw a skeleton with an eye patch, faded pirate hat and gold tooth holding a cutlass out to show how tall you had to be to ride. What caught my eye was how tall this ride needed you to be. I didn't even come close, and I'm almost six foot. Dragonman stands a solid 7 foot 6 inches and would be more than tall enough to pass this skeleton's criteria. I ignored the skeleton entirely because of what a rebel I am and walked past it. Just inside the entry cave were rows of cubbies, where guests could place items they didn't want to go flying on the ride. One of the cubbies was open, and a large black object was hanging out. I crept closer to it. It was a large leather jacket folded as neatly as it could and shoved into the cubby. The jacket was so big it hardly fit and looked like it was about to fall out. I ran my fingers over the material, feeling the pebbly surface, a mix of snakeskin and fish scales met my touch.

Dragonhide. This was the Mantle of Blackwing, Dragonman's melodramatic name for his trench coat. Because only the edgiest superheroes of the night have names for their coats. Nestled in the cubby with the coat were a pair of silver gauntlets and a thick leather belt covered in bulging pouches. I couldn't see the buckle, but I was willing to bet it would look like a Japanese ogre demon, an *oni*. Leaning against the cubby was a massive wooden club, the grip wrapped with leather straps and the whacking end wrapped with metal bands. Dragonman's iconic trusty club.

"Well," I said to myself. "Here are Dragonman's things. Now where is…" I started. Behind me, where the ride would normally stop to pick up and drop off riders, I heard a roar of water and a desperate gurgled cry. I whirled around to see a small mockup pirate ship with a skeleton mermaid figurehead (so cool) blast past with a drenched and soggy figure riding in the back. His arms hung limply, and his black hair was plastered to his gray face and muscular shoulders. He let out a gurgled cry as the ship rocketed past, not even slowing its pace.

"Shit. Hang on, buddy!" I called, racing out the cave. I ran past the pirate skeleton and followed the path of the ride. The boat briefly passed in front of the rest of the park, before veering right and heading deeper into the foggy jungle. I quickly drew my grappling gun from my belt and fired the cable at the back of the ship and dove in. I landed in the water with a splash and immediately started retracting the cable.

Holy shit, that water was cold. I felt my breath rush out in an involuntary gasp when the chill hit. I sank below the surface, gripping my little grapple gun tightly as the ride tugged me along. The gun pulled me closer to the departing ride. My hood was yanked off my head by the rushing water as I approached the little dinghy. I was thankful for my goggles, otherwise I wouldn't have seen the boat I was being dragged behind and probably would have concussed myself crashing into the damn thing.

As I reached the ride, I pulled myself up with one arm and flopped into the boat with all the grace of a trout being pulled onto a fishing vessel. I gasped and tried to stand up. The damn boat kept rattling back and forth so much, I fought to even crouch without falling off the side. Guess they have those harnesses for a reason. I managed to clamber up to the middle row where Dragonman was sitting. He wasn't moving anymore.

"Hey!" I yelled over the surging water. Christ, I felt like I was in the middle of a storm on the high seas. Water kept splashing onto the little boat. Dragonman managed to turn his head towards me. He looked absolutely miserable. Never mind the cold, the water was sapping his strength. His royal blue eyes looked unfocused, and his long black hair clung to his neck and cheeks. His normally immaculate beard was askew, and his arms hung limply at his side.

"Silver?" he managed to ask weakly.

"Yeah," I said. "It's me. I'm gonna get you out, okay? We're gonna get off this ride and go someplace dry, got it?"

"So... cold..." he whimpered.

"Yeah, I know. Don't worry. Think about, uh, hot coffee and steaks, okay? I'll get us out of here," I said. He whimpered something I couldn't hear and slumped his head against the headrest. Seeing him like this made me want to cry and punch someone. Dragonman was one of the toughest people I knew and seeing him laid low by a frigging pirate ride for children done pissed me off something foul. I looked around desperately for something I could use to get him free. I looked down at the straps holding him down. Plain nylon straps, the material used for seatbelts in cars, held him down.

The buckles looked odd, gleaming in the meager light of the torches. I frowned at them. Even being weakened by the freezing water, he should have been able to unbuckle himself. I tried them, and they popped off normally. I scowled at the buckles, then looked at his hands. His palms were covered in angry black blisters, the gray and blue skin marred and disfigured, as if something burned him.

Silver. The buckles were made from silver, which burns the skin of werewolves and repels creatures of the night. I ground my teeth at this. Someone kidnapped my friend and trapped him on a ride that splashed water on him to weaken him, and his only way out was a material that burned his flesh like acid. This was more than sick. It was deranged and sadistic. His hands looked horrible. My imagination gave me a brief image of a desperate and weakened Dragonman, pawing at his restraints and grimacing in pain at the burn of the metal. Like my restraints, anyone of us could've escaped easily and swam to shore, but he was trapped.

Cruelty is always painful to look at, but intelligent cruelty makes it so much worse.

I pulled the straps off him, making sure to keep the silver buckles away from his skin and placed them in the seat next to him. Now came the hard part. How the hell was I going to get him off this ride? Not only did water weaken him, but he also sank like a rock. I searched in vain for an emergency brake but found nothing. No way was it going to be that easy. As I said earlier, Dragonman is a big guy. He's over seven feet tall and has the bulk to match. His broad shoulders and muscular build made him weigh maybe 250 pounds, maybe even 300. I'm strong and in great shape, but I'm only human. I can't carry that much dead weight and still swim. Plus, any more exposure to water and it might kill our friendly neighborhood monster hunter. I looked in the water. Just under the surface, I could see a rail guiding the boat along. Other than that, the boat was floating on its own buoyancy.

If I could get the boat off the rail, maybe I could paddle it to shore and drag the brute onto dry land.

"Silver," I heard Dragonman moan. I looked up to see him pointing weakly ahead. I followed his finger with my gaze and saw something that made my eyes widen. Ahead of us was a sharp incline, and water cascaded down into the river we were riding. I followed the track to see that we would soon be going up a hill, pulled up by a chain, then drop down into a large splash and keep riding.

Without the threat of imminent death, that might be fun on a hot summer day at the park with a couple of friends. But when water was your biggest weakness and you had no seatbelt on, that might be a problem. The drop could throw us out of the ride, and we would both flop into the water. I might make it if I didn't hit my head and drown, but Dragonman definitely wouldn't survive.

"Shit. Shit shit shit," I muttered under my breath. I needed to get this boat off track *stat*. I looked around frantically for way to stop the boat. Ahead of us, right before we reached the incline, a pair of mangroves flanked the river, almost reaching our intended path. My mind started racing. The boat had to be able to fit, but just barely. I reached into one of my quivers and drew a net arrow. These things were tough, and I've used these things to stop speeding cars, mutant alligators, and a rabid tiger. I nocked the arrow and aimed. Hopefully, it was the right size, and hopefully it would expand at the right time. I mess this up, and Dragonman was going to die.

I took a steadying breath, aimed and released.

I watched the arrow fly in slow motion. It sailed right between the roots of the mangroves and burst. The carbon-fiber net sprang out, the hooked corners caught on the mangrove roots and stayed there, swaying slightly. I breathed a sigh of relief and got to work, drawing my cryogenic arrows. We reached the net and boat shuddered to a stop. I heard the motor whine in protest, and steam started to rise from the bottom of the dinghy. The hooks of the net bit deeper into the roots, and the wood bent and started to splinter under the stress of the boat. I started shooting ice arrows into the water, forming large ice floes, like the ones polar bears and seals like to hang out on. The ice floes started to crowd the little river, and they began to freeze together, forming their own iceberg. The boat strained against the net and growing glacier. The boat began to twist away to the left, towards the better (and drier) part of the park.

"C'mon," I begged. "Just a little more." The metal squealed underneath us, the steam mixing with the fog and obscuring even more of my vision. I got desperate and pulled out an explosive arrow. I moved towards the back and shot the thing down into the water at the rail. The arrow exploded with a loud burst of warm water, and the boat jolted left. The rail had snapped under the temperature flux and the shock of the explosive arrow. The sudden jolt of motion threw me off balance, and I almost toppled off the side.

Something caught my belt and pulled me back onboard. I looked back to see that Dragonman had hooked a claw onto my belt. He was already looking better. I grinned at him and drew my grapple gun to get us to shore.

Chapter 3: Nothing Soothes the Soul like a Cup of Joe

I managed to get Dragonman back to the shore, recover his weapons, coat, shield, claws, club and utility belt, and half drag half support him back to the food court. I settled him down at a table and broke into a few of the restaurants to get some food in his belly. Feeding the massive gargoyle was no easy feat. Fruits and vegetables made him sick, and he needed to eat animal products. Meat, eggs, fish, and simple grains were all he could stomach. And blood of course, the part vampire weirdo he was. Strangest of all was that he could handle processed crap like energy drinks, chocolate bars and Taco Bell just fine. Coffee wasn't an issue either, and neither was honey.

I managed to rustle up some burger patties, fries, and two cups of hot coffee. I returned to the table with my bounty and found Dragonman basking in the moonlight. The sun had sunk down below the horizon, and the waxing half-moon filled the courtyard with eerie silver moonlight.

"Feeling better?" I asked. Dragonman looked over at me and smiled gently.

"Bless you child," he said, his voice a deep rumble, like distant thunder. He grabbed a still sizzling burger patty and popped it into his mouth in one bite. "The moon helps. Perks of my werewolf father, I suppose," I cocked an eyebrow at that.

"You've never mentioned your father before," I said, sitting down across from him.

"Don't have much of a reason to," Dragonman said. "Never knew him."

"Sorry to hear that," I said sheepishly.

"Don't be," Dragonman replied, helping himself to another patty and a sip of coffee. "I had other father figures that did the job better than he." He rumbled deep in his chest, a sound I felt more than I heard. "I owe you my life, Silverbolt. Had it not been for you…"

"You don't owe me anything, big guy," I said, cutting him off. "You would've done the same for me."

"Without hesitation," he replied. "But I am still grateful nonetheless," he looked around, as if getting a good look for the first time. "Where are we?"

"Jester Park," I replied.

"Seriously?" he asked.

"Yeah, but it feels more like Walt Disney took a leaf out of Jigsaw's book," I answered. I told him about how I woke up on the carousel and escaped the lion.

"You freed the beast?" He said when I finished.

"Well, yeah," I said. "I couldn't just leave him there."

"You realize that now we have a hungry lion roaming the park now, as well as escaping and rescuing the rest of the team, right?" Dragonman pointed out. I bit my lip. Hadn't thought of that.

"Well, it's not like he could sneak up on you. You've tangled with worse than just a lion," I said after a pause.

"Mmm," Dragonman said thoughtfully.

"Hands feeling any better?" I asked. He flexed one hand, testing the pain and flexibility of his fingers. He flicked his fingers out to reveal a set of claws in the gauntlet.

"Adequate," he said finally. "Nothing I can't fight with."

"Good to hear," I said. "You know how we got here?"

"Hmm, last thing I remember before the ride was a warehouse," Dragonman said. He paused to take a sip of coffee.

"The one in Ohio," I prompted.

"Right," he said. "I don't remember much. It all gets hazy after we enter."

"You remember anything about the place before we got knocked out?" I asked. He closed his eyes and focused.

"Only that there was one heartbeat in there," he said, his eyes still closed. "The place reeked of blood and death. Other than that, nothing unusual.

"Huh," I said. "Any theories?"

"Nothing now," he said. He frowned in thought suddenly.

"What's up?" I asked.

"Lab Rat wasn't with you, was he?" he asked.

"Since we came here?" I asked. "No, you're the only person I've seen here."

"Hmm," Dragonman said. "That doesn't bode well."

"Why not?" I asked.

"We were knocked out by a gas, right?" he asked.

"Yeah, like chloroform or something," I said. "At least, that's what I think."

"Then where's Rat?" Dragonman asked. "That fishbowl of a helmet he wears would filter out a knockout gas, assuming there was one that could affect him."

Lab Rat was our resident techie. He wasn't just a Man in the Chair, like Alfred or Oracle. He was a certified badass in his own right. A few years ago, Lab Rat accidentally signed on with Alley Cat, that technology corporation. They used him as their own lab rat and tested all sorts of medicines, bioweapons and Lord knows what else. The result had been a person with genius IQ and the ability to survive any environment. He could survive extreme temperatures, radioactive areas, high altitudes, diseases and all sorts of toxins. He could even shrug off the strongest alcohols in a matter of minutes with no hangover. The more I thought about it, the less sense this made. Lab Rat was a paranoid brainiac with Savant Syndrome. A super genius who always has one eye looking backwards wouldn't be laid low by something as meager as chloroform. At the same time, anything strong enough to knock him out would be more than enough to kill one of us.

"What do you think?" I asked.

"I think that there's something else going on here," Dragonman said. "They could've killed him, but I doubt that."

"Because they could've killed us outright too," I said. It was a dark thought. If they could ambush and take us down non-lethally, they could've seen our faces, guess our identities, and sold it to the highest bidder. Plenty of people would pay top dollar for that kind of info. Like the FBI's Task Force 52, for example.

"Why bother with the amusement park?" I asked. "If they were going to kill us, why not do it in our sleep?"

"It's a good question," Dragonman said. He stretched his arms and groaned. "But enough sitting around. The other members are likely trapped in rides like we were."

"You're right," I said, standing. I reached into a pouch and pulled out a small, folded map of the park I snagged on my way back to the food court. "Any place we should check first?" Dragonman snorted smugly.

"No need," he said. "I can track down anyone's scent," I nodded, then folded up the map. He stood and closed his eyes, sniffing the air deeply. He turned in slow circles, moving his face around, trying for a scent.

"Got it," he said and started down the main road.

"Whose?" I asked.

"Lab Rat's," he said.

"Just out of curiosity," I asked, following him down the road. "What does Lab Rat smell like?"

"Chemicals and Cocoa Butter."

"Cocoa Butter?"

"You've seen how dark he is. His skin dries out in the slightest and he gets wicked ashy."

"Ashy?"

"Jesus, you need more black friends," Dragonman said, shaking his head in disappointment. "This way."

Chapter 4: Amazing Conditions

We followed the scent all the way to the hedge maze I saw on the map earlier. The entrance was decorated with white Roman columns of marble forming a large white arch with the words "Prepare to be a-MAZE-d!" written on the arch in blocky letters, like something from ancient Rome. The red brick path changed to gravel and round flagstones. Flanking the path were marble statues of the Roman gods. I recognized Neptune, Jupiter, Mars and Mercury, among others. I scowled at the statues. The whole thing looked like some rich billionaire's backyard.

"What the hell is this?" I asked. Dragonman rapped a claw on a statue.

"It's real," he said in amazement (no pun intended). "Real marble."

"Wait, what?" I asked. "Who the hell uses real marble in an amusement park?" Dragonman scowled, furrowing his brow in thought.

"Back in the pirate cove, there was a tunnel filled with real treasure," he said. "Mountains of gold and gems as big as apples."

"Seriously?" I asked. "How could you tell?"

"I'm part dragon," Dragonman said. "I can always tell." I looked around at the marble statuary, the perfectly smooth lawn, and the manicured hedges.

"Whoever built this place must have some serious moolah," I said.

"Do people still use that word?" Dragonman asked. "Moolah?"

"The point it, who have we pissed off who has enough money to blow on an amusement park with real gold and silver on its pirate attraction and marble statues in its hedge maze?" I asked.

"Not to mention real animals on the carousel," Dragonman said with a smirk. I glared at him.

"Yeah. That too," I said begrudgingly.

"We should discuss this as a team," Dragonman said, interrupting my train of thought. "Let's just focus on getting everyone out alive." I nodded, and we strode towards the entrance. To the right of the entrance was a beautiful carving of a man. I thought it was another Roman god, until I got a closer look at it.

It was a statue of Lab Rat. I recognized the flowing lab coat, rocket boots, gloves and belt. The statue was in an action pose, both hands holding Lab Rat's twin electro guns. It was a good likeness, given that Lab Rat dresses in all white, to begin with. The part that had me worried the most was the helmet. It wasn't caved from marble, but plexiglass and ceramic plating. My blood froze when I realized that I was looking at Lab Rat's *actual* helmet.

"Dragonman," I said sharply, pointing at the helmet. Dragonman looked and scowled at the statue. I reached out cautiously and removed the helmet from the statue. Underneath was smooth marble, like a store mannequin, only this one had a blindfold over its eyes.

"Creepy," I commented, handing the helmet over to Dragonman. He turned the helmet over in his hands, deep in thought.

"You think he's okay?" I asked nervously.

"I don't know," he said after a moment. "Is this his only piece of equipment here?" he asked. I checked the statue again.

"Looks like it," I replied. Dragonman's scowl deepened.

"This isn't good," he said.

"What do you mean?" I asked. "Isn't it a good thing he has all his gear?" Lab Rat was decked out in all sorts of useful gadgets and tools that helped him break into pretty much anything.

"Well, think about it," Dragonman said. "My weapons and armor were removed. If I had my claws or daggers, I could have cut myself free, superpowers or no. If you had all of your gear, you could have gotten free of the carousel in seconds."

"So?"

"So, either they forgot to remove all his gear, which I doubt, or none of his tools would be useful in getting him free of the maze," Dragonman explained. A thought suddenly occurred to me.

"Hey, isn't a maze a terrible place to keep him?" I asked. "I mean, he's like the smartest person in the world. Some maze isn't going to trap him here for long."

"I know. Which probably means there's more to this maze than we can see," Dragonman replied.

"Shit," I said. I looked up and noticed something. There wasn't a roof or overhead to the maze. Lab Rat could fly with his rocket boots or climb out with his grappling hook. I frowned. No way it was that easy. There had to be a way to keep him from going over the walls. I nocked an arrow and launched it into the air.

There was a sudden noise, like the world's largest bandsaw going off, and the arrow exploded into little silver shards. We both looked up at where the arrow was, then at each other.

"What the hell was that?" I asked.

"Some sort of AA gun?" he suggested.

"That can shoot an *arrow* out of the sky!?" I asked incredulously.

"Looks like it," Dragonman said. "Guess that leaves flying out of the picture."

"You think?" I said sarcastically. We both headed into the maze.

Normally, I love mazes. Not far from where I grew up, we had a haunted corn maze that opened up every Halloween. I had fond memories of wandering through the corn, the sides marked off with fake bloodstained police tape. People in cheesy zombie costumes would jump out to scare you, and there were little puzzles you could solve for fun every couple of feet.

This maze had no such feeling to it. The hedges were tall and ominous, and the path narrow and claustrophobic. Even stranger were the sounds. Every ten feet, there was a speaker mounted on a pole playing random sounds, like a cat was wandering across a cartoon soundboard. It was both creepy and annoying. I found myself missing the circus music from the carousel.

"Okay, what the hell is this?" I asked. "These sounds are just getting annoying." Dragonman looked up at one of the speakers, then down at the helmet in his hand. I saw his eyes widen in abject horror.

"What's wrong?" I asked.

"I figured it out," he said quietly. "Oh, those sick sons of bitches."

"What?" I asked. Dragonman turned to face me, his gray face looking more ashen than usual.

"You know that Lab Rat has autism, right?" he asked.

"Sure. I mean, I kind of guessed. So what?" I said.

"Okay, well, a lot of autistic people have a hard time with noise," Dragonman said. "They get these 'sensory fits' if there's too much noise, and they either throw a fit or just shut down." I frowned at that.

"Hang on," I said. "I've seen Lab Rat in some pretty noisy environments, and he handled it just fine."

"Because he had his helmet," Dragonman said, holding it up for emphasis. "The helmet plays soothing music when he's in a loud environment, like a shoot-out, for example." My eyes widened in shock as I realized what was going on.

"Holy shit," I said. "You mean he's somewhere in here, wandering around having some sort of fit, while this stupid music plays?"

"And he can't use his gadgets because he can't focus," Dragonman added. "These traps are meant to be insulting. We can focus just fine with this playing, but he can't. He loves mazes and hates excess. All the fine decorations are a waste of money in his eyes, and him being unable to solve a maze while being surrounded by expensive and pointless decorations is just pouring salt in the wound for him."

"Like the seatbelts on the pirate ride," I said. "Silver doesn't hurt us, only you."

"Or the leather straps on your carousel. Like you said, any one of us could have gotten out in seconds. It was only a problem for you," he said.

"Those... *bastards*," I said. We both took off running through the maze. Well, I was running. Dragonman was just jogging, and I still struggled to keep up with his longer strides. I didn't complain though. I hated the idea of Lab Rat trapped in a maze he wouldn't be able to escape. Sure, he was a weird little geek, but he was *our* weird little geek, dammit.

We ran for what felt like hours. Finally, we rounded a corner and Dragonman shouted, "There!" We saw a figure in white crouched down, their back leaning against the hedge. We ran up to them.

It was Lab Rat. He was dressed in white and silver, decked out in the world's most technologically advanced lab coat. His hands were pressed against his ears, and his eyes were screwed up in either pain or concentration. His lips were curled in a snarl, and his body kept rocking back and forth

"Rat!" I said, placing a hand on his shoulder. "Rat, it's us! We're here!" He didn't move.

"Lab Rat, move your arms," Dragonman said gently. "We have your helmet…" Lab Rat let out a sudden savage scream and jumped up. We both leapt back, startled. Lab Rat kept screaming and punched Dragonman in the stomach, knocking the wind out of him.

Lab Rat isn't that much stronger than the average person, but he knows how to throw a punch. Dragonman wheezed and dropped Lab Rat's helmet. He kept up the offensive, pounding on Dragonman in pure aggression and frustration. I acted quickly, scooping up Lab Rat's helmet and slamming it down on his head unceremoniously. The force of it knocked him down off of Dragonman, and he stopped for a second. I quickly started strapping it on, trying to remember how he did it. I managed to plug the helmet into the large mechanical backpack he had on when he grabbed my hands.

"Stop," he said. "You're doing it wrong," I froze and backed off. He reached up and redid everything I did.

"Rat?" I asked hesitantly. "You okay?"

"Better," he said shakily. "Didn't mean to hit you."

"It's alright," Dragonman said. "Not like you could hurt me anyways."

"I doubt that," Lab Rat said, turning to walk down the path.

"Hey," I said. Lab Rat ignored me. I nocked an explosive arrow and shot it at a nearby speaker. It erupted into geyser of sparks that crashed down onto the hedges and gravel. Lab Rat whirled around to face me.

"What?" he asked.

"We just saved your ass," I pointed out. "Maybe some gratitude would be nice?"

I know that when dealing with people who have autism, you need patience and an open mind. But I left most of my patience behind at the carousel.

"I… Thank you," he said, as if he had forgotten how to say it. "We should be going." Dragonman looked down at me and shrugged. I sighed and shook my head.

"Alright," I said. "Let's go."

We regrouped at a park bench outside the maze. Dragonman leaned against an empty vending machine, while Lab Rat and I sat on the dark green steel.

"So," I said. "You remember how we got here?" Lab Rat was quiet for a bit.

"Not really," he said after a pause. That was concerning. Really concerning. Lab Rat was one of the smartest people I know. He doesn't forget easily, if at all.

"What do you remember?" Dragonman asked.

"We were investigating the kidnapping of Brittany Howser, that billionaire heiress who went missing a month ago," Lab Rat said. "I got a message from someone saying they had info on the girl, and a potential meet up place."

"The warehouse," I said.

"Exactly," Lab Rat replied. "That's when they ambushed us."

"How did they pull that off, though?" Dragonman asked. "I thought you were immune to knockout gasses."

"I am, which is why they hit us with a mind bomb," Lab Rat answered.

"A what?" I asked.

"A mind bomb. It uses a type of negative brainwave that sends someone into a trance immediately. Alley Cat was working on a prototype for the military. Takes out an entire room non-lethally in a second. Gas masks would be useless and doesn't leave a gas-filled room. No evidence, no clean-up," Lab Rat explained.

"How did you know it was a mind bomb?" Dragonman asked.

"I saw it as soon as we entered the room. Those things are huge," Lab Rat said. "I recognized the logo," I said nothing for a while, thinking on it. Whoever trapped us knew us. They knew our greatest weaknesses and spared no expense getting us here to abuse us. There was an entire park here made to mock and humiliate us. And they had access to experimental paramilitary equipment. This was just getting worse and worse.

"We should keep moving," Dragonman said, pushing himself off the vending machine. "Any ideas?"

"Well, we still need Professor Magic, Blue Fox and Thundergirl," I said. I handed the map to Lab Rat. "Any thoughts?" I asked. He looked it over once, then tapped on one of the attractions. "This is where Professor Magic is." Dragonman and I leaned over his shoulders to look.

"The Christmas Village?" I asked. "What makes you think he's there?"

"Tell me, what are some of our Christmas traditions?" Lab Rat asked as he started walking.

"Well, Dragonman always sets up a nativity set that we all take turns sneaking *Warhammer* figures into," I said. Dragonman scowled at that comment.

"What else?"

"Blue Fox always gets KFC, you decorate the house with LEDs, Thundergirl and I always make gingerbread people that ends up into a roast session," I said, trying to remember everything we do on Christmas.

"And what does Professor Magic do?" Lab Rat asked. I thought back to our last Christmas.

"Well, last year he got trashed on eggnog and started arguing with everyone," I said.

"He gets mad about Yule," Dragonman said. "So?"

"The Professor has an axe to grind with Christianity," Lab Rat said. "I don't know why or how it started, but he's always arguing about old cultures being ruined by missionaries cutting out 'pagan' practices."

"Wait, he does this every year?" I asked. Dragonman nodded glumly.

"Wow," I said. "I thought that was a one-off."

"What makes you think he's in the Christmas Village?" Dragonman asked. "How would they know he can't handle his brandy?"

"How did they know about my autism, or your weakness for gold and seawater?" Lab Rat asked. "Or Silverbolt's inability to…"

"Shut it," I snarled. "Let's just go see Santa's Workshop.

Chapter 5: The Naughty, the Nice and the Pagan

The Christmas Village was located in a giant snow globe. It kind of reminded me of Epcot at Disney World, but smaller. The glass ball had fogged up, and we could hear machines whirring to keep the attraction cold. In front of the entry gate, there was a life-sized nativity set with very realistic models of Mary, Joseph and little baby Jesus. An angel in white robes with golden wings hung above the Newborn King, and real livestock wandered about on the straw.

"Well, look at this," Lab Rat said, investigating the nativity set. "And me without my dwarves."

"Oh, I *knew* you used the dwarves," Dragonman said angrily.

"Which faction do you use for Christmas?" Lab Rat asked me, ignoring Dragonman entirely. "Wood Elves?"

"Nah, Lizardmen," I said.

"I thought Blue used the Lizardmen."

"She uses Dark Elves, Thundergirl uses the Empire, and Professor Magic uses High Elves," I explained.

"You people are terrible. Why can't you let me practice my religion in peace?" Dragonman asked exasperatedly.

"Because it's funny watching you freak out over dwarves and elves witnessing the birth of Christ," I said.

"Yeah. What happened to 'all are welcome'?" Lab Rat asked.

"I hate you both," Dragonman said, shaking his head as we entered the giant snow globe. The sudden drop in temperature hit us all like a truck.

"Holy shit!" I exclaimed. Dragonman let out a snarl of discomfort.

"Tsk," Lab Rat said smugly. "Peasants."

"Oh, shut up, Mr. Immune to Everything," I said. The entry tunnel was lined with red and gold ribbons, expensive-looking wreaths, Christmas trees and tinsel. A red and gold carpet covered the floor, and the yellow lights looked like something out of a cheesy holiday movie. We walked through, staring at all the expensive decorations. Lab Rat kept shaking his head in disappointment. At the end, we were greeted with a set of oak double doors like something from a European castle with carvings of Santa Claus and his reindeer on one, elves slaving over toys on the other one.

"Oh, this would piss him off," Lab Rat said. "He hates how the elves are shown working in a sweatshop for greedy kids."

"Hey, weird question," I asked. "With all the magic and mythology blending into the world and all, is Santa Claus real?" Dragonman furrowed his brow.

"I don't know, actually. Some stuff was made up recently, like Slender Man and that Momo thing a while back, but Sinterklaas had some legends to it."

"Isn't Santa supposed to be based on Odin from Norse mythology?" Lab Rat asked.

"Some of it," Dragonman admitted. "But I haven't seen any indication that there is a real Santa. Why do you ask?"

"Just popped into my head. Figured you would know," I explained. Lab Rat pushed open the doors and we entered the Christmas Village.

Wow. They really spared no expense on this place.

The interior of the giant snow globe looked exactly as you would expect. Picturesque log cabins surrounded us, an ice-skating rink took up the center of the attraction, and little shops advertising merch, snacks and other souvenirs dotted the area around us. The path ahead of us branched into two directions. At the fork stood an animatronic snowman.

"Hello!" the snowman said in a dopey cartoon voice. "I'm Snowflake the Happy Snowman!"

"Hi Snowflake," I said. "What's up?"

"I'm so happy!" Snowflake responded eagerly. His eyes lit up every time he spoke. "It's so nice that it's always Christmas here in the Christmas Village. Is there anywhere you want directions to?" We all looked at each other.

"It can't be this easy," Lab Rat whispered.

"Oh, it is!" Snowflake exclaimed, making us all jump. "I'm here to help! I just love helping!"

"God preserve us, that's creepy," Dragonman said.

"I'm sorry if I scare you, Dragonman," Snowflake said, his head swiveling to look directly at him. The hairs on the back of my neck stood up.

"You... You know who I am?" Dragonman asked, backing up a little.

"Of course, I do!" Snowflake replied cheerfully. "You're the Dragonman, a creation of the Vatican in the 18th century to hunt the monsters of the New World and protect the colonies!" Dragonman's jaw dropped.

"Do you know who we are?" I asked.

"Yes! You're Silverbolt, the newest member of the Jesters! You are the greatest marksman in the world!"

"Markswoman," I corrected.

"You keep telling yourself that!" Snowflake replied, giving me a wink. I drew my bow and aimed an arrow at Snowflake.

"Alright jackass, just what the hell is…" I asked before something wet and cold slammed into the back of my head. I stumbled and spun around, the other two turning to face our surroundings. I felt the back of my head and felt a small amount of snow stuck there.

"Did I just get hit with a snowball?" I asked.

"Yes, you did!" Snowflake replied. I turned to face him. "We have the greatest security here in the Christmas Village! Any misdemeanors are met with correction!"

"Misdemeanors?" I asked.

"Yes! Anyone who uses foul language, threats or otherwise tries to compromise the fun environment for other guests is corrected!" Snowflake explained.

"With a snowball?"

"Or a 50-cal round to the back of the head," Snowflake said, the usual cheer gone from this statement. We all froze.

"You uh, kill people?" I asked.

"Only if they're being naughty!" Snowflake said. "Are you being naughty?"

"No! No, no one's being naughty here!" I said hurriedly. "Right, guys?"

"Absolutely!" Dragonman said, his eyes scanning the rooftops for hidden guns.

"Yep," Lab Rat said, typing something into his forearm.

"What was that Lab Rat?" Snowflake asked, turning his head to face him. "I couldn't hear you very well."

"I said I'll be Nice," Lab Rat said, putting extra emphasis on the last word.

"Oh, goody!" Snowflake said. "I'm so happy to hear that! Is there anything else you need?"

"Yeah, we were looking for a friend of ours," I said.

"Are you looking for Professor Magic?" Snowflake asked.

"Uh, yeah," I said. "Is he here?"

"Professor Magic is currently on the Christmas Express, learning all about the true meaning of Christmas!" Snowflake replied eagerly.

"Oh, that's uh, nice," I said. "Do you know where Blue Fox and Thundergirl are?"

"They're not here, although I'm sure that filthy Japanese heathen could use some real Christmas Spirit!" Snowflake said.

"The fu-" I said angrily before Lab Rat clapped a hand over my mouth.

"What was that Silverbolt?" Snowflake asked.

"Nothing," Lab Rat said. "She just wants to know where the Christmas Express is."

"Oh! Just follow the path to the right and go past the gingerbread house!" Snowflake replied cheerfully.

"Wonderful," Dragonman said. "We'll head right over. Thanks for the help, Snowflake."

"You are so very welcome, Dragonman," Snowflake said. "Have a Merry Christmas, you three!"

"You too," Lab Rat said.

"Mmph!" I said, as Rat still had his hand over my mouth. We headed down the right path, away from Snowflake, the

Way Too Informed Snowman. Once we were far enough away from the creepy thing, Lab Rat took his hand off my mouth.

"Gah!" I said. "What was that for?"

"I just saved your life," Lab Rat said.

"What do you mean?" I asked.

"Snowflake has a sorting algorithm, where it decides who's being naughty or nice."

"What?" I asked.

"While you two were playing 20 questions with the robot snowman, I hacked into the network of the village," Lab Rat explained. "Snowflake is a simple A.I. with access to a massive database on us, and a behavior recognition software. If you are being nice, it will be nice to you and offer you discounts."

"Discounts?" I asked. Lab Rat pointed to our right. We looked over to see a shop selling Christmas Village hats and t-shirts. Behind the desk was Snowflake.

"What the he-heck?" I said, correcting myself.

"That's creepy," Dragonman muttered. "Is it following us?"

"It's an A.I.," Lab Rat said. "The entire Christmas Village is automated. This entire area could be operated without a single employee, save some tech support.

"Wow. Like that café in Japan?" I asked.

"Exactly. But on an entirely different level," Lab Rat said.

"Meaning it can kill us," Dragonman mused.

"Exactly. Snowflake wasn't kidding when it said it would shoot you in the head with a 50 cal," Lab Rat said. He pointed up at the ceiling. Above us, I could see little boxes with tubes sticking out attached to the inside of the globe, space out every couple of feet.

"Are those…"

"Gun turrets, yes. They can shoots snowballs or 50 cal. rounds," Lab Rat said. "No telling how accurate they would be, but I don't want to risk it," Dragonman and I shared a look.

"Back at your maze, there was a gun turret that shot one of my arrows out of the sky," I said.

"It what?" Lab Rat asked. I explained what happened to him.

"Goodness," Lab Rat said when I finished, looking up nervously at the turrets.

"Yeah," I said, glancing at another shop being run by Snowflake.

"Look," Dragonman said, pointing. To our right was a gingerbread house and an archway saying 'Christmas Express'. We hurried down the path to see a truly gruesome sight.

Professor Magic was tied to a colorful train, like something you would see kids on. All around him, animatronic elves were singing songs about Jesus and his birth. The train was going around in a circle around a giant animatronic Santa Claus who was dancing and singing along.

"Jesus Christ," I said. "They trapped him in *Small World.*"

"C'mon," Lab Rat said. "Let's get him out of there," We ran down to the train tracks. The train was going very slowly, and the circle itself wasn't very big. We walked up to the train to investigate.

"Professor?" I asked him. Professor Magic is one of the world's most powerful sorcerers, and has been famous for a long time. His wrinkled face, hawklike nose and long white beard made him look like a classic fantasy wizard. His eyes were mismatched, one green and one blue. There was a metal clasp around his mouth with an electronic lock on it with a wire connected to the chair his was tied to. Surprisingly, his arms were free, and there was a keyboard and monitor in front of him. On the screen was a line of code, and rejected answers filled the rest of it.

It took me a few seconds to realize what was going on. Professor Magic is a powerful wizard, but he needs to speak the spells for them to work. This wasn't the first time he had been gagged to prevent his spells from working, and I'm sure it won't be the last. Also, he was a massive luddite. He's only in his twenties, but still types with one finger and still uses a flip phone. Dragonman is our oldest member, being over two centuries old, and still works technology better than him. My guess was that whatever the code was asking, Professor Magic wouldn't have been able to solve it.

Lab Rat walked up to investigate. He took one look at the code, went "Oh!" and leaned in and typed the answer. The train stopped, and the elves stopped singing. There was a click and the metal gag fell off of the Professor's face.

"Gah!" Professor Magic said, rubbing his mouth and working his jaw. "Bloody hell. Cheers Rat," he said.

Did I mention he's from the slums of London?

"You all right, Professor?" I asked, helping untie him.

"I'm alright, thanks for that," he said, standing.

"CHEATER," a voice rang out, echoing across the village. I looked behind me to see a stand selling Christmas Express merch. Behind the counter was Snowflake.

"LIAR," he called out. He was staring right at me, and his eyes were glowing red.

Gulp.

"You said you would be nice!" Snowflake said. "You said you would be good!"

"Umm," I said. "We're just here to pick up our friend…" I said sheepishly.

"He was here to LEARN!" Snowflake said. I heard a whirring and clicking sound echo from above. "He was being BAD! He needs to learn about CHRISTMAS SPIRIT!" Snowflake shook his head. "But I'm Nice. I can forgive. Professor Magic, if you apologize and say you were wrong about Christmas, I will let you go."

The logical thing to do would be to bow your head and say sorry. Admit you were wrong, and we would all live. But Professor Magic once told me, 'Magic isn't defined by logic. It's ruled by emotion.' So it shouldn't have surprised me when he looked the snowman dead in the eyes and said:

"Eat shit and Happy Yule, you bloody tin can."

I sighed. Nothing is ever easy with the Jesters.

"NAUGHTY!" Snowflake screamed, "KILL THEM ALL!"

Chapter 6: Everything has a Reason, Even if it Almost Kills You

Had it not been for Dragonman, I would've died in that snow globe, looking like a very meaty pasta sauce. As soon as the gun turrets went off, I saw blue lights flicker around Lab Rat as he jerked around, right before something black and leathery slammed into me, sending me flying into the Christmas Express merch store. I hit the back wall and fell to the ground, sucking wind. I looked up to see Professor Magic had been sent flying along with me. The sound of the gun turrets filled the air, the roar of gunfire drowned out any other sound. Finally, the gunfire stopped, leaving my ears ringing from the noise. A moment later, Dragonman limply hauled himself over the counter. He was covered in dark red blood leaking from the bullet holes covering his chest. He growled in pain as the holes started to close up.

"Hiding, are we?" Snowflake asked, turning his head to face us. Dragonman snarled and lashed out a kick, popping the snowman's head off, leaving exposed wiring sticking out and sparking.

"Goddammit, Professor," Dragonman hissed. "You couldn't have just said you were wrong back there?"

"Shut up," Professor Magic snapped. "You weren't here earlier. These fucking robots wouldn't shut up about Christmas."

"You self-centered bastard!" Dragonman yelled, grabbing Professor Magic by the front of his shirt. "You just got Lab Rat killed!"

"Hey," I managed to wheeze. "You remember that he has a force field, right?" They both stopped and looked at me.

"Lab Rat!" I called out. "You dead?"

"Nope!" I heard him yell back. I sighed in relief. "Managed to duck into a ticket booth. You guys alright?"

"We're fine," I replied. "Aren't we?" I asked the two with me. Dragonman narrowed his eyes at Professor Magic but nodded. Professor Magic gave him an equally venomous glare but nodded.

"Look, you two can duke it out later, but for now, let's focus on getting out of Willy's Winter Wonderland," I said, putting a hand on either one's shoulder. They both furrowed their brows at me, then looked at each other.

"I don't get that reference," Dragonman said. "You?"

"No clue," Professor Magic replied. I rolled my eyes. No one appreciates my humor.

"Hey!" Lab Rat called. "I have good news and bad news! Good news is that I hacked into Snowflake's algorithm and got into his IFF!"

"English please?" I called back.

"I can get us off the naughty list!" Lab Rat explained.

"And the bad news?"

"I can't get the Professor off! Just you, me, and Dragonman!"

"Shit," I muttered. "Why not?"

"No clue. Something about his profile on here! I keep getting an error message!" Lab Rat called.

"Brilliant," Professor Magic muttered. "So even if I did apologize to that bugger, we still would've been shot at!" He punched Dragonman lightly in the arm. "Looks like you owe me an apology."

"You didn't know that, and you still could've gotten us killed!" Dragonman snarled.

"Hey!" I said angrily. "We still have evil angry animatronics here! *With guns!*"

"What's going on over there?" Lab Rat asked.

"Tweedle Dumb and Tweedle Dipshit are arguing again!" I yelled back. Lab Rat was quiet for a bit.

"Which one is Tweedle Dipshit?" he finally asked.

"Not important!" I replied. I rubbed the bridge of my nose. God, I needed a drink after this.

"Oi!" Professor Magic called out. "Can't you just delete the profile it has on me?"

"Nah, it would still shoot you on sight," Lab Rat called out. "Unknowns still get shot on sight."

"What kind of park is this?" Professor Magic wondered out loud.

"One that has silver seat belts and live animals on carousels," Dragonman answered.

"Live what?" Professor Magic asked.

"Later," I said. "Lab Rat!"

"Yeah?"

"Can you turn the system off?"

"What?"

"Shut Snowflake down! Maybe reset the program?"

"Let me see!" Lab Rat replied. He was quiet for a bit, then called back.

"So, I can't shut it down remotely, it needs to be done manually, which we can't do from here," He called.

"Shit," I muttered.

"I can restart it, though!" Lab Rat called. "Problem is it will wipe our profiles and will kill us all."

"So, we have to leave before Snowflake comes back on," Dragonman said thoughtfully.

"How long until it turns back on?" Professor Magic asked.

"30 seconds!" Lab Rat replied.

"Shit," I said. "Any other ideas?" I asked the other two. They both shook their heads.

"Dammit," I muttered. "Alright, get ready to run." I checked to make sure I didn't leave anything behind. "Lab Rat! Give us a count down and reset it! We'll high tail it to the doors."

"Got it!" Lab Rat shouted. "Restarting in 3!"

We crouched down under the counter.

"2!"

I placed my hands on the counter, my muscles tensing up, ready to spring out.

"1!"

I tried not to think about those guns coming back online early.

"Go!"

I sprang up and vaulted the counter. I saw Dragonman and Professor Magic do the same on either side of me. I charged forward. The lights turned off, replaced by red emergency lighting. We sprinted down the path, veered left towards the ice rink and headed towards the door. Dragonman had longer legs and more muscle, and he passed us all. I saw him reach the doors ahead of us. He couldn't slow down in time and smashed right through the oak doors. Lab Rat was right behind him. He dove forward and unceremoniously crashed into a Christmas tree on the other side. Professor Magic and I were neck and neck. I tried to imagine this as high school gym class, or that I was racing Thundergirl to the bathroom for the hot water.

"Hurry!" Lab Rat called. "10 seconds left!" I was almost there.

Then my dumbass slipped on the remainder of the snowball that hit me earlier and fell.

I didn't even have the dignity to catch myself. My face hit the pavement, and I felt my teeth cut my lip.

"SILVERBOLT!" Lab Rat and Dragonman screamed in terror.

I could only look up to see the dozens of guns on the ceiling whir to life and take aim.

So, this is how it ends. Was my only thought.

"**ARAS!**" Professor Magic cried. I suddenly shot forward, yanked up by my belt. I almost lost grip of my bow as I flew towards the exit. I hit Professor Magic head-on and knocked him down. Dragonman and Lab Rat quickly pulled us into the exit tunnel as chattering machine guns tore up the pavement right where we were sprawled.

"Are you alright!?" Dragonman asked me panicked.

"I think I cut my lip," I said, touching my face through my mask.

"You had over 15 turrets firing at you, and all you had was a cut lip?" Lab Rat asked.

"Yeah," I said. "Crazy. What happened?"

"You fell!" Lab Rat said in shock.

"Yeah, I was there for that part," I said. "How did I get out?"

"Summoning spell," Professor Magic said. "Get off me, maybe?"

"Shit, sorry!" I said, pushing myself up. Lab Rat helped me to my feet while Dragonman helped Professor Magic up. We all left the tunnel and reentered the main park. On the way, Lab Rat and Dragonman got the Professor caught up on what was going on. We made our way back to the food court and got some food in our bellies.

"So, we're trapped here in a park specifically designed to exploit all of our weaknesses," Professor Magic asked between bites of pizza.

"Pretty much," I said. He stared ahead, seemingly deep in thought.

"Professor?" I asked.

"Hm?" he replied, looking back at me.

"Why were you trapped in a Christmas themed carnival?"

"What do you mean?"

"Why would that be your weakness?" I asked him. He sighed and wiped the grease off of his hands.

"After my parents died, I was sent to live with my great aunt," he said, not looking at me. "She was incredibly religious, and anything she didn't understand she deemed satanic and heretical."

"That sounds rough," I replied. He nodded.

"This was around the time my powers were developing as well," he continued. "I kept casting spells by accident, the magic words just appearing in my mind. I was foreseeing events before they happened and attracted all sorts of supernatural attention. She blamed me for it, and she would try to 'beat the devil' out of me."

"Holy shit," I said. "So around Christmas…"

"She was the worst. As I got older, I learned more about the customs and where they came from. We fought about it constantly. Also, my powers became stronger in that time. My spells just had more kick in them."

"And you two fought more and more," I surmised.

"Always. I started learning more about magic and sorcery out of spite, just because I knew it would bother her. Had I not found the Tower of Merlin, I could have gone down a dark path," he said. He looked forlornly at Dragonman, who was looking over the map with Lab Rat. "It's why witches were such a problem long ago. When people suddenly find the power to give themselves anything they want with no visible consequence, they can turn very bad very fast."

"I thought that dark magic would twist your mind to be evil," I said. "Like the One Ring."

"No," Professor Magic said seriously. "It's not the power itself, it's how you use it. Look at today's elite. How many billionaires use their power and influence for themselves and screw other people over? How many governments with complete control over their people abuse that power for their self-interest? That's what dark magic is, Silverbolt. Power, used only to serve oneself."

I chewed on that thought before another question popped into my head.

"I thought magic was a skill you learned?" I asked. "Not some predestined ability," Professor Magic squirmed slightly and looked over at Dragonman and Lab Rat.

"Normally, yes," he said softly. "But the Wizards are something different."

I was about to ask what he meant by that, before Dragonman and Lab Rat walked up to us.

"We think we know where Blue Fox is being kept," Dragonman said.

Chapter 7: The Not-so-Funhouse

"Oh, of fucking course," I said, staring up at the building.

"Yeah, it's pretty obvious," Dragonman said sheepishly. We were standing outside what looked like the unholy combination of an American funhouse and a Japanese Kabuki theater. A large red Shinto gate towered in front of the building, while a Zen garden graced the entrance. Cheap shamisen music echoed from the building, punctuated by the occasionally kabuki wooden block sound and someone going 'Yooooo' really loud. The building was three stories tall and built like a Japanese castle. There was a twisting slide going from the top floor the bottom floor, colored lanterns flickered with LED light. Like everything else in the park, this looked really cool and would be a fun place to visit. At the same time, it was probably loaded with traps and other deadly decorations.

"Oh, this is rich," Lab Rat said sarcastically, looking down at the sign posted by the Shinto gate. I looked over his shoulder and read the 'Rules of the Hall' post.

"No animals allowed," was the first rule, accompanied by a picture of a nine-tailed fox. "No weapons, such as katana, shuriken, nunchucks, or kunai, no fingernails longer than one inch.”

Oh, that was funny. One of Blue Fox’s favorite weapons were her nails, which she could grow and shrink at will, although I’ve never seen them shorter than an inch.

“No one over 5 feet tall allowed,” I said, and that got a rueful chuckle out of the guys. Blue Fox was tiny, barely reaching 5 feet. This was a source of humor for us, especially Dragonman, who kept storing her mugs and snacks on the top shelf.

“And finally, no public displays of affection,” I said. Oh, that was a stinger. Blue Fox is, how do I put this lightly? Very, ah, ‘affectionate’ when it comes to men. You remember that one girl in high school who went through boyfriends like fashion trends, had all the terrible ideas when it came to boys and tried bringing her friends along on her ‘adventures’? Give that girl the powers of a fox spirit, a ninja’s arsenal and a medical degree, and you have Blue Fox. She’s the daughter of a Korean kumiho turned human and a Yakuza thug, who is now possessed by a Chinese spirit fox called Daji. She’s capable of conjuring powerful illusions, shapeshifting into animals and people, and can seduce people with her words. Her magic is crazy potent, and she’s an Olympic level swordswoman, who, according to Japanese media, took down a massive sea monster on her own. 100% genuine badass.

"So, she's trapped in some tacky Japanese knockoff, I assume?" I asked. Professor Magic waved his hand in front of the gate, apparently feeling for something.

"Whoa," he said, his mismatched eyes shining. "Not so tacky at all. This is genuine Shinto power."

"Seriously?" Dragonman asked, cocking an eyebrow.

"Yeah. I'm no expert at East Asian magic, but this has the right feel for it," Professor Magic said.

"That makes no sense," Dragonman said, frowning.

"Why not?" I asked.

"Japan is fairly unique when it comes to magic," the Professor explained. "Japan was formed by the gods Izanagi and Izanami by pulling magma from the core of the earth with a spear. Most Japanese spells and power only work there."

"So?"

"So, you can't just uproot a Shinto gate and plop it here in America and get the same effect," Dragonman said.

"How is this relevant?" Lab Rat said shortly. Despite the staggering evidence of magic and mythology in our lives, he still remains skeptical of it all. Any claims of mysticism he tries to explain away with science.

"Because Blue Fox can't cross these gates," Professor Magic said. "Hostile spirits can't pass these gates, and the Yokai tucked away next to her soul is about as hostile as they come."

"I get it," I said. "If she can't pass under them or get past them, how did she get in there?"

"Do we even know she's in there?" I asked. "If these gates stop her so much, wouldn't this be the last place she could be?"

"Why have a Shinto gate at all if not to keep a Yokai trapped?" Professor Magic countered.

"Plus, her bag and sword are over there," Dragonman said, pointing to the interior of the garden. By the door, there was a mannequin dressed in a black and yellow kimono. Her face was obscured by a parasol, but I could see a large bulky blue purse hanging on her shoulder, and a katana lay sheathed at her feet. I couldn't tell if they were hers or not, but Dragonman's eyes were better than mine anyway. If he said they belonged to Blue Fox, they did.

"Would this gate impede any of us?" I asked.

"Unless you were a hostile spirit, no. It would have no impact on you, aside from maybe a slight sense of tranquility."

"Awesome," I said and stepped through the gate.

"Wait!" Lab Rat called. I froze, and we all looked at him.

"There could've been a land mine, or some other trap!" he said. I looked around.

"I doubt it," I said. "Seems a little too heavy-handed for these guys."

"The Shinto gate is an obstacle on its own. Why plant land mines next to the gate?" Dragonman asked. "That's just redundant."

"That's what they want you to think!" Lab Rat argued. Dragonman rolled his eyes, he stepped over. No explosions went off. Professor Magic walked through, and finally Lab Rat followed him, stepping gingerly and looking around nervously. We walked up to the mannequin, and I picked up the sword. Upon closer examination, I could tell it was hers. The wooden sheath was painted blue, and had decorative foxes worked into the top and the hilt. I drew the blade out a little, and I heard Dragonman let out a sharp hiss.

"Put it back!" He exclaimed. I put the blade back in the sheath and looked at him. His eyes were wide and staring at the blade.

"What's wrong?" I asked.

"That thing is a muramasa!" he said angrily.

"A what?" I asked.

"A cursed blade," Professor Magic said. "Those are the ones with demons sealed in the blade, right?"

"A what!?" I asked horrified, looking down at the blade nervously.

"Oh, I am gonna have a talk with her about this!" Dragonman said hotly.

"Does anyone else wanna carry this?" I said, offering it out. Professor Magic and Dragonman both stepped back, as if the blade was a venomous snake. Lab Rat sighed and tapped a button on his belt. A mechanical arm reached out from his backpack and plucked the sword from my hands and held it against his back vertically.

"Are we done being a bunch of superstitious little kids now?" Lab Rat said irritably. "Or do you guys wanna keep talking about spooky ghosts more?" No one said anything. I grabbed the bag from the mannequin's shoulder to remove it and the things head spun around to look at me. As I jumped back in fear, I heard a cackling laugh, and the mannequin collapsed into a pile of clothes.

"Okay, what the hell?" I asked. Professor Magic poked the pile of kimono with the butt of his staff.

"Weird…" he said.

"Weird?" I asked. "Weird!? '80s workout tapes are weird! People who put ketchup on steak are weird! That was so much more than weird!"

"Calm down, Silverbolt," Lab Rat said. "It's probably an animatronic that got pulled into a trap door. Look…" He bent down and moved the kimono out of the way. The floor beneath it was perfectly smooth.

"Um…" he said nervously.

"Magic," Dragonman said firmly, as if that statement settled what happened. "Let's go get Blue out of this place."

The inside of the funhouse was just as culture appropriationy as you would have expected. I think the designers were told 'make something Oriental' and literally just did that. We walked past Ming vases, jade dragons, those weird statues of lion/dog things you see outside Chinese temples, gongs, and samurai armor. Asian spa music played from speakers around us, and I say Asian because I have no idea what country it could have come from, it was *that* generic.

"This place bites," Dragonman said sullenly, adjusting the grip on his club.

"You're telling me," I replied dryly. "It's the same cheap decorations from before. How original." We soon entered a larger room. It was the size of a basketball court, and the far wall was taken up by a large funhouse mirror.

"Oh, I love these things!" I said as we got close to it. "Look how squat we look!"

"You are far too easily entertained," Lab Rat said flatly.

"Bah," I said dismissively. "I have simple tastes." I started waving my arms around and squatting up and down, making my distorted reflection shift and warp. Just as the others started to turn away, I noticed something odd in our reflections.

"Hey, guys?" I asked. "Does this look weird to you?"

"It's a funhouse mirror, Silver. Of course, it looks weird," Professor Magic said.

"No, look again." Everyone stopped and looked harder at their reflections. My reflection smoothed out and looked proportional. However, it was no longer dressed as me. It looked like me, but different. I was dressed in a camo hunting jacket with a camo snapback cap, dirty blue jeans and hiking boots. My face looked sort of the same, but my hair was cut shorter than I like it, and I looked… well…

Male.

"What the hell?" I murmured. I looked at the others and saw other differences. Dragonman's was almost ten feet tall, had large bat wings and bigger horns. Their jaw was more pronounced, and his lower fangs almost reached his eyes, which were glowing red. He was dressed in dirty blood-stained armor and carried a massive double-headed battle axe, both blades dark with dried blood. Lab Rat's was dressed in a white jumpsuit, and had wires hanging out from all over his body, with a mass of cables sticking out from the back of his head and reaching up into the ceiling. Professor Magic's reflection looked more or less the same, although his face was his normal one, not changed to look like an old man. His eyes looked sunken, and there was a starved gauntness to him, and he wore a black cape and hood rather than his black wizard hat. He had traded out his rune carved staff for a long and sharp looking spear, and trailing behind him was a host of dark smoky looking figures. I couldn't make out their shapes very well, but they appeared to be a mix of armed warriors and massive hounds.

Just as I was about to ask what the hell was going on, Dragonman's reflection let out a roar and punched

Dragonman in the mouth. It charged out of the mirror and swung it's axe at him, which Dragonman barely parried with his iron-shod club. Lab Rat's reflection let out a painful scream and the wires coming from his arms shot out to wrap around Lab Rat like constrictors. Professor Magic's reflection pulled out a hunting horn and blew into it, which let out an eerie echoing sound and signaled the shadow army behind him to charge. The force of the shadows sent the Professor sprawling into the wall behind us.

I looked around in confusion, then at my reflection. It just stood there and stuck its hands into its pockets and leaned back and forth on its heels.

"Sup?" it asked.

"You, uh, gonna come out and attack me?" I asked sheepishly.

"Hmmm, nah," it replied. It had the same southern accent as me, but way stronger. "I don't think I could take you in a fight. We can just talk this out."

"Talk what out?" I asked. Other Me laughed.

"About how *ridiculous* you are," Other Me said. "I mean, come on!"

"What the hell are you talking about?" I asked.

"Dude, come on," he said. "You run around in a dress and fight monsters? With a bow and arrow?"

"What's wrong with that?" I asked defensively.

"Dude, this isn't a comic book. A gun would work better."

"Guns kill people," I retorted.

"Right, because bows were invented for peace treaties," Other Me said, rolling his eyes. He pulled out a cigarette from behind his ear and lit it with a small lighter he pulled from his pocket. He took a drag and blew the smoke right at me. I saw the cloud pass through the glass and hit me in the face. I coughed and waved the smoke away.

"What the hell is going on here?" I asked. "Who the hell are you?"

"I'm you, Aiden," Other Me said with a smirk. "The real you, that is."

"The fuck you are," I snapped. "I don't smoke, and I don't dress like that." Other Me laughed at that.

"You've always wanted to give it a try, but I see your point on that. As for how I'm dressed, I just thought this outfit was more honest than the costume *you're* wearing."

"It's armor, dumbass. Not a costume," I snarled. He laughed again.

"Dude, you're wearing a *dress*."

"It's a skirt!"

"Is that any better? What's next, heels and a pearl necklace?" He asked. "What kind of a guy wears a fucking *skirt*?"

"Oh, hell no," I said. "We are not doing this right now!"

"Now's a good time as any. Who do you think you're fooling, dress like that? If you had adopted a female persona to keep your identity safe, I could at least understand that, if not condone it. But you *really* think you can put on a skirt and call yourself female?"

"Fuck. Off," I snarled. "I left this kind of shit in the past. Back home."

"No, you didn't. You packed it up in a little box and shoved it in the back of your head and acted like the problem never happened," Other Me snapped; his smug jovial nature gone. "You think you can live this lie and be happy? While you disregard everything and everyone who ever loved you?"

"Shut up!" I yelled. "They kicked me out for who I am!"

"You kicked yourself out! You left without a backward glance over your damn feelings! Over a lie you told yourself in a pathetic attempt to make yourself feel better!" Other Me yelled back. "You ruined Dad's reputation! You broke Mom's heart!"

"They couldn't accept me!" I replied, my voice weaker than before.

"They were honest with you," Other Me said venomously. "More honest than the cowards you call friends.

"You don't get to say that about them!" I said. "You don't know what I went through!"

"Yes, I do! You felt sad and alone because you thought no one knew how you felt! You made up problems and dug yourself into a pit of depression over something you thought made you different! News flash, princess! Everyone has those feelings! Everyone feels like they don't belong!" Other Me said. "You turned your back on your family, your friends, your home! Because you were sad! And weak!"

"I am not weak," I said quietly.

"Really? You could've been in the Olympics. You are the best damn shot in the world, and you squander your gifts on this ragtag group of mutants," he reached into his pocket and pulled out a golden medallion on a blue ribbon. "You see this? This could've been yours!"

"They wanted me to compete as a man!" I said, my cheeks burning.

"You *are* a man, you withering, pathetic coward!" Other Me spat. "You have the same parts and equipment as everyone else in this room."

"You don't understand…" I started to say, but Other Me cut me off.

"No, I don't understand. I don't understand how you could turn away from a life of fame and fortune, where your gifts and skills could earn you the respect of the ENTIRE WORLD, and you settle for living in squalor with criminals!" Other Me said, throwing his hands into the air. "I don't understand why you would turn your back on your own flesh and blood over your *fucking feelings*."

"We help people!" I protested.

"Really?" Other Me said. He reached out of the mirror and grabbed my face and turned me to face Lab Rat, who was being buried under a pile of writhing wires and cables. "He set off a bioweapon in Panama, killing an entire hotel of civilians. He regularly steals equipment and money just to satisfy his desire for revenge. Do you know how many people's lives he ruins just to satisfy himself? How many people lost their jobs to his vendetta and are now starving?" He turned me to face Professor Magic.

"How about him?" he asked. "He executed a man in the Tower of London because the guy put his hands on his girlfriend. He invokes the powers of demons and spirits to gain forbidden knowledge! He could conquer the entire world in an afternoon with the right rituals."

"Or how about the big one, the Dragonman?" he said, turning me to face the gargoyle. "He's born to be a killer, a savage brute that would burn down someone's home to get at one Ouija board. You think he saves people? Ask him how many witches he dealt with as judge, jury and executioner."

"You don't know them," I whimpered.

"No. *You* don't know them," Other Me said with disgust. "You've barely been with them for a year, and you think you know who they are?" He spat at my feet. "You are a means to an end for them. They needed a marksman, and they picked you. The guy before you? Your predecessor? The most notorious killer in the world. A fucking hitman. And they called him a friend."

I winced at the mention of the Nocturnal. He was a former member of the Jesters, a cybernetic assassin who delighted in the murder of others. I heard he killed his own father with a broken bottle. Or so the rumor goes. Other Me wasn't wrong about him. He used to be a member. Hell, I have his old room.

I fell to my knees. Fuck me, he was right. I ran away from home because my parents couldn't accept who I was, that I was transgender. I left them behind without saying goodbye. I bounced around places, occasionally fighting crime with my ramshackle equipment and a bow.

"How much do you think they need you?" Other Me said. He was crouched down to speak to me face to face. "These men and women are demigods. You've seen what it takes to beat them. They tied you to a fucking kid's ride and called it a wrap. You don't belong here. You never have."

He was right. I was the only vanilla human on the team. I couldn't lift cars, fly, cast spells or hack computers with my mind.

"You think they actually accept you?" Other Me whispered in my ear. "How do you know they aren't lying to your face? They will only accept you for as long as you are useful to them. They'll toss you out on the streets as soon as they are finished with you. Once you become a burden on the team. And how long do you think that will last?"

"God, I that was my worst nightmare. How did I know they weren't just pretending to accept me?" I looked over at my companions, struggling with their own inner demons. Professor Magic was being battered down with shadowy figures. Dragonman was pinned down, being beaten on by his doppelganger, and I couldn't even see Lab Rat anymore, just a squirming pile of colored wires.

I had no idea if they actually liked me. If they just put up with me for the sake of convenience. I looked up at Other Me, who was now smiling.

"Now you get it. Hang up the mask and skirt. Go home. Become a celebrity. Claim the fame you were promised. Leave all of this behind," he said.

"You're right about me," I said, the firmness in my voice shocking me.

"What?" He said, looking confused.

"I don't know if they truly accept me. Or if they are lying to me. I can never know for certain. But you know what?" I asked. "It doesn't matter."

"What!?" Other Me sputtered.

"It. Doesn't. Matter," I repeated slowly. "You know why?"

Other Me said nothing.

"Because I have faith in them. I have faith that they love me because I love them back," I said, rising to my feet. "I believe in them, and I would gladly give my life for them, and I know they would do the same for me. I know this, deep down in the core of my very soul. I know who I am, and I know a lot more about me than you think I do. I reached down and pulled him up to face me. He didn't look so different to me now.

"I know who you are. You're my Doubt. My Fear. You're everything I hated about myself and locked away so I wouldn't have to face it. You and I have a lot of work to do, but you're not better than me. You're not stronger than me. You *are* me," I said. I pressed my forehead to his and closed my eyes.

"And I'm sorry for leaving you alone for so long."

I opened my eyes, and he was gone. My reflection was back to normal, although I could see more about myself now.

I saw a lonely little girl, who grew up thinking something was wrong with her, that she was missing something. I saw someone incredibly gifted trying to find something to use her gifts for. I saw a rebel desperately seeking a cause to fight for. I saw…

… Me.

I blinked the tears away and looked at my friends. This mirror, whatever it was, showed you something you hated about yourself. It took all the darkness in your soul and threw it at you. I wanted to help my friends fight their demons so bad that it hurt, but this was their battle, not mine. I had no business fighting their fight, just as they had no business fighting mine.

I was glad to see that my fears were unfounded, because my reflection was barely defeated when Lab Rat burst out from beneath his pile of wires.

"WEAKNESS," a distorted voice called from his reflection. "YOU ARE WEAKNESS, A SCARED BOY FIGHTING A MAN'S WAR. YOU WILL NEVER BE FREE OF YOUR PAST."

"I already freed myself," Lab Rat said proudly. "I've been free of you for years. I did that with my own two hands, and I'll free myself a thousand more times before I lose to you!"

I heard an echoing boom, as Dragonman suddenly gained the upper hand in his fight.

"You stood by and silently let them suffer," Other Dragonman boomed. "You stood by and let your nation crush the people who needed you most."

"Yeah?" Dragonman snarled. "And this is me FIXING THAT!" he cried as he swung his club like a baseball bat and sent his demon flying back into the mirror.

"I AM WHO I CHOOSE TO BE!" Professor Magic shouted; the mass of black shadows flung away from him. A nimbus of blue light surrounded him, "MY POWER AND DESTINY ARE MY OWN!"

We all stood together, slightly out of breath from the effort.

Chapter 8: Inner and Outer Demons

"Alright, does someone wanna try and explain just what the hell just happened?" I asked. We all looked around. Dragonman and his double had made a huge mess in their fight, although the room was slowly rebuilding itself. Pieces of the tatami floor flew back into their spots, splinters returned to their walls, and a porcelain vase returned to its original form.

"The Mirror of Truth," Lab Rat said, pointing up at the mirror. I looked where he was pointing, where there was a small bronze plaque with something written in Chinese.

"I've heard of this before," Professor Magic said. "It creates a phantom of your deepest self."

"And makes it attack you?" I asked.

"No, it just manifests it. If you have deep-seated violence and dark ideals, then that's what you see," The Professor explained. Dragonman shifted uncomfortably at that. I looked back at the mirror. Then something occurred to me.

"If that thing reflects something dark and evil about you, what would happen if you were possessed by one of the most sadistic spirits in China and you looked in this mirror?" I asked.

"Oh shit," Dragonman said.

"We need to find her, now," Lab Rat said, and we all took off running down the corridor, until we reached a set of stairs. We raced up the steps to the second floor. Thankfully, Dragonman was able to track down Blue Fox's scent (cherry and vanilla) down a few winding corridors, until we came across a grisly sight.

The second floor had changed from Japanese teahouse and paper wall dividers to a gray hallway. Rough gray office carpet for the floors, white corkboard ceilings and machine gray walls. This would've been weird alone, but the walls were liberally decorated with splashes of dark red blood. A corpse lay on the ground a few feet from us, a man in his early forties with his neck slashed open. I ran up to him to investigate. The carpet squelched with blood under my feet.

Upon closer inspection, the man had a hand over his ruined windpipe in a vain attempt to stem the flow of blood. I reached out to check the wound, and my fingers passed through his face.

"What the hell?" I muttered.

"It's illusion," Dragonman said, squinting at the walls.

"Is Blue Fox making this?" I asked.

"Maybe," Professor Magic replied, looking around.

"I know what this is," Lab Rat said. We all looked at him.

"It's the Kitsune Massacre, isn't it?" Professor Magic guessed.

"I'm afraid so," Lab Rat said.

"The what?" I asked.

"This was Blue Fox's introduction to the world," Dragonman said sadly. "A brutal massacre of 20 people in the Gruman Orchestra over 10 years ago."

"Jesus," I breathed.

"She hadn't earned her moniker yet, and the survivors claim they saw a humanoid fox tear through the musicians and staff members like a demon," Dragonman continued. "She was never caught, and some people still think it was done by a maniac in a costume. But most people still believe this was the work of a Yokai," I stood and looked down at the man. Cut down by a woman he saw as a friend. I could feel bile rising in my throat. I took a deep breath and we continued down the hallway. We saw more bodies, and a few people fleeing the scene, frozen in time. Their faces contorted into visages of terror. Others simply sat on the ground, blank looks of horror on their faces. Most of the people we passed were Japanese, although there were a few people of different ethnicities.

We finally entered the auditorium, where we found Blue Fox. She was tied to a large bronze pillar with sticks and brambles piled at the bottom. Sitting at the bottom, a woman in a black silk dress was eagerly making out with a young man in a tuxedo. He was weakly pawing at her shoulders and was rapidly losing weight. As we got closer, his arms went limp, and his face was a sickly shade of pale green. The woman released the man and tossed his dried-up body off the stage. It hit the floor with a dry crackling sound before collapsing into dust. The woman looked over at us eagerly and smiled.

She was short, petite and kind of cute. Her hair was done up in elaborate curls and decorated with jeweled combs, and her dress was a semitransparent silk piece that seemed to extenuate her body rather than conceal it, like lingerie. She had thick black hair, cherry red lips and deathly pale skin. The strangest part was that behind her, nine black fox tails swirled and danced behind her. She had a wicked grin, dark eyes and vulpine features.

"Daji," Dragonman growled, baring his teeth and readying his club.

"The Dragonman," Daji replied, licking her lips. "It's nice to see that Tomoko's taste in men hasn't dulled with age." She had a thick Chinese accent.

"Let her go, demon." Professor Magic said, squaring his shoulders and striking the ground with his staff. Daji only laughed.

"Demon, you say?" she tittered. "Foolish Englishman, do you have any idea who I am? I am more akin to your angels. I served the will of Nu'Wa."

"You serve your own will," Professor Magic shot back.

"Don't we all?" Daji asked.

"Enough games, fox," Dragonman snarled. "Give us Blue Fox, or I cave in your skull."

"Hmm," Daji said playfully, looking up at Blue Fox's unconscious body and tapping a long black nail to her chin. "As interesting an offer that is, I'll have to decline. Tomoko is simply too sweet a treat to give up so easily. As delicious and offer that this, though."

Dragonman growled deeply, for real this time. A deep, lupine growl bubbled from his throat.

"Patience, dear hunter, patience!" Daji said with a laugh. "You westerners are so quick to violence! Let us not succumb to our darker natures. For now, anyways," she added with a wink.

"Okay, I've had it with the creepy temptress," I said irritably. I pulled a net arrow from my quiver and nocked it to my bow. Daji merely stared at me, and my body relaxed entirely. My mind felt warm and stuffy, like I was drunk.

Why were we here again? We were doing something important. I struggled to even form one concrete thought. What was it again…?

"You see?" I heard Daji say. She sounded a million miles away. "Why not lay down your weapons and rest? It's been a long night; you must be tired…"

My arms weighed a ton. I could barely hold my bow. I heard the others struggling to stand.

My eyelids started to droop. Still, I remained on my feet. I couldn't sleep now, not until we…

… Did… something. I know I was here for someone. Or something… It had to be important…

There was a loud crashing sound. I jerked awake and looked around. Dragonman had smashed a chair with his club to wake us up and break the spell. I shook the remaining sleepiness from my head. Holy shit, is that what Blue Fox's victims felt like? I'd seen her use this kind of magic before, bewitching guards to fall asleep or forget what they were doing. I've caught the side effects of the spells before when she did this, but I've never been the target of it. What scared me the most was how subtle it was. I didn't see it coming, it was just… *boom*. Tired.

Yikes.

"Is this the best you can do?" Dragonman snarled. "I've taken down succubi worse than you!"

"You dare compare me to those western harlots!?" Daji snarled. "I'll rib your heart from your chest, you overgrown toad!" She howled and surged towards him, her form blurring into a massive black fox. Dragonman brought his club down on her head, and it passed through her like a ghost. She growled, and bit him in the shoulder. Dragonman howled in pain, and I saw blood drip down from the wound.

"Aras Spectros!" Professor Magic cried out. There was a flash of blue light around Daji, but nothing happened. Dragonman screamed in pain, his claws passing through Daji's head harmlessly. Lab Rat pulled two devices from his pack and attached them together. His mechanical hand dropped the sword and helped attach the two devices together

"Hey! Slut Fox!" he yelled. Daji looked up from savaging Dragonman to growl at Lab Rat. He pressed a button on the device and a rippling cone of energy beamed from it. The ripples engulfed the fox, who shivered and snarled. She shook her head and broke free of the energy field. Dashing forward, she slithered between the seats faster than any creature her size ever could. She caught the scientist in her jaws and flung him against the wall. He smacked into it hard before falling to the ground.

"Silverbolt!" Professor Magic cried. "Get down!" I looked to see Dragonman on his feet, the bite marks already closing. An orange glow was building in his chest and moving up his throat. Professor Magic began a low chant, the runes carved into his staff started glowing like embers and smoking. I bent down and grabbed the fallen sword. Daji saw the two and charged them. She made it halfway across the auditorium before the two let loose with pillars of fire. Magical fire had succeeded where all other attacks failed. I heard her scream in agony, a mix of a fox's yelping and a woman screaming. The flames died down, and the fox was gone. Professor Magic waved his staff to cool it, while Dragonman looked out of breath.

"Did you kill her?" I asked, looking around.

"She's a projection," Professor Magic said. "She's not real, just an illusion with more…" He waved his hand while he tried to think of a word.

"Spunk?" I suggested.

"Sure. Spunk," he said. "Dragonfire and Wizard flame should keep her from manifesting for too long."

A bit of movement caught my eye.

"Behind you!" I shouted. The two magic users turned, but they were too late. Their shadows sprung to life and wrapped tendrils of darkness around them, pinning their arms to their sides and covering their mouths. The shadows pooled in front of me, getting between me and Blue Fox.

"You mortals *dare* burn me!?" I heard Daji snarl. She rose from the pool of shadows, her form a twisted mix of woman and fox.

"You *dare* strike me with western magic!?" She snarled, her voice no longer sultry and sensual, but ragged and animalistic. "I ruled the Shang Dynasty! I pulled the strings of the Celestial Empire! Shrines and cults were raised in my name! Who are you to stand against me!?"

"Silverbolt," I said simply. Don't give me that look. One-liners are tough to come up with when fighting a thousand-year-old spirit vixen. Daji growled at me, her nails lengthening and sharpening into black claws. I reached for an arrow, but then I remembered what the Professor said. Arrows weren't going to cut it, and yes, that was a painful thought to think. Fortunately, I had something that could beat her. Hell, it had been beating her all along. I drew Blue Fox's demon sword. The blade shined bright in the auditorium lighting, gleaming almost like a lightsaber. Daji laughed when she saw the blade.

"Is this your plan?" She said. "To die with another's weapon?"

"Oh, I don't do that," I taunted back. "Dying, that is. It's up there with missing."

"Missing?" Daji asked.

"My aim is perfect. I've never missed a target in my life. Doesn't matter what I'm using, shooting or throwing," I explained. "Darts, arrows, bullets, knives, even swords. Doesn't matter what it is, but when I throw this sword, you're finished." Daji laughed again.

"A bold claim, but foolish," Daji said. "I will remember your face long after I tear it from your skull."

I raised the sword over my head with one arm, using my other to focus my aim. I only had one shot, but I was confident in my skills. I hurled the sword with all my might...

… And it sailed past her head by a mile. Daji laughed and surged forward, grabbing me by the throat and lifting me up.

"What was that throw?" She asked with a smirk, which was just terrifying on her half fox face. "I thought that throw was supposed to finish me?" It was my turn to laugh.

"You stupid, self-centered *whore*," I spat. "What makes you think I was aiming for you?" Daji cocked her head in confusion, then turned to see where the sword had landed.

Right in Blue Fox's hand.

She held the sword over her head, still tied to the pillar, but she was awake now. Blue fire covered the blade, and was swarming over Blue Fox's body. She cried out, not in pain, but defiance. The Foxfire burned through her bonds, and she landed in a crouch on the stage.

"NO!" Daji cried out and dropped me to charge Blue Fox, who was beginning to chant. It wasn't Japanese, but something else. Something older, more ancient. Her hair began to glow, first orange, then paled to snow white. White mist formed around Blue Fox, which Daji couldn't seem to pass through, but she flailed her arms at it, screaming obscenities in some form of ancient Chinese. The mist formed foxes, nine of them, flanking Blue Fox. Suddenly, I could understand what Blue Fox was saying. It wasn't English, but the meaning just clicked in my mind.

"Daji, failed servant of Nuwa. Whore of Shang. Blight of Yinxu. By our honor, our pledge and power, you are bound," Blue Fox chanted. She let out a rending cry, and Daji screamed and shrank into a small black orb the size of a baseball. Blue Fox plucked the ball from the air and pressed it into her breast and vanished. The mist dissipated, and Blue Fox fell to her knees. I ran up to her to check on her.

"Blue!" I said anxiously. "Blue, are you alright?" She groaned and rubbed her temples.

"Ow," she complained. "I hate binding rituals," she blinked up at me in slight surprise.

"Hey Silver," she said. "Please tell me you have booze on you. I need a drink."

Chapter 9: Painful Memories

"So, you're telling me we got jumped in a warehouse, knocked out by experimental tech, and trapped in a theme park catered to our weaknesses?" Blue Fox asked through a mouthful of lettuce.

"That about covers it, yeah," I said.

"*Sugoi*," she muttered dryly. We were back in the food court, and Blue Fox had dug up a packaged salad pack from one of the food stalls. She was picking at it idly, occasionally taking a bite of lettuce.

"You gonna be okay?" I asked.

"Yeah," she said with a sigh. "It's not every day that someone throws all the shit you hate about yourself in your face like that."

"Yeah," I said with a weak laugh, thinking back to the reflection I saw. "What happened in there?"

"And who was that guy Daji was making out with when we got in there?" Lab Rat asked. "Was it another illusion?"

"Well, when I found the mirror, it showed me what I hated about myself," Blue Fox said, pushing her unfinished salad away. "A darker version of myself that enjoyed killing. The darkest, most toxic parts of my soul were laid bare."

"Daji," I guessed.

"No," Blue Fox said. "Daji is a separate entity. The mirror brought out my personal demons. The pain I was feeling was enough for her to protect herself from me. If you three hadn't shown up, she would've fully escaped."

"What happened to your inner demons then?" Professor Magic asked.

"Daji consumed them," Blue Fox said. "Or, well, the projection of them at least."

"Then she beat you?" I asked.

"Sort of," Blue Fox said sadly. "It was an unfair fight. I had scarcely fought off the Shadow Me when she crawled out and attacked. It was a two on one fight. After she beat me, she took out my reflection."

"And strung you up on the Paolao," Dragonman surmised.

"The what?" I asked.

"The giant bronze pillar," Blue Fox explained. "It was a torture device Daji invented in the Shang Dynasty. The pillar is heated with fire and a person either tried to balance on it while their feet burn or they're strapped to it and cooked."

"… Holy shit…" I said. "That's just barbaric. Why would she make something like that?"

"Daji got off to the sounds of people in agony," Blue Fox snarled, her nails cutting into the table as she tightened her grip.

"So… who was the guy?" Lab Rat asked again.

"Hmm? Oh, just an illusion. A little show for me, Daji was drawing strength from my own arousal. And showing off her powers as well," Blue Fox said.

"That… *bitch*," I said forcefully. "In every sense of the word."

"Daji is a vixen," Lab Rat said, sounding confused. "Not a dog."

"Okay, maybe not *every* sense of the word," I said. "But you know what I mean."

"What about you guys?" Blue Fox asked, cutting off Lab Rat's response. "Did you three look in the mirror as well?" No one said anything. Professor Magic's face tightened, and Lab Rat looked down at his hands.

"You did," Blue Fox said. It wasn't a question. "What did you see?"

"That's…" I began.

"You three just saw my own literal inner demon that thrives off of humiliation and degeneracy," Blue Fox said sharply. "You tell me 'it's personal' and I will be *very* upset."

"I saw my Guilt," Dragonman said. "For over a century, I stood by silently while this country continued its campaign west. I saw men and women born into servitude and die in chains. And I did nothing," I looked up at him in surprise.

"You're talking about slavery?" I asked. He sighed, letting out a white cloud of smoke.

"Yeah. I would love to say that I took part in the Underground Railroad, that the Silent Prayer abhorred slavery and that we fought back against the oppressors of the time, but we didn't. We didn't get political. We didn't bother with slaves unless one of them was practicing witchcraft. Hell, the Silent Prayer even purchased a few slaves back in the day."

"Jesus," I breathed. Dragonman shook his head sadly.

"It was only until after the Civil War did I really get a good look at what was happening," he said. "I could've stood up to it. I could've easily freed them. But I didn't."

"It's not your fault," Lab Rat said. We all looked over at him. "You were a product of your time. Slavery was normal back then."

"It was evil," Dragonman replied.

"True," Lab Rat said. "But you can't say that slavery in America was your fault."

"I'm not saying it is," Dragonman said. "But I regret not doing anything before."

"I heard what you told that thing," Lab Rat said. "That you are trying to make up for your past mistakes. I think that's the best path forward."

"Never thought I'd hear you defend someone who didn't do anything about slavery."

"Really?" Lab Rat asked. "Why?"

"Because…" Dragonman said awkwardly. "You're… you know…"

"What?"

"Black."

"Oh?" Lab Rat said. "Well, if you've been listening to Thundergirl, I'm not very good at being black. But I really don't claim much of the heritage. I'm just me." Dragonman let out a weak little laugh.

"What about you?" Dragonman asked. "I didn't get a very good look at what was going on with you." Lab Rat seemed to close up immediately.

"I saw me, back when Alley Cat had me in their claws," he said sharply, falling into his usual monotone. "I was their plaything, their little toy to do what they wanted with," he sighed and shook his head. "I was taken apart and put back together again, over and over again. I got horrifically sick constantly, only to be dissected and examined. I got cancer at least three times, tuberculosis, tetanus, kidney stones, and other diseases I'd never heard of. I got hit with a plague that drove me insane; another made me see in black and white. My body became a living battleground for bioweapon research. One team engineered a plague that would kill me; another would try and cure it so I wouldn't die."

"God preserve us," Dragonman muttered, making the sign of the cross.

"I finally managed to escape," Lab Rat said. "Freedom was the most delicious taste in the world. But the nightmare never left me. Some nights I wake up in a panic, thinking that my time in the Jesters was an illusion, a dream I invented to escape the horrors of Alley Cat," he started breathing heavily.

"And those *fucking cunts* still work to this day!" he snarled. My eyes widened. I've never seen him get this mad before.

"They keep up this charade that they are all about human research, when even now, someone is going through that hell," Lab Rat growled.

"Easy," Dragonman said. "Deep breaths. Try and relax…"

"I can't," Lab Rat replied, although he stopped breathing so heavily. "I can't forget anything they did to me. My memory is too good."

Holy shit, how had I not realized that? Lab Rat has savant syndrome. Forgetting something is an entirely foreign concept to him. For him, the pain of disease and scalpels would never cease. He would always know exactly how he was treated. He can't forget.

And he would never forgive.

"This might be the wrong thing to say," I ventured. "But you broke yourself out."

"I know."

"You did. Not us, not some government team. You pulled yourself…"

"I *know*, Silverbolt," Lab Rat snapped. I shut up immediately.

"I know what I did. Why I continue my vengeance. I applied logic to the problem. That's how I beat it," he said. "But I can never forgive them for what they did," he was looking right at Dragonman when he said that. Dragonman lowered his head.

"I know."

"I can't turn the other cheek, or whatever else…"

"I know," Dragonman said. "And I'm sorry I said those things to you. It wasn't my place."

"What are you two talking about?" I asked. I hate being the new kid sometimes because there's always something that happened before my time. To my surprise and confusion, Blue Fox looked confused too.

"Their first fight," Professor Magic explained. "Dragonman told Lab Rat to forgive Alley Cat and make peace with his past when he first joined the Jesters." I winced, and Blue Fox looked aghast at Dragonman.

"Why would you say that!?" She asked.

"I thought I could help him," Dragonman said sadly.

"It didn't," Lab Rat said sharply.

"Look, it's ancient history," Professor Magic said. "You two made up after that. Haven't you?" They didn't say anything, but Lab Rat nodded sharply.

"So, what about you?" Blue Fox asked. "What did the mirror show you?"

"My old self," I said. "Back before I came out."

"Came out?" Professor Magic asked. "Oh, you mean as transgender?"

"Yeah. I saw the person my parents wanted me to be. The son they thought I took from them."

"Yikes," Blue Fox said. "You don't talk about your parents much."

"No." I said heavily. "I don't."

"Weren't you almost an Olympic archer?" Professor Magic asked.

"Yeah, but they wanted me to compete as a man. The thought of being immortalized as a man disgusted me. If I was going to get a gold medal, I wanted it to be the real me."

"I take it your parents had something to say about that," Dragonman said.

"It started the whole fight. That was when I told them I was female. At first, they told me that I shouldn't joke about stuff like that. Then they realized I was serious. Dad got mad and Mom started crying. Few hours later, I was driving away with all my stuff. Haven't spoken to them since," I said. I waited to see their reactions.

"Oh," Professor Magic said. "How old were you?"

"19," I said.

"Is this when you started fighting crime as Silverbolt?" Blue Fox asked.

"Yeah. I was very open about being trans, and that draws the attention of some nasty people that far south," I said.

"The Holy Hand of God," Lab Rat said.

"Yeah. They almost killed me, and I managed to hit the Hangman's leg on the way out."

"Is that why his leg was in a brace?" Professor Magic asked.

"Who is this?" Blue Fox asked.

"The Hangman," I replied. "My nemesis. He leads a bloodthirsty hate group that wants to restore America by driving out people they deem 'deviants'."

"People who aren't straight, white or American," Dragonman explained.

"*Kuso rokudenashi*," Blue Fox spat.

"How about you, Professor?" I asked. "What was all that shadowy stuff?"

"… I don't know," he said after a pause.

"Bullshit," Dragonman said.

"Honestly," Professor Magic said. "I don't know what that was. Something about the Golden Line of Wizards, but I don't know what."

"Anyone with a shred of knowledge about European lore knows what that was," Dragonman said.

"I. Don't. Know!" Professor Magic said sharply. "I know what it looked like, but I don't know why it showed up!"

"Does it have to do with the Black Wizard?" I asked. A while ago, we ran into a former Jester, the Nocturnal, who knows all about our pasts and skeletons in our closets. He mentioned the Black Wizard before. Someone the Professor had killed.

"I don't know. I have a theory, about the origins of the Wizards, but I'll need to research it. Until I find out what it means, I don't want to talk about it. Understood?" Professor Magic said with a huff.

"Fine," Dragonman said, crossing his arms.

"Right," Blue Fox said, taking another bite of her salad. "So, we just need to find Thunder-chan and this heiress girl and we leave, right?"

"Brittany Howser," Lab Rat reminded us. "That's right."

"*Kakkoi*," Blue Fox said. "Fantastic. Where are we on that?"

"Not sure yet," Professor Magic said. Blue Fox frowned but said nothing.

It brought up a very uncomfortable question. Thundergirl is quite possibly the strongest person in the world. She's a supersoldier created by a man who sought to rid the world of evil. But evil is subjective, and when Thundergirl realized that her mentor and benefactor meant to rule the world to save it from evils like 'freedom' and 'equality' and 'religion' she got the hell out. At least, that's all she says. She usually deflects questions like that with humor.

Regardless, she's a warrior of the mind and body. She was born with something called the 'Goddess Gene', which gave her astounding psychic powers. Telekinesis, telepathy, pyrokinesis, energy manipulation and levitation. Her bones are nigh unbreakable, her skin as tough as steel, and she's way stronger than a human. Her eyes are more comparable to an eagle's, and she has a thunderous cry that can knock over a tank.

My point is, keeping her in one place against her will is no easy feat. If there was something capable of holding her in one place, it meant it was stronger than her. Which is a terrifying thought.

"She has any weaknesses?" Professor Magic asked. We were all looking at Blue Fox. The two of them were best friends, practically inseparable. Blue Fox finished her salad and pushed it in front of her with a sigh.

"Well, she hates gore," Blue Fox said. "Spiders, men with attitude…"

"There isn't some easily exploited Deus ex Machina weakness she has that turns off her powers, is there?" I asked Lab Rat.

"You can just say 'kryptonite' Silver. We know what you mean," he said.

"Well, does she?" I asked.

"Not really," Lab Rat said.

"She's terrified of magic," Dragonman said thoughtfully. "Well, black magic really."

"Hmm," Professor Magic said. "I know she hates them, but I can't see how that's going to keep her trapped."

"Well, let's think logically," Lab Rat said. "We were all trapped in an area that we couldn't escape, but the others could. Dragonman can't be in water, but we can all swim. Professor Magic needs to speak to use his powers, but we don't need to. We can all overcome our own demons, but Blue Fox has more demons in her."

"We get it," I said. "What's your point?"

"What is something we can all do that she can't?" he asked. No one said anything. I could shoot the wings off a fly at 50 paces, but that's just me. I tried going through old missions, what I knew of superpowers, but couldn't think of anything.

"Stealth," I said. Everyone looked up at me.

"She's snuck around before," Dragonman rumbled.

"Not very well. She's a living battering ram. Her only tactic is 'knock everything down and laugh about it'."

"Okay, and why would she sneak out of a trap when she could just tear down the walls and take a selfie with the rubble?" Lab Rat asked.

"That's an oddly specific statement," I said with a frown. "Has she ever done something like that before?"

No one said anything.

"Oh lord…"

"She can't sit through a horror movie," Blue Fox piped up.

"What?" I asked.

"I tried showing her *Ju-On*, but she left 15 minutes into it," She explained.

"*Ju-On*?" I asked.

"The original Japanese release of *The Grudge*," Dragonman explained.

"So?" I asked. "Japanese horror is in a class of its own. What of it?"

"If I was designing a trap to hold her in place, I would make it horrifying," Blue Fox said.

"That goes back to my original question," Lab Rat asked. "What kind of horror show could force her to stay?"

"Hey, I'm just guessing," Blue Fox said.

"Isn't there a haunted house here?" I asked. Lab Rat pulled out the map and we all leaned in to look at it.

"Boom," Blue Fox said, pointing at the haunted house. "Told you."

"Doesn't mean she's there," Professor Magic argued.

"You have a better idea?" she asked.

"… No."

"Alright then," she said, standing up to stretch. "Let's go get spooked!"

Chapter 10: Test of Courage

"No fair!" Blue Fox said indignantly. *"That's* their haunted house!?"

I looked up at the building. It was a massive gray cathedral, complete with gothic arches, stained glass, stone gargoyles, and wrought iron fences. It wasn't a cheesy knockoff, but an elaborate creation. The building gave off an eerie vibe of something best left alone.

"Wow," I said, gazing up at the tall steeple. "I've seen haunted mansions, but this is something else!"

"This is incredible," Dragonman said in awe. "Flying buttresses and pointed arches. Hell, it looks like the Leon Cathedral in Spain!"

"You're into gothic architecture?" Professor Magic asked.

"I'm a gargoyle. Of course, I am," Dragonman said proudly.

"There's something else creepy about this," I said, looking around. I couldn't shake the foreboding feeling. Like I was being watched or something.

"I feel it too," Blue Fox said, her initial awe vanished, replaced with uncertainty.

"I don't feel anything supernatural," Dragonman murmured. "How about you, Professor?"

"This place feels wrong," he said. "But I'm not detecting any magic…"

Blam!

We all jumped and drew our weapons, only to see Lab Rat holstering an electro gun. Next to him was a tombstone with the top blasted off.

"What the hell, man!?" I asked, stowing my arrow.

"Infrasound generator," he said simply. "Sounds between 19 and 20 hertz can cause feelings of uneasiness and paranoia. I was able to detect it with a sensor I built."

"I know what infrasound is, dumbass!" I said. "You couldn't have said something first?" He looked around at us, then at the tombstone, then back at us.

"Oh."

"Come on," Dragonman rumbled, keeping his club handy. "Let's check out the creepy church."

We followed him to the large oak doors. The path to the church was flanked by stone statues of angels with blindfolds. Some had some sort of liquid leaking from under their blindfolds.

"Weeping angels," Blue Fox muttered.

"Best not take your eyes off them," he said jokingly. She cocked an eyebrow at him

"Why?"

"You know, don't blink," he said. Blue Fox only looked more confused.

"Is that some sort of reference?"

"You've never seen that episode of *Doctor Who*?" He asked in amazement.

"I don't watch a lot of American shows," she confessed.

"American!?"

Their argument was interrupted by a high-pitched scream. Not some canned speaker, but a real desperate cry of pain and fear. The kind that makes your hair stand up and makes your skin crawl.

HELP.

The word echoed in my mind like a bell. Judging by the looks on everyone else's faces, I guessed they heard the same thing. We all know telepathy when we hear it. Or... feel it, I guess. Dragonman kicked open the door and stormed in. We followed suit, weapons out and ready for action.

Despite the vaulted arches outside, the inside was narrow and cramped. Flickering lights were the only source of light inside the church. No one was around. We slowly moved closer together, facing out. The only sound I could hear were the clicking of Lab Rat's hands adjusting their grip on his guns, the steady breathing of Blue Fox and Professor Magic, and Dragonman's lupine growling.

Then, in true horror movie fashion, the giant doors slammed shut.

"Bloody hell," Professor Magic grumbled.

Clank.

We all turned to face the sound. Something heavy and metallic was coming from our right.

Clank.

I readied my arrow, drawing it back so the fletching touched my right ear. I heard the familiar creak of the bowstring, and took comfort in the weight of my bow in my hand

Clank.

Dragonman moved slightly in front of us, adjusting his stance and regripping his club. Blue Fox added her own growls to Dragonman's, her body rippling with new muscles as she shifted to a more bestial form.

Clank.

"Sancte Michael Archangele, defende nos in proelio," I heard Dragonman mutter. I assumed it was a prayer. That, or a magic spell.

Clank.

"Come on," I heard Professor Magic complain. "Get on with it…"

Clank.

Then I saw it. Slowly moving into the weak light of the entrance, a humanoid figure was walking. Each step echoed loudly with a metallic step. As it approached, I saw golden armor with white fur trim, a dark purple bodysuit, a cape that reflected the light in rainbow colors.

"Thundergirl," I breathed. We all relaxed. She walked closer. Her face was completely neutral and emotionless. She kept walking closer, like she was in a trance.

"Thundergirl?" I asked. No reply. Everyone stepped back to let her pass. She made no indication that we were even here.

"Hey!" I said and jumped in her path "What the hell are…"

POW!

The world spun and I hit the wall, the blow knocking the wind out of me. I wheezed and tried to figure out what happened. Thundergirl kept walking past me, and it clicked. She just shoved me out of the way, and it almost broke my ribs. I winced in pain as I struggled to stand. Ow. Maybe not almost…

Lab Rat stooped to help me up as I struggled to regain my breath.

"Thundergirl!" Dragonman snarled. "What are you…"

In a flash, she grabbed him by the beard and dragged him down to the ground, his head smacking into the flagstone with a loud impact. Blue Fox moved to get in her way, but the Professor held her back

"Wait," he said. "Something's not right."

"You… think…?" I wheezed. Dragonman groaned in pain, steaming black blood leaking from his forehead.

"Look at her head," he pointed out. I managed to look up and see where he was pointing. Thundergirl's helmet can fold up into a little circlet, like what the elves in *Lord of the Rings* sometimes wear. I have no idea how it does that, but she wasn't wearing it. Around her head was a dull metal band with small LEDs on it.

"A neural monitor," Lab Rat said. "Someone's reading her mind."

"Follow her," Professor Magic said, walking after her. We all followed suit, Dragonman and I taking up the rear. My breath was coming back, and his head was mending itself.

In the dim flickering light, we passed a number of coffins. Thundergirl slowed her pace, only a little bit, but kept walking. I could feel a sense of dread emanating in front of me, and I realized it was coming from her. One of the coffins burst open to reveal a bloody zombie missing its lower jaw, lunging out at her. Thundergirl flinched, and the same scream we heard outside echoed from somewhere in the church. She kept walking, her body stiffer than before. The zombie, once mere inches from her face, retracted back into the coffin, which closed up.

"*Nandayo*?" Blue Fox muttered, which I assume means 'what the hell?' in Japanese. Lab Rat checked the coffin with his scanner.

"It's an animatronic," he said in amazement.

"*That's* an animatronic?" Dragonman asked.

"Bloody hell," Professor Magic said. "They had access to these, and I got the Disneyland knockoffs?" Lab Rat ignored him and was looking down at the coffins, then back at Thundergirl.

"I get it," he said.

"Get what?" I asked, wincing as I rubbed my side.

"I get how she's trapped here," he said. "You two were right."

"Quit stalling," Dragonman growled. "What is going on here?"

"We were wondering what would keep her from breaking out," Lab Rat said. "Why she wouldn't tear down this place in the first few minutes."

"So?" I asked.

"There's a hostage," he said. "That neural monitor is reading her mental state. She gets scared or tries to escape, it will pick up on it."

"Those screams we heard," Professor Magic said, his eyes widening in understanding.

"I think I know where Brittany Howser is," Lab Rat said. "Whenever she gets spooked or tries to escape, Brittany suffers for it."

"If she doesn't keep walking, Brittany gets hurt," Blue Fox said. "That's why she hit Silverbolt and Dragon-san."

"My thoughts exactly," Lab Rat said.

"How do you know so much about these monitors?" Professor Magic said.

"Because Alley Cat had me in one as well," he said bitterly. "Mine was surgically implanted though. Hers is just a wearable one."

"So, how do we free her?" I asked.

"Simple," Dragonman said with a shrug. "We find Howser and spring her. Thundergirl will have no reason to stay here and can leave."

"So, where is she?" I asked. Dragonman cocked his head and closed his eyes in thought.

"Above us, I think," he said slowly. "If I could pick up her scent, I could track her easily."

"Hang on," Blue Fox said. "Someone should stay with Thundergirl. She shouldn't have to go through this alone."

"I'll stay with her," Professor Magic said. "You four go find Brittany."

"I think I should stay," Blue Fox argued. "I can calm her down in case she gets scared again."

"If Brittany's getting hurt every time Thundergirl gets spooked or deviates from her path, she's gonna need medical attention. You're our best doc, and you'll need to calm her down there."

"But…"

"*Go*," Professor Magic insisted. "You aren't the only one capable of calming magic," he started walking down the path after Thundergirl before Blue Fox could respond. I walked up to her and put a hand on her shoulder.

"She'll be fine," I said reassuringly. "He'll look after her."

"I know," she replied sadly. "I just hate the idea of her being here."

"C'mon," Dragonman said. "Let's free the girl and go home."

We walked down the path that Thundergirl was taking. After scanning the animatronics, Lab Rat confirmed that they weren't connected to the neural monitor or Brittany. So, we managed to smash a few of them on our path. Less torment for our friend to deal with. Blue Fox decapitated a mechanical werewolf with a sort of enthusiasm I hadn't seen before. Lab Rat was scanning the place to generate some sort of map, while Dragonman was listening and sniffing, trying to get a read on where Brittany was being kept.

"Hey Blue," I said, suddenly having an idea.

"Yeah?"

"You demon fox, Daji, she draws power from pain and suffering, right?"

"Yes," Blue Fox said stiffly. "What's your point?"

"Can she sniff it out?" I asked.

"What?"

"You know, can she detect if someone's in pain to consume it?" I clarified. Blue Fox furrowed her brow in thought.

"I have no idea," she said. "I've never tried."

"Would it work?" I asked.

"I... I guess," she said. "I don't like the idea of asking her for help, though."

"It was just a suggestion," I said. "You don't have to..."

"No, if it means saving her, I'll do it."

"What are you two talking about?" Dragonman asked.

"Daji might be able to find Brittany by detecting her pain," I said. Blue Fox closed her eyes and started focusing.

"What!?" He said hurriedly "Blue, don't do that! You start relying on the demon…"

"That way," Blue Fox said suddenly, pointing up.

"What did you tell her?" Dragonman asked. Blue Fox said nothing, just started checking the wall.

"Blue!"

"I didn't promise her anything," Blue Fox snapped. "I'm not some kid playing with an Ouija board asking how many babies I'm gonna have. I know how to handle her."

"Everyone who deals with demons says that," Dragonman said. "Right up until it kills them."

"Are you really going to start this now?" She asked, whipping around from the wall to glare at him. In any situation, this would have been pretty funny, seeing how she's under 5' and maybe 100 lbs. soaking wet, but the grim lighting and creepy atmosphere of the tunnel took the humor out.

"I just don't want to see you fall under its influence," Dragonman said stubbornly.

"And I don't need some ancient lizard man telling me how to use my powers!" Blue Fox said. "You westerners might not understand this, but we handle our spirits with grace and respect! We don't start burning women because she knows how to communicate with spirits!"

"Is that why you carry a cursed blade then?" Dragonman spat.

"I... what?" Blue Fox asked, completely baffled by Dragonman's response.

"Guys..." I heard Lab Rat say.

"A Muramasa!" Dragonman said hotly, ignoring Lab Rat. "A cursed blade with a demon sealed in the metal! Don't act surprised, you know what I'm talking about!" Blue Fox stared at him in confusion, then drew her sword to show him.

"You see this?" She said, showing him a marking on the blade. "What does this say?"

"It says..." he said, squinting his eyes.

"It says 'Kogitsune'," Blue Fox said. "It means 'little fox'. Which is the name of my sword," she flipped it over to the other side. "This says 'Kokaji-Munechika'. That's the name of the blacksmith. Not Muramasa."

"I..." Dragonman said uneasily.

"Just because a katana has a marking on the blade doesn't mean it's a cursed demon blade," Blue Fox said sharply. "This blade was forged with the help of Inari, the goddess of rice, blacksmithing and foxes. The *only* goddess I get along with."

"Guys…" Lab Rat said more insistently.

"Not everything attached to spirits is evil," Blue Fox continued. "So, the next time you want to play inquisitor, do your homework first!"

BOOM!

A sudden explosion ripped through the wall to our left, where Blue Fox was investigating. I whipped around with an arrow ready, only to see Lab Rat standing there with a detonator in his hand.

"Lab Rat, what the hell!?" I asked.

"I found a way through!" he said innocently.

"What did I say about telling us first!?"

"I tried! No one was listening!" he complained. I sighed and peered through the hole he made. Apparently, this was once a door that had been sealed up after construction. Lab Rat and I walked through, with Blue Fox and Dragonman following in bitter silence. The area was clearly not meant for the public. Exposed insulation and wires lined the walls, with unpainted drywall appearing sporadically. The path led to a steep set of unfinished wooden stairs.

"Hey, here's something else we can do that Thundergirl can't!" Lab Rat.

"What's that?" I asked.

"Walking up these stairs!" he said jovially. "Because they would break under all her armor!"

"She can fly, Rat."

"I know. That's the joke."

"Ah."

"It was funny, right?" Lab Rat asked. I sighed.

"Kinda," I said. We went up the stairs and rounded a corner.

"Think she's close?" I asked.

"Maybe," Lab Rat said. "What does the demon say?"

"Rat…" I chided.

"What?"

"Not a good time. They just had a fight about it."

"But it's helping us find the girl."

"Dragonman doesn't like us asking spirits for help," I explained.

"… But it's helping us find the girl," Lab Rat repeated.

"It's fine," Blue Fox said gently. "This way," she started to lead the way. I looked back at Dragonman. He looked uncomfortable but followed behind her.

"Don't," he said softly when I opened my mouth to say something. I frowned. My mask covers my mouth.

"How…" I tried to say.

"I heard you take a breath in," he said. "Not now."

"You don't know what I was going to say."

"Something to explain why I shouldn't be telling her what to do," he said.

"… Lucky guess," I conceded. He smiled wanly.

"I try to help," he said.

"I know," I said. "But sometimes the best help is to be there when they fall."

"Starting to see that," Dragonman admitted. I patted him on the shoulder (the part I could reach) and we followed Blue Fox and Lab Rat. We reached a set of rooms and started looking inside. Some had controls for the animatronics, special effects and ambience. Another had CCTV and other security related stuff, and other was a janitor closet. Brand new stuff too, still wrapped in plastic. High end janitorial gear.

Don't give me that look. I wasn't *always* a crime fighter.

The last door in the hallway was labelled 'Private'. After nodded at Dragonman, who kicked it open. Sure enough, we found Brittany Howser.

According to the brief, Brittany Howser was the rich daughter of Brady Howser, the oil tycoon. That oil spill in Monterey Bay last year? His company. Brittany grew up wanting nothing. Wait, that's not right. Lemme try that again.

Brittany grew up wanting everything and getting it. Much better. She was a good-looking woman, just entering her twenties. Tanned skin, bleach blonde skin, big lips, and fake breasts. In the picture we had of her for the original mission, she looked like those queen bees in high school, the captain of the cheerleaders who ran the whole school. She had a permanent look of disgust on her face that no amount of cosmetic surgery could remove.

Now, she looked less fake and even less human. Her time in captivity cost her a couple of pounds she couldn't afford to lose. Her blonde hair was unkempt and outgrowing its dye, giving her a streak of mouse-brown hair in the middle of her head. Her mascara had run with tears, giving her a haunted look. She was locked in a glass box sitting in what looked like an electric chair. She had straps on her ankles, wrists, torso and head. The straps were on too tight, and I could see red chafe on her wrists. Her fingertips were losing circulation and were slightly blue. She was dressed for clubbing, a short sequin skirt, a pink crop top and stiletto heels. Her pink nails were chipped and peeling.

Sure, she looked like another entitled trust fund rich girl, but no one deserves to be treated like this. In front of her, a number of screens showed Thundergirl walking through the haunted church. On the screen, I saw Professor Magic walking next to Thundergirl. I couldn't hear him, but I could see him talking. A sarcophagus popped open, and an animatronic mummy burst out. Thundergirl twitched and Brittany's chair started buzzing. Brittany let out a blood-curdling scream. Sparks arced between two wires behind her head. On the screen, I saw Professor Magic blast the mummy with white prismatic fire. The screen got staticky, and when it cleared the mummy was melted into slag. After they passed, the chair stopped buzzing, and Brittany slumped forward. There was a faint hiss, and she jerked up in her chair with a weak groan.

"What the hell," I muttered.

"Adrenaline," Lab Rat said, pointing to her neck. A trio of IV tubes were connected to her neck, the other end attached to a large tank.

"Jesus, Mary and Joseph," Dragonman breathed. This wasn't a curse, it was a prayer.

"What sick, twisted sadist does this to a person?" Blue Fox said. "Hooking her up to adrenaline to keep her screaming in pain." Brittany glanced over at us.

"Please," she whimpered. "Please help me." Her voice was raspy from screaming. I felt my throat tighten and my blood boil. Whoever did this was going to *pay*. Dearly.

"It's okay," Blue Fox said. She pressed her palm to the glass. "We'll get you out of here in no time." Brittany's head slumped back, and I could hear her crying pitifully.

"Stand back," Dragonman said, raising his club. "I'll get her out."

"*Baka*!" Blue Fox yelled at him, "The shards would carve her up!"

"Please get out of the way, Blue Fox," Lab Rat said formally. "I will use my drill to remove the glass panes to get her out." We all looked at him in surprise.

"Oh. Uh, go ahead," Blue Fox said.

"I'm telling you because Silverbolt yells at me if I don't warn you before breaking stuff," Lab Rat said. Dragonman and Blue Fox looked at me in confusion.

"Thank you, Lab Rat," I said, facepalming. With a few bolts removed, we got the glass off her case and Lab Rat started working on getting Brittany free. Blue Fox started checking her for injuries and infection. Dragonman and I started looking around.

"Hey, Silver! I found Thundergirl's helmet/crown," he said, holding up a small golden circle. "Catch!"

"Why are you using two hands – OH SHIT!" I yelped and barely dodged the circlet. It slammed down on the ground heavily, sinking slightly into the wooden floor.

"Asshole!" I yelled. "What was that for?"

"I wanted to see you struggle under its weight," Dragonman said mischievously.

"How is something that small so heavy?" I asked, poking it with the toe of my boot

"It's a titanium-gold alloy that can stop a tank round condensed into a tiara," Lab Rat called from Brittany's chair. "All that mass has to go somewhere."

"And she just walks around with that on her head all the time?" I asked.

"Yep."

"Damn," I said, rubbing my neck self-consciously. "Sounds rough."

"Not for her."

"If you two are done playing catch, we need to get Howser-chan to a hospital," Blue Fox said seriously. "She's seriously malnourished and dehydrated. Not to mention the burns on her head, and possible brain damage from all the shocks. Her heart's off rhythm as well." She pulled a small canteen from her bag and helped Brittany drink it, who eagerly slurped it down.

"You have anything that can help her now?" Dragonman asked seriously.

"Some, but she needs a medical facility," Blue Fox said. "We need someone to carry her. I'll mix something up on the way out."

"We also need someone to carry this," Dragonman said, picking up Thundergirl's circlet. "We can't leave this here."

"Oh, hang on," I said. "I know what to do." I walked over to the glass case and looked up. On the top was a small microphone.

"Hey, Thundergirl! We freed Howser. Come on up here and I might forgive you for cracking my ribs." I checked the screens to see Thundergirl had disappeared. There was a faint rumbling sound beneath us.

"Stand back, y'all," I said. We all moved to the edges of the room, except Blue Fox who stayed by Brittany's side. The ground exploded as Thundergirl burst through the cheap unfinished floor.

"Is she okay!?" Thundergirl asked hurriedly.

"She needs help," Blue Fox said.

"Oh my God, Brittany. I am so so so *so* sorry for earlier!" Thundergirl said, grasping one of Brittany's hands in both of hers. "I couldn't think of a way to save you, I just had to keep moving or you would get zapped again, and I can't stand gore and zombies and monsters and…"

"Back up!" Blue Fox said, swatting Thundergirl away. "Let the poor thing breathe."

"You got Howser?" I heard Professor Magic say. I saw him slowly float up from the hole Thundergirl made, no doubt on a small tornado he conjured.

"Safe and sound," Dragonman said. "Here, this is yours, T."

"My helmet!" she cried, picking up the circlet. "Thank God this is safe." She reached up and pulled the neural monitor off and dropped it on the ground to stomp on. Just before her foot crushed it, Lab Rat yelped and scooped it up.

"Don't you dare!" he cried.

"What?" Thundergirl asked.

"This place just *reeks* of Alley Cat, and I'm picking as much evidence as I can." Lab Rat said.

"O-kay," Thundergirl said, placing the circlet on her head and pulling her dreadlocks back into a ponytail. The circlet expanded into a full helmet with a purple visor. Her hair poked back out the back as a small tail.

"Dragonman! Come be useful and carry Brittany Howser out of here!"

"Excuse me, I am *very* useful…"

"Now!" she yelled. Dragonman shut up and picked the girl up gingerly, and carried her out the door. Blue Fox followed him closely and was pulling stuff from her bag and mixing it. The rest of us followed them.

"Saw your handiwork down there," Thundergirl said. "Really helped me out."

"Figured it would," I replied.

"Yeah. Who was drawing smiley faces on the wall?" she asked.

"That was me," Lab Rat piped up. "The place needed some smileys."

"That it did, Rat. That it did," Thundergirl said. "Sorry about hitting you like that, Silver."

"Bah," I said dismissively. "It happens."

"I just couldn't let Brittany get hurt because I stopped tor tried to talk to you."

"Thundergirl, it's fine. I'll have Blue look at it later," I said. "I just owe you a punch."

"Oh alright," she said, lifting her arm to expose her side. "Not sure it will do anything."

"Not now, of course," I said. "Later. When you won't see it coming," Thundergirl lowered her arm slowly.

"Seriously?"

"Yep. And to make it fair, I'll have to find something so it'll hurt," I said mischievously. "Probably some kind of arrow."

"Ha ha," Thundergirl said nervously. "You're kidding, right?"

I spun around with an arrow nocked in the blink of an eye and aimed it at her. She yelped and tried to block.

"Maybe," I said, lowering my bow and walking away. "Maybe not."

"Silver? Come on Silver, it wasn't my fault! Guys, she's kidding. Right? Guys?"

Chapter 11: The Man Behind the Torment

We made it outside the haunted church, just as dawn was breaking. It was only then that I realized how tired I was. All-nighters weren't rare with us, but it had been a long night.

But we made it. Despite all the danger, emotional trauma, mazes and creepy AI, we were reunited and managed to save poor Brittany Howser as well. Not a bad ending.

Which is why we ran into *him*.

Right by the entrance to the park, just a stone's throw away from my carousel (ugh), was a short man in a suit. He was a little person, with stylish stubble beard, jet black hair slicked back and a pair of shades. As we got closer, he started slow clapping.

"Well done!" he said. "A terrific show, indeed!" We all looked at each other.

"Who are you?" Professor Magic said.

"No one you need to worry about," he replied with a toothy smile.

"Bullshit," I said.

"You can call me the Ringleader, if it pleases you," he said.

"It doesn't," Thundergirl said coldly.

"Oh, come now!" Ringleader said. "Every Jester needs a ringleader!" My blood froze when he said that. I suddenly recognized his voice from the carousel.

"It's you," I said. "You built this place."

"Guilty," he said playfully, spreading his hands.

"You?" Lab Rat said. "You put us here?"

"I did," Ringleader said. "Owner and proprietor of Jester Park."

"So, what's stopping us from pounding you into the pavement," Thundergirl threatened, cracking her knuckles aggressively.

"Because I know you," he said. "I know who you are, Athena Justice Freeman."

My jaw dropped when he said that.

"How…" Thundergirl said, stunned.

"He wrote the Snowflake program," Lab Rat said. "He knows who we are."

"How?" Blue Fox said.

"A magician never tells," Ringleader said with a wink.

"How I show you a real magician?" Professor Magic said, his staff blazing with blue fire. "See if you feel like talking then?"

"Because of this," he said, pulling out a small device. It looked like a detonator with a small red button on the top.

"The hell is that?" Thundergirl asked.

"I push this button, and all of your identities get blasted all over the internet," Ringleader said, his jovial manner evaporating. "The whole world will know who you are. Especially Task Force 52."

"They get fake leads all the time," Lab Rat said. "What makes your info so potent?"

"Should I read off your address, social security number, or the foster home you lived in until you turned 18, Soren Griffin Steele?" Ringleader said with a smirk.

"What do you want?" Dragonman growled.

"I want you to work for me," Ringleader said.

"What?" Thundergirl said.

"You work for me. I give you missions, you carry them out," Ringleader said. "Either you do as I say, or you have Task Force 52 breaking down your door.

"Who else has this info?" I asked.

"No one. I work alone. My resources are practically infinite. I can get almost anything I want, but you six have access to things even I don't have. You are the best of the best. Even when faced with your greatest weaknesses, you still managed to free yourselves," Ringleader said. "I will deal with you in good faith, of course. You work for me, I will compensate you for it. Wouldn't you rather work out of a manor with house servants, 5-star meals and the most advanced technology at your fingertips than that crumbling ruin of a house instead?"

"Don't talk shit about the Fortress of Destiny," I said.

"Yeah," Thundergirl said. "Only we get to bitch about it."

"Silver," Dragonman whispered.

"Yeah?" I whispered back.

"Behind him," he breathed. I looked and saw what he was talking about.

"Oh shit," I said.

"Told you this would happen," he hissed.

"Shut up," I hissed back.

"What's going on you two?" Ringleader demanded.

"Ringleader," I said, reaching for an arrow. "You might want to look behind you."

"How stupid do you think I am?" He asked. "You think I'm gonna fall for that?"

"Oh shit," Thundergirl said. "No, seriously, *turn around*."

"You're coordination is perfect," he said. "I admire your teamwork, but if you think I'm going to turn around so that Silverbolt can shoot this out of my hand, you are *gravely* mistaken."

"This isn't a trick," I said seriously as I raised my bow.

"Put that down, NOW!" Ringleader demanded. "Either you lower that bow, or I dox you and the entire team!" I lowered my bow begrudgingly.

"Goddammit, man!" Professor Magic said. "Either get out of the way, or it's going to get you!"

"Oh really?" Ringleader taunted. "What will?"

"The lion I let out," I said. He frowned at me in confusion, just as the beast leapt out from the bushes.

Ringleader didn't stand a chance. The thing ravaged him within seconds, staining the pavement red. I won't go into too much detail, but it was bad. He screamed in terror the entire time, until it crushed his windpipe.

"Oh my God…" I said, watching the carnage. Thundergirl dashed over to a trashcan to vomit. Like Blue Fox said, she doesn't handle gore very well. By the time any of us could act, it was too late. The lion had killed the Ringleader. His little doxing device tumbled from his limp hands as the lion carried his carcass away.

"That was…" I tried to say.

"Wow," Lab Rat said.

"Okay, so I know this sounds bad, but I don't think he deserved that," I said. "I know he threatened us with private information, and tormented us with our own weaknesses, but still."

"I'd like to agree with you," Professor Magic said. "But I think he earned that."

"Many that live deserve death. And some that die deserve life. Can you give it to them? Then do not be too eager to deal out death in judgement," Dragonman quoted.

"Are you seriously quoting Gandalf at me?" Professor Magic asked. "Me?"

"Come one guys," Blue Fox said. "Howser-chan. Hospital. *Now*."

After a brief bit of portal magic, we managed to get Brittany to a hospital and her parents. I'm sure we could've gotten a good amount of the reward money, but we left before they could offer that to us. We had a bigger problem.

"It makes no sense," Lab Rat said.

"Check again," I countered.

"I checked the servers four times. No breaks, no leaks, no hacks. That firewall I coded puts the People's Republic of China to shame. Nothing could have gotten through," Lab Rat said.

"Could Nocturnal have told him?" Dragonman asked. We were back at the Fortress, sitting around our busted hockey table. After a well-earned crash, we were all trying to find out how the Ringleader managed to learn that much about us.

"I doubt it," Lab Rat said. "He didn't know my last name."

"None of us did," Professor Magic said. "Besides, he hasn't been seen since I sent him to Helheim."

"Maybe he struck a deal with a demon," Blue Fox suggested.

"Maybe," Professor Magic said. "But this place is warded well. Dragonman and I made sure this was shielded from the supernatural went we first bought this place."

"Bought?" I asked.

"Well, not really. No one owned it, or even knew it was here," Professor Magic said. "We just took it."

"We're getting off topic," Dragonman grumbled. "Lab Rat, you're sure you've recovered everything?"

"Yes, I'm sure!" Lab Rat said. "The device linked back to a server room in the park. I made sure I cleared it. Three times."

"Are you positive, Soren?" Thundergirl teased.

"Don't. Call me that," Lab Rat said coldly, glaring daggers at her.

"Alright, damn," she said, raising her hands in surrender.

"Oh, while we're on the subject, if anyone calls me 'Aiden', I will personally ensure you will have enough arrows up your ass for you to legally be called a porcupine," I said.

"No one is going to be using any real names here," Professor Magic said evenly. "And we aren't going to start doubting each other. I trust that Lab Rat has recovered everything, and that our data is secure."

"Thank you," Lab Rat said appreciatively.

"We're safe for now, but this accident could happen again," the Professor said. "If the Ringleader didn't get it from us, he got it from someone else."

"Which means someone else has our secret identities," Thundergirl said darkly.

"Exactly," Professor Magic said.

"Shit," Dragonman muttered. No one said anything for a while.

"You think there's a conspiracy?" I asked.

"What?" Professor Magic asked.

"Look, someone was funding Sawyer," I said. "That pedo pimp was selling kids and women to someone. Maybe there's a connection between Sawyer and the Ringleader."

"That's insane," Thundergirl said with a nervous laugh. "Isn't it?"

"Not really," Lab Rat said. "I've been going over some of the data you recovered from Sawyer's church. Apparently, there were some people we didn't save."

"And you bring this up now!?" Blue Fox asked.

"Look, it was only one email, and I didn't see it until recently. Anyways, they were talking about recruits," Lab Rat said.

"Recruits?" Dragonman asked.

"Yeah. Didn't make sense to me. But I don't remember any young men on Firefly Island," Lab Rat said.

"Don't forget Silverback and the Soviet monkey army," I said. "How does a kiddie pimp manage to hire someone like that?"

"Are you telling me someone was using Sawyer to get recruits for, I assume, an army and gave our identities to a psychopath billionaire to blackmail us into working for him?" Thundergirl asked. "Why?"

"Why else?" Dragonman said darkly. "Someone's trying to take over the world."

THE END

321

Story 3: Frustration – A Dragonman and Professor Magic Adventure

Prologue

"Goddammit!" Thundergirl howled. I laughed.

"Wow," I said calmly. "You suck at this game."

"No, you're… argh! Cheater!"

"I'm not cheating. You just suck," I said with a smirk. Thundergirl glared at me, and I could feel her frustration emanating off her in waves. One of the downsides of being a telepath as powerful as her means her emotions radiate off her. I took a dramatic sip of my coffee, then quickly no-scoped her in the game.

"What the fuck?" Thundergirl said.

"Wow," I heard Dragonman say behind me. "That was embarrassing."

"Shut it, you big lizard," Thundergirl said, scowling at the game. "You would be getting stomped just as bad as I am." Dragonman smiled and took a swig of his coffee. Video games were harder for him, given that his hands were too big for the controllers. He preferred to watch and make comments on our gameplay instead.

"What's going on in here?" a sleepy voice said. I looked over to see Blue Fox walk in. Wow, she was not a morning person. Her hair, normally immaculate, was a tangled mess.

Her eyes had dark circles under them, and she was dressed in baggy sweatpants and sweatshirt.

"Morning, Blue!" I said, headshotting Thundergirl without looking.

"What the fuck!?" she yelled.

"Holy shit," Dragonman said, sounding impressed.

"You're playing this game again?" Blue Fox asked.

"Thundergirl was talking shit, so we had to settle this like adults," I explained. Blue Fox came over and checked the score.

"Silverbolt. You know you're not allowed to use the sniper rifle in game," she chided.

"She's not," Dragonman said. "She's using the pistol."

"Wow," Blue Fox said. She walked over to curl up on the couch next to Dragonman. Thundergirl looked up from the game to look at Blue Fox.

"Isn't that my mug?" she asked.

"Yeah, because *someone* keeps putting mine on the top shelf," Blue Fox said, glaring at Dragonman.

"Damn," he said, hiding his smile poorly. "That's mean," she punched him in the arm.

"Is that green tea?" I asked, recognizing the smell.

"Yeah," she said. "It's better for you than coffee. How come you Americans never drink tea?"

"Tea belongs in the harbor in this country," I responded. Dragonman laughed.

"Atta girl!" he boomed proudly.

"Mail call!" Lab Rat said, walking in with a bundle of mail.

"Did I get anything?" I asked, firing a shot in the game to blow up a barrel and killing Thundergirl again, drawing out a stream of cuss words from her.

"No." Lab Rat said. "You know, hiding behind explosive barrels isn't a good way to win."

"Shut up, Rat." Thundergirl snarled. Lab Rat frowned.

"I'm only trying help," he said innocently.

"What came in the mail today?" Dragonman asked, changing the subject.

"Uhh, *Sports Illustrated*," he said with confusion. "Who…?" Blue Fox leapt up and snatched it from him, only to sit down and eagerly sift through the pages.

"Uhh, okay." Lab Rat said. "More bills, some deal offer from a computer store for the Professor… a package for Thundergirl… and this letter came for you, Dragonman."

"Ah, I was getting worried about this. They're not normally this late," he said.

CRUNCH!

"Dammit!" Thundergirl said, holding up her controller she had accidentally crushed. Super strength isn't kind to most electronics. She sighed and opened up the trash bag next to her and tossed it in with the other controllers she broke. I paused the game so she could dig up a replacement.

"Who's the letter from?" I asked.

"The Silent Prayer," he said, breaking the wax seal and pulling out a slip of paper.

"Who?" I asked. He looked up with concern.

"You don't know who the Silent Prayer is?" he asked.

"Should I?"

"Well, no. Not really. But you've probably heard me talk about them before, haven't you?" Dragonman said.

"Once or twice," Thundergirl said.

"Wait, you don't know either?" he asked. "Does anyone?"

"They tried to kill me a few times," Blue Fox said, her eyes locked onto her magazine. "Past that, nothing really."

"Lab Rat, you know who the Silent Prayer is, right?" Dragonman asked desperately.

"Only that they pay you a sizable chunk of money every month," Lab Rat said. "I've tried looking them up, but never found anything.

"Good Lord, none of you know this? No one knows how the Jesters got started?" he asked incredulously.

"Well, you and Professor Magic started it," I said. "Past that, no one really knows."

"Yeah, wasn't that the point?" Thundergirl asked, looking up from her search for her controllers.

"From the public, sure," Dragonman said. "But at least you guys should know this story."

"Well alright then, old man." I said. "How did the Jesters form?"

Chapter 1: Red Tape

It all started one cool spring morning, just before dawn. We had been hunting a possible warlock who had been murdering children and using their blood to draw horrifying satanic symbols when…

"You have got to be kidding me," I said. "You want me to just walk away?" I asked angrily.

"The instruction is clear on this scenario," Mentor Myers said. "The killer isn't a witch. Thus, this is a problem for the police and FBI now." I crossed my arms. My team and I had just returned from the latest crime scene of the Devil's Advocate, the media's name for a serial killer we had pegged as a witch/warlock on account of all the demonic imagery found at every murder. I was still dressed in my combat gear, black and white camo pants, a black trench coat made of dragon's hide, silver gauntlets with retractable claw attachments on the fingers, and silver boots shaped like a dragon's talons. I never wear a shirt, despite the constant teasing I get for it. But if you can regenerate, wearing armor there would just get in the way. My sword leaned against the side of my chair. The hilt was designed to look like a dragon with its jaws opened 180 degrees with the blade coming out like a long metal tongue. The Dragonblade was a powerful weapon against darkness. Only the worthy could wield such a weapon.

"The FBI have been after this psychopath for almost a year!" I argued. "They aren't any closer to catching him than they were six months ago!"

"I know, but we hunt monsters here," Myers said. "The instruction says…"

"He's butchering children, Myers!" I yelled, cutting him off. "This guy *is* a monster!"

"You told me there was no sign of witchcraft in that room, despite the demonic imagery on the walls, correct?" Myers asked, crossing his arms defiantly. Myers was an average-sized man, his chestnut brown hair receding to the top of his head. He wore a pair of birth control glasses, making him look like an average-looking salaryman, except for the deep scars running across the side of his head. He was dressed in the uniform of the Silent Prayer, black trench coat, black cargo pants, steel-toed boots, and black shirt with the Silent Prayer's logo stitched onto his chest. His left arm had been torn off years ago, leaving him with a prosthetic.

"Yes," I growled reluctantly.

"Then this isn't the actions of a witch or demon," Myers said plainly. "Drop the case and pray that the FBI gets a break soon. The killer can't hide forever."

"But we have resources the FBI can only dream of!" I said, rising from my chair, towering over Myers. "If we only…"

"No," Myers said. "We have rules here, Grimm. We don't have jurisdiction over criminals."

"But we do over witches, werewolves and hobgoblins?" I asked spitefully.

"You know just as well as I do that the FBI has no means of catching a supernatural predator. We provide that kind of service to humanity. But the government has means of catching killers like this," Myers said, pointing at me with his prosthetic arm for emphasis.

"But…"

"But nothing. Return to your office, Mentor," Myers said. "I'll forward your report to the Council, and let you know when your next assignment is. In the meantime…"

"You don't outrank me, Myers," I snarled. "You don't get to order me around like that." It was Myer's turn to glower at me.

"You are still a Hunter, Grimm. I handle your team's assignments. If I remember correctly, you were the one who insisted on actively hunting. Had you chosen to stay behind and focus on lessons, perhaps I wouldn't have to give you orders," Myers said. I growled at him, a low rumbling sound like distant thunder. I gave Myers my best glare, then turned and left Myer's office.

Sitting in the chairs outside Myers' office was the rest of my team. Winters, a young blonde woman in her twenties, popped up to her feet as soon as I left the office.

"Well?" she asked. "What's the plan?"

"They're saying to drop it," I said angrily.

"*WHAT!?*" My team shouted all at once and began bombarding me with questions.

"Calm down!" I said, and the clamoring stopped at once. "The official call is to drop the case entirely and let the FBI handle it."

"Oh come on!" Clarke, a young man with dark skin and cornrows, said hotly. "The FBI couldn't find their way out of a hedge maze!"

"Look, this wasn't my decision, alright?" I said. "Trust me, I feel the same. But the Silent Prayer hunts monsters, not serial killers."

"The Devil's Advocate has already killed 42 children." Wong piped up. "That sounds pretty monstrous to me, am I right?"

"Grimm…" Winters asked, lightly touching my arm. "You can't seriously expect us to do nothing about the killings, can you?"

"Look," I said with a sigh. "For now, if you want to send anonymous tips to the FBI about what we know, I won't stop you. But officially, we aren't pursuing the Devil's Advocate, okay?" No one looked at me. "Everyone, just head back to your quarters. I have a lesson plan to look over. If anyone needs me, I'll be in my office grading papers."

"Yes, sir." They said dejectedly, before walking away down the hall. I sighed and turned the opposite way, towards my office.

I hated this. The rules, regulations, the bureaucracy that shackled us. Back in my day, when I first arrived in the colonies (yes, I am that old), things were different. You didn't need permits or orders to hunt monsters. You grabbed a rifle, hung a cross around your neck, and shot whatever hairy monster had arrived to eat your livestock or steal your children. But times change, and as this country rose in power and population, more regulated infrastructure was required.

"Grimm!" I heard a voice call. I turned to see a heavily scarred older man approach me from down the hall.

"Reynolds," I answered, giving a small wave to my fellow mentor.

"You're back early," he replied. "Hunt go alright?"

"There's no hunt," I said with a huff. "Guy's a mundane."

"Seriously?" Reynolds asked, walking in step with me.

"Yeah," I said.

"You were investigating the Devil's Advocate, right?" Reynolds asked.

"Yep."

"But wasn't the murder scene covered in satanic symbols?"

"It was."

"Damn," Reynolds said. "That sucks."

"You're telling me. Guy kills almost 50 children, and the council wants me to do nothing." I grumbled.

"Well, what *can* you do?" Reynolds asked. "Chop off the Advocate's head like a vampire?"

"If I have to," I said.

"That's cold, man," Reynolds said, shaking his head. "We're here to save humanity, not kill them off."

"We kill witches all the time, Reynolds," I argued.

"Witches sacrifice their humanity for power," Reynolds said. "They don't count." I sighed.

"I just hate not being able to do anything about it," I said.

"Don't let it get to you," Reynolds said. "Look on the bright side, you could get Jeffries' old hunt."

"Jeffries?" I asked. "What happened to her?"

"You didn't hear? Her whole team got butchered by a nuckalavee in Cape Cod. Could be your chance for some action."

"Jeffries is dead?" I asked.

"Yeah, we had her memorial service last week. I thought you were there?" Reynolds asked.

"No, I was investigating this damn psychopath," I said hotly.

"Oh," Reynolds said sheepishly.

"I liked Jeffries," I said sullenly. "I figured her for the next Mentor."

"Shit man, we all did," Reynolds said. "It was a shock for all of us."

"Did anyone recover the body?" I asked.

"Not much of a body left to recover," Reynolds said. "All they found were her glasses and the remains of her coat. Biggest piece of her team was a hand."

"Hers?" I asked.

"No, one of her hunters. What was his name… that big sumo looking guy…?"

"Jacobs?"

"Yeah. Jacobs's hand, missing a few fingers."

"Jesus…" I said. "How's her husband holding up?"

"As well as you would think," Reynolds said, shaking his head. "Anyway, you have any plans tonight?"

"I did, but they got canceled because a maniac apparently wasn't saying magic words," I said.

"Ah," Reynolds said. "I was going to go out with some of the other Mentors for a beer and some wings. Interested?"

"Ehh, not tonight," I said. "Think I'll hit up Doomsday and pay my respects to Jeffries."

"Fair enough," Reynolds said. We were silent for a few steps.

"You got a class this afternoon?" Reynolds asked.

"Yeah," I said. "I was hoping Brewer could cover for me because of the hunt but it looks like I'll be teaching it."

"What class?"

"Witchcraft, ironically," I said.

"Remedial?" Reynolds asked.

"No. Greenhorn," I said.

"Good Lord, this is not your day," Reynolds said with a wince. "I hate teaching newbies."

"Some Mentor you turned out to be. You do realize that's your job now, right?"

"Yeah, but I prefer teaching Hunters who have some experience under their belts," Reynolds said, waving his hand. "Greenhorns just ask too many questions."

"Someone misses the hunts," I said with a chuckle.

"Fuck you, Grimm," Reynolds said. "You think I like being parked behind a desk teaching 20-something-year-olds about the life I used to live?"

"I heard you are one hell of a drill instructor." I pointed out.

"And I heard you hate turning reports in on time," Reynolds said with an evil smile.

"Up yours, scarface." I said with a smile. "Myers tell you that?"

"Please. You think I want to spend my time around that windbag? Makes me want to tear off my own arm." Reynolds said with disgust.

"Try tearing his off," I suggested sarcastically. "Just tell him you're evening him out." Reynolds let out a bark of a laugh.

"Ha! Maybe I will. Sure to be worth getting dismissed," he said, his smile taking years off his face. "Well, I have to go patrol the barracks again. Apparently, another hunter got pregnant again."

"Sounds about right," I said. "Barracks are barracks. Take care of yourself, Reynolds."

"You too, Grimm. Good luck with your class this afternoon."

Chapter 2: Magic 101

"Magic!" I said, writing the word on the whiteboard behind me. "Who here can tell me the Silent Prayer's definition of magic?" I turned towards my class, looking for an answer. No one said anything.

"Anyone?" I asked. Finally, a girl towards the back raised her hand.

"Hunter Mackenzie!" I called. The girl stood up nervously.

"Mentor, t-the Silent Prayer defines m-magic as the ability to a-alter reality using mental t-tricks," she stammered. I sighed.

"Exactly right, Hunter," I said. "I couldn't have defined it better myself, although I wouldn't have stuttered so much," Mackenzie blushed bright red as the class laughed to themselves.

"You can sit, hunter," I said gently. She quickly resumed her seat. "Magic is the skill to alter reality. With magic, a spell caster can rewrite the laws of physics as they see fit, with certain restrictions. Who can tell me one of the laws of magic?" I asked.

"Mind control!" One of the guys blurted out. I sighed dramatically.

"Hunter Baker, I swear to God, you blurt out another answer like that again, I will chop you up and use you as mermaid bait," I said.

"Sorry, Mentor."

"Not yet you're not, Hunter," I said. "But yes, you can't use magic to control someone's mind. You can make certain actions or ideas more appealing, but in the end, you still have control over your own actions. Someone give me another. And raise your damn hands this time!" Another hand shot up. I gestured for him to answer.

"Raising the dead," he said confidently.

"Good," I said. "Ghosts are not the souls of the dead, only an echo of their life replaying itself." Another hand went up.

"You can't change your eyes," she said when I pointed at her. Everyone looked at her like she was crazy.

"Interesting," I said. "You sure about that one?"

"Yes, Mentor," she said. "Eyes are the window to the soul. The soul cannot be touched with magic. It's why mind control and raising the dead are impossible."

"Even if you shapeshift?" I asked.

"Yes, Mentor," she said. "If you were to assume the face of another person, your eyes would remain unaltered."

"Well said, Hunter," I said. "What's your name?"

"Krieger, Mentor," she said. "Sarah Krieger."

"Hunter Krieger is correct," I declared. "As absurd as it sounds, a spellcaster is incapable of changing their irises. Magic is similar to science only in that it follows a set of rules. Science is defined by logic, while magic is ruled by emotion. While there are some things people can change about themselves, shapeshifting is never permanent. Eventually, your true self will always come out."

"What if you get turned into a toad?" one hunter asked.

"If you manage to survive long enough as a toad, you will eventually recover," I explained. "Moving on. Who knows the difference between a witch and a Wizard?" No one raised their hand aside from Krieger. I pointed at her.

"Aren't wizards male and witches female?"

"And I had such high hopes for you, Krieger," I said with a sigh. "This is a huge misunderstanding when it comes to magic. A witch is a mortal in the service of a magical being. These can be demons, faeries, Yokai or other kinds of spirits. Once the bond is formed, the witch channels that being's power through themselves. Depending on the bond and spirit, these witches can vary in power from small-time conjurers and folk healers to full-blown sorcerers and spellcasters."

"Wizards, however, are in a class of their own," I said, writing it down on the board. "No matter what, there are only seven Wizards at a time. When a Wizard dies, their power gets passed on to another person. This is normally someone of a similar mindset or shares traits with the previous Wizard."

"What does it mean when a Wizard passes on their power?" Baker asked. "Isn't magic a skill you can learn?"

"That is true. But Wizards pass on their memories, experiences and skill," I explained. "For example, imagine if one day you suddenly received the skill and muscle memory of every MMA champion at once and someone tried to throw a punch. You would take that person apart in seconds without even realizing what you just did." The class murmured amongst themselves.

"The Wizards are divided into different Lines and given a color," I explained. "Each Line also has a speciality. These are as follows: The White Line is mostly oracles and soothsayers, the Green Line nature magic, the Black Line necromancy, the Red Line combat magic, the Blue Line handles healing magic and alchemy, the Silver Line deals with exorcism, and the Golden Line elemental magic."

"How does nature magic differ from elemental magic?" one hunter asked.

"The Golden Line is the most stereotypical one," I explained. "Most wizards you see on TV or in video games are based on Merlin, who was a Golden Wizard."

"Ohh," the class said in unison.

"Now, with your usual backyard spellcaster, they don't pose much of a threat. Using your mind to bend the laws of nature with your mind is no small order. This is why many people rely on familiars and make deals with spirits to work their magic. A Wizard, however, has the knowledge of thousands of generations of magical experience to work with. To them, spellcasting comes as easy as breathing. They are exceptionally powerful and should not be dealt with alone."

"Doesn't all that power cost them something?" Krieger asked. "Mentor Reynolds told us all power comes at a price."

"It does. Their sanity," I said. "Each Wizard is carrying thousands of years of experience, but also thousands of years of trauma. Many suffer constant nightmares as a result and depending on how young a Wizard is when they receive their powers."

"This can happen to a *child*?" Baker blurted out.

"We have reason to believe the late Black Wizard, Bartholomew Page, was an infant when he received his powers," I said.

"How?" Krieger asked amid the hubbub of voices talking at once.

"Quiet!" I commanded, and the greenhorns went silent. "We don't know, and we can't confirm it to be true, but study of Wizards is patchy at best."

"How come no one knows about these Wizards?" a hunter asked. "Why wouldn't they flaunt their powers, or try to take over the world?"

"To answer the first question, they do. But very rarely do people believe them. Grigori Rasputin was one, and he was killed because of his powers. Cleopatra, the Oracle of Delphi, Merlin, Alistair Crowley, Alexandria of Hypatia and Abe No Seimei are but a few. These people appear and use their powers to influence the world and direct history. But what happens more often is their minds crumble under the weight of all those memories and they go insane. That insanity then carries on, until a more stable Wizard manages to tame it. As for your second one, they are still human, and the Silent Prayer has found long-range weapons or a quiet approach to be an effective way to kill one. Not to mention they still need to speak the magic words in order to cast, so if you can silence them, you cut off the bulk of their power.”

Just as Krieger opened her mouth to ask another question, a loud gonging sound rang out. I winced, my sharper hearing made that sound that much more painful. The class all got up and began packing away their notes.

“Everyone read up on ancient tomes and grimoires! We’ll be continuing this lesson later. Witches are the most common foe you will face, and if you don’t know your basics, you’ll end up and some hag’s pet newt!” I called out. I started packing up my stuff and prepared to head back to my office and go over some more reports.

“Mentor?” someone asked. I looked up to see Krieger standing at my desk.

“Yes?” I asked.

“Have you ever met a Wizard before?” she asked.

“Once. Isaac Stone, the Silver Wizard,” I replied.

“What was he like?” she asked.

“Unlucky,” I said simply. “He was a walking, talking example of Murphy’s Law.”

"Why?"

"Every Line has a curse. The Green Line gets burned by metal, the Blue Line needs to drink sea water to live, the Red Line is a demon magnet, and the White Line keeps predicting the death of everyone they meet."

"What about the Golden and Black Lines?" she asked.

"Each other. If the Golden Wizard and Black Wizard meet, one of them will end up dying. The most famous case was Merle Ambrose, known today as Merlin, and Morgana Le Fay. In that clash, Merlin ended up dead," Krieger looked down at her boots thoughtfully.

"Why do you ask?" I asked.

"Just... Curious..." she said. "Have a good afternoon, Mentor," she said hurriedly and walked out the classroom briskly. I watched her leave with my own questions popping up in my head. I sighed and shook my head. She was the daughter of one of the council members. I knew the name Krieger pretty well. Her entire family had been monster hunters, all the way back to when Germany was known as Prussia.

"That's all it is," I told myself. "Just wants to do her clan proud."

I hoped.

Chapter 3: Doomsday

'Til Doomsday is, by all appearances, your typical dive bar. It's a hole in the wall building with a barely lit neon sign. The bar itself is half-hidden by a copse of trees next to a crossroads. It was an old speakeasy back during the prohibition when I found it and has blossomed into a haven for rough biker gangs and college-age hipsters. You might be wondering how toughened bikers and young metrosexual hipsters get along in a place like this. Simple.

They don't.

Fights break out all the time, but I remember when this bar had mobsters and other hardened criminals shooting each other. One of the walls still has the bullet holes from the last time someone shot the windows out with a Tommy gun. The bikers here weren't One-Percenters, just tough guys acting the part. They were usually harmless but didn't always appreciate the new kids and their lofty views on craft beers.

I come here because mostly out of habit, and the fact that they serve the greasiest, meatiest nachos on the planet. These things could clog a person's arteries at 50 paces, and the portion sizes could serve as a Thanksgiving feast on its own. I think I'm the only patron to finish a plate by myself.

I was sitting at the bar, where one of the stools had been reinforced for someone of my weight (It's mostly muscle, don't give me that look). I raised my glass in a small toast.

"Miranda Jefferies," I rumbled. "The Prayer never knew a finer hunter." I downed my glass in a single pull, then signaled for a refill. The bar had its usual fill of bikers and hipsters, and the age-old ritual of 'Who's playing that garbage on the jukebox?' had begun. I could hear the grumblings of some of the old patrons as they expressed their distaste at the pop song that had come on. I couldn't keep up with music that well. Genres sprung up, split apart, merged and died so fast, I couldn't possibly pick a favorite. Hell, I remember when rock and roll was first invented, and when people were burning Beatles records because one of them said the wrong thing. The sixties were a weird time.

"This seat taken?" a voice at my elbow asked. I glanced over to see one of the hipsters had found his way to the bar. To his credit, he didn't look nearly as bad as the rest of them. He had his hair up in something I had recently learned was called a 'man-bun.' I don't hate new fashion trends, but they do confuse me. He was dressed in tight jeans, sneakers, a hoodie, and shirt with a blue police box on it. He was clean-shaven, which made him stand out already. It was an unspoken rule that part of the dress code of the bar was for all men to have a full beard.

The most striking feature of his face was his eyes. One was blue, the other green. Oh, and he had a cockney accent, which I knew was going to get annoying.

"Oi, this seat taken?" he repeated, and then I realized he was talking to me. Most people ignore my presence, which isn't their fault. A gift from my goblin heritage is that it's hard to notice me. Despite my stature, horns, gray skin and fangs, I can blend in with a crowd better than anyone I've met. It's useful when staking out a vampire hideout, but absolutely brutal trying to flag down a waitress.

"… No," I said slowly. The only time I ever get noticed is either I make an effort to be seen (which doesn't always work) or if someone is trying very hard to find me. And I planned on being alone this evening.

"Stellar," the hipster said eagerly and hopped up on the stool next to me. I watched him as he ordered a mug of Guinness and started watching the TV, which was showing the news coverage of the Devil's Advocate. The anchor was talking about the latest killings, a teenager and her little brother. I groaned and tried to focus on my upcoming drink.

"Bloody mess, innit?" the hipster said. Again, I realized he was talking to me.

"I guess," I muttered, hunching my shoulders and closing my body language. Hopefully, the kid would pick up on this and shut up.

"I mean, how does someone like this manage to kill a dozen kids like this anyways?" He continued. "You'd think someone would catch them."

"Yeah," I growled. "Look kid, I'm not really in the mood to…"

"This type of sick shite just pisses me off," he said, his accent getting worse. Ugh. "How come no one's stepped up to this creep?"

"Now is really not…"

"And what's with the devil worship angle? Their symbols are all correct, not that useless Leviathan Cross bollocks," he blathered on.

"What?" I asked, suddenly paying attention to him. No one knows this kind of stuff. Not unless…

"I mean, they know what they're doing, they're just not doing it. Weird, innit?"

"How do you know that?" I asked, narrowing my eyes.

"Look at that photo, yeah? Upside down pentagram with the points outside the circle, but they have the esoteric symbols around for protection," he said, pointing at the TV. "You can't see it too well, but someone with your eyes should have noticed it, Mr. Grimm."

I grabbed him by the collar and slammed him onto the bar.

"Who are you!?" I demanded, shaking him a little.

"Easy! Easy bruv!" He choked, eyes wide in shock. Everyone in the bar was looking at us. No amount of goblin magic could cover the noise I was making.

"Who sent you?" I continued.

"My name is Berengar Black!" he managed to say. "I was sent by the Professor! I'm here as a friend!" I stopped shaking him and glared at him. The brit looked more startled than scared. I let him go and sat back down. He slid down from the bar and returned to his seat.

"Bloody hell," he muttered, smoothing out his shirt. "The Professor said you might react badly, but I wasn't expecting that."

"What Professor?" I asked flatly.

"Professor Magic," he said, pulling out a small business card and handing it to me. I took it gingerly and read it. It was black on one side, white on the other, with a pentacle on each side in opposite colors. No name, no number.

"I thought he was dead," I replied. Berengar laughed.

"Reports of his death were greatly exaggerated," he said. "He still lives and is interested in meeting you."

"And what does the Wizard of the Golden Line want with me?" I asked.

"He's been investigating the Devil's Advocate and wanted to parley with this country's top investigator," Berengar replied.

"The Silent Prayer is staying out of this," I said, hating myself. "It's been ruled a mundane."

"Mundane or magical, people are dying," Berengar said seriously. "The Professor isn't here to hunt a witch, he's here to stop a killer."

"If he wants to investigate this, he is free to do so," I said. "But it would be between him and the police."

"He doesn't want help from the police or the Silent Prayer," Berengar said. "He wants help from you." I blinked in surprise.

"Me?"

"Yes, you," Berengar said. "You are the Prayer's greatest hunter, and the longest living one as well. The

Professor would greatly appreciate your experience and talent to bring the killer to justice."

"I've been barred from this investigation," I said. "If the Professor is willing to take up talks with the Council…"

"The Professor has a certain respect for the Silent Prayer and its hunters, but he has an unfortunate history with them. I'm sure you can understand," Berengar said uneasily. I frowned.

"Look, tell your master that I would be more than willing to work with him. I've got nothing against the Wizards, but my hands are tied. Without leave from the Council, I won't be able to help him."

"Unable, or unwilling?" he asked cryptically. "The only thing necessary for the triumph of evil is for good men to do nothing, after all."

"Edmund Burke," I said slowly, recognizing the quote. It was something I told my team and my students countless times.

"Think on this proposition. Should you accept, simply tear the card I gave you in half, and the Professor will tell you where to meet him. If you reject, do nothing. The Professor is a patient man, but he cannot abide by these killings. Whenever you feel that you can join him, rip the card," Berengar said. He finished his beer and left. I stared down at the card, wondering what to do.

By the time I got home, I still hadn't made up my mind. On one hand, I really wanted to catch this maniac. It killed me seeing those missing kid photos, the silence in suburban yards where children normally ran and played. I hated seeing weeping parents on the news and the Amber Alerts coming in when another kid vanished.

On the other hand, I couldn't ignore the Council. The Silent Prayer has stood for centuries, and their rules existed for a reason. To disobey them would mean my dismissal. And given that I've worked the same job since the late 1700s, I wasn't sure how well I would survive the current job market.

I sat on my bed and looked down at the card, idly flipping it in my hands.

The right thing to do…

People fought wars over something so simple. Many have died pursuing that or had been killed for it. The right thing, whatever it was, had a lot of blood spilled in its name. But what was it? Could I really defy the laws that had bound me for centuries, all for one person?

No.

Not one person. Innocent lives. People who wanted nothing more than peace and happiness. Could I walk away from everything I had ever known for the sake of a child's safety?

At that moment, everything changed. The question I had asked myself suddenly became so simple.

I grasped the card and tore it down the middle.

I waited by my phone. I don't know how the Wizard would contact me, but I knew they had their ways. If his little pet hipster could track me down at Doomsday, getting my phone number wouldn't be out of the question. After a while, I started to get impatient. Surely, I had done it right, didn't I? Berengar said to tear the card in half if I wanted to help, so why hadn't they…

The sound of my TV turning on startled me. I muttered a curse and went to investigate. My widescreen TV was showing static, and garbled voices could be heard among the static.

"42… Pleasant Drive… 5 o'clock… in the morning…" I heard. The message repeated itself three times, before the screen went black, and bluish smoke started leaking out the back. I sighed and unplugged the TV.

"Damn Wizards," I hissed as I checked out the damage. The back of the TV had overheated and melted partially.

"It's for the kids," I told myself. "Think of the children…" I grabbed my bag of monster hunting gear and headed for the door.

It was time to see the Wizard.

Chapter 4: Professor Magic and the Tampered Crime Scene

I drove down to where Professor Magic had asked me to meet him. As I got closer, I saw the yellow and black police tape on the door of the house. It was a modest two-story building with dark green paint, overgrown lawn and shuttered windows. I pulled up to the building, where another car was parked. It was an old-fashioned pickup truck that reminded me of the trucks they drove back in the 30s. I'd like to say it was beautifully restored, but it looked like it was held together by rust and sheer willpower.

Or magic.

Standing outside the truck was a man I instantly recognized. Professor Magic was one of the world's most iconic superheroes. While some might claim that characters from comic books and movies are more iconic, there are a small number of people who actually live those lives. Stinger, Professor Magic, Captain Chernobyl, and a few others came to mind. A rare breed of crazy drove these people to stick their necks out and use whatever strange abilities and talents they had to fight to protect people. All for the sake of altruism. I know there are a few 'superheroes' who work for governments, but I don't consider them to be heroes like the others. I know I don't count.

"Professor," I said. The Wizard turned to face me. He was dressed in his iconic getup of loose-fitting black tunic and pants, black gloves and boots with red trim, black wizard hat, and black cape with red interior. He had a white beard down to his collarbone, a white pentacle emblazoned on his chest, and a monocle over his right eye. The monocle had an odd shimmer to it that obscured his right eye, but his left eye was bright green. He wore a thick belt with pouches on it and carried a staff with runes carved into it. It looked like it was made of ash, but I'm not so good with types of wood.

"Dragonman," Professor Magic said. His voice was smooth and echoed with wisdom. "I'm glad you decided to help."

"You could've just called me instead of blowing out my TV," I said.

"Ah," the Wizard said. "My apologies, friend. I sometimes have issues with modern technology."

"You could've had your minion ask for you," I pointed out.

"Minion?"

"The kid. Berengar."

"Ah, yes him. Wouldn't quite refer to him as a minion."

"Whatever," I said, looking up at the house. "Shouldn't there be a bunch of police out here standing guard?"

"There were," Professor Magic said. "They're just on break."

"All of them?"

"Indeed. I can be very persuasive when I want to," the Wizard said.

"Mind magic?" I asked, bristling.

"Nothing of the sort. I just managed to convince them that coffee and donuts were more important than guarding this crime scene," Professor Magic said. "Shall we enter?" I grunted in assent and we walked in.

"You know," I said. "I don't really trust spellcasters."

"Why not? You use magic yourself."

"Not like you do. Mine is limited to a few inborn tricks."

"I'm not a witch," Professor Magic said plainly.

"But you are a Wizard," I pointed out. "Which can be worse."

"Worse than someone who pledges their service to a demon in exchange for power?"

"Someone with immense power whose mental state is questionable," I said.

"You're referring to all my memories," Professor Magic said. He raised his staff and muttered a word under his breath. The police tape snapped, and the door opened.

"That much knowledge crammed into a brain can't end well," I pointed out.

"Is it that much more dangerous than a super soldier sworn to a secret brotherhood that allows its members to execute people on a rumor?" Professor Magic asked venomously.

"We need more than a rumor to kill someone for witchcraft," I said. "And we don't kill them on the spot. We have trials."

"By the time some amateur spellcaster makes their way to the Silent Prayer's Judgement Hall, their fate is sealed," Professor Magic said. "And to be fair, I don't trust career monster hunters."

"So, why ask for my help?"

"Because this case is bigger than either of us," Professor Magic said as we entered the house.

"This isn't a magical case," I pointed out. "The FBI can handle it." Professor Magic let out a bark of a laugh.

"If they could, they would've caught the killer by now. Some villains don't need the supernatural to be true monsters. Now, if you are done accusing me of being a witch, I'd like to investigate this killer before they harm another family. Coming?" Professor Magic said plainly before walking into the house. I swore under my breath and followed him.

The smell of blood filled my nostrils, that sickly sweet metallic smell. I know humans' sense of smell is much weaker than mine, but I knew Professor Magic could smell it. His face tightened into a mask of disgust. I led him upstairs, following the smell into one of the bedrooms.

Oh God…

It was a nursery. The walls were painted pale pink, and a crib was in the corner next to a diaper-changing station. A large bloody pentagram covered the white carpet with black wax candles on each point with the chalk outline of a body in the middle. Esoteric symbols graced the walls in dark dried blood. The crib was stained with blood, as if someone had poured it into the top. Streaks of it dripped from the interior. I felt my own blood boil at the sight of it. Smoke leaked out from my mouth, a bad habit I got into back in the 50s. 1850s, mind you.

"What kind of sick…" I began.

"Hang on," Professor Magic said, walking forward into the room. He checked the crib and seemed to relax.

"What is it?"

"Look around. Aside from the blood stains, see anything else out of place?" he asked. I glanced around. All I could see was blood and satanic imagery.

"No toys," I said. "This is a child's room."

"Exactly," Professor Magic said, walking around. He checked the dresser and closet.

"Not a lot of clothes in the dresser, and adult clothes in the closet," Professor Magic said.

"You think this is a fake?" I asked.

"Maybe," Professor Magic said thoughtfully, looking at the symbols on the wall.

"Then why are we here?"

"Because this *is* the scene of the latest Advocate kill," Professor Magic said.

"You read that in entrails or something?" I asked sarcastically.

"Tea leaves, actually," Professor Magic said, looking more intently at the runes.

"You've got to be kidding," I said. "Can't believe I'm risking my job for something you saw in a *teacup*."

"Look at these runes," Professor Magic said. "How much do you know about dark magic?"

"A fair amount," I replied. "Why?"

"What kind of spell do you think this ritual was for?" He asked. I frowned at the runes.

"Not sure," I said. "We just checked for magical resonance and got nothing."

"Well, let's assume these are supposed to be used for a spell," Professor Magic said. "What do you think it was for?" I checked the runes.

"Well, the Solomon Seal is mostly used for containment," I said. "And that circle over there says something in Old Norse…"

"It's a type of seidr," Professor Magic said. "A negating spell."

"Negating?" I asked. "Negating what?"

"Good question," Professor Magic said. "Most of these spells would be for locking down something, another for blocking."

"You're right," I said. "This isn't a summoning spell. They look more like wards."

"You know a lot about wards?" Professor Magic asked.

"It's the closest we come to spell casting," I said. "Good way to keep the demons out."

"So why place warding spells at the scene of a murder?" he asked.

"Here's a better question," I said. "Why set up spells you're not going to use?"

"What?" Professor Magic asked.

"There's no magic in them," I pointed out. "They set up the ritual, but never turned it on. It's just creepy paintings on the wall without any magic pumped into it."

"You're right," Professor Magic said. "What if we turned it on?"

"I'm sorry?"

"I could activate this spell, see what is meant for," he said.

"That doesn't sound wise," I said.

"Nonsense, it would only be for a little bit," he said. He raised his hand and started muttering.

"Wait!" I cried, but the runes flashed with a brief red light, and my vision blurred. I felt nauseous and heavy. I could hear Professor Magic gasping in pain, but he sounded lightyears away.

Then the sensation passed. My body felt normal, and I could see and hear just fine. I regained my composure and took a steadying breath.

"What was that?" I asked. Professor Magic moaned and rubbed at a temple.

"No clue. Felt like hell though."

"Told you it was a bad idea," I snarled.

"What was it for?" Professor Magic asked, looking up at the runes in wonder. "Felt like my connection to magic had been cut off." That got my attention. My abilities are based on magic. Without it, it made sense that my senses would fail. Was that what normal human's vision and hearing were like? No wonder you all scream when you talk.

"Hang on," I said. "If this ritual is to clear out all the magic in a room, would that clear out any residual resonance?" Professor Magic furrowed his brow.

"That's… possible…" he said. He closed his eyes and waved his arm around.

"You're right," he said. "There's nothing left. Like the spell never happened."

"Damn," I said. This changed everything. We were told to back off due to the lack of magic, but if there could be magic involved, I could get the Silent Prayer to reconsider opening the case back up. I could pursue the killer with my team and the full resources of the Silent Prayer backing me up.

Suddenly, I heard a noise from downstairs. I perked up my ears and started looking around.

"This is incredible," Professor Magic was saying. "But why kill the magic in a room?"

"Hang on, Professor," I said, trying to listen."

"The spell kills itself in a few seconds though," Professor Magic went on, thinking aloud. "Why bother with such a potent spell that collapses on itself?"

"Professor, I'm trying to…"

"Unless it was merely a distraction? No, it's too well done to be a mere distraction…"

"Professor!" I hissed sharply.

"What?" he asked harshly.

"Would you shut up?" I asked.

"*Excuse me*!?" he asked indignantly. "I am trying to solve the crime!"

"I'm trying to listen for something! I think the police are coming back."

"Oh, don't be ridiculous! That spell should have them gone for another half an hour. We have plenty of time!"

Just then, the door opened and a short woman with brown hair and round wire frame glasses stepped in.

"Sorry I'm late, Agent Mathers!" she said, easing the door open with her elbow as she carried a cup of coffee in each hand. "Traffic was a mess and the line for coffee was…" She stopped when she saw us in the room. No one said anything. Then she dropped her coffee and reached inside her jacket suddenly.

"Shit!" I said and dove out the window, shattering the glass.

"Dragonman!" I heard Professor Magic cry out.

"Agent Kane to all stations!" the woman shouted. "I have two suspects fleeing the scene!" Professor Magic leapt out the window and landed more gracefully than I did. I started running towards the woods in the back.

"What are you doing?" the old man panted.

"I thought she was going for a gun!" I confessed. "You said we still had time!"

"She… wasn't… there… when I cast… the spell…" He wheezed. I stopped to let him catch his breath. We had gotten far enough away from the house.

"Look, we need to lay low," I said, checking my phone. "Shit, I'm late for work!"

"What?" Professor Magic asked between deep breaths.

"Look, I'll call you, okay? You have a number I can use? Social media account?"

"Hang on," he wheezed, before pulling out an old flip phone.

"Oh, you have to be kidding me," I groaned. I know I'm old, but I do my best to keep up with the times. He pushed a few buttons, then read his phone number to me.

"Alright," I said. "I'll call you later." I started making my way back to my car.

"Where should we meet up?" Professor Magic asked, still breathing hard.

"I'll let you know. In the meantime, try and find out what you can about the spell," I said. "We can work from there."

"So I have your full cooperation?" Professor Magic asked.

"You do. I'll see if I can get the Council to back us," I said. "If this is truly the work of a sorcerer, then there's no reason they'll refuse me."

Chapter 5: Death by Paperwork

"You can't be serious," I said.

"Oh I am," Myers fumed. "Late for duties, missing a class, and late on your reports! Again!" I growled and crossed my arms. It had taken me a bit longer than I had planned to get my car back from the FBI. Thankfully my goblin magic was able to help me get in unnoticed. Sadly, it doesn't always apply to my car. I was able to slip out relatively unseen, but I had to rely on some quick thinking to get past the beat cop who stopped me for (you won't believe this) directions to the crime scene. By the time I got to the Silent Prayer's HQ, my usual parking spot was taken by a car I didn't recognize. After parking further away than I liked, I found Myers in my office looking pissed.

"I have a very good reason," I said.

"Oh, do you?" Myers asked. "What reason could that be?"

"I…"

"Is it a good enough reason to delay *my* work because I had to cover for *your* class? That you missed?"

"If you…"

"Because of that, I had to turn *my* reports in late, and find a reason for why yours weren't in!" Myers shouted. "I had to explain myself to the Council why we were behind *ON AN INSPECTION DAY!*"

I grabbed Myers by the collar and slammed him against the wall. My office is so small that I almost crushed his head against the ceiling.

"Let me make something absolutely clear, you dried-up secretary. I've slain vampires more threatening than you. I've dealt with lichs, werewolves, satanic cults, ancient curses, and spirits of the damned more than you ever could. I've done more for this organization than you ever could hope to achieve. So I will not sit here while someone whose day consists of signing papers and typing yells at me," I said, my voice lowered to a deadly whisper. "You will not speak to me in that tone of voice. *Ever.*"

"You dare lay your hands on a Mentor like this?" he snarled. I flattened my ears back against my head and roared. Right in his face. I screamed until I was almost out of breath.

"Get out of my office," I snarled, dropping him. He stared at me with a mix of fear and contempt.

"NOW!" I bellowed, punching the wall. He got up and tried to leave with as much dignity as he could after being pinned to the wall like a mouse. I sat down at my desk and sighed. My throat hurt and I could feel my blood storming around. I tried to relax. I hadn't had any coffee yet, but that battle cry had stirred me up better than any amount of caffeine could.

God, I hated Myers. He only cared about his career, having retired from hunting after losing his arm. He was part of a problem that had been growing in the Silent Prayer since the second World War.

Career Hunters. People who joined not for the sake of safeguarding their fellow man, but for their own gain. Selfish bastards who only cared about advancing their status and pay. Myers had his eyes on the Council for years. Ever since he had been assigned to my team, he has been nothing but trouble. I took another steadying breath.

He was a pain in the ass, but he was always right. Every time I bent the rules just a little to make my life easier, he jumped down my throat. I was in a weird position in the Prayer. Normally, a mentor is assigned to a hunter team to manage their hunts. When a hunter gets too old or injured to hunt, the normal move is to promote them to Mentor. I had been in the Silent Prayer since the 1800s, just over 200 years. I had retained my strength, so I was allowed to hunt, but my expertise made me an ideal Mentor. Mentors also work to teach new hunters, relying on their experience to better the next generation of hunters. Myers and I didn't exactly outrank each other, and I know that infuriated him. He hates everything that doesn't follow proper protocol and order, which made him an abysmal hunter. But paperwork and bureaucracy? He was in his element as Mentor.

A knock on the door interrupted my musing.

"What?" I snarled, the caffeine headache starting to come in. The door opened and a man entered. He was of average height, and despite his advanced age, was in excellent shape. He had snow-white hair, crow's feet, and narrow eyes. I jumped to my feet instantly, recognizing the white robes and blue stole.

"Councilor!" I said. "My apologies, sir. I thought you were someone else," he laughed.

"It's alright. I just came down to investigate the noise," he said. I winced.

"My apologies, sir," I said. "Another Mentor and I had a disagreement."

"I see," the Councilor said, his eyes looking up at the hole I punched into the wall. "You must be the famous Roman Grimm. The Dragonman."

"Yes sir," I said. He held out his hand and I gingerly shook it. I could feel the strength in his grip.

"Councilor Miyamoto," he said, introducing himself. "What was the disagreement about?"

"Paperwork," I said simply.

"Just paperwork?" he asked with a playful smile, gesturing for me to sit. I did, and he sat at the chair across from my desk.

"Well, that and my tardiness," I admitted sheepishly.

"Ah," Miyamoto said. "And why were you tardy?"

"I was investigating a lead," I said. "I had gotten a tip about a possible warlock."

"Surely something like that would excuse being a bit late," Miyamoto said. I sighed.

"Not with Myers. He wants hunters to call in if they find something out."

"Isn't that proper protocol?"

"Technically, yes," I said through gritted teeth. I eyed my coffee maker with longing. I really needed a cup now. Miyamoto saw my gaze and smiled at me, then rose to make himself a cup.

"Sir, I can take care of that," I said hurriedly. He laughed.

"Please, allow me. I fear you might accidentally trample me in this tiny office," Miyamoto said warmly. "Let us not worry about protocol and station." That statement alone made me like this guy even more. Most Councilors were stuffy old windbags like Myers. Meeting one like this was refreshing.

"How do you take it?" Miyamoto asked.

"Cream and sugar," I said. Miyamoto nodded and started making the coffee.

"So, did your tip pan out?" he asked.

"Sort of," I said. "FBI showed up and we had to flee the scene."

"We?" Miyamoto asked.

"My tip," I said, choosing my words carefully. Wizards were sort of a gray area with the Silent Prayer. I wasn't sure how well the Council would react to having a Wizard working with a Hunter.

"And what scene was this?" Miyamoto asked. I sighed.

"The Devil's Advocate," I said. Miyamoto froze.

"Oh," he said finally. "That one."

"I know it's been declared a mundane, but I may have found new evidence…"

"Mentor Grimm," Miyamoto interrupted. "Do you know why the Silent Prayer doesn't hunt serial killers?"

"I… No sir, I don't," I said, disarmed by the question.

"It's because we have limited resources," Miyamoto said. "Our pockets only go so deep, and we need to focus on the threats that only we can handle."

"But we are here to help people," I argued. "We are a Silent Prayer for those who live in fear."

"I know the motto," Miyamoto said, returning with the coffee. He placed mine on my desk and pushed it over to me. I picked it up and took a sip. Wow. This guy knew how to make a proper cup of joe.

"Mentor, I have nothing but respect for you," Miyamoto said. "Most people on the Council do. You are our best hunter, but we need you hunting monsters, not mundanes."

"We may have found something at the latest scene," I said. Miyamoto lowered his coffee and scowled.

"Like what?"

"Possible magic," I said. I explained what we had found at the crime scene, leaving out the part with Professor Magic. Miyamoto said nothing, just sipping at his coffee and looking more and more concerned.

"This is serious," Miyamoto said when I was finished. "Who was this spellcaster you were working with?"

"I can't say," I said. "They wished to remain anonymous."

"Roman, I am a member of the Council of the Silent Prayer," he said. "If a hunter is working with a possible witch, we need to know. How do you know this weakness spell wasn't conjured by him?"

"It wasn't," I said.

"How do you know?" he asked again.

"Because…" I said, searching for an answer.

"Roman, the words of a witch are dangerous. All spellcasters pose a danger we cannot ignore. Those sites were found to be devoid of magical resonance," he said. "I read the report that you yourself wrote."

"If there's a chance…" I said.

"We can't afford that," Miyamoto said. "I know someone like you doesn't need some old veteran like myself telling you what to do, especially after all you have done for this organization and humanity as a whole. But consider this: You don't know this spellcaster. They could be a witch in disguise, or even worse, one of the Seven. Those who seek magical power rarely do it for a good cause. And that power over other men corrupts whatever reason they had. The Wizards can hardly count as safe or sane."

"What about me?" I asked defensively. "I use magic."

"You are an exception," he said. "There are those who wield magic due to their own heritage, and with careful supervision, can learn to use their powers for good. I apologize if I upset you. It was not my intention to offend you." I blinked in surprise. No one ever speaks to me with such politeness.

"Oh, it's fine," I said.

"Let me impart some advice," Miyamoto said. "Save your passion and skill for a truly evil threat. What is happening to these children is deplorable, and I pray that the FBI finds this killer soon. But we must let them do their job, and we do ours." I sighed.

"I respect your desire to protect an ally, but they do sound suspicious," Miyamoto continued. "We must be ever vigilant in the face of dark magic. I would cut off all communication with this mage, and let the other Mentors know about him."

"Why?" I asked.

"Spellcasters can turn wicked, and if we can prevent loss of life from happening at the hands of a sorcerer, it is our sworn duty to do so," Miyamoto said. "Or don't," he added, seeing my face harden. "Do what you think is right. You certainly have the experience to know what that is. Just think on what I've said," he stood and placed his coffee on my desk. I rose as he walked towards the door.

"Thank you for the coffee, Mentor Grimm," he said, bowing slightly. "It was truly an honor to meet you."

"You too, sir," I said as he left. I sat back down as the door closed and I thought about it all. It was certainly a possibility that Professor Magic wasn't who he said he was. I had seen his death announced on the news two years ago. I even went to the U.K to pay my respects. Despite the Silent Prayer's attitude towards magic, he had earned the respect of many hunters around the world, being the only supernatural superhero. Winters and I left roses on his grave as our sign of respect.

And yet here he was, healthy as ever in America. With some college kid sidekick in tow. There was certainly something off about Professor Magic, that was for sure. But what he said had the old 'ring of truth' to it. Despite what Miyamoto was saying, I know warding runes when I see them. And that spell was an anti-magic spell that I can't imagine any spellcaster would cast. Why waste time learning a spell that can easily take away your greatest ability? It would be the same as tearing off your arm to use as a club. I sighed and checked my phone. There was a text from Professor Magic on it. I read it, and at first, I thought he was using some sort of code, until I realized he just spelled everything wrong.

"Luddite," I muttered, shaking my head. I managed to translate his garbage text into a message asking me what the Council had said. I decided to call him rather than get a headache from his texting.

"Ah, bollocks. Hello?" Professor Magic said.

"It's me," I said. "Council said no."

"Are they mental?" he asked hotly.

"No, they just aren't buying the whole 'anti-magic' bit."

"Saw that coming. Bloody twats," he cursed. That got a smile out of me.

"I know."

"So, you still on?" Professor Magic asked. I thought about it.

"Yeah, I'm still on. Let's catch this bastard."

Chapter 6: We All Scream for Ice Cream

I met with Professor Magic around lunchtime. I had to explain myself to the Senior Mentors, but thankfully Councilor Miyamoto had put in a good word for me. I was given barracks patrol as punishment, which sucked, but I can usually cage some snacks from the senior hunters. Yes, I take food bribes. As long as no one is getting killed or knocked up in the barracks, I really don't care what goes on. If some hunter has some extra fries or a burrito they don't want, I am more than happy to look the other way while he and his buddies bend some of the rules. I gave the other Mentors some crap excuse about getting food outside the HQ, claiming I wasn't in the mood to deal with other people. They believed it, as the entire compound heard my roar. Some were even taking bets on whether or not I killed Myers. Some were even a little disappointed that I hadn't.

I showed up at the Professor's meeting place, which happened to be a playground in the heart of some suburban neighborhood. I brought my lunch with me and decided to dig in while I waited for the Wizard. I was halfway through when a large black raven landed in front of me. The raven swelled in size and turned into the Professor.

"Good lord, is that all for you?" he asked, gazing at the carnage of my meal. I stifled a belch and nodded, picking up another taco and wolfed it down.

"Want one?" I asked, offering a meat taco dripping in grease and cheese. He looked sickened.

"No thanks," he said and sat on the bench next to me. I shrugged and devoured it.

"Your loss," I said through a mouthful of steak, pork and chicken.

"Those can't be good for you," Professor Magic said, staring at the rest of my meal in shock and disgust.

"Not good for you, but for us carnivores, it's perfect."

"I thought tacos were supposed to have lettuce and tomatoes in them," he asked.

"I told them to leave them out," I said.

"Why?"

"Because I can't digest vegetables," I said. "I subsist on animal products, simple sugars and fungus."

"I didn't know gargoyles were carnivores," he said. I wiped my mouth and bared a grin, showing off my sharp teeth and fangs. He leaned back at the sight.

"It's the main problem with gargoyles," I said. "We're expensive to feed. My body requires almost five times the caloric intake of most humans."

"I can see," Professor Magic noted.

"You hungry?" I asked.

"Not anymore," he said simply.

"So…" I said, stuffing another taco into my mouth. "The great Professor Magic comes to America."

"I have."

"Mind if I ask why?"

"The Devil's Advocate has been at large for far too long," Professor Magic said, his gaze lingering on the playground, where a horde of screaming children ran around playing.

"Careful," I said. "One of their moms might see you eyeing up their kids and call the cops."

"Why's that?"

"Because kids have been going missing a lot recently, and they might not like the look of some old guy in all black sitting at a park bench," I said. He chuckled.

"That won't be a problem. I took a leaf out of your book and masked myself like you do. Goblin magic is dead hard though," he said. We were quiet for a while.

"So, why are we out here?" I asked. Professor Magic sighed.

"While you were getting chewed out by your supervisors for doing the right thing, I did some investigating. The victims' deaths are spread pretty far out, and the victims all have one thing in common: they are all young," he said.

"You think they're gonna strike here next?" I asked.

"Maybe. This neighborhood hasn't had any deaths or disappearances," he said.

"Tea leaves tell you that?"

"No. The internet."

"Did Berengar help you with that?" I asked.

"No. He's not very good at computers. Thankfully his girlfriend is," Professor Magic admitted. I said nothing for a bit.

"Alright, final question."

"I doubt that."

"Did you fake your death?" I asked. He looked at me.

"Why do you ask?"

"Because I visited your grave. One of my Hunters is a big fan," I said. "You had my respect as well."

"I thought you didn't trust Wizards."

"I don't. But that doesn't mean I don't think you did good work," I admitted. "But I saw your death on the news. I left flowers on your grave. You died," he looked away again.

"There was a parade. The entire world mourned your death," I said.

"Is there a point to this?" he asked uncomfortably. I finished the last of my tacos and started crushing up the paper into the box they came in.

"Yeah. Either you faked your death for some reason, or you aren't the real Professor Magic," I said. "I want to know which one it is and why," he looked back at me and met my gaze.

Before he could answer, the air was rent with a piercing scream. We leapt to our feet and saw the kids fleeing back to their parents. One mother was screaming louder, chasing after an ice cream truck. I swore loudly. I had been completely focused on our discussion. A kid had been nabbed right in front of us.

"Go!" Professor Magic said. "You're faster than me! I'll catch up later."

"But…"

"Go!" he implored. "If that truck leaves the neighborhood and gets on the main road, we'll never catch them! Go!" I nodded and sprinted after the truck. My powerful legs felt refreshed after the meal. All that grease and meat might slow down a human, but I felt like I had just gotten a good night's sleep and a shot of espresso. The truck wove down the twisting streets of the neighborhood, but I was right behind them. Just as they were making their way to the exit of the neighborhood, I pushed off from the ground and leapt after the truck. With a loud clang, I landed on top of it, my clawed gauntlets digging into the steel roof with a muted scream. The driver immediately noticed my presence and floored it, fishtailing the truck in an attempt to throw me off. I grinned to myself.

"Finally, some action," I muttered. I held on tight and tried to ease myself to the back of the truck. If I took out the driver, the truck would crash, and the kid might be killed. I couldn't risk that. I hooked my clawed boots into the back of the truck and slowly climbed to the back. We were on a straightaway and going well over the speed limit. A fall here would mean they would get away and stay gone.

I managed to hang onto the back of the truck, where the back doors would open to allow the ice cream to be onloaded. I punched the lock, shattering it, and opened the door.

I was immediately greeted by a giant of a man wearing an Easter Bunny mask who threw a punch right at my face. I felt my tusks cut his knuckles and my sharp fangs cut my lip. Bunny man cried out in pain, slinking back into the truck, the hot dragon's blood from my lip burning his hand.

I let out a fierce cry and charged the man. I threw my own punch, catching him in the face, putting a gash in his cheap plastic mask. He grunted in pain and punched me back. We kept this up for a bit, trading punches and running the risk of falling out the back. He seemed to be tiring, but I was loving it. I hadn't had a good fight in a while, and this monster of a man could hold his own against me. I ducked one of his punches and caught him right in the breadbasket. He wheezed and fell back. I laughed and threw my head back, flicking my hair out of the way.

"Oh, come on," I said with a grin. "That's all you got?" I heard a faint whimpering and looked down to see a little girl looking up at me, her big brown eyes wide with fear. I suddenly remembered why I was here in the first place. I bent down and offered her my hand. She recoiled, and I can't say I blame her. Some gray-skinned giant with a fierce beard, fangs, horns and blue markings just ripped open the door and started fighting.

"It's okay," I said. "I'm here to help." I tried a smile and she started crying. Oops.

"Don't let her escape!" a gruff voice called from the driver's seat. I looked up to see an average-sized man wearing a cheap plastic Santa Claus mask driving. I frowned. He smelled familiar…

Easter Bunny recovered enough to grab me from behind. I roared in frustration, which wasn't helping the kid warm up to me. I threw my head back and caught Easter Bunny in the face with my horns and he recoiled in pain. He released me to grasp at his face. I leaned down and picked the kid up. She screamed and struggled against me.

"Dammit kid, work with me here!"

"No!" Santa yelled from the driver's seat. I held the girl tight and leapt out the truck back first. My coat spread out and formed two giant batlike wings. The wings caught the air and acted like a parachute. I landed safely as the truck vanished around a bend. I put the little girl down and she ran over to the guard rail and started crying. I let her go and looked around. Where the hell were we? I figured the kidnappers would take the kid on the highway. We were in the middle of the damn woods. I looked down at my hands and saw the killer's blood on them. Or at least the Easter Bunny.

Two killers. This wasn't good. Two killers working together to murder children. Hell, there could be more. And Santa Claus. I swear, he smelled familiar, but I couldn't put my finger on it. I heard a rush of wind and looked up to see Professor Magic fly in on top of a small tornado. I waved him down and he landed.

"Is she alright?" Professor Magic asked.

"She's in one piece," I said. "But traumatized."

"I understand that," he said. He knelt down next to the girl, who had broken down into tears. In the distance, I heard the familiar sound of police sirens coming from the direction of the playground.

"Cops are coming," I told the Wizard.

"Good. They can get her back to her mum," he said with relief.

"That might be bad for us," I warned.

"As long as the girl is safe, I really don't care," he said. He started talking to the girl in a soothing voice, and she stopped crying. I saw blue and red lights flashing.

"Professor…" I said. He looked up and saw the police cruiser speed towards us. He waved them down and the cop pulled up next to us. Another cruiser sped past us after the ice cream truck.

"Freeze!" The cop said as he jumped out of the squad car. We both put our arms up, although his gun was fixed on Professor Magic.

"Officer, we…"

"Shut it!" he snapped. Professor Magic scowled at him.

"Sir, we are only trying to help."

"I said shut it, old man!" the cop snarled. "Where's the kid?"

"I'm here!" the little girl said. "He saved me from the bad men!"

"This man here?" the cop asked.

"Not him. *That* one!" She said, pointing at me. The cop looked confused.

"Who…?" he started, then jumped when he realized I was there.

"Holy shit!" he yelled and fired a round into my chest before I could speak.

"Argh!" I yelled, grabbing at the wound. "Trigger discipline, asshole!"

"You… You're the Dragonman!" he stammered. "You're real!?" Oh great. Another one. I swear, I'm gonna sue whoever made that documentary about me not being real.

"Yes, I'm real," I snarled.

"Dispatch, I got…" he said before freezing up entirely. I frowned at him, then looked at Professor Magic, who had lowered his hand.

"He shot you!" he said incredulously.

"Yeah," I said. "That happens sometimes."

"You weren't doing anything! You just saved a child's life! Why would he just shoot you like that?"

"Welcome to America," I said. I flexed and popped the bullet out. The wound started closing up immediately. "Come on. I know where to find them."

"You do?" Professor Magic asked. "How?" I grinned and licked the blood from my gauntlet. Immediately, I felt a slight tug on my subconscious, pulling my attention somewhere down the road.

"Vampire powers. I got a taste of the killer's blood. He can't hide from me for another 24 hours," I said.

"Wicked," Professor Magic said. "Let's get back to your car. We can follow him in that."

"That's a bit of a hike," I said. "Might be faster to walk from here."

"Nonsense," he said. He held up his staff. "This is a cutting from Yggdrasil, the World Tree. I can get to anywhere in the nine realms with this. We can pop into Asgard with this, and back to the playground from there." My eyebrows shot up at that.

"Seriously? I thought that was just a focus," I said. "How the hell did you get a piece of the World Tree?"

"Long story. Had to fight a dragon and a giant squirrel for this," he said. He raised the staff and it glowed blue like a sliver of a nebula. A golden circle appeared before us, showing a giant ruined city inside.

"Come on. Let's go stop this murderer."

Chapter 7: Childhood Trauma

After taking a shortcut through Asgard, we recovered my car from the playground parking lot and followed my psychic link with the Easter Bunny. As I drove, I filled the Professor in on what happened in the ice cream truck.

"Bloody hell," he said. "There's two of them?"

"Maybe more," I said. "Could be a cult."

"Bloody fuckin' hell," Professor Magic said, dropping back into cockney. "And this Easter Bunny bloke was as big as you?"

"Almost," I said. "But not as strong."

"I hope not," he said. He sighed. "The fact that they're doing this with those masks is worse. Dressed up as children's icons and all."

"Yeah," I said.

"So, you're part vampire then?" he asked.

"Yep."

"So how come you don't burn up in the sun?" I sighed.

"Some Wizard you are. Vampires don't burn up in the sun. That's just a modern superstition," I said.

"What about garlic?" he asked.

"Burns my skin and makes my throat close up," I said.

"You're allergic to garlic?" he asked.

"Yep."

"So, how do you kill vampires then?" he asked.

"I pull their heads off like dandelions," I said. "Or I burn them. Or stake them."

"So you really can breathe fire then," Professor Magic said.

"Yes, you idiot," I replied. "Where do you think I got the name 'Dragonman'?"

"Maybe you picked it out yourself to sound tough," Professor Magic said with a smirk.

"Please. I could've picked a better name than that," I said.

"How did you get that name, anyhow?" Professor Magic asked.

"Some colonist saw me charge the enemy lines back in… oh when was it… 78? Yeah, 78. I charged an enemy line breathing fire. He started talking about the General's pet 'Dragonman' and the name stuck."

"I thought you had that name longer than 40 something years," Professor Magic said with a frown.

"That was 1778, knucklehead."

"Oh. Wow, you're that old?"

"Yeah. I was born in Tuscany, Italy, in 1760," I replied.

"Holy shit!" Professor Magic said. "You're..."

"256," I replied. "Give or take a few years."

"Wow."

"Yeah," I said. I felt the link grow stronger and I almost drove past the entrance to the driveway. It was a tiny dirt driveway nestled in a thicket of woods. I could barely see the rusted mailbox that had been covered by vines and grass. I pulled over to the side and we got out. I looked around and took a deep breath.

I couldn't hear anything outside of the ordinary forest sounds. Professor Magic's heart was pounding. I was surprised at how strong it sounded. The old man must've kept himself in good shape. The faint smell of blood led further down the driveway, and we started walking. I was grateful for my goblin magic muffling the sound of dirt crunching under my boots, but the Professor's sounded so much louder in the quiet woods. The long driveway eventually led to a dilapidated house that looked like it was about to collapse. A large oak tree had grown in the front yard. The lawn had been reclaimed by the woods, and the grass had grown up to the Professor's knees and covered in dead leaves. The windows had all been boarded up, yet the door looked brand new. I crept up the porch, signaling the Wizard to hang back. The wooden slats that made up the old porch were old and rotting, but still held. I checked the door. It had been recently installed, but the wood surrounding it was rotting away. A grown human could easily knock this thing down, but a child would have difficulty. The smell of blood was stronger here, and I noticed a bright red drop on the ground. I knelt and sniffed it. Yeah, this was the Easter Bunny's. I crept back to the Wizard, who was scanning the second floor carefully for any sentries.

"Door's brand new and there's blood on the porch floor," I whispered. He nodded.

"This must be the place then," he whispered back. "What's the play?"

"Seek and destroy," I said. "I'd burn this thing down myself, but they're might be kids in there."

"You would burn this place with the killers inside?" Professor Magic asked, looking horrified.

"Why not?" I asked.

"Because they are still people!" Professor Magic said hotly. "You can't just go around killing whoever you want!"

"These aren't people. They're monsters who kill indiscriminately."

"Like you?" Professor Magic asked. I frowned at him but didn't say anything.

"We can't condemn people for being killers while being killers ourselves," Professor Magic said seriously. "That would make us hypocrites." I grunted in agreement, then looked around for the ice cream truck. I noticed a set of tire tracks leading around towards the back. I pointed them out to Professor Magic, and he nodded back at me. I drew my sword, and we walked around back.

We found the ice cream truck parked unceremoniously in the backyard, where the back of the house opened up to some sort of warehouse. I could hear two people having an argument.

"Tell me again what happened," a high-pitched female voice said.

"It was some sort of demon," a man's voice replied.

"Bullshit," the woman replied.

"I'm telling you, that's what it was. A giant gray man covered in blue stripes with horns and fangs. Like some sort of orc or gargoyle."

"An orc?" the woman asked, giggling slightly. "You got jumped by something from *World of Warcraft*?"

"Don't laugh, Fairy," the man said. He grunted in pain. "Fucker almost poked my eyes out."

"With what?"

"With his fucking horns, bitch! Are you listening to me or not?" the man sputtered angrily. I realized this must be the Easter Bunny. I heard a slap.

"Don't call me a bitch when I'm the one stitching your hand back together," the woman called Fairy snarled. I crept closer and looked in the open door.

It looked like some sort of stable, with cement floors and rusted iron drains. The Easter Bunny was sitting on a three-legged stool, his right hand being wrapped in gauze by a small, wiry woman wearing a plastic mask of a bright-eyed woman with a creepy looking smile, rosy cheeks and blonde pixie cut hair. She was dressed in dirty overalls, work boots, a flannel shirt and a pink tutu. Her own skin was tanned by the sun, and her hair was dark brown and curly. The Easter

Bunny had gotten a new mask and was dressed in similar work clothes to the Tooth Fairy, only he wore dark blue coveralls with a toolbelt around his waist. I couldn't see Santa Claus anywhere.

"So," the Tooth Fairy said. "Did Santa say when he was gonna be back?"

"No," Easter Bunny growled. "Said something about keeping up appearances."

"The hell does that mean?" Tooth Fairy asked.

"No clue," Easter Bunny replied.

"Fantastic," Tooth Fairy said. "We were supposed to kill that kid tonight."

"I know."

"So, did this monster of yours eat it or something?"

"How the hell should I know?" Easter Bunny asked, throwing his left hand up in the air. "All I know is that snatched the kid up and flew out the back."

"It flies now?"

"Well, it had massive black wings and jumped out the back with them," Easter Bunny said.

"Did it breathe fire?" Tooth Fairy asked.

"No. If you keep making fun of me, I'll kill you instead of one of these brats," Easter Bunny threatened.

"I'm not! If it flew, I think you got jumped by the Dragonman," Tooth Fairy said.

"The what?"

"Christ, you really aren't from around here, are you?" Tooth Fairy said disapprovingly. "The Dragonman is this folk monster the locals talk about sometimes. He's a massive hulking brute that lurks in the woods, seeking the blood of the wicked to drink."

"That's ridiculous," Easter Bunny said.

"That's how the stories go. He's like Bigfoot to these people."

"I did not get beat up by Bigfoot."

"I didn't say that," Tooth Fairy said gently. "My guess is that you got attacked by someone in costume anyways."

"What, like a superhero?"

"Maybe."

"Oh please, that's even crazier! What superheroes work out here?"

"Maybe this is a new one, someone who wears a Dragonman costume and can fly," Tooth Fairy suggested.

Oh, hell no. I will not have bad guys thinking I'm someone *dressed* as the Dragonman. I *am* the Dragonman. I rose and walked into the room with them. They hadn't noticed me, and I stomped my foot and roared. The two killers jumped back in surprise.

"Heard you were talking about me," I growled.

"Fuck! That's him!" Easter Bunny shouted, backing up.

"Shit!" Tooth Fairy said, reaching into her pockets. Once inside, I saw a chicken wire fence against the wall. It was full of whimpering, wide-eyed children watching in fear. I felt my blood boil and I let out a deep wolflike growl.

"You will both pay for this," I snarled and leveled my sword. The blade shimmered and burst into flame. The heat made the air ripple around me. I could smell the fear coming from the killers.

"He's got a fire sword!?" Easter Bunny asked.

"I guess!?" Tooth Fairy asked. Easter Bunny grabbed a sledgehammer from the wall behind him and readied himself for a fight.

"Listen here, asshole," he growled. "If you expect me to just lay down and surrender, think again."

"I expect you to die," I growled. He let out a cry and charged me. I saw a glint of metal and the Tooth Fairy dive at me with a knife. Before she could reach me, she was thrown back by an invisible force. I saw Professor Magic standing in the doorway, the runes on his staff glowing.

"Nice," I said.

"Behind you!" Professor Magic cried. I turned and barely blocked the hammer blow from the Easter Bunny. I roared again and swung the blade at him. He was faster than I expected from someone of his build, and he dodged out of the way, keeping the hammer between us.

I kept swinging, and he kept out of the blades reach. We both knew that if he tried to block, the sword would cut right through the wooden shaft of the hammer. I swung wide and gave him an opening. He took it and slammed the head of the hammer right into my left shoulder, dislocating it. I snarled in pain and swung the blade at him. The attack was sloppy, and he nimbly stepped out of the way. He managed a kick and sent the blade spinning out my hand. Once free of my grip, the sword's flame died, and it clattered onto the ground. Easter Bunny wasted no time in hitting me in the chest with the hammer, forcing me onto the ground.

"Not so tough now, huh freak?" he taunted. I growled and dove at him, sinking my teeth into his knee. He let out a high-pitched scream of pain as I sunk my teeth deeper and deeper into his flesh. I felt fangs pierce bone and meat. My mouth filled up with the iron taste of his blood. I clenched my jaws and bit harder. With a loud snap, my teeth met, and I tore his leg off with a twist of my head. I rose to my feet and spat out his severed leg. He screamed and screamed, grasping at the wound. I growled at him and raised my foot up to stomp on his throat.

"Wait!" Professor Magic yelled. I froze and looked behind me. He had made short work of the Tooth Fairy. She was slumped against the wall, wrapped in chains made of sparks.

"He's bleeding out," I said. "He either dies now quickly or slower later."

"I can heal him, you idiot," Professor Magic snarled. He knelt down next to the weakening serial killer. The blood was coming out much slower now. I heard the Wizard start chanting, and the wound began to close, until it was a pale stump. The killer stopped moving now, his body grayer and more relaxed. The Wizard sighed and rose.

"Well?" I asked.

"He'll live, but just barely. What the hell were you thinking, biting his leg off like that?" Professor Magic demanded angrily.

"I was thinking I was stopping a killer," I growled.

"By becoming one!?" Professor Magic demanded. "Look at you!"

I glanced down and looked at my chest. Blood covered my bare chest, soaked into my beard and was staining my pants.

"You look like a monster!" Professor Magic yelled. "What do you think they think!?" He jabbed a finger at the caged children. I looked over at them. If they were scared before, they were truly terrified now. Their eyes were as wide as dinner plates, and the whimpering had stopped. They were completely silent. The stench of fear was coming off of them in waves.

This was primal fear, something that still lingered in the human psyche since we were apes. The fear of a predator, of being eaten.

I looked down at myself and felt a deep burning sensation. Not the burning of rage or battle fever, but shame. Deep, smoldering shame.

"I…"

"Don't," Professor Magic said icily. "Go outside and wash yourself. I'll get these kids freed."

"Can't you just magic this stuff off me?"

"I could. But you need to see how hard it is to wash the blood from yourself."

"This is hardly the first time I've had blood on me."

"That's not what I meant," Professor Magic snarled. I nodded, understanding and stooped to pick up my sword. I frowned when I picked it up. It felt heavier than usual. I sheathed it and went outside to the hose.

I snarled when the cold water touched my skin. Dragons have powerful control over fire. Their very blood burns like acetylene and can burn through flesh like acid. Being creatures of fire, dragons had a hard time with water, and I was no different. I clenched my jaw and set about scouring the blood from my chest. The cold water burned like fire on my skin, and I scraped more and more blood off. I took off some chest hair in the process, but it was better than being covered in blood. As I washed, I thought about what Professor Magic said. I thought about what those kids had seen.

They had been snatched from their homes and families to be shoved into a cramped cage with other children and kept in filthy conditions. Then, a giant monster with a flaming sword arrives, screaming and roaring like a demon. They watched while I fought the man who kidnapped them and watched me chew his leg off. For the first time in my life, I felt disgusted with myself. I had always embraced my nature as a monster of good. Charging the lines back in the late 1700s with General Washington had felt good. Killing vampires felt good. Killing witches felt good.

But that doesn't mean it was right.

I returned to the Wizard with a heavy heart. The children were gone, and he was stepping out of a portal showing a verdant green field.

"I thought about what you said."

"And?"

"And you were right. I shouldn't have lost control like that," I said humbly. The Wizard seemed to relax after that.

"Good," he said. "Now, let's ask our little friend here what's going on before the FBI shows up," he nudged the unconscious Tooth Fairy with the butt of his staff. She groaned and looked up at us.

"Oh shit..." she gasped, recoiling.

"Oh shit is right," Professor Magic said, kneeling down to look her in the eye. "Now, you're going to tell us everything we need to know."

"Fuck you, I'm not saying a word," she snarled. I growled, deep and loud. She looked up at me and pulled her legs closer to her chest.

"Hear that?" Professor Magic asked, jerking a thumb back at me. "You don't start talking, I feed you to him."

"Shut up! Where's Bunny?" she wailed. I bared my teeth at her, showing her my blood-stained fangs. I was blocking her view of the Easter Bunny. She didn't need to know he was still alive. Not now anyways.

"Oh fuck! Oh no, oh shit…" she whimpered.

"Now, he's got room for your scrawny ass, so start talking," Professor Magic said evenly. She was trembling, her eyes flicking between the two of us.

"It… it wasn't my idea!" she cried. "It was Santa's!"

"Who?"

"I don't know! We never learned each other's names! It was all his idea! He got us together so we could help people!"

"Help people?" I growled. "You're killing children!"

"Only the bad ones!" she said. "These kids grow up to be drug addicts and criminals!"

"How the hell could you know that?" Professor Magic said.

"Santa said he figured it out!" she said. "The world is filling up with people too fast. There's not enough to go around, and people get desperate! That desperation breeds crime and criminals! We're making the world a better place by culling the population!"

"Bullshit," I snarled. "You've killed only 42 in a six-month period. You've hardly made a dent in the population."

"We had to dodge the FBI! They wouldn't understand our mission," Tooth Fairy said. "The plan was to make the kills look like satanic sacrifices to fool the police! That takes time, but even a little bit can help!"

"You're insane," I said. "You're murdering children. How can you justify that?"

"Naughty children get punished," she murmured. "Naughty children get punished. Naughty children get punished..." she kept repeating this to herself over and over again, rocking back and forth.

"Dammit," Professor Magic swore, standing. "I don't think we're gonna get anything else out of her." I sighed.

"Now what?" I asked.

"We need to find Santa," he said. "Easter Bunny said he left to maintain appearances, right?"

"He probably has a day job as an alibi," I said.

"Right. We should come back to this place later, see if he shows up," Professor Magic said. He suddenly frowned.

"What?" I asked.

"What time is it?" he asked.

"Why?"

"Don't you have to be back at work?" he asked. I swore and checked my phone. I had missed three classes, my barracks patrol and had three missed calls from Myers, 12 from Winters, and one unknown number.

"Dammit!" I said.

"I can get you back now, if you want," Professor Magic said.

"No. I'll drive," I said. "Get out of here before the cops find out."

"You sure?"

"This will only look worse if I return with a Wizard," I said. I looked uneasily at the missed calls.

"How bad will this get for you?" Professor Magic asked. I groaned.

"Pretty bad," I said. "But I don't regret it. This had to be done." Professor Magic nodded. I set my shoulders and strode out to my car.

Time to face the music.

Chapter 8: Judgment Day

There was a group of Enforcers waiting for me back at the compound. Enforcers are sort of like Military Police, but they answer directly to the Council. I parked and got out of my car slowly. One of them approached me carefully.

"Roman Grimm?" he asked.

"Yes?" I replied, knowing what was coming next.

"You've been summoned to appear before the Council of the Silent Prayer," he recited. "You will accompany us in chains or your free will. What do you choose?"

"I will walk with you of my free will," I said. The Enforcers visibly relaxed, and a few took their hands off their weapons. They escorted me through the compound to the Lodge, the Council's area of work. Many hunters stopped to stare at us. A few cried out in protest but were quickly shushed and herded away by the Mentors. I kept my head high and my eyes locked forward. I just hoped that Winters and the rest of Dragon Squad wouldn't see me.

We reached the doors of the Lodge, a massive single-story wooden building made from logs, like a giant log cabin. The lead Enforcer opened the door and held it open for us. After escorting me to the Council Chamber, they backed off and I was led in by the lead Enforcer.

The Council had convened and was seated in ringed stands, the lights dimmed so that the accused would be the center of attention under the single spotlight. I stood under the light and crossed my hands behind my back.

"Mentor Roman Grimm answering Summons," I declared.

"So, you can follow orders," a Councilor said. I remained silent.

"I take it you know why you are here," another said. "You stand accused of disobeying orders, neglecting duty, and failure to report. Do you deny these claims?"

"No," I answered.

"Where were you?" Councilor Brooke asked. She was an older woman with gray hair and missing an eye. "You were supposed to perform your sacred duties as Mentor this afternoon and patrol the barracks an hour ago!"

"With all due respect, Councilor, these duties are hardly sacred. Especially after we split from the Vatican a hundred years ago," I said. Councilor Brooke looked at me like I slapped her daughter.

"You dare speak to the Council like this?" Councilor Thomas asked. "You were asked a question, now answer it! Where were you!?"

"Doing my job, you windbag," I snarled.

"Hunter, you will mind your tongue in this chamber!" Councilor Thomas shouted. "Your job is here, hunting monsters and teaching students!"

"My job is defending humanity, which you clearly forgot!" I replied.

"I will not warn you again!" Thomas snarled. "You will keep a civil tone in front of this Council! You have been given a tremendous amount of leeway here, but do not allow this to go to your head!" I glared at him, but kept my mouth shut.

"I was hunting," I replied.

"We know that," a familiar voice said. I looked up to see Councilor Miyamoto staring down at me in disappointment. "Now, tell this Council who you were hunting."

"The Devil's Advocate," I said through gritted teeth.

"Despite being given orders not to?" Councilor Miyamoto asked. "And can you explain *this*?" He pressed a button on a remote and a screen behind me lit up. I turned to see a video taken from someone's cellphone play. It was shaky, but it was a clip of me running from the playground after an ice cream truck.

"A child had been taken right in front of me," I said. "I pursued and managed to rescue them, as well as track down the killers and free other children they had taken."

"Impressive work, hunter," Miyamoto said disdainfully. "But care to tell us who your companion is?" He rewound the video and paused it right when I first ran past the camera. Right behind me, clear as day, was Professor Magic. I winced. Goblin magic can cloud the minds of mortals, but it has no effect on technology.

"Is that who I think it is?" Councilor Brooke asked, leaning forward.

"Professor Magic, also known as Meriwether Hill," Miyamoto said. "Hill gave his life two years ago defending the Queen of England from a terrorist attack at a soccer match. Yet here he is, in America. Next to you."

"Professor Magic has proven himself useful during this investigation," I admitted.

"You have been working this entire time with a Wizard?" Councilor Thomas demanded. Other Councilors began shouting all at once.

"Enough!" Brooke called out, and the Council fell silent. "This changes everything, Hunter," she said.

"Bad enough that you were disobeying orders but working with a dangerous sorcerer," Thomas said, his face paling in fear. "Normally, you would be put on probation and kept on the compound, but now…"

"How has this changed?" I demanded. "I've worked with the Silver Wizard in the past with no consequence."

"Professor Magic is dead," Miyamoto said. "This is either an undead or an imposter. If you can't tell the difference, then you are at best useless to us and at worst a liability."

"You would dismiss me for working with a Wizard?" I asked.

"No. We would execute you as a precaution," Brooke answered. I froze.

"… Execution?" I asked weakly.

"Your mind in the hands of a dangerous Wizard would be a threat to us all," Thomas said. "We can't afford that risk."

"This is insane! The Golden Line has been hailed as heroes in the past! Do you truly fear the work of Merlin, Cleopatra and Meriwether Hill?" I demanded.

"We fear your mind in the hands of Samuel Blake," Miyamoto said. "A dangerous cultist in the 60s who came before Hill."

"Blake's insanity still lives in the mind of the Golden Wizard," Thomas explained. "The late Professor Magic had managed Blake and other mad Wizards before him. But if this truly is the newest Golden Wizard…"

"You'll kill me because you don't know who the Wizard is?"

"Hunter, he is here in a foreign country seeking a killer. Professor Magic always worked with the Crown as the Royal Wizard. What is he doing here, and why is he wearing another man's face?"

"Or why did Professor Magic fake his death and come here?" Miyamoto asked. "These are questions a seasoned veteran like yourself should be asking," I growled back at him.

"Snarl all you want, Hunter," Thomas sneered. "You won't be able to bully us with your bestial nature."

"I am a Mentor," I snarled at him. "Not Hunter."

"You haven't been acting as a Mentor," Thomas replied. "This Council finds the accused guilty of disobedience, witchcraft and vigilantism. The sentence is death, to be carried out at the Crossroads tonight! Take him away!"

"You think I'll let you!?" I snarled. I stomped my foot and roared. "Fools! Cowards! I'll take you all on! I've been slaying monsters when your ancestors were young! I won't go down easily!" Miyamoto simply reached into his pocket and withdrew a golden medallion.

Oh my good God, it was the most beautiful thing I had ever seen in my life. Words cannot describe how it caught the light and shone, or how perfectly it had been sculpted. I felt my body relax and a slack grin appeared on my face. How could I fight others when something as beautiful as this existed? I could stare and watch this piece of pure beauty and art forever.

I felt something strike my cheek, and the world went black.

Chapter 9: Darkness

I awoke to find myself locked in a cage. I groaned and rose to my feet. My clothes were all gone, save my boxers. The room smelled of mildew and blood. I recognized the place.

This was the dungeon, where we kept dangerous witches and warlocks who were awaiting their execution. The events of before suddenly came back to me.

I was going to die. All for not killing a wizard on sight and trying to stop children from dying. I snarled and pounded on the cage bars. I recoiled in pain, grabbing my hand. Black burns blossomed where my skin had touched the metal.

"Impressive, isn't it?" someone said. I looked up to see Miyamoto walking down the stairs toward me.

"You fucking snake," I snarled.

"It's an alloy of silver and tungsten. Practically unbreakable and burns the flesh of monsters. Very tough to get, and even more expensive to make," Miyamoto continued. He looked over at me disapprovingly. "How someone like you managed to join will always mystify me."

"I was recruited by Benjamin Franklin," I growled. "This is what I was built for."

"The fact that you were built at all disgusts me," Miyamoto sneered. "I've said this for years. Magic has no place in this organization." I growled and paced back and forth in the cage like a tiger.

"What do you want?" I asked.

"To let you know, we found your little Wizard friend. Used your phone to contact him and tell him to meet up. Stupid little spell chucker fell for it, hook, line and sinker."

"You're making a mistake," I said. "He's the only one who can catch the Devil's Advocate."

"I don't care," Miyamoto said. "That warlock will get what's coming to him. To every witch and heathen that dares work that evil power!" I glared at him.

"I understand not trusting mages," I growled. "But you're going too far."

"You understand nothing!" Miyamoto snarled, tearing into his pocket. He dug out a worn photograph and thrust it in my face. A pair of young Japanese women smiled back at the camera.

"My daughter and her friend, Tomoko," he said. His fury was fading, and I could hear sorrow creeping in. "They became friends in the Gruman Orchestra."

"The Kitsune Massacre," I said, my eyes widening in horror.

"Three years ago, a member of the orchestra went savage and brutally attacked everyone there. My daughter died of her wounds in the hospital.' Miyamoto said, tears streaming down his face. "Do you know what her final words were?"

I shook my head.

"Tomoko," he whispered. "It was Tomoko," His face screwed up with rage.

"I did my research. Did everything I could to find that bitch. Then I learned something," he said. "Magic isn't just learned. Tomoko was the descendant of a clan of Fox-Employers. Her mother was a Korean fox herself. I never caught her, but I found out many of the witches and warlocks we hunt have similar bloodlines. Go back far enough, and you'll find a faerie, changeling, Yokai, djinn or demon eventually. These monsters are only human on the outside, but deep down, they thirst for human blood. It's just a matter of time before they sate it."

"Miyamoto, the Kitsune Killer was possessed," I pointed out. "A kitsune possessed a young woman and drove her insane."

"Don't give me that!" Miyamoto shouted, getting in my face. "Possession is a myth! A lie! You can't make someone evil! They're born with it! All these witches are ticking time bombs!"

I took a deep breath in and realized something.

"You don't have a scent," I said curiously.

"What?" Miyamoto growled.

"I can't smell you," I said.

"It's an old Shinobi trick," he said with a sneer. "I don't eat meat, so I don't have as strong a body odor. What of it?"

"That's it," I said. "Santa didn't smell familiar. He didn't smell at all…"

"What the hell are you muttering?" Miyamoto asked.

"It's you," I said, the truth dawning on me. "You're the Devil's Advocate."

Miyamoto said nothing.

"All those kids," I said, thinking out loud. "This wasn't about overpopulation. That was just some bullshit lie you told your helpers. All those kids had magical potential, didn't they?"

"Deviants," Miyamoto hissed, his voice dripping with hatred. "Mutants, all of them."

"The wards," I said, my thoughts racing. "You painted wards on the wall to shut down the kid's power in case they fought back."

"Proof of their degeneracy."

"You… MONSTER!" I roared. Miyamoto said nothing and pulled out the medallion again. I instantly went slack and couldn't focus on anything else.

"Dragon gold," I heard him say but it sounded like he was underwater. "You can't look away or think of anything else. I'll leave this here for you. You'll be taken to your death without a fight. Like a sheep," he let out a sharp laugh.

"One less monster in the world."

Chapter 10: On Death's Door

My next coherent thought was the Enforcers opening my cage and blasting me with cold water. I felt my strength wane and I could smell the faint scent of garlic. Deteriorated by two of my weaknesses, the Enforcers forced me out of my cell. They carried spears with silver tips, and I was in no state to fight back against them. Meekly, I let them chain me and escort me up the stairs and to the Crossroads

The Crossroads was the center of the Compound, where we carried out executions. Crossroads in general were places where magic was stronger, but people killed there would be claimed by Hekate and not produce a ghost. Having it on a new moon was also significant, as my powers grew under the moonlight.

The Crossroads were lit with torches, as the entire compound had turned up to see the execution. Many hunters cried out in protest at my sentence, but the sound of jeers and insults coming from the other side of the procession caught my attention. I glanced over to see Professor Magic, walking as dignified as he could with his mouth gagged and his wrists bound. Hunters threw rocks, rotten food and other trash at him as he walked, but he showed no reaction.

"Eenin'," he said politely through his gag.

"It's Miyamoto," I wheezed. The garlic in the water was making it hard to breathe. "Miyamoto is Santa Claus."

"Whaa?" Professor Magic asked, his eyebrows going up.

"We need to stop him," I gasped.

"Quiet you!" the Enforcer said, punching the back of my head. Ahead of us, I saw the guillotine that would cut my head off on the stage. Next to it stood Councilors Thomas, Brooke and Miyamoto.

"Brothers and Sisters!" Thomas cried out. All jeering and protest died down. "We are here to see justice against humanity done right!"

"Death!" one hunter cried out.

"Kill the Witch!"

"Murderers!" another yelled out. I don't know who that was for. Thomas raised his hands for silence.

"We are here to witness the death of Professor Magic, who, under torture, refused to give up his name," I looked at the Wizard in shock. They tortured him?

"And we are here to regrettably carry out the sentence of Hunter Roman Grimm, who until recently, had served this holy crusade with honor," Thomas continued. "Do you, the

Answer to the Silent Prayer, wish to see Justice done against the apostates and corrupt?"

"YES!" came the deafening response. I felt my knees go weak. It had nothing to do with the water or garlic. I had served this organization for two centuries. Now the same people I fought to protect were crying out for my death.

"WAIT!" a voice screamed. Everyone stopped.

"WAIT!" the voice cried out again. I saw the crowd part to allow a small man with a receding hairline and prosthetic arm sprint towards the guillotine.

"Mentor Myers, what is the meaning of this?" Brooke asked.

"You can't do this!" Myers protested.

"And why not?" Thomas asked.

"Roman Grimm is a victim of witchcraft, not a practitioner!" Myers shouted. "Your decree was that he disobeyed orders due to magical interference."

"And?" Miyamoto asked irritably.

"And we don't execute the victims of witchcraft. We help them," Myers said hotly. Whispers and murmurings broke out in the crowd. I felt hope rise in my chest. He was right! Whenever we found someone who had their mind scrambled with magic, we helped recuperate them.

"Roman Grimm is far too gone to be helped," Miyamoto said quickly. "He must be put down."

"He has been imprisoned for less than a day!" Myers argued. "He should be put under observation for his condition to be properly assessed!" More outcries broke out. Miyamoto's face started turning red.

"Be silent, Mentor!" Miyamoto shouted. "Keep this up, and you'll be dismissed!"

"You can't dismiss me, Councilor," Myers shot back. "I am reminding you of your station. Kill the Wizard all you want, but you can't touch a hair on Grimm's head," Miyamoto glared daggers at Myers.

"What's going on here, Miyamoto?" Myers demanded. "I am not so blind and stupid to believe that someone as stubborn as Roman Grimm to be swayed by magic." More outcries broke out.

"You have something to say, Mentor?" Miyamoto spat.

"Councilor Miyamoto Kenji! I accuse you of murder, corruption and abuse of your station!" Myers shouted.

"With what proof?" Miyamoto spat.

"Dragon Squad!" Myers called out. I saw my team step forward. Winters was carrying the Dragonblade, and Wong stood next to Myers and cleared his throat.

"Councilor Miyamoto has not been seen in his office for several days over the past six months," Wong yelled nervously. Poor kid, he hates crowds. "When confronted about this, the Councilor told me to 'Mind my damn business.' I reported his behavior to Mentor Myers, who launched his own investigation of Miyamoto."

"Councilor Miyamoto approved the report of the Devil's Advocate without getting the additional signatures required to call off the hunt," Myers stated. "More importantly, he is the owner of 42 Pleasant Drive, the last murder site of the Devil's Advocate. His disappearances align with the murders of over 30 deaths attributed to the Devil's Advocate, as well as evidence of black mail of Councilors Thomas and Brooke." Gasps broke out in the crowd, and I heard the scraping of steel from sheaths and the cocking of guns echo through the throng.

"Councilor Miyamoto! What say you to these claims?" Myers demanded. I watched a vein bulge in Miyamoto's forehead as his face turned red, then purple.

"Fuck you, Myers! I'll kill them myself!" he howled. He ripped a spear from a surprised Enforcer's hands and charged at me. I was too weakened by the water, silver and garlic. With my hands bound, I couldn't defend myself.

FWOOSH!

Flames flashed in front of me, and Miyamoto went down screaming. I saw the spear go flying with two burnt lumps stuck to it. Miyamoto fell onto his back, writhing in pain. I looked up to see Winters standing over me, the Dragonblade drawn. I looked back at Miyamoto and gasped.

She cut off his hands with a single swipe.

"Enforcers!" Myers called out. "Seize that traitor! And the Councilors as well." The Enforcers snapped to action, detaining a shocked Brooke and Thomas. Myers walked up to me and looked me in the eyes.

"You alright?"

"Myers," I gasped. "Never thought I'd see the day you stick up for me."

"Neither did I," he said as he unbound me. Professor Magic started grunting and waving his arms eagerly. Myers frowned at him.

"Free him," I said.

"You sure?"

"You kinda proved him innocent as well," I said with a shrug. Myers sighed and undid the Wizard's binding.

"Ahh!" Professor Magic said, rubbing his wrists and working his jaw. "Cheers, mate! Got us out of some Barney Rubble, eh?" Myers looked at me pleadingly.

"No clue what he's saying," I said.

Chapter 11: Aftermath

After exposing Miyamoto as a killer, Myers was able to take his position on the Council, something I knew he was after for years. I wasn't sure what surprised me more; that he got it in my lifetime, or that I was happy to see him get it.

Miyamoto was handed over to the police. When asked about his hands, the Silent Prayer claimed they had no idea, and any claims of him being a monster hunter were written off as insanity.

Councilors Brooke and Thomas were demoted to the Library, where they were put to work doing research on supernatural threats. Their families, however, were safe. The only loose end left was, well…

Me.

"Mentor Grimm," Myers said on his first day on the Council. He was sitting in his new office, which he wasted no time in making it his. That is, removing all and any decorations from the previous owner. "You've put us in a difficult situation."

"I think I was in the worse one," I replied.

"Yes, and the Council does apologize for that," Myers said. I folded my arms.

"Screw the Council," I said evenly. "You're the only one on there that has any of my respect now."

"And to think I hated you before," Myers sighed, shaking his head. "On one hand, you disobeyed direct orders and assaulted a Mentor."

"That Mentor had it coming," I said with a smirk.

"On the other hand, you did everything you could to catch a killer in our midst and save the lives of dozens of children," Myers said, ignoring my snark.

"So, what now?" I asked. Myers sighed again.

"If we dismiss you outright, the junior hunters will rebel at the decision, and we could have a riot on our hands," Myers said.

"Seriously?" I asked.

"There's already a petition to clear the charges of you. For some reason, the younger crowd seems to idolize you," Myers replied.

"Can't imagine why," I said lightly.

"Neither can I," Myers said, missing my sarcasm. "If we keep you on, we set the precedent of ignoring people who break the rules."

"And let me guess, the council doesn't want its newest member to pop a blood vessel?"

"No, they don't want hunters going off on a hunch and getting themselves killed," Myers said icily. "You got lucky, but a police officer shot you, and the FBI is already looking for you as a suspect."

"Suspect of what?" I asked.

"Accessory to the Devil's Advocate Killer. You were seen by an agent at the crime scene."

"Oh."

"That's my point. You're not like the other hunters here, Roman. You can regenerate, breathe fire, lift a car over your head and see in the dark. No one can hear you coming, and no one can sneak up on you. The rest of us are only human," Myers said gently and saw his left arm twitch. Suddenly, I realized why someone missing an arm might not like a guy who can regenerate.

"So, what does the Council think should happen to me?" I asked.

"You have two options. One, we put you on the Council to keep an eye on you," Myers said with disgust. I winced.

"How nasty did those words taste?" I asked.

"Worse than I'd expect," Myers said. "Two, you leave the Silent Prayer on your own."

"You're not kicking me out?" I asked. Myers shook his head.

"Like I said, we don't want to incite the Hunters. This has the serious possibility of turning ugly," Myers said. "Despite your constant claims, the Council *does* care about the junior ranks."

"Are these my only options?" I asked.

"I'm afraid so," he said. "You want my advice?"

"Is it to leave?" I asked.

"You're not Council material, Roman. You're a fighter, a warrior. You belong out there, hunting bad guys and saving lives. Not behind a desk writing reports and going to meetings," he pulled an envelope from his robes and handed it to me.

"What's this?" I asked, turning it over. Nothing was written on it, and it was sealed with a wax seal bearing the symbol of the Silent Prayer.

"Incentive. I convinced the Council to give you a little bonus," Myers said.

"A bonus?"

"Roman, you have over 200 years of service. I say that earns you a little retirement package," Myers said with a smile. I looked down at the envelope and thought.

"Myers, this isn't the Council telling me to keep up the fight?" I asked. "This can't be their blessing to go hunt more bad guys and serial killers, is it?"

"Of course not," Myers said. "That would be aiding and abetting vigilantism. Which would make us criminals. We can't tell you how to spend that money, of course."

"Of course not," I said with a smile. I placed the envelope into my jacket pocket and stood.

"It's been an honor, Councilor," I said, holding out my hand.

"The honor is all mine, Dragonman," Myers said, shaking my hand.

"They can't do this!" Winters complained.

"They didn't do anything," I said. "I'm choosing to leave."

"Don't bullshit me, Boss!" Winters said. "They wanted you out!"

"No, I wanted to leave," I said. "I've been fighting this war almost my whole life. I just want some peace." I packed another set of clothes into my duffel bag. I was back at my apartment packing my stuff. The building was owned by the Silent Prayer to give the Mentors somewhere to live outside the barracks, which meant I had to leave to make room for another Mentor.

"Boss, you hate peace," Winters said.

"I know."

"I can't believe they bought you out," Winters steamed. "I can't believe you *took it!*"

"The offer was too shiny, Winters. You know how much I love shiny stuff," I said with a wink.

"This is really happening, isn't it?" She asked sadly.

"I'm afraid so," I said. She looked up at me sadly.

"Don't go," she said. She threw her arms around me. I hugged her back.

"I'll miss you too, Winters. But don't cry for me," I said.

"Because this isn't really goodbye?"

"Well, yeah. But mostly because you're ugly when you cry," I said. She punched me in the ribs and let me go.

"Fuck you, Boss," she sniffled.

"I love you too, kid," I said with a smile. She held up the Dragonblade to me.

"Keep it," I said, pushing it away. She looked at me confused.

"But this is your sword."

"Not anymore. I'm no longer worthy of the blade," I said. "It chose you."

"What do you mean?" she asked.

"The Dragonblade is the single most powerful weapon in the supernatural world. It chooses a worthy champion to stand up to the darkness. I am no longer that champion," I said.

"How can you tell?" she asked.

"Because I am no longer fighting its war," I said. "I'm fighting my own. It doesn't ignite like that for just anyone. The fact that you can lift it at all is a sign." She stared down at the blade.

"I can't be worthy of it," she said.

"Because you think that makes me more certain that you are," I said, ruffling her hair playfully.

"But what will you use?" She asked. I looked around the apartment for a bit before I saw it.

"This will do," I said, hefting up a large club with iron bands wrapped around it.

"That old thing?" she asked, wrinkling her nose. "Didn't you pick that up from some ogre?"

"A troll," I replied. I balanced it in my hand. Not as good as the sword, but a decent weapon.

"Boss, it's a stick."

"It's got metal bits."

"It's still a stick."

"It's my stick," I said. "Now run along. Your team is gonna need you. I hear there's a nuckalavee in Cape Cod that need's killing."

"My team?" she said.

"Yeah, I named you my successor. Unless you want Clarke to be in charge?"

"No!"

“Then shut up and get to work,” I said. She hung the sword on her belt. It looked better on her than it ever did on me.

“Do I get the jacket too?”

“Hell no, this is mine,” I said aghast. “It’s the only jacket that fits me,” she smiled at me, and we both shared a laugh.

“Good luck out there, Boss,” she said, giving me one final hug.”

“You too, kid,” I said, blinking away the tears.

Chapter 12: Teamwork

As far as hideouts go, the Professor did a pretty good job. The house he was staying in was tough to find, and it wasn't in bad shape. I knocked on the door and waited. Moments later, it opened to show a surprised Berengar Black standing there in sweatpants and a t-shirt.

"Dragonman," he breathed. "What are you doing here?"

"Afternoon, Professor," I said. "I figured since you cost me my job, I could crash here with you for a bit."

"I'm sorry, but the Professor isn't here right now…"

"Don't give me that crap, I know who you are," I said.

"You do?"

"You are Berengar Black," I said. "And you inherited the Professor's powers. Now can I come in?"

"Oh, of course," Berengar said, letting me enter. I walked in and looked around. It was a modest house but looked unfinished. No carpeting, the walls needed new paint, but it was clean. A little dusty, but manageable.

"How did you know?" Berengar asked.

"At the trial," I said. "Your monocle came off and I saw your eyes. Both of them. Hard to miss something like that."

"Bollocks," he said bitterly.

"Plus, you kept slipping back into cockney," I said. "Old Meriwether Hill was way more posh than that."

"Alright, alright," Professor Magic said. "So, they fired you?"

"Officially, I'm retired," I said, holding up my envelope. "They pay me half my old salary as a thank you for my lengthy period of service." The Professor nodded, and led me to the kitchen, where he had set up a small card table. He brought out a kettle.

"Tea?" he asked.

"Is it caffeinated?"

"Of course."

"Sure, why not," I said, sitting down gingerly. The chair held my weight, but just barely. He brought out a humble tea set and started pouring. We drank in silence for a bit.

"So, mind telling me why you really came to America?" I asked.

"I told you. To catch the Devil's Advocate."

"That's it?"

"Well, crime in America has been on the rise…"

"So has Venezuela. Brazil. The Middle East. Hell, why bother here and start hunting warlords in the Congo?" I asked. "And don't say it's about hunting bad guys," he sighed.

"This isn't how I planned on this happening," he said to himself.

"You planned this?" I asked. He sighed and started pacing.

"The world is full of villains," he said. "There are plenty of threats that get superheroes killed all the time. Ever since Stinger rose up and started fighting cartels, masked vigilantism has been on the rise. My predecessor was one of them. But how many times do you see the good guys win?"

"I don't know," I said mildly.

"Never. Only Stinger, myself, and that Thundergirl in New York. Three people," he said, counting them on his fingers.

"So?"

"So, I figured a group effort might solve this," he said sheepishly. I lowered my drink and stared at him.

"What?" I asked.

"I know, it sounds ridiculous, but I figured, 'hey, bad guys make gangs to do crimes better, why not form a gang of good guys to fight crime?'"

"Do crimes better?" I asked with a smirk.

"I don't know!" Professor Magic said, throwing his hands up. "I figured I could get someone well connected like you, the Nocturnal, and maybe some independent heroes and we could pool our efforts and make some real change!" He sat back down and sighed.

"Only you got fired…"

"Retired," I corrected.

"Yes, retired," he said. "And I can't get in contact with the Nocturnal."

"Who?"

"A hitman, takes out criminals for a price," he said dismissively.

"Didn't you give me flack about killing people?" I asked. "Why do you want a hitman?"

"He's a cyborg, and we need a tech expert. Besides, you were a killer. I still wanted you."

"Touché."

"But now it's all gone topsy turvy!" He said. "I hoped we could have the best of both worlds. The resources of an official superhero and the freedom of an independent one."

"Hate to break it to you, but the 'official' superheroes are bound by red tape to the point that they choke on it," I said.

"Yeah, I'm seeing that now," he said sadly.

"So, you came all the way to America, bought a house in the middle of nowhere, just to make your own super team?"

"I didn't buy it. It was abandoned for being haunted."

"Is it?"

"Is that really a problem for you?" he retorted.

"Hmm, not really," I said, sipping more tea. We were quiet for a bit.

"It's a fool's errand," I said.

"I know."

"But not a bad idea," I said. He looked up.

"I thought you said…"

"Oh, it's nuts," I said. "Superheroes aren't the type to let people find them. It's foolish, but possible."

"You're not messing with me, around you?" he said.

"I don't think we know each other well enough for that," I said. "But I have nowhere else to go, nothing to do, and I can't imagine any place is willing to hire a 7'4" giant with horns and a caffeine addiction." Professor Magic's face lit up.

"Are you saying what I think you're saying?" he asked.

"I am," I said. "I'll join your little team of fools."

"Not fools," he said. "That makes us sound like idiots."

"We'll think of something," I said. Just then, there was a knock on the door. We frowned at each other, and I grabbed my new club and shouldered it. Berengar's face blurred, and standing before me was the Professor Magic everyone knew. He grabbed his staff and walked over to the door. I listened. I heard a bizarre heartbeat on the other side. Some sort of blend of a heartbeat and a machine. A pacemaker? The Wizard opened the door to reveal a pale man dressed in all black, with a shock of orange hair and a pair of shades on, holding a gun to his face.

"Professor Magic," the man said. "Heard you were looking for me."

"Depends," Professor Magic said. "You the Nocturnal?"

"I am," the man said. He grinned and holstered his gun with a spin worthy of any Hollywood gunslinger.

"Awesome," he said with a smile. He looked at both of us and asked:

"So, where do we start?"

Epilogue

"So that's how you two met?" I asked. "He cost you your job, so you became best friends?"

"We are not best friends. Besides, he had a point. America is the superhero capital of the world," Dragonman said.

"The hell you aren't best friends," Thundergirl said. "People don't argue like you two do unless they liked each other. Right, Blue?"

"Shut up, bitch," Blue Fox said with a smile. Thundergirl beamed at her.

"Also, you mean to tell me there is a dope ass bar not far from here serving massive plates of nachos, and you never told us?" Thundergirl asked.

"Yeah! What the hell man, I love dive bars!" I said.

"That's your takeaway?" Dragonman said. "I just told you how my life changed dramatically, and you focus on the bar?"

"Yes," I said.

"We should totally go," Lab Rat said. "How are the IPAs there?"

"You ask for an IPA there, it will start a fight," Dragonman warned.

"Promise?" Thundergirl asked eagerly, her eyes lighting up.

"Anywhere that has plenty of toughened manly men with beards and no female competition sounds like my kind of place," Blue Fox said. "I never could say no to a man with a beard."

"Can you say no to anyone?" Thundergirl asked. Blue Fox flipped her off.

"So, we are going to this Doomsday place then?" Lab Rat asked.

"Sure," Dragonman said. "If it matters that much to you."

"You guys want to go to that dump?" Professor Magic asked. He must've come in when Dragonman was telling his story.

"Hell yeah," I said. "Dive bars are the shit."

BANG!

"Ha! Got your pale ass!" Thundergirl cried triumphantly.

"Shit!" I said, quickly picking up my controller. "You never said we were resuming!"

"Get good, scrub," Thundergirl said smugly.

"Oh, tough talk from someone losing 1 to 45," I said. "Now I'm gonna start actually trying."

"Thundergirl, did you seriously challenge Silverbolt to a shooting game?" Professor Magic asked.

"She was talking shit!"

"You know she can't miss a shot," Professor Magic said. "How did you think this would turn out?"

"Hey Professor," I asked. "How did the name 'Jesters' come about?"

"The Wayne Brown show," he said. "He called us a pack of fools on national television. I called in and told him, 'Only a Fool can laugh at a King'."

"That's where our motto comes from?" I asked.

"Sort of. It sort of stuck after that. Nocturnal started leaving little calling cards with jester hats on them. The media picked up on it and started calling us the Jesters."

"I forgot about his calling cards," Thundergirl said.

"How come we stopped using those?" I asked. "It sounds pretty cool." "We kept forgetting to pack them," Dragonman said sheepishly. "Besides, after Thundergirl joined, we started getting seen more."

"That is *so* not my fault," Thundergirl said.

"You knocked down a building on your first day," Dragonman argued.

"It was a poorly built building anyways," Thundergirl said dismissively. "I was doing everyone a favor."

"Boom!" I cried. "Headshot!"

"Dammit!" Thundergirl cried. I laughed.

"So, the media called us idiots for teaming up, and you guys just ran with it?" I asked.

"Pretty much," Dragonman confessed.

"Nice," I said. "That sounds like us."

"It certainly does," Dragonman replied.

"Do you regret it?" I asked.

"Regret leaving your old life behind to slum it with us?" He asked. He looked over at us all. Blue Fox gazing intently at her magazine of muscley athletic men, Thundergirl loudly proclaiming me a cheater, Lab Rat insisting that we go to Doomsday, and Professor Magic trying to talk him out of it.

"Not for a second."

THE END

<u>Story 4: Dude in Distress</u>

Chapter 1: Princess Syndrome

"Now, just focus on your breathing," Blue Fox said. I took a deep breath and leaned into the stretch. I felt the muscles tighten, then loosen. Blue Fox was helping me with yoga, which doesn't sound like usual superhero training, but when we weren't fighting crime and corruption, we were keeping our bodies in top shape. This meant dieting, fitness, and mental exercises. Since coming here, I've eaten less processed food and less meat. It pained me to say it, but Blue Fox's diets worked wonders. Each of our bodies had been sculpted to near peak physical fitness, drawing out more strength than I thought we could. I was afraid of getting too bulky, but Blue Fox had accurately figured out my body type and got me in the right kind of shape for stealth and combat. Some people would just write her off as a slut, but she was also a doctor, and knew the human body inside and out. Wait, that came out weird…

Yoga was something I was having issues with, so Blue Fox had decided to give me a one on one lesson. I took another deep breath and felt a wave of tranquility wash over me. I finally felt like I was getting it.

"MOTHERFUCKER!"

I jumped at the exact wrong time and fell on my ass, twisting my back in the process. I groaned in pain as Blue Fox tried to help untangle me.

"This fucking *moron!*" Thundergirl shouted, storming into the room angrily.

"Calm down!" Blue Fox said. "What's wrong?" Thundergirl thrust a slightly crumpled paper at Blue Fox with a sound of disgust.

"Oh no," she said. "Not again."

"Hey T," I said. "Also, ow."

"This fucking idiot!" Thundergirl said, ignoring me. "I swear, this is the last time he pulls this bullshit!"

"You say that every time. You love the guy," Blue Fox said. Thundergirl made an incoherent sound of anger while making claws with her fingers.

"What's going on?" I asked, rising to my feet. I twisted around, testing how bad I messed myself up. Nothing permanent, but ow. That hurt. Blue Fox handed me the paper. It was a photocopy of a ransom note with letters taken from cuttings of magazines.

"We have your..." I said, squinting at the text. "...sneak?" I frowned. "Meet us at Central Park at 5:30 PM if you want your thief back."

"This idiot…" Thundergirl snarled.

"Okay, I'm lost here," I said. "Who's this 'sneak' they're talking about?"

"My boyfriend," Thundergirl said. "Tommy Thompson."

"Two things," I said. "One; I refuse to believe that is his real name. Two; shouldn't you be more worried than scared?"

"Tommy is a private investigator and reporter for a conspiracy theorist organization," Thundergirl explained. "He's been kidnapped 17 times since we started dating."

"What?" I asked. I looked at Blue Fox, who simply nodded sadly.

"And *every* time he does this, I have to take time out of my day to save his dumbass!" Thundergirl said. I checked the note again.

"Where did you get this from?" I asked.

"His boss sent it to me. Wanted to know what he should do," Thundergirl said.

"I know this is a stupid question," I said. "But why not get the police involved?"

"This is a group of conspiracy nuts," Blue Fox said. "They don't trust the establishment at all. Chances are, Tommy once again uncovered some sort of corruption and got caught."

"I swear, he does this on *purpose*," Thundergirl growled.

"Alright, calm down. No need for us all to get pissy," I said. Thundergirl took a shaky breath, and I felt the tension in the room ease. Thundergirl's emotions can be contagious, one of the drawbacks of being a powerful telepath like her.

"Now, who was he investigating last?" I asked. She sighed.

"No idea. He always keeps his cases to himself. Says he doesn't want to get me involved in case something goes south."

"He knows you're bulletproof, right?"

"I've told him several times to just *ask*. I would gladly help him if he ever needed help, but nooooo. 'I've got it, Athena. No need to worry about it, babe. Ol' Tommy's got it covered'," Thundergirl said.

"Relax," Blue Fox said. "He lives back in New York, right?"

"Yeah," Thundergirl said.

"Alright," Blue Fox replied. "Let's start there.

"How are we going to get there?" I asked. "Professor Magic is out with the guys working some case." The girls looked at each other.

"We could take the Flier," Thundergirl suggested.

"You guys got it to work?" Blue Fox asked. Thundergirl see-sawed her hand.

"Marvelous," I said. "Let's go."

Chapter 2: Homecoming

The Flier was our name for a flying machine that Lab Rat and Thundergirl had been working on for a few months. It was made from an old army troop transport and flew like a giant RC drone. The thing rattled and clanged the entire flight. I kept on hand on the handle above me, the other on the pull-string my suit had to deploy a pair of glider wings. By the time we landed in New York, one of the rotors had caught fire, something fell off, and Blue Fox had vomited over the side. To anyone in New Jersey who got hit with that, I apologize.

Despite the dangers of flying a helicopter truck made of garbage, we were soon walking the streets of New York to Thundergirl's neighborhood. Rather than risk her secret identity by going in costume, we were in civilian disguises courtesy of Blue Fox's illusion magic. I was dressed in leggings, a plaid skirt, loose-fitting hoodie, high top sneakers, and a pair of sunglasses. Blue Fox was dressed similarly, but with black leather high heeled boots, a gray skirt and jacket. Thundergirl wore skinny jeans, a Wonder Woman shirt, sneakers, thick frame glasses, a thin scarf, and her hair done up in a messy bun. Only now did I see she had faded scars all over her arms. Scrapes and scratches across otherwise flawless skin.

"These illusions are nuts," I said, looking over my arms. "It doesn't even feel like I'm wearing my armor."

"A proper illusion covers all five senses," Blue Fox said proudly. "Lab Rat is always crowing on about how good his holograms are, but my illusions can mimic touch, sound and even scent." I cocked an eyebrow at her, then sniffed my arm.

"Pine?"

"You love the wilderness," she said. "Thought you might like it."

"I do. Just an odd choice for clothes is all."

Thundergirl didn't seem to be in a good mood to be home. I could feel her discomfort radiate off her, and the people passing by seemed to be picking up on it. The crowds parted before her like the Red Sea, and we reached our destination in no time.

We stopped in front of a small barber shop. The window had gold lettering on it, saying 'Ray's Barbershop.' We walked in, the bell hanging in the door announcing us with a cheery jingle.

"Uncle Ray!" Thundergirl said brightly. A man dressed in black smock and slacks looked up from his client at her. He was a large, heavy set man. His skin was darker than Thundergirl's, and his well-trimmed beard was a good mix of silver in it. His hair was buzzed short, and he looked like he was a lineman or a wrestler in his younger years. He smiled broadly and let out a croaky laugh.

"Athena!" he said jovially. His voice was scratchy, likely from smoking too many cigarettes, but I thought he sounded like an old school jazz singer. He was a staple of the community, someone you could spill your life's problems to, and he would listen and give his own sage advice. He was a father figure to many young men who didn't have the luxury of growing up with one, and he had the respect that came with it…

I shook the thought from my head. Where had that come from? I had never met Ray Freeman before, but somehow, I could just tell by looking at him. I frowned. There's reading people, which I'm proficient at, but that's more along the line of telling how well someone can handle themselves in a fight. But this? This was something new.

While I was pondering this revelation, Thundergirl and Uncle Ray were catching up. Thundergirl was leaving out all the parts about her being a superhero, instead keeping the conversation about her webcomic series.

"Well, I didn't expect to see you here," Ray said. "Who're your friends?"

"Uncle Ray, this is Tomoko, she's from Japan," Thundergirl said.

"*Hajimemashite*," Blue Fox said, bowing at the waist. Everyone looked impressed by that.

"And this is…" Thundergirl said, pausing slightly.

"Friday," I said, leaning forward to shake his hand.

"Friday," Uncle Ray said. "Nice to meet you. Where you from?"

"Down south," I said. "Athena and I met online a few years back."

"Well, ain't that nice," he said genially. "Should've guessed that from your accent."

"Yeah, it's pretty obvious, ain't it?" I said, hamming it up. Uncle Ray chuckled and turned his attention back to his client.

"So, what brings you back home?" Uncle Ray asked, lining the man's hair up. I had to admit, I didn't know much about black hairstyles, but the guy was looking good. Uncle Ray knew his work.

"Something's happened to Tommy," Thundergirl said, her previous warmth leaving. "Have you heard anything about him recently?"

"Tommy…" Uncle Ray said, pausing his work briefly to think about it. "I'm afraid not. He doesn't come to this part of town much."

"Why not?" I asked. Uncle Ray looked at me uncomfortably.

"I'm not sure how things normally work down where you're from, but here…" he said, fishing for the right way to say it, before letting out a weak sigh. "There's no right way to say this…"

"He's white," a cold female voice said. I looked up to see a woman walking towards us from the back room. Her hair was immaculate, a shoulder-length set of curls. She looked just like Thundergirl, only a shade darker. She wore an outfit identical to Uncle Ray and she carried a pair of silver scissors in her hand.

"Chauntelle," Thundergirl said coldly. The two women glared daggers at each other.

"Athena. I see you have deigned to grace us with your presence," Chauntelle said, crossing her arms.

"Chauntelle," Uncle Ray said. "That's no way to talk to your cousin."

"Oh, she's my cousin now?" Chauntelle said. "I must've forgotten. It's not like she acts like it."

"Chauntelle!" Uncle Ray said.

"This is how you act when I come home?" Thundergirl asked. "We haven't talked in years, and this is how you greet me?"

"Seeing how you left us behind to run off with that weird French guy without saying goodbye to your own family?" Chauntelle asked. "I'd say it's pretty deserving."

I squirmed at that. I had left my own family without a backwards glance, and I knew I had the same hostility waiting for me if I ever returned. I glanced over at Blue Fox for help, but she was sitting between two handsome men waiting their turn for a haircut and was chatting away with them. I rolled my eyes. Classic Blue Fox…

"I did what I had to," Thundergirl said, crossing her arms.

"Oh, I'm sure. And what brings you back home? Oh, that's right. Your white boyfriend. Why you can't date someone your own color, I'll never know."

"At least I can keep a man," Thundergirl snarled. "How many boyfriends have you had since I was gone?"

"ENOUGH!" Uncle Ray boomed. All eyes were on him, even the men Blue Fox was entertaining.

"I will not have you two bickering like children in this shop!" Uncle Ray said. "This is a place of community and respect! You two are family, and as long as you are in my shop, you will act like it!" The two women said nothing but glared at each other.

"Athena, I haven't seen Tommy recently. But I know he has been talking with Granny. Try asking her," Uncle Ray said. Thundergirl winced.

"I was hoping to avoid that," she said softly.

"Anything that happens in this town, she hears about it. You know that," Uncle Ray said. Thundergirl sighed.

"You're right," she said. "Come on, girls." We turned to leave, when Chauntelle just had to open her mouth again.

"That's right, walk away," she called. "Walk out with your new white friends!" Thundergirl whipped her head around and glared at her with pure venom. I thought she was going to hit her, but instead the air thickened with tension and rage.

"You ever say that again, cousin, and I will fucking bury you," she said. I gulped. Last time I saw Thundergirl give someone that look, she punched him hard enough to dislocate his jaw and sent him flying ten feet. Chauntelle's eyes widened, and the entire barbershop went deathly silent. Thundergirl held her gaze until Chauntelle looked away, then Thundergirl turned on her heel and walked out.

I waited until we were a couple blocks away before breaking the silence.

"Soooo…" I said. "You wanna talk about what just happened?"

"No," she said evenly.

"Because I think we should talk about that. How you threatened your cousin like that," I said.

"Silver, there's nothing to talk about. Chauntelle is a petty, jealous bitch who only cares about herself," Thundergirl said.

"She's your cousin," I said. "That has to count for something, right?" Thundergirl sighed.

"Chauntelle and I grew up together. Our family is really close, so she was like a sister to me. When my powers started manifesting, we started drifting apart. Psychic powers run in our family, and she was always jealous of the things I could do," Thundergirl said.

"Do they know that you're…?" I asked.

"No. Only Granny does. Still, a fair number of my aunts and cousins have some ability. Granny is a powerful telepath, my Aunt Diana can predict the future, and my cousin Anna could tell animals what to do," she said. "Chauntelle never developed any powers."

"Why the women?" I asked.

"How much do you know about psychic powers?"

"I know you can lift a bus with your mind."

"So, nothing. Alright, the way it was explained to me was this: psychic ability is decided by a few genes in your X chromosome. Women are twice as likely to develop psychic powers. You've heard of women's intuition? That myth comes from psychic women," she explained.

"Can men be psychics?" I asked.

"Sure, but it's rarer. Psychics are rare enough on their own, and men just have a lower chance of developing it. Most psychic powers manifest as some small ability, like moving small objects, intuition of certain events, or hearing people's thoughts," she said. "But even more rare are women like me. Women with the psychic gene on *both* X chromosomes."

"Double the power?" I asked.

"Way more than that. Dr. Gaspard, the foremost researcher on psychic powers, called it the 'Goddess Gene.' Most girls that are born with it burn out their neurons in infancy. In the entire world, there are only three people who survived it and can use it safely," she said. "Including me."

"Wow," I said.

"Yeah. The other two are a set of identical twins, Bella and Ella Gaspard."

"Let me guess, the Doctor guy's kids?"

"Yeah. A pair of sociopaths," she said with a shudder.

"You've met them?" I asked. She nodded.

"Remember when Chauntelle said I left with some French guy?" she said. "That was him. Dr. Lucas Gaspard. He recruited me to help him rid the world of evil and gave me my physical enhancements. My family thinks I left to go study science with him in Paris."

"Ah," I said, piecing it together. "She thought you were living in the lap of luxury in France while she was left behind."

"Exactly," Thundergirl said.

"While we're on the subject, you should cut her some slack," Blue Fox said. "Not all women are meant to be with one person." Thundergirl looked at her with confusion.

"She's not like you, Blue," she said. "You do it simply for the sake of sex. She does it for attention, luring in guys to buy herself stuff and pay rent. She wants to marry a rich man and get out of town."

"Oh," Blue Fox said, still looking uncomfortable.

"That's why her talk of family pissed me off. She thinks I screwed my way to the top before she did."

"That's messed up," I said.

"Yeah. Now you see why I didn't want to come back," Thundergirl said. "And I have a question for you."

"Go ahead," I replied.

"Friday?" she asked. I laughed.

"It's a nickname I picked up when I started working. I spent most of my free time hunting or practicing archery. I could only work on Friday's, so all my co-workers called me 'Friday.'" I said.

"Where did you work?"

"This small-time diner in a town called The Dirty Spoon," I said.

"How did it get that name?" Thundergirl asked with a grimace.

"No one knows, but it's been there since the 50s," I said. "Hasn't really aged since then. Great food though. After I let home, I kept using the name until I picked up the moniker 'Silverbolt.'"

"It's a nice name," Thundergirl said. "Fits you."

"That's what I thought," I replied.

Soon, we reached a set of apartments. I shivered. It felt like we were being watched. I glanced around, but no one was near. Still, I couldn't shake the feeling. The other girls looked tense as well. Blue Fox was making a soft growling sound.

"She knows we're here," Thundergirl said. "Come on. Time to introduce you to my grandmother."

Chapter 3: The Queen of Queens

The apartments were small and cramped. Thundergirl's footsteps resounded through the wooden floors. Her body has a much higher metal count than us, and that made her heavier by default. Cracks about her weight always ended in smacks, and none of us were strong enough to fight her off. Still, I was worried about her falling through the floorboards.

We reached the last room on the third floor, and Thundergirl walked up to the door and raised her fist to knock. Before she could, the door opened to reveal a short, portly woman with dark skin, white hair in curlers, and wearing a housedress. She wore no makeup, and her eyes were completely gray.

"Well, look who finally decided to show up!" Granny said.

"Hey Granny," Thundergirl said sheepishly.

"Don't you 'Hey Granny' me, girl!" She said. "Come in, you and your friend." She quickly waved Thundergirl and Blue Fox in, and almost closed the door on me.

"Excuse me, ma'am," I said, catching the door. Granny jumped and faced my direction.

"Who!?" she said, waving a hand towards my voice. "Oh! I couldn't feel you. My, that's impressive," I stared at her. Thundergirl watched us nervously.

"May I come in?" I asked hesitantly.

"Of course you can, sugar," she said sweetly. "You mind is different, that's all," I walked in after Granny.

"She always been like that?" Granny asked Thundergirl.

"Mhm," she said.

"Speak up, girl! Lord, did I raise a heathen or something?"

"Yes Granny," she said. "Silverbolt has a tough mind to read," I looked at her sharply when she said my superhero name.

"You can relax, Silverbolt," Granny said. "I know who you are. You too, Blue Fox. There's not much that I don't know about a person." She led us into the kitchenette and told us to sit. Only after sitting did I realize that she didn't say it out loud. I just knew that she wanted us to.

"So, Granny…" Thundergirl said.

"Ah!" Granny said, cutting her off. "None of that now! I know why you're here, and Tommy isn't in as much trouble as you are, girl!"

"What?"

"'What', she says! You gone dumb after leaving? Did all that time with the Jesters turn you into a fool as well?" Granny said.

"Granny…"

"Girl, you up and left us to follow some hair-brained scheme to save the world!" She said. "I told you that man was no good! That snake had nothing but venom and lies coming out of his mouth! And your dumbass ate up every word like you was starving. I told myself, 'June, when that girl shows her face around here again, you smack her into next week!' But now that you're here…"

"Granny…"

"Don't you interrupt me! I oughta smack the black out of you! But I would just break my wrist on your metal ass! What would your daddy think of you running off with that man?" Granny said. Thundergirl wilted under her words.

"You didn't think of that, did you? And to think you're my granddaughter! Lord, I can practically taste the emotions coming off you! And now you got memories coming out too! You wanna save time and tell the whole world who you are?" Granny said. "You had poor Silverbolt here thinking she was a psychic!"

"That's what happened?" I blurted out. Thundergirl looked at me in confusion.

"Back at…"

"Back at Ray's, she knew what you knew about Ray," Granny said, interrupting me. "Didn't I teach you better?"

"It's harder around people like Uncle Ray," Thundergirl said weakly.

"Don't give me that about 'hard'! You're a Freeman, are you not? Our family doesn't fold like a house of cards when things get hard! Did your ancestors make excuses when they fled the south to come up here? No! Did your great grandpappy complain when he fought off the slavers in the south during the Civil War? Never! So I think you can easily reign in your emotions when you see your Uncle. Lord!" Granny said. She took a deep breath after that tirade.

"Now, who's hungry?"

Soon, we were digging into bowls of chili. Granny made it extra spicy, but I grew up on southern cooking, where spicy was default. Poor Blue Fox was struggling, but I think she was reticent about eating a meat sauce on a diet day. Me, I didn't care. Only a fool turns down free food. And this chili was totally worth the extra miles I would have to run. While

470

we ate, Granny filled us in on the proud warrior legacy of the Freeman family. Ever since the Civil War, the Freeman males served in the military, despite all the stigmatism from their white compatriots.

"Silverbolt, you want seconds, sugar?"

"Yes please," I said. She beamed.

"See, Silverbolt is a proper lady. Minds her manners and says please. Calls me ma'am. You do your generation proud," Granny said, refilling my bowl. "Blue Fox, you hardly touched your bowl! You need more meat on those bones, girl!"

"I'm fine, Freeman-sama," she said.

"See? Another fine woman. Athena, you could learn a thing or two from your friends," Granny said.

"I will, Granny," Thundergirl said. "Have you seen Tommy?"

"Tommy? Why yes, he was here last week. You know he still visits? He is such a gentleman. Best thing you ever did was get with that man. I was so afraid you'd turn out like your cousin," Granny said. "Tommy is a fine young man. Don't you lose him, you hear?"

"I know, Granny. That's why we need to find him," Thundergirl said exasperatedly.

"Don't you take that tone with me, young lady," Granny said. "He was investigating that Morning Star building uptown."

"He told you?" I asked. "I thought he kept that kind of stuff to himself."

"Oh he tries, sugar," Granny said. "But I heard his mind, clear as if he said it himself."

"That sounds useful," Blue Fox said.

"Oh, it is. Athena could do it too, but she's too busy ripping up the streets and throwing cars to practice any subtlety," Granny said.

"Granny, I have a question," I said.

"You want to know why it's harder to read your mind?" she asked. I nodded, then remembered she was blind.

"It's okay, I can read you just find. I see better than most people with working eyes anyhow. The truth is, that your mind is more subtle. You don't like being seen, don't you?"

"No, ma'am."

"So polite," she said with a smile. "You close your mind so much, you do it reflexively. It's a rare skill that I try to teach Athena to protect her, but she can't close herself to others very well. You have a quieter personality than others. That's all."

"It's not a superpower?" I asked.

"Depends on what you would call a superpower," Granny said simply. "Sometimes a skill can be so impressive that it appears supernatural. Personality plays a factor as well. I had a hard time picking out from the background thoughts of others in this building. Next to Athena and Miss Blue Fox here, you were practically invisible."

"Huh," I said.

"Freeman-sama, how is it your powers are so strong?" Blue Fox asked. "Do you have the Goddess Gene as well?"

"Oh no. I'm just a telepath. I've had years and years to hone my skills to what you see today," Granny said. "If you dedicate your life to a skill, you can make it seem bigger than it really is. Just like Silverbolt's aim."

"It's just practice?" I asked.

"Exactly. The Goddess Gene is powerful, but that requires skill and finesse to properly use, just like any gift. It's what sets my dear Athena apart from those demons Gaspard owns."

"Have you met them?" I asked.

"Not directly. I checked Athena's mind when she escaped from Gaspard," Granny said, patting her granddaughter's hand. "You did the right thing, walking away from them."

"Thank you, Granny," Thundergirl said. "But we should really get going."

"Oh, alright!" Granny said. "Go save that young man. But you should come home more often. Come spend time with your old Granny. I don't have many years left, you know."

"Granny, you are going to live to be 1,000 years old," Thundergirl said with a smile. "Someone like you doesn't just keel over and die."

"Bah!" Granny said. "Still, it would be easier for you to come home more often. I know Chauntelle can be a prickly little troublemaker, but she misses you. We all do."

"Okay," Thundergirl said, taking her grandmother's hand in hers. "I will."

"You better, or I'll send that FBI team after you and beat you myself."

"Yes, Granny," Thundergirl said.

"And don't go getting yourself killed either! You die before me, I will climb all the way to heaven and smack you back down here myself!"

"Yes, Granny."

"Good. Miss Blue Fox and Miss Silverbolt, it was wonderful meeting you. Next time, bring the rest of the Jesters! I want to meet the people who kept my baby away for so long."

"Yes, Granny!" Thundergirl said impatiently. "We need to go now. I love you."

"Hmph. Always in such a hurry. Fine then, darling. Take care of yourself," she said in a huff. Thundergirl quickly ushered us out before Granny could speak up again.

Chapter 4: Siege Tactics

I looked up at the Morning Star building. We had ditched the disguises in favor of our costumes and were planning our assault on the building.

"What can you see?" Blue Fox asked. I had my bow up and was using the mini-HUD on my goggles to get a better look at the building. My bow has tons of sensors in order for me to calculate wind direction and speed to better my aim. There was also a camera that fed right into my goggles, letting me be even more accurate. It's not quite the same as a sniper rifle scope, but it works just as well.

"Not much," I said. "Standard looking security. Should take us 15 minutes," I said. "You sure he's here?"

"That's what Freeman-sama said," Blue Fox replied with a shrug. I frowned and glanced at Thundergirl. She was levitating in place with her legs crossed. I couldn't see her face through her helmet, but I could tell she was focusing.

"He's here," she said, moving her feet to the ground. She sounded relieved.

"How can you tell?" I asked.

"I could feel his mind," Thundergirl said. "Let's go."

"Hey now!" I said, stepping in front of her. "We need to think this through."

"Not really," Thundergirl said. "Chances are they've already seen us."

"Actually, I had us cloaked this whole time," Blue Fox said. "No one will take notice of us."

"Alright then," I said. "See? Let's not rush this."

"The note said they wanted to meet in Central Park at 5:30. That was half an hour ago," Thundergirl said. "We don't have time to plan."

"Here's an idea," Blue Fox said. "You two head for Tommy, I'll handle the distraction."

"Wait, this won't be like last time you handled the distraction," Thundergirl said. "There's a reason it's mostly up to Lab Rat."

"He's not here, and I think it would be best for you to save your boyfriend, not two strange women whom he's never met before," Blue Fox said. "Besides, this is going to be even *better* than last time," she said with a mischievous smirk.

"What happened last time?" I asked.

"You don't want to know," Thundergirl said. "But it's better than nothing. Let's go."

We walked through the front doors, Thundergirl in full bad bitch mode. A security guard walked up to her to stop her. Before he could get a word in, Blue Fox grabbed him by the tie and pulled his lips down to meet hers. Her face flushed with color and he collapsed with a pleased-sounding whimper. Blue Fox smiled and closed her eyes.

"Ahh, now this I can work with," she said sensually. I looked at her nervously, already guessing what she had in mind for the building. We reached the center of the skyscraper. The building was effectively a hollow tube; the middle of the building was open, and the floors ringed the central area. A pair of glass elevators ran up and down ahead of us, and the center area was designated as some sort of plaza. Blue Fox immediately broke off and headed to our left, following the sign saying 'Cafeteria.' Thundergirl walked into the middle of the plaza and looked up. She was getting a few stares from the salarymen and businesswomen around us. We waited a few moments, then I heard shouting coming from the cafeteria. Workers streamed past us to get there. I felt a tingle on the back of my neck, and a slight pull in that direction. I shook the feeling off and focused on the task at hand.

"Where is he?" I asked. We needed to move fast before security called the cops, and the cops called Task Force 52.

"The highest room of the tallest tower," Thundergirl said.

"I think there are taller buildings…" I started, before she crouched down and leapt up three floors. I heard a crash of glass as she shattered the glass railing. There was a commotion, and I saw her leap across the gap to higher floors. I sighed. I guess levitation would be too slow for her, and her rocket boots too hard to control. I shrugged and made my way to the elevator. I pushed the button and waited. With a ding, the elevator doors opened to show a shocked looking secretary. I stepped in and pushed the button for the top floor. The secretary stared at me.

"Hi," I said. "I'm Silverbolt."

"Hi…" she said weakly.

"What's your name?"

"Uhh, Katie," she said.

"Nice to meet you, Katie," I said. "How long have you been with the company?"

"Um," she said, torn between keeping an eye on me and watching Thundergirl tear through floors of an office building. Security had already engaged her, and the sound of semi-automatic fire sounded in the building.

"Well?"

"It's my first day," Katie said.

"No kidding? Me too," I said. "Well, first time in this building."

"Am I a hostage?" she whimpered.

"What? No, we don't do that," I said. "What floor are you going to?"

"I was about to go home…" she said.

"Ah," I said. "My bad. It's quitting time, ain't it?"

"Um… yes. Time to go home."

"Again, sorry about that. You wanna get off?"

"Well, I don't want to get in your way. You sure I'm not a hostage?"

"Pretty sure," I replied. There was a ding, and the elevator doors opened. I saw a battalion of armed guards in riot gear lined up with assault rifles aimed at us. Katie squeaked and fell to the ground.

"Hands up and on your knees, Jester!"

"Which is it?" I asked, putting my hands up. "My hands up or on my knees?"

"On your knees!" the lead guard barked. "Now!"

"Here? Now? In front of all these people?" I said, faking a nervous stammer. "Why, this is so forward of you…"

I was answered with the clicks of guns being taken off safety.

"Alright, alright!" I said. "Just let Miss Katie here go!" I said.

"The hostage?" the lead guard said.

"What is with you people and hostages? She's not a hostage," I said. I nudged her with my toe.

"Go on," I said. "Git!" she stammered something and crawled out of the way. Once she was free, I played my card. I dropped the small steel ball from between my fingertips and it exploded into a thick white mist. I dropped down and expanded my shield. Just in time too, as bullets roared past me, hammering into the shield.

"Cease fire, cease fire!" the lead guard called out. The bullets stopped. I retracted the shield and threw my boomerang out the side.

"Down!" I heard a guard yell. I could see them all watching the boomerang. And not me. I quickly nocked an arrow and fired it into the crowd of them. It burst into thick pink foam, rapidly expanding until it held them all.

"Gah!" one of the guards yelled. "What the hell is this stuff?"

"Rock foam," I said, catching my boomerang on the return. "Expands and solidifies in seconds. Little invention of mine. Hard as stone." One of the guards seemed to be panicking. He kept snarling and scraping at the foam desperately.

"Relax," I said. "It won't last more than an hour. You'll be free before…."

He let out an inhuman scream and broke free.

"… You know it," I said. "Um…" I said, stunned. He screamed again and tore off his helmet. His eyes were glowing blue, and bluish light was glowing within him, showing off his skull. Black lines traced his nervous system, like a lightning scar. He growled at me, and I could see his breath fogging the air. He dropped his gun and charged me like a bull. I ducked under his fist, then rolled out of the way of his next. His fist careened into a cement support pillar and tore out a chunk.

"Holy shit!" I cried, keeping on the move. If one of those punches connected, I was done. He kept screaming and punching. I ducked another fist and pulled out one of my new bolos. The cables were carbon fiber, a little project Lab Rat and I cooked up. I flung it at his feet, tying them together. He howled and fell to the ground. I fired a sleep dart into his neck, and he slowed down. I frowned. I fired another, then two more. After that, he stopped, and the glow died down.

"What the hell," I muttered and did a quick scan of him. His body temperature was through the roof, over 120 degrees Fahrenheit. His hands were in ruins, the bones bent and warped. I scowled at that. Bent? That couldn't be right. Since went did bones bend like that?

"Thundergirl," I said on my comms. "We've got a problem."

"Hang on!" She said. I saw a purple and gold blur slam into the wall behind the guards. Thundergirl had one of the maniac guards pinned, while another one dressed in business attire was on her back. She punched the guard in the face twice, which only seemed to piss him off. She snarled and flung the salaryman off her back onto the marble floor. The guard clawed at her face. She let out a shout and head-butted him, finally knocking him out. The salaryman leapt at her and she nimbly jumped out of the way like a matador. Before he could recover, she grabbed him by the collar and belt and lifted him high over her head. With a cry, she slammed him into her knee, breaking his back Bane style. I heard his spine snap, making me wince. The man let out a soft groan, and she dropped him.

"You alright?" I asked.

"Yeah," she said, staring down at him.

"What the hell are these things?" I asked.

"No clue," Thundergirl said. "But this place is full of them."

"Shit," I said. I looked over at Katie, who was quietly crawling away.

"Hey," I shouted. She started crawling faster. I nocked an arrow and fired it at the floor in front of her, missing her ear just enough for her to feel the breeze on it without getting cut. She yelped and flinched back.

"What the hell is going on with the guards here?" I asked her.

"I don't know!" she whimpered.

"Don't give me that bullshit!" I shouted.

"She doesn't know," the lead guard said behind me. I turned to face him. Thundergirl and I walked over to him.

"You do?" I asked.

"She doesn't," the guard said. I looked him in the eye, watching his reaction. He still looked defiant, his jaw set. "She just started working here. If you are going to interrogate someone, don't pick her."

"Interrogate…?" I said. "Dude, I just want answers. I'm not here to hurt anyone."

"You just fired an arrow at her!" he argued.

"That's just how I say hello. Tell him, T."

"It's true," Thundergirl said solemnly. "And very annoying."

"So, you gonna talk?" I asked.

"I'm not telling you a damn thing. I swore to protect this building and I don't give my word lightly," he said with a snarl.

"Well well, we have a man of honor and dignity," Thundergirl said. "And here I thought this was just a job to you."

"To some, but not me," he said. The other guards watched us with rapt attention.

"That's cute," I said. I pointed over at one of the maniacs who attacked me. "You see that? Your guard, the man you swore to protect, just tried to eat me. And there are more in here as we speak." The guard didn't say anything.

"You got a name I can call you?" I asked.

"I'm not telling you a damn thing," he repeated.

"Sergeant Richards!" his walkie talkie chirped. "What's your status?" Sergeant Richards winced.

"Alright, Sarge," Thundergirl said. "We're here for an investigator who was checking this place out. Someone you folk had kidnapped."

"This might surprise you, but this is a pharmaceutical firm. We make and sell medicine. We're not into kidnapping," Sarge said.

"Look, the higher-ups might not have told you much," I said. "But his name is Tommy Thompson."

"Him?" Sarge said blinking. "Yeah, he's here. I checked him in myself."

"You what?" I asked. "You sure?"

"Yeah, I remember because I thought it was a fake name. But he wasn't kidnapped. He scheduled an interview with one of the managers," Sarge replied. Thundergirl and I looked at each other in surprise.

"Why did you think he was kidnapped?" Sarge asked. I drew an arrow and aimed it at him.

"Wait!" he cried. I fired it into the foam near his shoulder. The arrowhead burst, shattering the foam, and freeing the guards.

"Sarge, get these people to safety," I said.

"Why the hell should I listen to you?" he asked.

"Because we've all been used, you moron," Thundergirl said. "Everyone in this building just got hoodwinked, and now innocent people are dying."

"Because of you!" Sarge argued.

"Because someone just pulled a fast one on us, and we need to get going. Now!" I said. "You don't have to believe us, but these maniacs are rampaging through here and killing the people you swore to defend. Focus on evacuation, we'll handle the monsters." We ran past him and his goons before he could retort.

"What do you think is going on here?" I asked, my breathing getting labored.

"My guess is that someone faked Tommy being kidnapped to lure us here," Thundergirl said. Her voice was steady, despite our running speed.

"You think they know who we are?" I asked. Ordinarily, I wouldn't have even considered it. However, one maniac had guessed our secret identities and used it to threaten us. In an amusement park catered to our weaknesses I might add.

"Doubt it," she said. "The ransom note was sent to his boss, not us. We've responded to kidnappings this fast before, despite not having any connection to the person before."

"Benefit of Lab Rat's vigilance, no doubt," I said.

"This way," Thundergirl said, heading further down towards some nicer offices. She ran up to an office door and smashed through it. Remember how I said that I was scared of Thundergirl breaking through the wooden floors back at Granny's? All that mass she has means that her inertia can get in the way. The faster she runs, the harder it is for her to stop. I stopped right at the door she blasted through. Inside the office, Thundergirl stumbled and tried to stop herself, only to go tumbling through the window. I peeked inside to see a pair of well-dressed people. At the desk, an older woman dressed in a pantsuit with a bobbed cut was looking at us, trying to figure out who the gold plated battering ram was. Tommy was unfazed.

Upon seeing the person whom we've been looking for all this time, I couldn't help but be impressed with Thundergirl's taste in men. He was just shy of six feet, had rich black hair, a strong jaw, and a stylish amount of stubble. He was dressed in a baby blue collared shirt, striped tie, khaki pants, and brown leather shoes. He looked like he belonged to a country club, which might not endear him to Thundergirl's family. He wore a pair of thick frame glasses, which threw off his handsome football captain look, making him look way nerdier.

"Hello," he said. He had a smooth, deep voice. "Was that Thundergirl who just ran past?"

"Maybe," I said. He beamed, showing off bright white teeth. Lord, he could've given Thundergirl a run for her money with those pearly whites.

"You must be Silverbolt," he said, holding out his hand.

"Actually, I'm Dragonman," I said, shaking his hand. "People make that mistake all the time." Tommy laughed.

"It's a pleasure to meet you," he said. Thundergirl floated up and through the broken window.

"You good?" I asked.

"I'm fine," she said.

"Hey, didn't expect to see you here," Tommy said. Thundergirl reached up to retract her helmet into a circlet.

"Hang on," I said. I reached out and fired a knockout dart at the woman behind the desk. After a moment of shock, she collapsed. Thundergirl nodded at me, then retracted her helmet. She glared down at her boyfriend, then flicked him in the ear.

"Hey!" he said. "What was that for?"

"I have been looking for you all day!"

"Why?" he asked. "I've been working."

"Your boss told me you had been kidnapped!" Thundergirl said.

"What?" he asked.

"And because you don't use a phone or the internet, I had to get Silverbolt and Blue Fox to come track you down!" Thundergirl spouted. Tommy frowned at her, then looked over at me in confusion.

"Yo," I said, giving him a small wave.

"Look, smartphones are how the government tracks you down for your private information, babe. I know it's difficult…"

"Don't 'babe' me now, asshole!" she said, sounding almost exactly like her grandmother. "I'm the one who is being hunted by the government, and I manage just fine." She took a deep breath, then kissed him full on the mouth.

"You ever pull this kind of shit again, and I will never forgive you," she threatened after they separated.

"I have no idea what you're mad about, but the next time I don't get kidnapped, I will let you know," he said seriously. She kissed him again.

"Aww," I said. "And they say true romance is dead." Thundergirl flipped me off, still kissing her boyfriend. They broke off, Tommy still looking confused.

"So, what's been going on?" he asked. "They said there was some sort of a security breach, and that we needed to stay put."

"Well, that might work if it was a crazy drug addict who broke in or if the intern finally snapped and brought in a gun, but this is something else," I said.

"Some of the employees here Hulked out and started trashing the place," Thundergirl explained.

"Wait, what do you mean by 'Hulked out'?" he asked. Right on cue, one of the maniacs burst through the wall, roaring and snarling. Without missing a beat, I fired a net arrow and got it tangled up. It fell heavily and started thrashing about, straining against the carbon fiber netting.

"Holy shit," Tommy said, his eyes wide with shock. "That was…"

"A reason to leave," Thundergirl said. She scooped Tommy up and carried him bridal style out the office. I sighed and retrieved my sleep dart.

"Oh no, Thundergirl. It's cool, I'll handle the cleanup. You just focus on your boytoy. It's no biggie," I said to myself sarcastically.

"Grargh!" The maniac snarled in his net.

"Right?" I said to him. "No respect at all," I walked out the door and followed Thundergirl and Princess Tommy. Without warning, Thundergirl leapt over the railing and dropped down to the first floor. I heard Tommy scream the whole way. I leapt off myself, waiting a few floors to pull a string on my suit to deploy my glider wings. I circled around a bit and landed gracefully in the plaza.

"Right, let's go get Blue and get out of here," I said, walking towards the cafeteria.

"You can put me down now," Tommy said. "I can walk just fine."

"Hell no. I'm not letting you out of my sight until we get you home," Thundergirl replied. I pushed open the cafeteria doors, and my jaw dropped in surprise.

A full-blown orgy had broken out, where most of the employees and security had ended up. Clothes had been strewn all over the place, and a mass of writhing naked bodies moaned and groaned in the center of the room.

"Oh my God…" I said. I tore my gaze away to see Blue Fox leaning on the wall next to the coffee machine, sipping tea with a smug look on her face.

"Blue…" I said, horrified. She glanced over at us and smiled.

"Well, what do you think?" she asked, gesturing to her handiwork.

"*This* is how you make a distraction!?" I asked.

"Hell yeah! What's more distracting than this?" she asked.

"Oh my God, I knew you would do something like this," Thundergirl said with disgust. "It's like the University of Arizona all over again!"

"Oh please, this is much better," she said, framing the scene with her fingers. "Probably my best work yet."

"I honestly can't say I'm surprised," I said, shaking my head in dismay. "How hard was this to set up?"

"Easier than you'd expect. These people are so pent up, they all needed a little release," Blue Fox said. "I fired up some hormones, set up some illusory couples, and the rest just fell into place."

"Setting up an orgy like this can't be that easy," I said.

"I could've done the same thing with a keg and three strippers," she said with a wink. "I know what I'm doing."

"What about the maniacs?" I asked.

"The what?" Blue Fox asked.

"The people turning into monsters and destroying everything. The ones with glowing blue eyes," I said.

"Oh, them!" she said. "There's a few of them in there, but they seem to be having fun." I risked another glance to see a woman with glowing blue eyes doing… something really aggressive. I'm not going into detail.

"So, you saved the princess?" Blue Fox asked, looking over at Tommy. Her eyes lit up and she broke out into a smile. "Why, hello there, young man," she said sensually.

"Hello, Blue Fox," he said, his eyes firmly on the wall to his left.

"Watch it," Thundergirl said to Blue Fox threateningly. She turned on her heel and walked out. I sighed.

"If it makes you feel better, I could carry you out like a bride," Blue Fox offered. I laughed dryly.

"You? Bitch please, I could carry your scrawny ass in one of my quivers," I said. She punched me in the arm.

"Bitch," she said. "Last time I offer you something." She glanced back at her work and sighed forlornly.

"Such a shame to leave it behind," she said.

"Surprised not to find you in the middle of that," I said as well left.

"You Americans have a saying: 'Never get high on your own supply," she said. "Besides, I'm too selfish for groups."

"Gross."

"How is it gross? Sex is simply the most intimate thing two or more people can do. Such a thing should not be reviled but celebrated. I don't see how something like this could be revolting," she said.

"STIs and pregnancy," I said.

"There are plenty of options to prevent unwanted pregnancies," Blue Fox said. "And proper health and hygiene keeps disease at bay."

"Abstinence is a pretty good solution to both."

"Chocolate can rot your teeth and make you fat, but do you refuse chocolate? No. If you want to enjoy nice things, you need to do the necessary work for it. The human body is beautiful. It should be celebrated and maintained, not shunned and hidden away," she said. I thought about that for a second.

"You've got a weird mind," I said.

"Bah! My mind is normal. Everyone else is weird," she said.

Chapter 5: Not Again…

We reconvened back at the Flier, where Thundergirl was trying to get it working again. The rotor that had burst into flames on the way over was unresponsive, and Thundergirl was trying to fix it.

"Grrr!" she snarled, her golden gauntlets covered in grease. "Work, you stupid thing!"

"You guys really flew here in that thing?" Tommy asked.

"Yeah," I said.

"How?"

"Sheer hope, duct tape and no small order of luck," I said.

"Shut up, Silverbolt!" Thundergirl said. "It was working fine earlier!"

"We could just call Lab Rat," Blue Fox said.

"No, I can fix it. I'm not running off to call him every time something breaks," Thundergirl insisted.

"He built it," I said. "Makes sense to call him about it."

"He HELPED build it. I did most of the work," Thundergirl argued.

"The heavy lifting?" I asked innocently.

"No. He's not the only genius in the group. I made your supersuits, remember?" Thundergirl said.

"Yeah, about that," Blue Fox said. "I had some design changes I wanted to make to mine…"

"Blue Fox, for the last time, I am not lowering your neckline," Thundergirl said, not looking up from her work.

"Why not?"

"Because it won't be able to protect you. What happens if you get shot in the chest and you aren't wearing armor there?"

"Dragonman shows off more skin than any of us," Blue Fox argued.

"Dragonman can regenerate. You can't," Thundergirl said.

"What about showing my midriff?"

"No."

"Shoulders?"

"No."

"You are no fun," Blue Fox said, crossing her arms. There was a clang, a flash of sparks, and Thundergirl let out a stream of cuss words.

"That sounded expensive," I said, walking over to the Flier to check on Thundergirl.

"Silver, you stay over there and keep an eye on Tommy," she said.

"Why? You think he's gonna get kidnapped again?"

"No, I don't trust Blue Fox around him," Thundergirl said. "You know how she gets around hot guys."

"Oh please, I know she's shameless, but do you honestly think…" I started, before being interrupted by the sound of loud kissing. We both turned (Thundergirl faster than me) to see Blue Fox standing a good way away from Tommy. She was making kissing sounds with her mouth and smirking. She waved impishly at Thundergirl. Thundergirl glared at her, then made the 'eyes on you' gesture and went back to work on the Flier. Tommy looked nervously at Blue Fox and Thundergirl, before focusing on his notepad. I sighed and walked over to Blue Fox.

"Why are you like this?" I asked. She laughed.

"She gets so defensive when it comes to her boyfriend," Blue Fox said. "With all the teasing I get from her about my sex life, this is my way of getting back at her."

"You wouldn't actually try anything with him, would you?" I asked.

"Never! I respect Thundergirl too much. She knows this but can't help but wonder," Blue Fox said. "Consider it my way of making sure their relationship holds out. If he can resist me, then he can resist any woman."

"Someone thinks highly of themselves," I said.

"Hey, I have experience. I know what I'm doing," she said. "What about you?

"What about me?"

"Anyone special in your life?" she asked. I blushed.

"Not really," I said.

"No one?" she asked. I sighed.

"Alright, there was a guy I had a crush on a while ago."

"Oh ho ho! Alright, what was he like?" Blue Fox asked, her eyes lighting up with interest.

"His name is Alistair. He was the local pastor's son. Nice guy, always had a smile on his face," I said.

"Did you ever talk to him?" Blue Fox asked. I opened my mouth to answer, then a roar sounded from the rotor Thundergirl was working on.

"Ha ha!" she crowed. "Told you I could fix it!"

"Awesome," I said, looking over at Tommy. "Alright, let's…"

He was gone.

"Uh, Tommy?" I called, looking around.

"Oh no," Blue Fox said. "Tommy?"

"What's going on?" Thundergirl asked. "Where's Tommy?"

"He was right here," I said. I looked around, then heard muffled yelling. I peeked outside the alley and saw Tommy being forced into the back of a limo. I quickly nocked a tracking arrow and fired it at the back of the car. The men kidnapping Tommy looked up to see me readying another arrow. They started moving faster and took off.

"T!" I shouted. "Some thugs just stole your boyfriend!"

"What?" She asked. "How? I thought you were guarding him!"

"I was, but we were talking about some guy I knew back home…"

"YOU LET MY BOYFRIEND GET STOLEN BECAUSE YOU WERE TALKING ABOUT GUYS!?" She thundered.

"Look, this is my fault, I get it," I said. "But I got a tracking arrow on the car, so we can follow him." Thundergirl let out a scream and punched a nearby dumpster, denting it with a resounding crash.

"Let's go," she said, climbing into the flier and prepping for takeoff. Blue Fox and I barely had any time to get in before she blasted off after my signal. I uploaded my signal tracker to the Flier's computer, which was built solely by Lab Rat, so it worked perfectly.

"I cannot believe you let him get kidnapped after we *just* rescued him," Thundergirl fumed.

"I can't believe they did it so quietly," Blue Fox said in amazement.

"I *still* can't believe it's not butter," I said. Everyone glared at me. "Bad time?"

"Who were these guys?" Blue Fox said, ignoring my awesome joke.

"Chances are it's the New Ice Gang," Thundergirl said.

"I'm sorry, the what?" Blue Fox asked.

"When I got back from Dr. Gaspard, I went on a crime-fighting binge," Thundergirl said.

"As you do," I interjected.

"Shut it," Thundergirl snapped. I shut up immediately. "Anyways, I drove crime down to pretty much nonexistence. The New Ice Gang rose after I left, running just about every vice in the city. I knocked out their competition, then left to join the Jesters. They've pretty much taken over the city."

"Why New Ice?" I asked.

"I think it's named from the bar they used to operate out of," Thundergirl said. "The high-ranking members all wear diamonds, so it might be because of that."

"This gang takes over your city, and you didn't tell us about it?" Blue Fox asked.

"Look, they aren't normally that bad," Thundergirl said. "As far as street gangs go, they do more to protect the little guys than the cops do. Since they're the only gang in New York, violence has all but vanished. They do charge for protection from small business owners, but they actually protect it. They have the infrastructure to make sure the streets are safe. Cops think twice about beating down on minorities with New Ice members lurking around."

"Right," Blue Fox said suspiciously. "Where do they get their money?"

"Drugs, weapons, racketeering," Thundergirl said.

"I knew it. Thunder-chan, a street gang can put on the face of a guardian for the little guys, but it's a system that chews up the undesirables. Trust me on this," Blue Fox said with disgust.

"How do you know?" I asked.

"It's how the Yakuza operate back home," Blue Fox said. "Less violence, but they still buy and sell women as sex workers. They offer protection, but still extort the people they protect. No matter its pattern, a snake is still a snake."

"What would you have me do?" Thundergirl said. "Last time I tried to clean up the city, I created them. If I came back and tried it again, I could make it worse. They keep people safe as best they can. Besides, they know if they raise hell, I could come back. Their leader is scared shitless of me."

"Are you seriously trying to justify a street gang?" Blue Fox asked.

"Why did they kidnap Tommy?" I asked. "If they care so much about protecting people and maintaining safe distance from superheroes, why nab someone right from under their noses?"

"I don't know, but given Tommy's nature, he probably pissed them off somehow," Thundergirl said. The tracker beeped, letting us know we were getting close. We circled around an old warehouse by the harbor, triangulating the position of the car.

"Right, let me go first," I said.

"Why you?" Thundergirl asked.

"This is going to take some finesse," I said. "They may have changed cars, and I can check for tracks if they have. If not, then Tommy's here."

"If he is, I should be the one to rescue him," Thundergirl argued. "Let me just check for him with telepathy."

"We don't have time for that. If they see you charge in, they might kill him," I argued. "It's my fault he got nabbed, let me be the one to scout it out. I'll let you know when to charge in and wreck the place. Just wait for my signal." I got up and dove out the back before she could argue back.

Chapter 6: Silverbolt, Going Dark

I dropped down towards the warehouse, silently gliding in the dusk. I landed on the roof of the building and activated my active camouflage. My suit is normally green, given that I spent most of my time hunting bad guys in rural areas. However, the Jesters spend more time in cities and other urban areas, and I wasn't about to give up my camo advantage. My suit changed from green to a dull gray, matching the cement ground and steel beams around me. I wasn't completely invisible, but it was harder to see me.

The guards were in alert mode, a term I came up with after my extensive time breaking into places I shouldn't.

Guards have three modes, which I call Relaxed, Alert and Active. Relaxed is when the guards are most vulnerable and easiest to get by. They aren't paying attention as much as they should, and this can be easily exploitable. You see this on military bases, museums, and banks. The guard isn't carrying their weapon, and patrols might be chatting with each other casually.

Alert mode is when they are more alert than relaxed mode, but not looking for a fight. They don't chat but are actively looking for a threat. They know something is out there, but don't know what. This is when you need to be careful, as they can slip into Active mode quickly.

Active mode is when they know something is here and figure out where it is. This is when you get caught and the base goes on full alert. When this happens, you will be fighting. Get in cover, and either start taking out guards, rush your objective, or leave. Stealth is no longer an option.

I could tell by the guard's body language that they were ready for a fight. They had just grabbed someone from a trio of superheroes and got caught doing it. Retribution was coming, but they didn't know when or where it was coming from. Most of their attention was directed at the street, which is from where they figured Thundergirl would attack. Knowing Thundergirl, it made sense. She's the type to just walk into a fight with all eyes on her. Me, I prefer the better part of valor.

Humans are terrestrial creatures, meaning we think in two dimensions. Don't believe me? Without looking, describe your ceiling. Now look. Not quite what you remember, right? First rule of stealth is this: No one looks up. It's why I use a grappling hook and gliders in the first place. And also, why I prefer climbing in from above.

The building I was on had a lower and higher part. It seemed to be some sort of office area and storage area. I had landed in the office area, and luckily for me, I had a window leading into the storage area. I crouched down by the windows lock and drew my knife. I had upgraded it since our time at Jester Park, and while it still couldn't take down lions, it could cut through locks with ease. I pressed a switch on the handle and the blade started humming softly. I pressed it to the lock and snapped it in half. Deactivating the blade, I put it away and slowly opened the window. A set of rafters greeted me, and I smiled at my luck. Christ, this place was easy to break into. Might as well have given me a seat and refreshments. I pushed that thought away. Complacency has burned me before, and I still have the scars to remember that fight by. I climbed through and slowly and carefully made my way through the rafters.

Below me, I saw Tommy tied to a chair. He had a burlap sack over his head and was being watched by three gangsters.

"Well, well, well," the lead thug said. "Finally caught your punk ass."

"Mmm!" Tommy replied. I pushed a button on my earpiece to activate my microphone.

"I bet you thought you were safe with your superhero pals," he said. "Too bad the Jesters couldn't protect you from us." He ripped the bag from Tommy's head, and I saw a large blue bruise around his right eye. His mouth was taped shut, and I could see evidence of more roughness. I winced. Thundergirl was gonna be pissed.

"Charles!" A voice boomed from the entrance. I looked over to see a large man dressed in a large white fur coat, gold chains and diamonds enter, flanked by two gangsters.

"Boss!" Charles the lead thug said. "Look who we found!"

"Is that who I think it is?" The Boss said, pointing at Tommy.

"Tommy Thompson. The same bastard who exposed our drug trade to the FBI," Charles said.

"Huh," Boss said, walking around Tommy and examining him. "He's a slippery one, isn't he? Where did you find this eel?" Boss asked, placing a hand on Tommy's head.

"You're not going to believe this, but he was just chilling in an alleyway with the Jesters," Charles said with a laugh. Boss looked up at Charles sharply.

"What?"

"Yeah. They were arguing about something and working on this weird ass vehicle. Looked like some sort of helicopter," Charles said.

"Which ones?" Boss said coldly. "Which Jesters?"

"Lemme think, I saw Silverbolt, Blue Fox, and Thundergirl," Charles said.

"Thundergirl is here!?" Boss asked.

"Yeah, so?" He said. "Silverbolt fired at us but missed. Darius took the arrow as a souvenir."

"Charles, you fucking idiot!" Boss howled. "You kidnapped this guy from the *Jesters!*"

"So?"

"So, you moron, they're going to come looking for him!" Boss said. "I told you fools to keep an eye out for superheroes!"

"Boss, these are only six people wanted by the FBI for corporate espionage and vigilantism," Charles said. "You're scared of these punks?"

"Yes, I'm scared of them," Boss said. "I'm fucking terrified. You realize that only *one* of them took out every criminal organization in this city on her own! And you're telling me that there are *three* of them in this city, *and you took someone they were protecting!*"

"I've got guards posted up all over this building," Charles said, crossing his arms. "There's no way in without me knowing it."

"Goddammit Charles, Thundergirl is a bulletproof monster who can crush you into the size of a cantaloupe with her mind, rip this building apart like wet clay, and shatter every bone in your body with her voice. *Her fucking voice!*" Boss said. "Not to mention Blue Fox, who killed one of those sea monsters in Japan on her own and can shapeshift into literally anything."

"I heard she's a whore," one of Charles's thugs piped up.

"She's a whore who will tear your arms off," Boss snapped. "And Silverbolt, who never misses a shot!"

"She missed me, Boss," Charles argued.

"Did it ever occur to you that maybe she wasn't aiming for you?" Boss said. "Where did the arrow hit?"

"The back of the car."

"There was probably a tracker in it, and you led them right here!" Boss shouted. "For all you know, Silverbolt could be in here already!"

"Oh please," Charles said. I dropped down from the rafter onto one of the shelves silently. "They're all hype!

There's no way that everything they say about them is true." I crept out of the shadows and stood right behind Charles.

"Psst," I said, right behind Charles. He turned around to see me with an arrow nocked and aimed right at his face.

"Let's see how much hype I live up to, amigo," I said.

"S-Silverbolt!" Boss squeaked. There was a thunderous roar above us, and something hit the pavement outside. Hard. Shouting and gunshots broke out. I heard a loud crack of thunder, and the windows rattled and shattered at the shockwave. The wall to my left exploded, and Thundergirl strode in. I could feel cold waves of fury pour off her, and her glare was like a searchlight. Boss fell to his knees and started stammering. His thugs all drew weapons and fired at her. Charles glanced over at them and started to reach for his own weapon.

"Ah ah," I said. "Watch." The bullet pinged off Thundergirl and spun away slowly as if they were being pulled into her orbit. Each step she took cracked the cement ground. Bullets and debris circled around her like Saturn's rings. She flicked a hand out and one thug flew back and slammed into the wall, falling unconscious. The other's panicked and tried to run. She raised her other hand and they all slowly lifted into the air, as if their gravity suddenly vanished. She reached Boss, who had been reduced to groveling at her feet.

"P-please, Thundergirl!" he sobbed. "I had no idea about this!" Thundergirl made a disgusted sound and kicked him in the collarbone. He flew, ass over teakettle, into the shelves with a clatter. She saw Charles and held out her hand like Darth Vader. He flew into her grasp and she held him by the collar.

"You were the one who took him," she said icily. It wasn't a question, but he still tried to lie out of it.

"N-no, I swear!" he cried. I saw a dark stain slowly growing on his groin. Pathetic.

"Don't lie to me, scum," Thundergirl hissed. "I can hear your thoughts."

"P-please..." he stammered.

"This is my city. These are my people. You ever hurt any of them, I will destroy everything that you ever built. No one will know who you were apart from the smoldering crater left in my wake," Thundergirl growled. "And in case you forget..." She held her hand up to his face and placed it gently on his cheek. Her hand glowed, and Charles screamed in pain. She took her hand away to show a nasty handprint burned into his skin. Charles fell back, writhing in pain.

"Poor baby," I said sarcastically. "Can't handle a little burn mark." Thundergirl looked around, checking to make sure all the guard were out cold, then retracted her helmet and flew to Tommy's side.

"Oh my God baby, are you okay?" she asked, her voice full of concern. She gently pulled the tape from his mouth and he winced in pain.

"Have I ever told you how hot you are when you go full goddess mode on people?" He said. I wrinkled my nose in disgust. Good lord, he sounded like he meant it. I left the love birds alone to be gross together. Outside, Blue Fox was on cleanup duty, beating down the remaining resistance.

"*Konbanwa,*" Blue Fox said genially.

"Tommy's fine," I said. "A little roughed up, but he'll live."

"That's good," Blue Fox said. "Decided to give the odd couple some privacy?"

"Yeah. He said he liked when she went all psycho on everyone, and I knew it was time to leave," I replied.

"Sounds about right. He seems the time to like being dominated," Blue Fox said.

"I choose not to think about stuff like that," I said.

"For some reason, everyone seems to think I'm into stuff like that," Blue Fox said.

"Like what?" I asked, instantly regretting the question.

"BDSM," Blue Fox said. "I'm surprisingly vanilla. Granted, I tried bondage once…"

"You can stop now."

"… But it just felt weird and uncomfortable. I don't need all the tools and accoutrements to have an orgasm…"

"Seriously, you don't have to keep talking."

"… The sadism parts are weird too. One time a guy asked me to step on his…"

"STOP!" I said, covering my ears. "Christ Almighty woman, I don't want to hear about your BDSM experiences!"

"Oh, sorry," Blue Fox said. "Guess I got carried away again."

"Seriously, read the room better," I said with a shudder. "You're as bad as Lab Rat."

"Oh come on, I'm not that bad. Besides, I always thought Americans were more prom…" She struggled. "Promis…"

"Promiscuous?" I suggested.

"That one," she said. "*Kuso Eigo*," she muttered. I chuckled.

"I keep forgetting English is your second language."

"I take that as a compliment," she said proudly. "Let's go get Thunder-chan and Tommy-kun."

"Yeah, they might start sucking face if we leave them alone for too long," I said.

"Hey, if they start screwing here, I get to make fun of them for it for *years*," Blue Fox said eagerly. "Then she can't tease me for that one time in the parking lot."

My dumb ass came *very* close to asking her to elaborate, but thankfully my brain got ahead of my mouth for once and I kept silent. Ignorance is bliss, after all.

Chapter 7: Homefront

We managed to safely navigate the Flier home, and Blue Fox had gotten Tommy some ice for his black eye. She even managed to be a lady about it and not flirt with him, showing that even she had lines she wouldn't cross. Soon, I was down in the living room alone with Blue Fox. She had insisted they get some time alone, and that she didn't need a spirit fox to know what they had in mind.

"You know, it's bad enough that Professor Magic brings his girlfriend over all the time," I said. "If this becomes regular, no one's getting any sleep."

"You have nothing to worry about," Blue Fox said. "Those two led such busy lives, they hardly get any time to spend together. I just wanted to make sure they enjoy the time they do have to share."

"That was almost sweet," I said.

"It *is* sweet," Blue Fox said, looking insulted. "*Baka.*"

"I still don't get how someone who sleeps around as much as you do can still have a romantic view on sex," I said.

"How could I not? I love the idea of bringing pleasure. Passion is passion, love is love. Life is too short to be miserable and secluded all the time," she replied, sitting down on the couch with some tea.

"You don't think that having it all the time cheapens it?" I asked.

"Does a food critic hate fine dining because he eats good food all the time?" She countered. "I'm a loving person. I have a lot to give, and I like the anonymity of it. I know that getting into a relationship would be a bad move for me, and unfair to my partner."

"I don't buy it," I said. "I still think you want to look somewhat innocent."

"You don't have to believe me," she said with a sigh. "But I live my life the way I want to. I've never felt the need to hide who I am from the world."

"You wear a mask and use a moniker."

"You know what I mean," she said. I chuckled.

"Yeah, I know. But I wasn't going to pass that up," I said. "I can respect that line of thought."

"Good to know," Blue Fox said. "So, tell me more about this Alistair-san."

"No," I said.

"What? Why?" Blue Fox said.

"Because it didn't work out the way I wanted," I said, feeling the mental walls go up. "Alistair is one of many reasons I don't go home or talk about my past."

"Silver…" Blue Fox said gently.

"Look, you might be all about free love and all, but not everyone feels the same way," I said. "If you ask someone to sleep with you, what's the worst thing that they could say?"

"No?" she guessed.

"He got sick. Physically sick," I said coldly. Blue Fox's eyes widened, then it clicked.

"Oh," she said. "I'm sorry, I wasn't thinking."

"It's okay," I said. "Romance isn't something that interests me anymore."

"I understand," she said softly. She straightened and tried a smile. "Hey, do you wanna watch a movie?"

"Sure," I said, recognizing the olive branch she was extending. "What do we have?"

Just then, a golden circle emerged in front of the fireplace. Lab Rat, Professor Magic and Dragonman came tumbling out.

"Argh!" Lab Rat groaned as Dragonman flopped onto him.

"Sorry!" The big guy said, trying to lift himself up. I saw Professor Magic's hand reach out and close the portal. All three were smoking, and parts of their costumes were still smoldering. The three guys managed to untangle themselves.

"You just *had* to burn the place down!" Lab Rat complained.

"I didn't see you coming up with any genius ideas!" Dragonman argued. Professor Magic only laughed.

"Did you see the look on that twat's face when the place went up in flames?" Professor Magic asked, pantomiming a look of horror. He laughed again.

"Alright, no more magic powder for you," Dragonman said, standing up and helping the Wizard to his feet.

"The hell have you three been?" Blue Fox asked.

"Mexico," Lab Rat said.

"Why?" she asked. Professor Magic giggled again.

"We were tracking down a drug ring," Dragonman said, dusting himself off.

"And what happened to Professor Magic?" she asked, putting her hands on her hips like a pissed off mother. I sipped my cocoa and watched the show.

"He got a minor blast of some of the stuff they were cooking," Dragonman said idly.

"These gloves feel fucking *weird!*" the Professor said, opening and closing his hands and staring at them.

"How much of what?" she asked, sounding more and more upset.

"40 cc of…" Lab Rat started before Dragonman nudged him to be quiet.

"It's nothing," Dragonman said hurriedly. "He just needs some rest, that's all."

"Oh, right. We're supposed to give him water and rest," Lab Rat said. It sounded like he was reciting practiced lines, but it was hard to tell with his monotone.

"Hey, Professor," I said, holding up my phone to film him. "How are you feeling?"

"Silverbolt!" He said happily. "Did you know that the mushrooms make plans?"

"Will you shut up about that?" Dragonman said harshly. "Get back here, you're going to bed."

"Mushrooms…" he whispered, as if he were sharing a private joke between us. I nodded at him knowingly. He winked at me, then Dragonman picked him up and slung him over his shoulder.

"Dragonman, get back here!" Blue Fox said, stomping after him. "You are going to tell me *exactly* what the hell you three were doing in Mexico!" After they left, I looked over at Lab Rat. He removed his helmet and let out a sigh of relief.

"Alright, tell me what happened," I asked.

"Dragonman said not to," Lab Rat said. "Blue Fox won't like it."

"Dude, do I look like Blue Fox?" I asked. "I want to know what Professor Magic is on and how I can get some for myself."

"He said you would say that too," Lab Rat said sadly. He looked around, frowning.

"Where's Thundergirl?" he asked.

"We had to rescue her boyfriend," I said. "She's… ah, 'attending' to him upstairs."

"Is he hurt? Blue Fox would be a better person to look after him," Lab Rat said with concern. "She has a medical degree after all."

"They're having sex, Lab Rat," I said flatly.

"Oh. You could've just said that," Lab Rat said. "Who kidnapped him this time?"

"Tell you what. Story for a story," I said, holding out my hand. "I'll tell you what happened to us if you tell me what happened in Mexico." He stared down at my hand, thinking about it.

"Alright," he said, shaking my hand. "Deal. Here's what happened…"

To be continued…

Story 5: Drug Money

Chapter 1: The Lads

"You are so full of it," Professor Magic argued.

"Look, Triceratops is a punk," Dragonman said. "One on one, I could easily take it."

"That thing charges you, you're dead," Professor Magic replied. "Rat, how big are they?"

"About 30 feet long," I said, not looking up from my work in the back of the van. I fit another cable in and turned the machine on again. I heard the fans spin up, but nothing on the display. I scowled at the device. What was I missing?

"30 feet is nothing," Dragonman said. "Triceratops was a social creature, it had a herd to back it up. Alone, I could get around its horns and flank it."

"Not if it can turn fast enough," Professor Magic said. "Rat, what were the rules?"

"It was what dinosaurs you think you could take in a fight. No preparation, standard equipment only," I replied for the third time. Forgetting things always terrified me. The idea of information leaving your brain just gave me the shivers.

"How much space do we get?" Dragonman asked.

"Same as the Roman colosseum," I said. Again.

"See?" Dragonman said. "Plenty of room." Professor Magic crossed his arms.

"Alright, tough guy. How about a T-Rex?"

"Easy."

"Oh, come off it!" Professor Magic said. "You've said you could take every dinosaur I've mentioned."

"Yeah, because I totally could. T Rex is all hype," Dragonman said. I shook my head and turned on my music so I could focus better. I've got odd tastes, but my usual playlists had 80s synthwave, classical music, and anime theme songs. I knew I was missing something for this thing to work. I looked up at the giant black box we nabbed from the last hideout we raided. The Hijos de Salomon, or the Sons of Solomon, were a cartel we were hunting. I had dug up some info on a drug ring they were running out of the middle of nowhere in the Chihuahua Desert. We found one of their locations, but it had been abandoned. I recovered a server terminal and loaded it into the back of the van while we drove around looking for where the Sons had run off to. I bit my lip in frustration. The fans would come on easily enough, so there was power going into that. I wasn't seeing any warning lights, so what was wrong with this thing? It wasn't that old. I fished around the inside of the server and checked for any loose wires or broken pieces. Maybe there was something I missed. I felt a loose wire and checked it. I frowned at the cable, then plugged it in and powered it up. The screen lit up and the server lights flickered on. I wanted to kick myself. I've been called the smartest person in the world, and with good reason. I've outsmarted criminals and masterminds for years, even the FBI and the best hitmen a CEO could afford. I've built astonishing machines out of scrap and trash for the last five years.

And I didn't plug in the damn monitor. I frowned at the machine, and then at my friends. I wondered if their idiocy was rubbing off on me. I turned off my music and leaned into the front seats.

"Fixed it," I said, interrupting Professor Magic.

"I… Oh," he said. "What was wrong with it?"

"Operator issue with the display function. Had to reroute necessary power to it," I replied simply. Professor Magic just stared at me.

"Forget I asked," he said. Professor Magic is probably the worst when it comes to technology. He has thousands of years of experience and knowledge, yet he still types with one finger. It's infuriating.

"What did you find on it?" Dragonman asked. Dragonman is better with tech, even if he doesn't truly understand it. He grew up in the late 1700s, and he finds technology fascinating. He still stares at airplanes in awe sometimes, and excitedly watches shows about sports cars. He marvels at how fast mankind is adapting and inventing. The only problem is that he stays up late drinking and watching DIY videos. I've caught him in our scrapyard at 3am drunkenly trying to make his own coil gun. He would've lost his hand had I not shown up in time.

"Hadn't had time to check," I said. "Seeing how I literally just finished it."

"Ah," Dragonman said. "Hey Rat, I've got a guy question for you."

"What is it?"

"You a breast man or an ass man?" he asked.

"What?"

"Don't ask him that!" Professor Magic said sharply.

"Why not?"

"It's sexist and degrading to women," Professor Magic asked.

"Oh please," Dragonman said. "There's nothing sexist about appreciating the female form."

"The most attractive part of a woman is her mind and personality," Professor Magic said stubbornly.

"No shit, Professor Obvious," Dragonman shot back. "I'm asking you guys to be disgusting pigs. Be filthy, uncultured barbarians for 3 seconds with me. Now: Tits or Ass?" Professor Magic was quiet for a bit before saying:

"Arianna has a nice ass," he said quietly.

"There we go! Was that so hard?" Dragonman said. "How about you, Rat?"

"I'm more of a legs guy," I replied, loading a hacker program onto the server.

"Oooh, nice," Dragonman said. "That's a rare one, but just as valid."

"You?" I replied.

"Breasts. Call me old-fashioned, but that's how I like 'em," Dragonman said.

"I can't imagine someone like you gets a lot of women," Professor Magic said.

"I don't, but it's about quality, not quantity," Dragonman said sagely.

"Well, that's something we can agree on," Professor Magic muttered darkly. I ignored them and focused back on the server. My hacker program, Labyrinth.exe, shut down the servers' defenses in seconds. I started sifting through files, my eyes flickering across data sheets and info. I've always been good at figuring out data and making calculations. Math and science came as naturally to me as breathing, and my idea of a good time was spent in a dark room in front of a screen calculating. Formulae, coding, and making something new were what gave me the biggest highs. I know some people find this type of thing boring, but to me, it was as exciting as a rollercoaster or a good movie. I saved useful data like shipping manifests, personnel, and ingredients onto my personal hard drive. I checked over a list containing something I found interesting. It was a chemical formula that looked oddly familiar. I frowned at it and ran it by other formulae I had seen before.

According to my knowledge of chemistry, this was some sort of steroid. It promoted aggression, muscle growth, and sociopathic tendencies. What were the Sons of Solomon doing with a drug like this?

"Hey, who's hungry?" Dragonman asked, cutting off my train of thought. "I'm starving."

"You're always starving," Professor Magic complained. "But I could eat."

"Well, we're in Mexico. There should be a place we could get some decent grub at somewhere around here," Dragonman said. "You guys been to Chihuahua before?"

"Until we got here, I thought it was just a breed of dog," Professor Magic said.

"Go north," I said.

"Why?" Dragonman asked, already making the turn.

"The Sons moved up to Juarez," I said. "From there they've been sending drugs up into El Paso."

"Has it been just to America?" Professor Magic asked.

"Previously, they have been smuggling weapons into Venezuela and Colombia and getting cocaine out of those countries," I said, reading off their shipping manifests and trade deals. "The Sons have made a ton of money from setting other cartels up with each other. They take a percentage of sales made between cartels they set up."

"Like a matchmaker for drug dealers?" Professor Magic said.

"A bit pedestrian, but yes," I said. "They've risen in power relatively unseen for years. But now they've got something else going on."

"Meaning?" Dragonman asked.

"Two years ago, they started mass-producing their own kind of drug, instead of smuggling other cartels'. Something I've never seen before," I said. "Whatever it is, it looks like some kind of steroid."

"That doesn't sound good," Professor Magic said.

"No, it doesn't," I agreed. "It seems they've… Oh no."

"What's wrong?" Dragonman asked.

"I know this person," I said, pointing at the screen. Dragonman kept his eyes on the road, while Professor Magic twisted around to look at it.

"Dr. Alice Alvarez," I said. "Didn't know she got her doctorate."

"How do you know her?" the Professor asked.

"We were lab partners in high school," I said. "Brilliant kid."

"You sure it's her?" Dragonman asked.

"Of course," I said. "I remember all my classmates from all my schooling." Dragonman merely grunted.

"What is your old high school lab partner doing with a Mexican drug cartel?" Professor Magic asked.

"Good question," I said. "She was always gifted when it came to chemistry. Maybe she's helping them with this new drug."

"What does it do?" Professor Magic asked.

"According to my calculations, it strengthens the skeletal and cardiovascular system, promotes muscle growth, aggression and immunity," I said.

"That doesn't sound like a drug," Dragonman said with a scowl. "That sounds like a super soldier serum."

"Not another one…" Professor Magic muttered.

"I wouldn't call it that," I said. "According to this, it really messes up your brain."

"How so?" Professor Magic asked.

"Well, it lowers inhibitions while ramping up aggression. It kills nerve endings, which ups pain tolerance," I said. "It would make you stronger but turn you into a drooling monster."

"How the hell are they making money off of something like that?" Professor Magic asked.

"What do you mean?" Dragonman asked.

"If they are mass producing it, then someone is paying for it," Professor Magic said. "Who the hell would be interested in buying a drug that turns you into an uncaffeinated Dragonman?"

"Hey!"

"It's worse than that," I said. "The side effects on this are brutal. Organ failure, acne problems, fertility issues, light sensitivity, blood clotting, baldness, and overheating."

"Overheating?" Dragonman asked.

"It can cause your body's thermoregulation to spiral out of control, and your body literally cooks itself to death."

"So a fever," Professor Magic said.

"A fever that could fry an egg," I said.

"Oh."

"Professor Magic's got a point," I said. "Who the hell would want to buy this?"

"Well, we're about to find out," Dragonman said. "Welcome to Ciudad Juarez."

Chapter 2: The City of Juarez

The suburbs of Juarez were massive. Houses sprawled across the dusty desert for miles in every direction. I had only seen satellite photos of the place online, but in person was something else entirely. Dragonman was still hungry, and I needed time to compile the data I had extracted. We drove around, looking for a place to eat and likely buy out. We headed north into the city proper and found a small hole in the wall restaurant, the kind of place we usually went to. I liked them because the small area meant we were more likely to see an attack coming, and places like this weren't normally targeted. Dragonman swears up and down that food cooked by a family-owned small business tastes better than any processed crap, and Professor Magic prefers to support local businesses than corporations, which is something I strongly agree with. Whatever it was called, the name painted on the side of the building had peeled off years ago, but the sign said they were open, so we walked in. It was only a tiny bit cooler inside the building, given that we were now out of the sun, and an old worn fan stubbornly spun in the corner, turning left and right slightly. There were only three tables in the dining area, and no one else was dining. Steam rose from the kitchen area, where we could see an older woman slaving over a stove. The entire restaurant smelled strongly of spices, chilli peppers, and roasted meat. A tired-looking woman was sitting on a plastic chair by the door. She wore jean shorts, a t-shirt and an apron with a notepad tucked into the pouch. She was on her phone when we entered and looked up when we entered.

"Welcome to Abuela Rosa's," she recited, pulling out menus. "Three?"

"Yes please," Dragonman replied in perfect Mexican Spanish. She looked surprised at that but led us to one of the tables.

"Not that one," I said to her in Spanish. "The one in the corner," she paused, rolled her eyes, and led us to the corner table.

"Could've said that better," Professor Magic whispered to me in English.

"I always take corner seats when I can. It's safer in case we get attacked. Here, I can see everything that goes on in here."

"I know," he said. "But you came off as a rude American tourist."

"Oh. Should I apologize?" I asked.

"Too late now," he said as he looked over the menu. I sighed. I can calculate an entire calendar year in advance, sketch a perfect image of a person, memorize entire languages, and create an arsenal of equipment and tools out of everyday items. I've withstood poisons, disease, and other technological horrors, but people always confuse me. I've always been direct, saying what's on my mind and telling people how I feel. I know it comes off as rude or insensitive, but it's just me. I never mean to insult people, but it still happens. I frowned and pulled out the menu. I checked it over and decided to order something small and meager. My metabolism was augmented from my time in Alley Cat, and I get more nutrition than normal people from the same amount of food. It also lasts longer.

Knives plunged into my flesh, blood spurting out from the incision as another growth was extracted. The scientists discussed how best to treat it, as I groaned in pain.

"Swap out its heart again. This one's no good…"

"Rat!" Dragonman said.

"What?" I snapped.

"You okay?" he asked gently. I took a steadying beath.

"Yeah," I lied. "I'm fine."

"You sure?"

"Of course," I said. I pulled out my latest invention, a type of pick that could vibrate to shatter stone and cement with a touch. I just needed to adjust the frequency.

"You looked like you saw a ghost," Professor Magic said.

"I told you, I'm fine," I said, growing irritated. "If you must know, the fan was getting too loud and bothering me."

"We can ask them to turn it off…"

"No, I'm fine. I'll just get a water and some chips," I said, focusing on my pick. I started rocking back and forth, which always calmed me down.

Fucking Alley Cat. I could never escape the nightmares of that horrible place. Where I was objectified and humiliated, nothing more than a test subject for cruel scientists making bioweapons and curing them, again and again. Augmenting my body with chemicals and hormones in order to test the full limits of human resistance and survivability.

"Igneous rocks make up 90% of the Earth's crust, formed from magma flows from the mantle…" I muttered, focusing on my favorite subject: Geology. I could talk about rock formations for years on end. It was an interesting subject that brought me joy. I rocked back and forth and focused on my tool. I could feel Dragonman and Professor Magic's gaze on me. I hated to make them worry, but I knew how to deal with this. I had been dealing with sensory overload my entire life, and the abuse I got from Alley Cat was ancient history. In order to move past it, I focused on what I could do. Build, invent and solve problems.

"What can I get you?" The waitress asked us.

"I'll take the carnitas," Professor Magic asked.

"I'll have the pork tacos, steak tacos, the shrimp…" Dragonman trailed off. "Actually, one of each meat dish you have. Hold the lettuce and tomato." The waitress stared at him, then looked at me.

"I'll have the shredded beef tacos, and the strongest tequila you have," I replied.

"We have El Luchador, is that okay?" the waitress asked me.

"Sure, why not," I said, watching the other guy's reaction. One bonus I got is that my body processes toxins way faster than they could. I once drank bleach and other cleaning chemicals from under the sink with no ill effect because I was mad at Blue Fox. I drank the entire team under the table without a headache and pounded an entire keg of beer in order to distract a group of college kids while

Thundergirl stole some data from one of their laptops. I can't get drunk, so I do this to remind the other Jesters that I'm not some child they need to protect. Once the waitress left, I put down my pickaxe and pulled up the data I got.

"Alright, so we're looking for a place where they synthesize this drug. My guess is that it's somewhere close to the border, seeing how they only care about getting it into America," I said.

"Why here?" Professor Magic asked.

"Because El Paso is just across the border. Chances are they have some place to receive it. Mexico is in a unique area, where they have access to a lot of drug trafficking. Corruption in police and other government bodies here means it's easier for them to smuggle drugs around the Americas," I explained. "They make the serum here, then export it to America."

"So they likely have the cops off their backs," Dragonman surmised, his attention partially on the kitchen, where the waitress was trying to explain Dragonman's massive order.

"Which is where we come in," I said.

"So, how are they making it?" Professor Magic asked. "If we could trace where they get their ingredients from, we could follow it to where they are synthesizing it."

"I like that idea," Dragonman rumbled thoughtfully.

"Let's see," I said, checking the lists. "Here's something. A company in Brazil created a chemical compound that's used to reduce myostatin."

"Myo-what now?" Professor Magic asked.

"Myostatin is a hormone in the body that reduces muscle mass. You remember that kid in Asia who was really buff at the age of 6?" I asked.

"I think I heard about that," he said thoughtfully.

"Well, that kid had a naturally low amount of myostatin," I explained. "Therefore, his body packed on more muscle than he needed."

"Was he in pain?" Dragonman asked.

"Apart from some muscle tightness, he was perfectly fine. But this chemical from Brazil, called Bright 32, was designed for cattle."

"Cattle?"

"More muscle means more meat. More meat per cow means more money," I said.

"Ah," Dragonman said. Mine and Professor Magic's meals came, which Dragonman looked at forlornly. I pounded back half of the tequila in a single pull and set it down roughly.

"Ahh. Anyways, Bright 32 is being used to make this new serum," I continued. "If we can follow the shipments, we can follow it to where they're making it."

"So where is it coming in from?" Professor Magic asked, digging into his taco. I removed my helmet and dug in as well. Holy shit, that was good. The meat was tender and juicy, the rice light and fluffy, and the salsa was fresh and full of plump chunks of tomatoes. Dragonman saw the looks on our faces and turned his attention fully on the kitchen.

"Good question," I said between bites. I gulped down more tequila and checked my data. "No ports nearby, so it's either by truck or air."

"We passed an airport on the way in," Professor Magic pointed out.

"True," I said. "I can check for recent flights from Brazil, see if it's being smuggled in through there." As we were discussing this, a group of rough-looking men entered the building. They were covered in muscle, scars, and tattoos. Sure, that doesn't guarantee they were thugs. What tipped me off was their posture. Constant awareness of their surroundings, one of them spoke to the waitress while the others looked around. I put my helmet back on and ran a facial recognition scan on them. Sons of Solomon, all five.

"Hola!" One of the sicarios called out as he walked up to us. "What's with the get-up?"

"Excuse me?" Professor Magic asked.

"Hey, I'm not one to judge, but it's a little hot to be walking around in all black! And a cape too!" He said with a laugh. I monitored his accent and placed him somewhere in Tijuana. According to his record, his name was Juan Sanchez-Carro. I checked his Facebook, Instagram, and Twitter, then started compiling a profile for him. All hands-free, mind you. Thundergirl calls it 'technokinesis', which is a ridiculous term for my ability to manipulate technology. Alley Cat installed a neural monitor in the back of my head so they could check on my mental state during their experiments. I refitted it to be a neural transmitter. I can use all my devices as long as they are connected to my transmitter, which is controlled by my brain. In a few moments, I knew everything I needed to about Juan Sanchez-Carro.

"Listen, Senor Sanchez-Carro," I said. "Or can I call you Juan?"

"What was that, midget?" he asked harshly.

"I asked you if I could call you Juan," I repeated. "My friends and I are currently enjoying lunch. By ourselves. I suggest you go back to your friends before Senorita Bella Rodriguez finds out about Senoritas Anna, Judith, and Maria. Both Marias." His jaw dropped open in shock.

"What did you just say?"

"You deaf or something?" I asked. "I said, walk away or I cancel your wedding with three pictures and a message to your fiancé, sicario. I can't imagine your future brother in law will be too pleased to hear you broke his sister's heart with your whoremongering." Juan glared at me, clenching his jaw. I popped my helmet off and took another swig of tequila. He swung his hand out to knock it out of my hands. I spat what tequila I had in my mouth into his eyes. He yelped and clapped his hands over his eyes. I stood up and donned my helmet again. His friends heard us and drew their weapons. Professor Magic rose to help me, but I waved him down.

"Don't worry, I got this," I said as Juan reached into his pocket and pulled out a switch blade.

"You're fucking dead, American!" I kicked him in the jaw, then cranked up my forcefield to the max. The bullets slammed into it and fell to the ground harmlessly. I drew my taser guns and fired a few blasts at them, forcing them to stop and seek cover. I ducked down. The forcefield was down more power than I usually use, but I couldn't let the bullets ricochet in here. I crept around the table in the middle and fired a blast of knockout gas in one of the sicario's face. He gasped and fell unconscious.

"3 left," I muttered. One of the sicarios leapt and shouted, taking aim at my head. My shoulder cannon whirred to life and aimed at his gun. Before he could fire, a blue blast of light fired out, shattering his gun into tiny shards. He fell to the ground, screaming in pain at his broken fingers. My motion sensor went off behind me, and my pack's robot arm reached out and caught the sicario by the throat. He gagged, but I held him there. The last one made a break for the door. I flung my bolo at him, something Silverbolt and I made recently. It tied his hand to the door handle, and I fired another electro blast at him and knocked him out. I walked calmly up to the man whose fingers I broke, dragging the other sicario with me by his neck. I kicked him in the temple with just enough force to knock him out. My mechanical arm swung the sicario around to face me, and I looked him in the eyes.

"Who sent you?" I asked.

"Fuck you, I'll never talk," he gasped in English. I punched him in the gut, making him choke.

"I'm going to ask you again," I said. "Next time, I ask my friends if they want a turn. Now, tell me who sent you or else."

"Or else what, pendejo?"

"Or else you get to learn firsthand how much pain and injury a human body can endure without dying," I threatened. I whipped out my acetylene torch and ignited it for emphasis. He stared at it fearfully, then swallowed.

"Orders came from up top," he stammered. "Someone broke into one of our old bases and stole intel. We were told to look for the Jesters."

"Why the Jesters?"

"I don't know! Apparently, they knew you'd be there, and they told us to look for you in Juarez!"

"How many are looking for us?"

"I don't know!"

"You don't know much, do you?" I asked.

"Not really," he admitted. I sighed and let go of his throat.

"Fine. First thing that's going to happen is that you and your goons are going to pay these people for wrecking their restaurant. Then, you will all go and have a nice day out doing nothing. 24 hours, or I tell your kids what their papa does for a living," I said.

"How…" he started. I held up a holographic photo of his family.

"Investment broker, really? With facial tattoos? Come on," I said. This time, he looked truly terrified. "Also, if I find out you and your goons try and get your money back, I will *personally* ensure that Thundergirl finds your house and tears it apart piece by piece. I don't have to read out your address aloud for you to understand how easy it would be for me to find it, do I?" He shook his head.

"Good. Now pay the nice woman back there and let us eat," I said. I walked back over to our table and sat back down. The guys were staring at me.

"Wow," Professor Magic said. "That was impressive."

"Told you I could handle it," I said. The waitress timidly walked up to us with Dragonman's massive meal. She placed it in front of him and scurried off to start putting the chairs and tables back up. I stood and started helping her. She looked up at me fearfully.

"I'm sorry about this," I said. "I didn't want your place to get trashed, honestly."

"It's… okay," she said. "I thought you guys were here in for some costume party or something."

"We get that a lot," I said.

"So, you're the real Jesters?"

"Half of them. I'm Lab Rat, and over there is Professor Magic and Dragonman."

"Yeah, I figured that out. You guys are kinda famous," she said.

"More like infamous. We're considered criminals back home," I admitted.

"Really? I thought you were heroes," she said.

"Depends on who you ask. Seeing how American laws are made with millions and millions of dollars, we're the bad guys," I said.

"How so?"

"I've exposed a lot of wealthy corporate leaders," I said. "Cost them a fortune just to get one picture of me."

"Is that the one of you flipping off the camera?" she asked.

"So you've seen it before," I said. She laughed.

"Everyone's heard of you guys. A bunch of crazy Americans who fight bad guys. I wasn't sure how true it was."

"A lot of it isn't," I said. "Some of the rumors are just plain crazy." I picked up the fallen bullets.

"Which ones?" she asked.

"Mostly the ones about our financial status. We don't have billions of dollars to spend on tech. I stole most of mine from a scrapyard," I said. She smiled at me and laughed.

"Guess you can't always believe everything you here," she said.

"Guess not. What's your name?" I asked.

"Maria," she said. "It's a horrible, common name."

"I think it's pretty," I said. "Like your earrings."

"My earrings?" she asked, touching them self-consciously. "These ugly things?"

"Ugly? That's aquamarine. It's a beautiful type of beryl stones. It's March's birthstone and was said to calm the seas," I said. "It's a truly beautiful stone."

"My friends always made fun of me for buying them."

"Well, looks like you have better taste than your friends," I replied. She looked at me nervously, still fiddling with her earrings.

"Will… Will you be in Juarez long?" she asked.

"Probably not," I admitted. "Long enough to take out these creeps and head back up north."

"Oh," she said. "Well, maybe you could come back here before you leave?"

"Maybe," I said. "But most of our exits involve us dodging gunfire."

"Oh. Well, can I get your number then?" she asked. Immediately, alarm bells started sounding in my head. Threat analysis began instantly. Why was she asking for that info? Was she part of the cartel? Could she be luring me into a false sense of security? What if Task Force 52 got their hands on it?

I looked at her face, and she looked genuine. Just like the rest of them…

I had lucked out with the Jesters, although they were in the same boat as me. This girl, a waitress tucked away in an empty dilapidated restaurant had everything to gain my selling me out. Then again, I had redundancies in place…

"Here," I said, and I gave her the number to one of my burner phones. "I can't promise I'll call, but I won't forget you." She beamed at me and gave me hers. She wrote mine down, but I didn't bother with hers. I remember it perfectly.

"Maria!" the chef called. "Get back here and help your brother with the dishes!"

"Coming, Abuela!" She called back and walked back to the kitchen. I walked back over to our table and sat back down.

"Damn," Professor Magic said.

"What?" I asked.

"You are a lot smoother with women than I thought," he said.

"Oh, don't give me that," I said.

"I'm serious! She looked like she was into you."

"So?"

"You gonna call her?" Dragonman asked.

"Maybe. We have a drug cartel to take down first," I pointed out. Dragonman shrugged and took another bite of his meal. He had already finished half of it during my conversation with Maria.

"Lab Rat, you better take this seriously," Professor Magic chided. "It would be cruel to get her hopes up like that."

"Look, I'll call her if I remember," I said.

"Lab Rat…" he warned.

"Look, we have a mission to take care of," I said. I glanced back over at where Maria had disappeared. I hadn't noticed it before, but she had *very* nice legs.

Chapter 3: Air Delivery

After paying for our meal and driving off, I started checking things online. Criminal records, social media posts, pictures, police accounts, and other extraneous data to create a map of where the Sons of Solomon would normally group up. It was a difficult and time-consuming process, but I started seeing patterns emerge. God bless the new generation and their obsession with selfies. There was an airport just outside of Juarez that had a fair amount of Sons activity around it. I gave the address to Dragonman, who nodded and started driving us there.

"So if I understand this correctly, the Sons of Solomon have normally been doing small-time smuggling and making deals between other cartels, right?" Dragonman asked.

"For the last 10 years, yeah," I said.

"So why make this new drug?" He asked.

"That's the million dollar question, isn't it?" I replied. "They had a fairly successful racket going before, but now they're trying something new."

"Hmm," Professor Magic said.

"Something on your mind?" Dragonman asked.

"Do you think someone requested they make this drug?" Professor Magic suggested.

"What do you mean?" I asked.

"It's like a commission. Someone orders this drug to be made and pays them for it," Professor Magic said. "It makes more sense than people just shooting up with this shite in the streets."

"Maybe," I said. "Any reason for this line of thought?"

"Nothing in particular," he said thoughtfully. "Just occurred to me."

"We shouldn't assume anything until we know for certain," Dragonman said wisely. We pulled up to the airport and parked. It was a small place, likely for small planes and private jets. Chicken wire surrounded the property, topped with barbed wire to keep people from climbing over it. The place looked deserted.

"Lab Rat, who owns this place?" Professor Magic asked.

"Esteban Ramirez," I replied.

"Is he connected to the Sons?"

"He runs them," I said.

"Wait, this airport is owned by the guy who runs the Sons of Solomon?" Professor Magic asked. "Why didn't we check this place first?"

"He also owns several businesses, three golf courses, and a shipping company in the Gulf. You want to check those places too?" I asked.

"We're looking for an airport for them to smuggle drugs in, why wouldn't we look into his personal airport?"

"It's not his personal airport, it's used by the public. Also, just because he owns it doesn't mean it's related to his cartel. We're here because several of his goons have been here and forgot to turn their Location function on their phone off," I replied.

"Location?" he asked.

"Smartphones have trackers in them for GPS navigation," Dragonman explained. "Some apps use them as well, like the dating one Blue Fox tried."

"Huh," Professor Magic said. "Didn't know that."

"Good Lord, how do you not know this kind of stuff?" Dragonman asked. "You're younger than me."

"I just never got along with technology," Professor Magic admitted sheepishly. "I was raised by my very conservative aunt. She didn't think highly of computers or other tech."

"That's depressing," I said. "Technology is a beautiful subject."

"If you say so. I just don't have much use for it. Why bother with the internet when I have a library in my head? Why look something up when I can scry it?" Professor Magic asked.

"C'mon," Dragonman said. "Let's go check this place out." We all climbed out of the van and started looking around. I walked into the main building and scanned for security. All the cameras were set up to view the outside, not the inside. Interesting…

I disabled the cameras and started poking around. Dragonman leapt over the fence to investigate the airstrip. Professor Magic started working a spell to check for 'resonances'. Whatever that meant. I tried the door to find it locked. I frowned, then saw that it was closed for 'renovation'. Odd. I took out my small circular saw and cut through it in seconds.

Inside the building were a few luggage carousels, a ticket counter and a security checkpoint. I slipped past the checkpoint and started scanning for clues. Occasional fingerprints on handles and door knobs belonging to members of the cartel, a closed coffee shop with the shutters down, and a small restaurant. Nothing outwardly suspicious, apart from the lack of security.

"Lab Rat," I heard on my comms. It was Dragonman.

"Yeah?" I replied.

"There's an odd scent on the tarmac where something spilled. It's a clear shiny fluid. Kinda like oil. Think that's the bright stuff?" he asked.

"Could be. Describe the scent to me?" I asked, bringing up the chemical compound on my display.

"Very chemical smelling, like bleach or formaldehyde," he said. "Hint of metal, like blood or iron."

"Yeah, that's it," I said. "Can you follow it?"

"Sure," he said, hanging up. I thought it over. So, we at least have the Bright 32 present at this airport. No security, apart from something to keep an eye out for the cops. Public access, but they probably hired their own men to protect the airport themselves, as well as keep the public from seeing their illicit activities. Not a bad front. Senor Ramirez wasn't a fool.

If they were getting the drugs in from Brazil via airplane, then they must be loading them onto a vehicle to bring them to their lab to make the serum. Which meant there was a loading area. I looked around for a sign or map to use. I found a small 'You are Here' map and scanned it. My suit generated a 3D map of the place and I put it on my helmet's HUD. I checked the area and found a place that didn't match the satellite photos I had gotten from the internet on the way here. Cross-referencing it, there was a place the general public wasn't supposed to see or know about. An area connected to the road.

Bingo.

I headed over to the missing zone and found an 'Employees Only' sign on a door. Once again locked. Electronically this time. I scanned the keypad and found four numbers with fingerprints on them. I arranged them in different orders, until I saw one that looked significant. Ramirez's wedding anniversary. I tapped it in, and the door unlocked. I shook my head ruefully. People always seem to make the same mistakes when it comes to security.

I walked inside to see a fairly open area where trucks could come and load up. I heard a soft clanging sound and turned to see Dragonman kick one of the doors down. His magic powers made it quieter, but still left evidence behind. I sighed.

"Subtle as ever," I told him.

"Scent leads here," he said, ignoring my jab. "How did you find this place?"

"Floorplan doesn't match satellite images," I replied. "This is a place they don't want people knowing about."

"Figures. My theory is that someone dropped a case or packet of the bright stuff and it spilled all over everything. Lead me straight here," Dragonman said.

"Makes sense. Human error is the usual downfall to systems like this," I said. I started scanning where the trucks would stop for tire tracks.

"Trail goes cold," Dragonman said. "They must've cleaned it up. You got something in mind?"

"I hope so," I said. Scans weren't showing anything useful.

"If I could get some of their blood, I could follow them no problem," Dragonman said, looking around the warehouse.

"Should've thought of that at the restaurant."

"Nah, that wouldn't work. I track where they are, not where they've been. Besides, I can't imagine your little girlfriend would be too pleased with me biting necks and drinking blood," Dragonman said.

"She's not my girlfriend. I just met her," I pointed out.

"Yeah, but she looked like she was into you," Dragonman said.

"I know she was," I said. "I'm not an idiot."

"I never said you were."

"Good," I said. "If you are done examining my love life, we have a cartel to take down."

"Fair enough," Dragonman said. He went quiet for a bit, and I looked over at him. He was checking some boxes that were stacked up, and he was biting his lip. I sighed.

"What?" I asked him.

"Hmm?"

"You have something you wanted to ask me. Ask."

"It's not important."

"Just get it out. It's gonna bother us both if you don't ask."

"Alright. You ever been with a woman?"

"I've been around women. The girls in the Jesters, females on the street, occasional allies," I said. "I'm familiar with female psychology, if that's what you meant."

"No, like… in a biblical sense."

"At church?" I asked.

"No, like… intimate," he said.

"Are you asking if I've slept with anyone before?" I asked him.

"It's okay if you don't want to answer," he said.

"Once."

"I mean, I'm not judging you if you haven't…" he started. "Wait what?"

"In high school, I was elected Prom King, and my date Prom Queen. She was invited to a party, and I went with her. We snuck off together and did it there," I said simply.

"You were Prom King?" he asked.

"Does it surprise you?" I asked, checking more data from my scans.

"Well, yeah. You don't seem the type," he said.

"It's not uncommon for special needs kids to win. It was a pity award, something the student body did, as if they felt bad for the autistic kid who freaked out when the cafeteria got too noisy," I said. "That, or some of them thought the idea of the geeky awkward kid was matched up with the cheerleading captain would be funny."

"That's… messed up," Dragonman said, sniffing around the shuttered doors.

"At the time, sure. I always stuck out in school. The only black kid in a small town, the kid without a dad, the kid with autism who watched cartoons too much. I was a high school bully buffet."

"You didn't have a dad?" Dragonman asked.

"My mother had me when she was 17. My grandfather was the local pastor, and the idea of his daughter having a kid out of wedlock embarrassed him. He wanted her to marry my father, but no one knew who he was or where he went. I was born, despite all the birth control my mother took. It was harder for the old man when he found out I was autistic," I said.

"That's horrible!"

"Yeah, but senior year was the best. I had gotten tons of college requests, I qualified for the best scholarships for the best schools, and I got with the queen bee at my school, who was incredibly nice to me after Prom. If I got Prom King as a prank for people to make fun of me more, it backfired horribly," I said. "When I left for college, I laughed in my grandfather's face, asked him what he thought of me then."

"What did he say?" Dragonman asked, lifting a few crates to look underneath.

"Told me if I thought so highly of myself, that I should leave. Get out of town and never come back," I replied.

"That's rough," Dragonman said. "High school sounds brutal. Glad I never had to deal with it."

"It's a bunch of children metamorphosizing to adulthood. It's gonna get weird," I replied. I sighed at the data streams. "Dammit, I got nothing here. You?"

"Nothing," Dragonman said sadly. "This place is dead. They must've scrubbed it before emptying the place out."

"Must've," I agreed.

"There you two are!" Professor Magic said. "I was wondering where you lot went."

"You could've called us on comms," I pointed out.

"Couldn't figure out how to work it," he admitted.

"You push the button and talk," I said simply.

"Oh. Well, good news. I found out how to track them," Professor Magic said.

"Excellent," I said. "What do you have?" Professor Magic grinned and held up a tiny person by the ankles. I started back in shock.

"Is that what I think it is?" Dragonman asked.

"El Duende," Professor Magic confirmed. "Local sprite."

"Let me go!" the tiny creature shrieked in Spanish. Its accent was a mix of Mexican, European Spanish and something else. Older, maybe Mayan? It looked like a garden gnome or a leprechaun. It wore a simple vest and loincloth, scavenged from trash and old cloth.

"Tell them what you told me," Professor Magic said sternly.

"Never! Liars! Cheats! I'll take your toes!" El Duende howled. I frowned at that last part. Maybe my Spanish isn't as good as I thought it was.

"I thought Duende were house spirits," Dragonman said. "What's he doing here?"

"This was a home, warm with food and hearth!" Duende wailed. "But nasty humans came and tore it down! They arrived in trucks and wagons that ate the earth! Poured hot liquid stone and burned the grass! Oh, how horrible!"

"Enough caterwauling," Professor Magic said, giving the tiny thing another shake. "Tell them what you told me."

"Foul Wizard! Accursed godling!" El Duende cried. "Fine! The thieves who lived here took boxes and crates from their metal birds and carried them here!"

"Where do the boxes go?" Dragonman asked.

"North!" El Duende said. "North, north they go!"

"And what did you take from them?" Professor Magic asked, as if scolding a child.

"It's mine!" El Duende yelled, thrashing about. "It's mine, I took it!"

"What did he take?" I asked.

"One of the sicario's phones," Professor Magic said.

"Seriously?" I asked excitedly. "That would be huge!"

"Yeah. All we need now is El Duende here to tell us where he hid it."

"Never! Foreigners! Thieves! I'll cut off your toes while you sleep!"

"You're in no position to be cutting off anyone's anything," Dragonman snarled. "Talk spirit!"

"Papist!" El Duende spat. "Your kind ruined this land!"

"Enough threats," Professor Magic said. "All we need is the phone and we'll let you go."

"No!" It wailed. "I stole it! Those foul men corrupt this place and hurt people! They shoot down birds and let the meat go to waste! They abuse their wives and children, but I cannot stop them!"

"Wait, you're fighting against the cartels?" I asked.

"I don't know what that word means, but I hate the men here!" El Duende said venomously. "I won't give them back their little squares, no matter what!"

"We don't need the phone, just the data on it," I said. "We're trying to find the evil men who were here so we can stop them."

"Truly?" El Duende asked, pausing his thrashing.

"Truly. All I need is the data on the phone, and you can have it back," I said.

"Lies! You're trying to trick me!" he called.

"No tricks," I said. "Just tell us where the phone is so I can copy everything on it, and we'll let you go."

"Hrrmmm," El Duende said, thinking it over. "Let me go, and I will show you."

"No," I said. "You'll just run off and leave us here. Tell us where it is."

"Fine," he said hotly. "There is a small tunnel made of metal down on the floor. I hid everything behind the metal door."

"Metal tunnel…" I said. "Oh, a vent?" El Duende just stared at me. I walked over to one of the vents and checked the grate. It was loose and could be lifted up like a door. I opened it, and a snake lashed out and bit me in the arm. Thankfully, my suit was tough enough to prevent the snake's fangs from getting into my skin. El Duende cackled.

"Ha!" he crowed. "Got you!" I pulled the snake from my arm and put it down. It slithered away and out the doorway Dragonman made.

"Anyways," I said and reached into the vent and fished around. "Here we go."

"Wait, you were bit by the snake!" El Duende said. "You should be dying now!"

"It only got a mouthful of my armor," I replied. "The fangs never reached my skin. Besides, snake venom doesn't even affect me anymore."

"What!?" El Duende shrieked. "No!"

"Now, let's see," I said and I tried to unlock the phone. Nothing. Must've died after it was stolen. I popped the back off and pulled out the SD card and slotted it into my gauntlet.

My HUD showed all the files on the card, and I started checking locations, contacts, and messages.

"Hey! What's he doing?" El Duende asked. Professor Magic squeezed harder on his ankles.

"Quiet you. You already tried to kill him," Professor Magic said. "Maybe we should feed you to Dragonman." Dragonman bared his teeth in a snarl, giving the gnome a good look at his sharp fangs and tusks.

"No! Wait! I dealt with you in good faith! I gave you the square!" El Duende begged.

"You didn't mention the snake," Professor Magic said.

"Leave him," I said. "We got what we needed."

"You sure?" Dragonman said.

"Yeah," I said. "Before you go, little man…" I said, getting in his face. "I don't forget. When I hold a grudge, I hold on tight. So you remember that, because I will remember how to tried to get a Fer-de-Lance snake to bite me."

"Your threats mean nothing to me, human," El Duende said. "I was here long before your filthy kind came here, I will still be here after you are gone!"

"Then you will have a long time to remember me when I cut off *your* toes," I threatened back. I nodded to Professor Magic, who dropped the gnome-thing onto his head. He scrambled to his feet and scurried out the door.

"Well, that thing was creepy," I said, repressing a shudder.

"Yeah," Dragonman said, letting out a pent up breath. "I hate dealing with the Wee Folk."

"So, what did you get?" Professor Magic asked, wiping his gloved hand on his cape.

"Drop off location," I said, reading the message.

"Nice!" Dragonman said.

"North from here, like the gnome said," I continued. "Just shy of the border."

"They're making drugs that close?" Professor Magic asked.

"Looks like it," I said.

"That's awfully bold of them," he said with a scowl.

"Yeah, but it fits," I replied. "Makes it easier for them to get the drugs over the border."

"Well, what are we waiting for?" Dragonman said. "Let's finish this fight!"

Chapter 4: Borderline

"That's the border?" Professor Magic asked.

"Yep," I said.

"With all the fuss I hear about it, I figured it would be bigger," Professor Magic said. "I mean, it's a fence."

"Well, they never got that wall built," Dragonman said. "Can't say I'm surprised."

"So, where is the drop off location?" Professor Magic asked me.

"There's a small lab not far from here," I said. "According to the message, they just drop off the shipments and leave."

"They don't stick around? Get paid for their actions?" Dragonman asked.

"Let me rephrase that," I said. "They're *supposed* to just drop off the drugs and leave."

"Ahh," Dragonman said, a grin spreading across his face. We were walking down the street, a place where most American tourists would dare venture. Graffiti covered the walls around us, and people walked fast and didn't try to draw attention to themselves.

"Hey hey!" a young man called out. I looked over at where the voice came from. A group of young men were walking up to us.

"Keep walking," Dragonman hissed. "Just ignore them."

"Were you three-headed?" he continued. His goons were now blocking the way. Professor Magic tried to walk past him, but the man sidestepped to block him.

"Hey now! Senor, I'm trying to talk to you!" he insisted.

"I'm not," Professor Magic replied coldly.

"Oh ho! Look here, we got us a Spaniard!" he said with a laugh, looking back at his goons with a smile. "Where you from, old man?"

"He said we're not interested," Dragonman snarled, stepping up and lowering his head to look the guy in the face.

"What's the issue, big guy?" the man asked. "I'm trying to be welcoming here! I've never seen you three in this part of town before. You lost?"

"No, we're not," Dragonman said. "We're in a hurry, and I hate being interrupted."

"We're not looking for trouble," I said. The man laughed.

"You came to the wrong neighborhood then! There's nothing but trouble here!" He gestured to his goons, and they all pulled out knives and small weapons. We readied ourselves as well.

"I'm gonna say this once. Turn around and find a different path to your costume party," he said, his voice colder and threatening."

"You are either going to move yourselves across the street," Professor Magic said. "Or I will move you across the continent."

"Try me, old bastard," the man snarled. Professor Magic lowered his staff and aimed it at the man's collarbone.

"Auras!" he cried. A ripple of air shot out from the end of his staff and struck the man in the chest, sending him flying back. The other thugs sprang into action One of the men charged forward with a chain swinging over his head, only to be hit with Dragonman's iron-shod club. I heard bones crack as he flew. The other thugs backed up, eyeing us nervously.

"Oh, what's wrong?" I taunted. "Seven to three, and you guys get cold feet?" I walked forward, and some of them shuffled back.

"Weak shit man," I said, shaking my head. "Just weak. Now run off before we get serious."

"Hold your ground, pendejos!" the first man called. We all looked over at him. He had stood up and was walking back to us, no worse for wear. The front of his shirt was torn, and he was dirty from where he landed, but he lacked the usual bruise that comes with a spell like that.

"Doctor de la Muerte fixed us up with the good stuff," he said, as a blue glow filled his eyes. "Just do as she said, and these putos can't touch us!" He knocked his fist into his chest and his muscles swelled. The other men started doing the same, and we were soon surrounded by angry glowing eyes. The three of us stood back to back. Dragonman stomped his foot and growled, psyching himself up for the fight. I heard Professor Magic start muttering a spell under his breath, and the air around him hummed with power. I pulled out a small baton that extended into a full-size staff. With a tap on the button, the end of it cooled and froze the air around it until a chunk of ice formed around it. I swung the Kelvin hammer around a bit. Man, this would be a perfect test of the new weapon.

"Well then, Jesters." The lead man said. "Any last words?"

"Yeah. This is a new invention, so can I get some feedback and criticism after I kick your ass?" I asked. He snarled in frustration.

"Kill them all!"

I ducked the first punch from the nearest guy and slammed my hammer into his kneecap. It bent out and he fell to the ground. Rather than scream out in pain, he growled in frustration and tried to sit up. Before I could hit him again, I was grabbed from behind by another thug and thrown across the street. I landed awkwardly on my back, my mechanical pack digging into my spine painfully. The goon who threw men pounced on me, pinning me with his legs. I tried to douse him in knockout gas, but he grabbed my forearm and crushed the dispenser in his grasp.

"Shit!" I hissed. My mechanical arm lashed out and tried to push him off, but he stayed firm like a mountain. I changed tactics and jammed two fingers of the metal arm into his eyeball. He grunted in pain and flinched, giving me enough leverage to get him off of me. I grabbed my Kelvin hammer and slammed the frozen head into his head. The blow was enough to knock him down, but he stayed conscious. I let out a cry and hit him again and again. It took three blows to put him down. I panted in effort. This wasn't good. These guys were tough, tougher than they had any right to be. A broken knee only slowed them down, and getting their eyes literally poked out was a minor inconvenience. Our only chance of stopping them was killing them.

Killing is a touchy subject with us. We're not eager to dole out death, and our no murder policy has earned us a lot of respect and support. Without that support, we ran the risk of being a bigger risk to the US government. These guys weren't giving us much of a chance and would easily snap our necks if we let them.

No, killing wasn't the only way. They were tough, but the laws of physics still held. Without their limbs, they would be unable to pursue us.

"Guys!" I shouted. "Carpe Pedes!" Hopefully, they could hear me. Professor Magic was dueling with two of the supermen, his staff blazing with white light in his left hand, a sword made of fire in his right. Dragonman was dealing with three of them, one on his back clawing at his head, the other two dancing around his legs. The men had all ditched their weapons in favor of tearing us apart with their bare hands. Unfortunately, my friends hadn't heard me.

"Right," I said to myself. "Time to even the field." I ran up to one of the thugs attacking Dragonman, who had his back to me. I swung my hammer right into the base of his spine. I heard a loud crack as his spine split, paralyzing him. He screamed and went down. I turned and swung the hammer down onto the shoulder of one of the men attacking Professor Magic. His arm went limp as I popped it from his socket. He glanced down at his arm, distracting him long enough for Professor Magic to catch him in the face with his staff. The man staggered back, blinded by the light. I drew an electro gun and cranked it up to just shy of lethal and fired it into his back. He grunted in pain but started thrashing and went down. I panted. Fighting is exhausting, but these guys showed no signs of stopping. My hammer swings were getting slower and weaker. Thankfully, the guys pulled through. Dragonman grabbed the man off his back and slammed him against the pavement. Unlike the movies, the pavement didn't break. The man did. I heard bones pop and snap, and blood shot from his mouth. The other guy caught Dragonman's club right in the chest and was launched into a telephone pole. I saw him bend and almost wrap around it. His spine was clearly broken, but he was still moving.

"Heyge!" Professor Magic cried out. A blast of dazzling prismatic light shot out and enveloped the man. He screamed in terror as he shrank down. Hair and spines sprouted out of his skin. Within a few seconds, the last man had been turned into a tiny hedgehog. I dropped to my knee and panted. Christ, most fights don't normally last that long.

"Everyone okay?" Dragonman asked. I gave him a tired thumbs up. Professor Magic mopped sweat from his face and nodded.

"So, I assume that these guys had taken the serum," he said.

"Would appear so," I said. "Are they dead?"

"Surprisingly, no," Dragonman said. "I can hear them all breathing," he sounded just fine. Battling off several superhumans at once was something Dragonman not only handled but thrived at. If anything, he sounded more relaxed. The hedgehog was still snarling and biting at Professor Magic's ankles, but he paid it no mind.

"That was intense," Professor Magic said, getting his breath back. "Think we should call in the girls?"

"We can handle this ourselves," Dragonman said. "Besides, Silverbolt said she was taking the day off."

"We could use Thundergirl's help," I said. "Wouldn't mind having a psychic supersoldier on our side."

"We'll be fine," Dragonman said, offering me a hand to help me up. I took it and he pulled me up to my feet.

"Besides, you handled yourself pretty well. Love the hammer."

"Oh, this?" I said, holding it up. The ice on the end had turned pink with blood and had bits of skin frozen to it. I pressed a button on the handle and the head melted off.

"Yeah. It's pretty cool," he said with a smirk. Professor Magic and I winced at the pun.

"We should get moving." Professor Magic said. "The cartels are probably watching this place and might be sending more guys."

"Or the cops show up," Dragonman said.

"Or both," I replied. "The Sons have police on the take." On that cheery note, we started moving down the street towards where the lab was.

The fight had taken too long, and the place was empty. The lab had been in a classic crack den with a dead lawn, a broken car in the front yard, graffitied walls, the front door hanging by a hinge.

"Shit," Dragonman said. "We're too late."

"Maybe not," I said. "They couldn't have been gone too long." I jogged up to the front door and walked in.

Thankfully, my helmet filtered out the acrid smell of burnt chemicals. Dragonman wrinkled his nose as he entered.

"Ugh, smells like death in here," he said. I checked the door.

"Recently broken," I said. "The wood underneath is still fresh." I checked deeper in the house. The other two followed me.

"Ground floor wouldn't be safe for the lab equipment to be used. This place would burn up in seconds," I muttered to myself. I checked a door and found stairs leading to the basement. I walked down, my mind racing. The basement was mostly empty, aside from a few barrels, a card table, and some lab equipment. I saw the barrels and froze.

"Wait," I said, holding up my hand. The two froze in place, watching me. I shifted my helmet display to infrared.

"Thought so," I said. "Laser trip wires."

"Let me guess," Dragonman said. "Those barrels are wired to explode if someone comes down here to check and they get blown up in a fiery explosion?"

"Along with any evidence as well," I said.

"Can you disarm it?" he asked.

"Maybe," I said. "It's a wireless connection, so maybe I can tap into it." Professor Magic scowled at the barrels.

"What's in them?"

"Jet fuel," I replied. Professor Magic nodded and closed his eyes. I heard him mutter a spell and walk forward.

"Wait!" I shouted. I tackled him to the ground and fired up my force shield. I was running low on power, but hopefully it would be enough to keep us alive. Dragonman could handle fire just fine, I only hoped his wounds would heal fast enough. I braced myself for the explosion and waited.

Nothing.

I frowned and looked around. The basement was intact, and the barrels hadn't gone off. What the hell?

"I appreciate the concern, but you can get off me," Professor Magic said.

"What?" I asked.

"I turned the jet fuel into harmless mineral water," he said simply. "The detonator short-circuited itself and didn't explode. I stared at him. Dragonman, who had previously been crouched down bracing himself for the explosion, walked over to a barrel and opened it up.

"He's right," Dragonman said in amazement. "It's just water." I got up and glared at Professor Magic.

"You could've said something, you dick," I said hotly.

"My apologies," he said. "I was about to, but you tackled me to the ground."

"I meant before," I said.

"I had a perfectly good one-liner ready, before you jumped on me," Professor Magic asked.

"Which was?"

"Well, I'm not going to say it now! You missed your chance," Professor Magic said stubbornly.

"Guys," Dragonman said, checking the evidence. "Come look at this." We walked over to check over the documents.

"They clearly left in a hurry," Dragonman said. "All electronics were taken away, but some papers were left."

"Sketches and diagrams," I said, checking them over. "This is Alvarez's handwriting."

"You're sure?" Professor Magic asked.

"I told you, I remember everything," I said. "Electronic models are good and all, but sometimes you need to write it out yourself." I leafed through the notes, checking the diagrams and formulae.

"Well?" Dragonman asked.

"She's still testing it out," I said. "Some sort of work order…"

"Wait, really?" Professor Magic asked. "Wow, I should've put money on it."

"No kidding," I said. "According to this, she's trying to solve the mania that comes from it. Isolate parts of the human mind related to empathy."

"Make it so it's easier to kill people," Dragonman said in horror.

"Exactly. But the problem is that without empathy, her test subjects are going insane. They start killing at random," I said.

"Isn't that what she wants?" Professor Magic asked.

"No, she wants soldiers, not monsters," I replied. "Men who will kill on command, who can fight for days without exhaustion, and won't complain when it gets tough."

"Who the hell is this for?" Dragonman asked. "The military?"

"No clue. Doesn't say," I said. "This is just the science behind it."

"So where did they go?" Professor Magic asked.

"Well, let's see," I said. "They set up a lab down here close to the border to smuggle it into the states for a client. A super fight breaks out between goons set up to guard the place and the Jesters. They know we're coming for them and set a trap for us. As far as they know, this place will destroy all their evidence."

"Except it didn't, and we're still fine," Dragonman said.

"What if it did?" Professor Magic asked.

"What do you mean?" I asked.

"If the bomb did go off, it would likely kill us and destroy their evidence, right?"

"Presumably," I said.

"Well, they would lower their guard once they thought we were taken care of," Professor Magic said.

"Not until they knew for certain," Dragonman said. "They would check the place for bodies to confirm our deaths."

"So if the place did blow up, they would send someone to check it out," Professor Magic said. We all perked up at that.

"Professor, you sly bastard," I said with a grin. "You can turn that water back into jet fuel, right?"

"Sure can," he said. "But the detonator is still shot."

"Leave that to me," I said, pulling out a pack of C4. "I never miss a chance to blow something up."

Chapter 5: Fireworks

The explosion was terrific. A brilliant column of fire and smoke rose into the air with a blast of hot air. The shockwave shattered windows and glass in the entire block, which was regrettable, but this had to look convincing. Once the blast had subsided, we waited in cover to see who arrived. After what felt like forever, a police car showed up to check the scene. Professor Magic looked disappointed, but I motioned for him to be quiet. It was only one cop, which didn't seem right to me. I pulled out one of my drone mice and steered it to the cop silently. I activated its microphone and connected it to our comms so we could all listen in.

"Mother of God…" the cop said, shaking his head at the smoke column. He grabbed his radio and hit a button.

"Dispatch, this is Cardenas. I'm at the site. Yes sir, the house just blew up. Must've been a gas leak or a meth lab. It's a miracle no one was hurt," he went quiet for a bit. "Yes sir, I'll stand by." He hung up the radio and pulled out his cellphone.

"Hey boss, it's me. Yeah, I'm at the house. Blew up just like you said. What? Hell no, I'm not going in there! It's a million degrees, I'm getting cooked just standing next to it!

No, I don't think they're alive. How could they? Look, they might be superhumans, but if they're anything like the ones we have, they would have blundered right into it..." he winced. "My apologies sir, I meant no disrespect. Yes. Yes. Yes sir. It would take a genius to identify the corpses, even the big ones. No sir. Yes, I understand. I will. You too. And hey, Happy Birthday to your daughter. I'll drop off her present once I get off. Yes sir. I will," he hung up, and Dragonman crept up to him silently.

"Evening, Officer," he said. The cop spun around and Dragonman clamped a hand over his mouth. "Scream, and I break your neck." Cardenas froze, and nodded. I walked up to him and scanned him.

"No other electronic devices. He's good," I said. Professor Magic stepped through a portal to go get the van.

"What the hell? How are you alive??" He asked.

"A magician never reveals his secret," I said mysteriously. "Cuffs," he shook his head, so I hit him in the gut and plucked them from his belt. Dragonman spun him around and shoved him against his car. I cuffed his hands behind his back as Professor Magic came back with the van.

"I will never adjust to how you Americans drive on the wrong side of the road," he said, moving over to the passenger side. I opened the sliding door and pushed

Cardenas in. Dragonman hopped into the driver's seat and we took off down the road.

"So, who were you on the phone with?" I asked. I sat across from the officer and moved some of the equipment out of the way.

"No one," he said. "I no speak English…"

"Don't worry, we all speak Spanish just fine," I replied in his native tongue. He wilted at that.

"I'm telling you, no one! I was just checking out an explosion!" He said. I leaned forward and took his phone out.

"Let's see about that," I said. I tapped on his phone a bit, and I was in. "Jesus man, you have Esteban Ramirez saved as a contact on your phone?"

"That's my cousin," he said quickly. "It's a common name."

"Oh, I'm sure," I said. "So, how about you stop messing around and tell us where the drug lab got moved to."

"Drug lab?" he asked. I hit him in the stomach again.

"I said stop messing around. Where did the Serum get dropped off at?"

"I don't know! They don't tell me anything! I just look the other way when something happens and tip them off to raids! Please, they'll kill my son if I don't work with them!" he sobbed.

"He telling the truth?" Professor Magic asked.

"Mostly. He doesn't have a son, but I don't think he knows anything about Alvarez," I said. "How about Esteban?"

"What?"

"Esteban Ramirez. Head honcho of Juarez. The only son of Solomon Ramirez. King pin of Chihuahua. Where can we find him?" I asked.

"You... you want to talk to Ramirez?" he asked fearfully.

"You dumb or something?" I asked. "That's exactly what I asked. Now, where is he?"

"I-I can't tell you that! He'll kill me if he finds out I told you!" he sobbed.

"Blame the Wizard," Dragonman called from the front. "It's what I always do."

"What?" Cardenas asked. I punched him in the nose.

"I hear you say 'what' again I will throw you out of this van," I threatened. "You can deny helping us, but I frankly don't care what happens to a cop who sold out to the cartels. Now, where is Esteban Ramirez?"

"He… he lives up in Lomas del Pedregal!" He finally said. "He has a mansion up there!"

"See? That wasn't so hard," I said.

"But it's his daughter's quinceanera!" he said. "Security will be tighter than ever!"

"Not a problem for us," I said. "You just worry about what you're gonna do once the Sons stop paying you after we tear the cartel down."

"What?" he said.

"Okay, that's it," I said. I opened the van door and shoved Cardenas out. He screamed the whole time, even though Dragonman slowed down enough to not kill him.

"You know where to find Lomas del Pedregal?" I asked Dragonman.

"I've been there before, hunting a tlahuelpuchi once," he said.

"A *what*?"

"A type of vampire," he said. He turned and started driving faster. Soon, we were out of the dangerous part of town and passed more and more expensive houses and manors. Soon, we found the biggest house in the neighborhood. The house had a massive yard, and cars were parked up and down the street. It was perched up on a hill, and we could hear the thudding of dance music from down the street. We circled around until we found a place to park and walked up to the gate. A lazy looking security guard was on his phone, not paying attention to us.

"Invitations?" he asked, stifling a yawn.

"Hi, we're here as entertainment," Professor Magic said.

"Oh?" he said and looked up at us. His eyes widened in shock.

"Yeah," Professor Magic said. "Could you tell the boss that a trio of Jesters arrived and need to speak with him in the kitchen? Something in our contract we have to work out before we perform." The guard fumbled for his gun and I hit him with an electro shock. Thankfully, he wasn't a superhuman, so he went down easily. I reached into the shack and grabbed a radio. I relayed the message to the head of security, then put a virus on the security monitors that played a loop of the last hour of footage over and over. We walked up to the mansion and headed for the kitchen.

"What the hell is this about!?" Esteban exclaimed, storming into his lavish kitchen. "I didn't hire any clowns!"

"Esteban!" We all called out jovially. He froze when he saw us. We had made ourselves at home and had dug into the food out on display for guests. We had made a bit of a mess, but figured he could afford it.

"You…" He started.

"Us," Professor Magic said. "Come, sit with us! We were celebrating your daughter's birthday. Fifteen, that's a huge milestone." Esteban's eyes shifted from each of us to the door.

"Wouldn't try to run if I were you," I said. "Your security has been dealt with."

"I assume you're here to kill me?" he asked evenly.

"Kill you?" Dragonman said through a mouthful of pork. "Nah, we told you. We're here to celebrate."

"Celebrate, mingle, talk," Professor Magic said. "Come, sit with us." Esteban slowly approached us and sat himself down. Dragonman had availed himself of almost all the meat available. His goblin powers made all but invisible in a crowd, so no one had noticed a 7 foot tall giant with horns, gray skin, and a trench coat waltz into the thick of the party and steal half of the pig they were roasting. He had finished off several carnitas, quesadillas, and other Mexican dishes I didn't recognize. He wasn't being neat about it either, dripping sauce and grease all over the marble table and floor.

"So," Esteban said, eyeing us with disgust. "What did you want to talk about?"

"Aside from the fact that you are disgusting criminal scum that profits off of ruined lives and lives in excess?" I asked. "Well, how about we talk about the super soldier serum you've been making?"

"I don't know what you're talking about," Esteban said tightly.

"Cute," Professor Magic said. "Real cute."

"Hey, guys! He's got glass bottle Cokes in here!" Dragonman said, investigating the fridge. "The good kind, made with real sugar cane. You guys want some?"

"I'll take one," I said. Dragonman tossed me a bottle. I didn't react as it sailed past my head and shattered on the floor, brown sugary liquid spreading across the expensive stone floor, and into the carpet of the neighboring living room. A vein bulged in Esteban's forehead, but he kept his cool.

"Oops," I said. "I missed it. Toss me another one." Dragonman chuckled and tossed me one. I waited until the last possible second before snatching it out of the air.

"You think this is funny?" Esteban said. "Breaking into my home and making a mess?"

"Hey, we're called the Jesters for a reason," Professor Magic said. "But all things considered, you *did* try to kill us."

"It's only fair," Dragonman said before noisily gulping down a bottle of Coke and belching loudly.

"Anyways," I said. "Back to what I was saying. There is a powerful serum being developed by your cartel, one that almost got us killed by some street thugs I assumed you hired to guard your lab."

"I don't know what you're talking about," Esteban repeated.

"Still playing dumb, eh?" Professor Magic asked. "Running the Sons of Solomon for this long without getting killed by another gang or getting caught by Interpol takes brains. You've either survived this long by luck or intelligence, and no one's luck lasts this long. Now, quit acting like an idiot."

"You really think you can get me to talk by making a mess?" Esteban said with a laugh. "What happens if I don't speak, you spill milk on my floor?"

"Lab Rat, how's his healthcare?" Professor Magic asked.

"Outstanding. Has access to the best hospital and doctors in North America," I replied.

"Perfect. Dragonman?" Professor Magic said, gesturing towards the kingpin. Dragonman, who had silently made his way behind Esteban, slammed his gauntleted fist onto Esteban's wrist, snapping it. To his credit, the drug lord didn't scream. He bared his teeth and hissed. His broken wrist began to swell and bruise instantly.

"And for the record," Dragonman said as he pulled out a carton of milk from the fridge. "Thanks for the idea," he lobbed it into the living room where it burst against the wall and spilled all over the carpet.

"So, you can start telling us where to find Dr. Alvarez, or we start breaking bones," Professor Magic said.

"You think you can threaten me?" Esteban hissed, reaching for the ice bucket where champagne was kept. Professor Magic muttered a word and the bucket slid out of reach. Esteban scowled at him, but continued. "I've killed dozens of men to get to where I am. There's nothing you can threaten me with because I've done worse than you. I've killed a man with a belt sander, used a drill to open a woman's skull because her husband owed me money. I've seen men die in excruciating pain. I know who and what you are. Cowards. You fail to pull the trigger because you're scared. Death terrifies you, and you can't bring yourselves to make that plunge into darkness. You call yourselves warriors, but cannot bring yourselves to kill," he spat onto my helmet. I let it sit there, then calmly grabbed a napkin and wiped it off. Then I looked him in the eye, and grabbed his broken wrist and twisted it 180 degrees. This time he howled in pain.

"Let's see how much you can endure, Esteban Ramirez. Let's see how far I can push your body, test your anatomy. I want to see how well you can handle pain. I've seen men taken apart and put back together again. I've heard women scream and beg for death. I've craved death myself, been plunged into that black abyss over and over like a yo-yo. You think death is the worst thing a person can grant?" I whispered in his ear. "Do not doubt my capacity for cruelty. I've seen things that make your little business dealings look like children's programing."

"You're all talk…" Esteban gasped.

"Am I?" I asked. I grabbed his phone from his pocket and unlocked it. "How much does your lovely daughter know about you?"

"What?"

"You heard me. Does she know this little party was paid for by girls her age being sold into slavery and kept loyal through drug addiction? Does she know how many men and women met their ends at your hands? What would she think of her doting father being the demon that keeps this city afraid?"

"You wouldn't," Esteban said hoarsely. I pulled out his phone and called his daughter.

"You tell me everything I want to know, and I don't turn your little princess against you forever," I said, my voice dripping with venom as the phone rang. Little Rosa Ramirez answered. I put her on speakerphone.

"Papa?" she asked. "Why are you calling me?" Esteban opened his mouth to answer her, and I hung up.

"She's looking for you, Ramirez," I snarled. "She finds us, I will show her everything that you've done. I have mountains of evidence. Nothing your lawyers can't handle in court, but enough to turn her away from you forever. She finds her way in here, and you will never get her back. Ever." Esteban looked scared now.

"Talk!" I said, and I squeezed his broken wrist.

"She's in El Paso!" He gasped. Tears streamed down his face. "She knows the Jesters are after her, her boss was hunting you all!"

"Who?" I asked. I let go of his wrist. He was broken now, no need to keep pushing him.

"I don't know! She never told us! We were given a vast amount of money for her protection! The Death Doctor works for him, all we had to do was let her work! Keep her safe, bring her ingredients and test subjects!"

"What else?" I asked.

"That's it, I swear! We were hired to protect her, that's all! I don't know who he is or what he wants, but I've seen the monsters she makes! She used her drugs on my men and made them loyal to her! Told me to stay out of her affairs or she would send my own top men after me and my family! I never asked," he sobbed. I stared down at him. In less than 20 minutes, he went from a proud and dangerous man to a sobbing pathetic wretch. He broke down crying and weakly clutching his broken wrist. We weren't getting any more info out of him.

"Come on," I said. "Let's get gone." The others got up in silence and walked out. I stayed back to look at the broken man. He had sinned, greatly. He hurt others, profited off of their pain and death. He was an evil man. Evil, through and through. I had read his profile. All the claims he made before were true. I kept files on major criminals back at the Fortress of Destiny. I knew exactly what kind of man he was. It would be wise to eliminate him. Put down the rabid dog before he killed again.

"Papa?" A young female voice called out. I looked over to see a young Hispanic girl in a bubblegum pink dress and tiara walk in. "Papa!" she shrieked when she saw her father. She ran to his side as fast as she could, stumbling in what had to be heels.

"Hey, princess," Esteban choked out, forcing a smile.

"Papa, what happened?" She cried. "Are you alright?"

"I'm fine. Just hurt my wrist a bit, that's all," he said, hiding his shattered hand. "Nothing to worry about," Rosa wasn't buying it.

"Why did you call me?" She asked. "What are you doing here, and why is there soda all over the floor?"

"Oh that?" Esteban said. "I just slipped, that's all. I must've called you by mistake."

"Papa, you need help," she said.

"No, I'm fine," he said. Rosa looked around at the mess we had made. She would've seen me too, had I not activated my cloaking device as soon as she entered. She looked right at me though, as if she knew they weren't alone.

"Rosa," Esteban said, rising to his feet. "You know I love you more than anything, right?"

"Of course!" she said, looking back at her father.

"And you love me back, right?"

"Of course I love you Papa," she said. "Why do you ask?"

"I… nothing. Just wanted to…" he struggled to say. I turned and left. I accidentally stepped on a piece of broken glass as I left, and Rosa whipped her head around to face me. I kept walking and left them behind. I had done enough damage to this family for one night. Her father had sinned, but there was no reason to punish her for his misdeeds.

No reason to deprive her of a father. For now.

Chapter 6: El Paso

We drove towards the border in silence. The others had heard my threats to Ramirez and were trying to think of something to say. I scared them, and I didn't blame them. I scared myself, probably more than they realized.

"I'm not a monster," I said, more to myself than them.

"What's up?" Dragonman said.

"I'm not a monster," I said again.

"We know," Professor Magic said.

"It's just…" I struggled. "Hearing him say those things, after reading about them, it just hit me differently. He knew what he was doing, and he didn't care. He wanted to hurt and kill those people. It just made my blood boil."

"Same here," Dragonman said. "I hate that he's been doing it as well, and getting away with it."

"But what got me the most was when he called me a coward," I said. "Why did that get me more than him talking about killing people?" No one said anything.

"I'm not a proud person. I can take an insult. It's just…" I struggled.

"It's when someone like *that* calls you one," Dragonman said. "A true bastard through and through calls you a coward. You, who have dedicated yourself to a cause that is just and noble, has their life's work spit on, and he laughs at it. He knows who we are and what we do, the good we bring and the hope we inspire. It's when someone like that calls you a coward for resisting what he never could, and fighting for the people he stepped on. That's what he insulted. Not you or your pride, but everything you had fought for."

"How… how did you know all that?" I asked.

"I've been doing this for a while kid," Dragonman said with a chuckle. "It's happened to me a couple times before."

"Was all of that off the top of your head, or did you give that speech before?" Professor Magic asked.

"It's a superhero thing. Ask Thundergirl, we're supposed to give motivational speeches like that on the fly."

"Yeah yeah," Professor Magic said dismissively. "It's a bit rich coming from someone who denied being a hero for 200 years."

"Hey, only recent years count," Dragonman argued. "Most of my life, it was for a paycheck."

"You guys don't think I went too far, did you?" I asked.

"With scum like that guy, going too far meant chopping his head off and giving it to his daughter," Dragonman said. "Threatening to expose him like that was probably the best move."

"Yeah, that was bloody brilliant," Professor Magic said, sounding impressed. "All that about being dipped in and out of the abyss was dark and depressing, but I have to agree with you. You've been through some shit, mate."

"I thought I was going to kill him too," I said. "I'm always afraid my past will get to me and turn me into a monster."

"Look, I'll tell you the same thing I tell Blue Fox. You won't turn into a monster if you are scared of being one. The real monsters are the ones who don't care what kind of carnage they unleash. They aren't concerned about how other people feel, only about themselves," Dragonman said.

"He's right," Professor Magic said. "You won't be able to understand how a mind like Esteban's works because you couldn't possibly bring yourself to hurt someone like he does."

I didn't know what to say. I knew the others had suffered in their past, maybe not exactly like I had, but they understood my pain. And they knew how to ease it, as if they had suffered as I had. I smiled. They were good friends.

Good friends are the ones who see you in pain and understand it like they felt it, because they did. It hurts seeing a friend in pain. Sometimes you have to remember that your pain is a friend's pain too, and they can help you heal from it. It's easy to forget, but always worth remembering.

We soon approached the border, and instead of waiting our turn to be searched by the border patrol, we simply cut through Asgard and popped out into El Paso.

"Welcome to Texas," I said dryly. "All guests receive a cowboy hat and complementary gun."

"Okay, so I've heard of this place before, and my knowledge of all the states is rudimentary at best," Professor Magic said. "How much of the rumors about Texas are true?"

"What have you heard?" Dragonman asked.

"They all have guns, wear cowboy hats and boots and spend all their time grilling and reading the Bible," Professor Magic said.

"Sounds right to me," Dragonman said.

"Oh Lord..." Professor Magic said.

"The best part about Texas is that we can blame all our stereotypes on them," I said. "Guns everywhere? That's just Texas. Bible-bangers? Texas. Unhealthy eating? Texas."

"I get it," Professor Magic said. "Hey, is it true that Americans have to swear a pledge of allegiance to the American flag?"

"We don't swear it, we just recite it every day in school," I replied.

"Seriously!?" Professor Magic said. "I thought Thundergirl was just messing with me."

"I didn't think they actually went through with that," Dragonman said. "I remember when it was first written."

"How creepy was it then?" I asked.

"I found it a little cultish, but people were loving it," Dragonman said, shaking his head.

"So, our clue is 'somewhere is El Paso', right?" Professor Magic asked.

"Pretty much, yeah," I said. "But I can check to see where the Sons drop off their shipments to and look from there."

"Anything else we should be on the lookout for?" Dragonman asked.

"They know we're coming," I said. "They will likely be heavily fortified and…"

I was interrupted by all of our electronics going dark. My suit seized up, the servos that enhanced my strength froze.

"What the hell?" Dragonman snarled. He pulled over so we didn't hit anyone. A message scrolled across my helmet as a voice played on our comms.

"Greetings Jesters," the voice said. It was altered to sound deeper and menacing. "I know you are looking for me, and that anyone who gets in your way tends to get beaten. Poor Hector got the brunt of it. Nothing I can't fix, of course."

"Death Doctor," Professor Magic breathed.

"In the flesh," she replied. "I offer you a parley. Meet me at the Sun Bowl Stadium in one hour and we can discuss this like adults. Or, I send as many Barbarians as it takes to grind you into a paste. Choice is yours. Oh, and unlike you, I'm not too sentimental about the citizens getting caught in the middle."

Everything in the van powered back up, my suit unlocked itself, and the radio went back to playing the thrash metal Dragonman had been playing earlier. He muted the radio and sat in silence. Hell, we all did.

I was terrified, mortified, and embarrassed. I had just been hacked as easily as I hacked the villains we faced. My firewalls, once seen as invincible barriers of cyber-defense, had been bypassed with ease. My hands, which had always been steady, now shook. What the hell happened?

"Lab Rat?" Professor Magic asked. "You okay?"

"I…" I stammered. "We got hacked…"

"Yeah," Dragonman said. "You think she had anything to do with the Ringleader?"

The Ringleader was a villain we faced a short while ago, a nasty piece of work who not only knew our secret identities but made a theme park dedicated to our greatest weaknesses. I had been trapped in a hedge maze that played random sounds that sent me into a sensory overload. God, I could barely breathe in there…

"I don't think so," I said. "I checked our servers and files. Nothing had been hacked or broken into."

"Well, you also said your firewalls were unbreachable…" Professor Magic said.

"You trying to say something, Professor?" I snapped.

"No! I'm just saying that maybe we're out of our depths here," he said. "That maybe we're up against something stronger than us."

"No," I said. "I refuse to believe that there is someone out there who can hack our communications and data and not get noticed by me. No way in hell."

"Lab Rat, it's okay if you're not the smartest person, or the best hacker," Dragonman said gently.

"No, it is not okay if someone is better than me, and they're breeding a race of monsters!" I snarled. "I have to be the best to keep you guys safe! If these assholes dox us, we're finished! We'll all be locked away in separate prison cells for life!" They both stared at me.

"I will not allow those *morons* running this country keep us apart!" I said, furiously typing away at my datapad and holographic display. "No way!"

"… That's what you're scared of?" Professor Magic asked. "Being separated?" I sighed.

"This might come as a shock to you, but I don't have any friends outside the Jesters," I said. "Not a lot of kids wanted to be friends with someone who freaks out if a restaurant gets too loud, or doesn't always understand social cues, or someone who won't shut up about rocks. The closest thing I had to friends as a kid were a few jocks who paid me for test answers. Here, though…" I took a deep breath.

"You guys are nice to me. You listen to me. When things get too loud and overwhelming, you guys want to move somewhere quieter. I spent almost an hour talking to Silverbolt about rocks and geology once, and she just let me go on. Never interrupted me," I said. "You two always try to include me. I'm valued here. I belong, for once in my life. I'm not giving that up without a fight."

"Hell yeah," Dragonman said. "So, are we going to meet this psychopath at this stadium or what?"

"I say we go," I said. "I want to see this woman face to face. See the person who got past *my* firewalls."

"This sounds like a trap," Professor Magic said. "You sure we should just walk in?"

"Or run the risk of her setting those things loose on the city?" I asked. "That's not a question."

"Yeah," Dragonman said. "We let the trap spring closed on us, then pry them open and punch them in the face."

"That's not a plan."

"Then maybe you'll like this one," I said. I told them what I had in store for Dr. Alvarez when we arrived.

"That's insane," Professor Magic said. "And foolish."

"Yeah well, we *are* called the Jesters for a reason. A pack of fools," I countered.

"It's risky, bold, and could easily backfire at any given moment," Dragonman said. "I love it."

"Alright then," Professor Magic said with a sigh. "Looks like I've been outvoted."

"So we're in agreement then?" I said. They nodded, Professor Magic's nod more reluctant than Dragonman's. "Cool. Let's finish these bastards."

Chapter 7: American Football

The sun had sunk far below the horizon by the time we arrived at the stadium's parking lot.

"This is so stupid…" Professor Magic was saying as we exited the van and walked up to the stadium.

"You have a better idea?" Dragonman said.

"… No…" Professor Magic said.

"Then shut up," Dragonman said. "We can't afford to show these things any weakness."

We walked through the gates into the stadium itself. It was a large bowl-shaped structure, standard of pretty much all football stadiums in America.

"Bloody hell," Professor Magic said, looking around in awe. "What team plays here?"

"The UTEP Miners," I said.

"Is UTEP the name of their league, or…?"

"It stands for the University of Texas El Paso," I replied.

"Wait, this is all for a *school*?" he said. "This stadium belongs to amateur players!?"

"I wouldn't call college football players amateurs," Dragonman said.

"But these are students, right?" Professor Magic asked. "Not professionals?"

"Correct," Dragonman admitted. Professor Magic looked around some more and shook his head.

"The longer I stay in America, the less I understand it," he said. We walked around some more. The lights were all on, but the stadium itself was empty.

"Alright, where the hell is she?" Dragonman muttered. Right on cue, the speakers squealed to life.

"Well, I'll admit it. I didn't think you would show," Death Doctor's voice called out. "If only Task Force 52 had threatened more hostages, we could all be free of your meddling."

"Hey, don't blame us," I called out. "Someone else would've stepped up to stop you."

"Oh really? Who? Don't say the Stinger, he's been out of commission for years," Death Doctor replied.

"I thought this was a parley, Doctor," Dragonman said. "Yet you hide in the shadows, like a coward. Hardly a way to settle this like adults."

"You'll have to forgive my caution, Dragonman," Death Doctor replied. "I couldn't afford to take that sort of risk. Had I simply sat out in the open, Lab Rat would've found some way to take me out from a distance."

"You find her yet?" Professor Magic whispered to me.

"She's in the box seats," I whispered back.

"How much more time?" he asked.

"12 minutes, I think."

"We're here, Doctor," Dragonman said. "So you can come and meet us, or we come to you. I don't plan on shouting myself hoarse here!"

"Fair enough," she replied. "Come on up to the box seats. And in case it's not clear…" the lights dimmed, and small groups of people started filling in the seats. We could see their eyes glowing from here.

"This goes south at all, and I will give the order. Don't make me give the order," she warned.

"I bet that sounded way cooler in her head," Dragonman said as we walked towards the box seats. We made our way to the top-notch upper-class seats, high above all the peasant seats.

I never understood the appeal of sports. A group of people run around chasing a ball for millions of dollars, and people go buck wild for it. I mean, it's a game. If you love to play it, that's fine. But I would have an easier time understanding how to make a working warp drive than understanding how a sports team losing a game can ruin a person's weekend. Your favorite team of meatheads lost. Why are you crying?

Regardless, we made past the leering squads of what the Death Doctor called 'barbarians.' It was a fitting name. They were burly and raring for a fight. Our own barbarian kept growling and blowing smoke at them as we walked past, and more than once, Professor Magic and I had to stop him from starting a fight with one. We didn't have enough time to get into it with them. Not yet anyways…

Once we made it to the box seats, we finally met the Death Doctor. She was dressed in a skin-tight black latex dress, which I supposed was her idea of a black lab coat. She wore black lipstick, a pair of half-moon glasses, a nose ring connected to her right earring by a thin chain, and stiletto heels. Her hair was done up in a bun. The whole look made her look like the evil scientist from a porno. I couldn't help it, I burst out laughing when I saw her. My laughing and her stunned reaction drew laughter out of the other two, and soon all three of us were cracking up. She scowled at us and blushed slightly, her tanned skin hiding most of it.

"What the hell are you laughing at?" she demanded.

"What are you *wearing*?" I asked, calming down enough to breathe. "You look like a prostitute!"

"I am the Doctor of Death!" she insisted.

"Jesus Christ, I needed that laugh," Dragonman said, wiping away tears. "Someone get a picture of her, please."

"Okay, you want some constructive criticism?" Professor Magic said, cleaning his monocle on his cape. "First off, no one is threatening in heels like that. When shite hits the fan and you have to run, you are going nowhere in those foot traps."

"And the dress is too tight," I said. "Sure, it shows off your figure well enough, but there is no way you are going to put up a good enough fight. Can you even breathe in that?"

"I've created an army of supermen and threatened to unleash them on the unsuspecting public. I have the most notorious cartels eating out of the palm of my hand, and you are criticizing my wardrobe?" she asked.

"Having a proper look can work wonders," Dragonman said. "Trust us on this. But you just look ridiculous."

"I'm not about to take fashion tips from a guy wearing a trench coat, no shirt, black and white camo pants and metal gloves!"

"The coat is made from dragonhide, and is impervious to most weapons. It can turn into a set of wings I can use to glide," Dragonman said. "The pants are from an old monster-hunting uniform I used to wear, and they have enough pockets for my various tools and equipment. The gauntlets have retractable claws and protect my hands from harm. I don't wear a shirt because it would get burnt by my fire breath, be torn to shreds by attacking monsters, or be soaked in blood constantly. I can regenerate wounds easily, so it's cheaper and easier to go without one."

"I thought you worked hard for your abs and pecs, and that you weren't going to hide them behind clothing," I asked.

"Not now, Rat…" he hissed at me.

"Enough!" Alvarez said. "I didn't call you here to criticize my clothing!"

"True, but maybe you should've…" I muttered.

"I said enough! I have all the cards! I have the army of monsters! I am in control!" Alvarez fumed. "I am the Doctor of Death! The bringer of destruction! And I will have my revenge!"

"Oh no…" I heard Professor Magic say. I grinned. This was going *perfectly*.

"Revenge?" I asked. "Against what?"

"I'm glad you asked," she said with an evil chuckle. Oh, this was too easy. I got hacked by *this*?

"I know you, Lab Rat," she said, which caught me off guard. Did she recognize me from high school? This could get awkward.

"I remember when we first met. Of course, I didn't know your name. You were just Test Subject 21 to me," she said imperiously.

"What?" I asked.

"Yes, that's right. I, Dr. Alice Alvarez, the Doctor of Death, was once a humble scientist working for Alley Cat!" she declared proudly. I blinked at her. My old lab partner was one of my torturers?

"You probably don't remember me…" she said with an evil grin that belonged on an anime villain. "But I remember you well. Our best subject, the survivor. Our best lab rat. To think you kept the moniker we gave you."

"You were there?" I asked. "I don't remember your face."

"I always had to wear a hazmat suit," she admitted. "I was part of the bioweapon defense team, finding a way to counter the attacks with human augments. My steroid got its start with you, actually," she laughed. "Say hello to your brothers, Rat."

"First off, I don't see you as a mother figure, that's just creepy. Second, only close friends can call me 'Rat.'" I said. "Third, did you practice this in a mirror?"

"Stop that! Stop comparing me to cartoon villains!" She said, stomping a foot in anger. I expected her heel to snap off, but it held. Damn…

"Anyways, where was I? Ah yes, Alley Cat. Your escape ruined me. Alley Cat was looking for someone to blame, and they placed it on us! They said that we made you too strong, that you escaped from us because we made you a superhuman. Can you imagine the humiliation? The stigma that followed me in the scientific community? I would never work another lab again because of you!" she wailed dramatically.

"You sure that's because of me, or the fact that you were part of an unethical human experimentation experiment?" I asked.

"Oh please, you think Alley Cat is the only one? Plenty of other labs do the same to test subjects. Besides, you volunteered!" she argued.

"No, I was tricked," I said. "Besides, normal human lab rats have meager, humane experiments run on them, like behavior tests and social experiments. They don't get cancer or organ replacements."

"Bah!" She said dismissively. "It's not important! What is important is that… Are you on your phone!?" I looked over to see Professor Magic tapping on his phone.

"Sorry, my girlfriend just texted me. What were you saying?" he asked.

"I was explaining my dark and tragic backstory!" she yelled.

"Right, about how you abused people for money?" he said. "Look, I've heard all I need to about Alley Cat from him," he said, jerking a thumb over at me. "As soon as you said you were a part of that, I stopped listening."

"But… that was the most important part!" She said, deflating a bit. "You guys seriously don't care?"

"Ma'am, as soon as we saw you and your stilettos, we stopped taking you seriously," Dragonman said. "You look like you're dressed for a bachelor party, not world domination."

"You mean bachelorette party," she said. "Not bachelor."

"There are women at bachelor parties," Dragonman said.

"Oh my God!" She said with disgust, finally figuring out what he meant. "Did you just call me a whore!?"

"No, he said you were dressed as one," Professor Magic said.

"Of course not," Dragonman said. "But this is a costume, one for a drunken college Halloween party."

"With frat boys," I added.

"Lots of frat boys," Dragonman said seriously.

"I…" she started, but couldn't figure out what to say. Honestly, getting mocked by people you are trying to kill had to toss a wrench into her plans pretty well, which was my plan. I just needed her to keep talking.

"Hey, how did you break past my defenses like that?" I asked her.

"Huh?" she asked, which was the final nail in the coffin of her looking like a real villainess.

"No one has ever hacked me like that before," I said. "One techie to another."

"Ha! It was simple. Your defenses are not as mighty as you claim!" she said, getting her villain stride back. I heard Dragonman groan and take a seat, ready to wait her out. She noticed, but didn't say anything about it. "I knew you would go after one of our server farms, so I left a little surprise for you. Nestled in with the rest of our data was a virus that would open your system to me. I could track you and message you as much as I could."

"Huh," I said. "You know what, that's actually really smart. I'll have to check for that next time."

"Ha ha!" she said, regaining her former zeal. "And now, I shall exact my revenge!"

"Oh no," I said dryly. "And how would you do that, I wonder?"

"Simple. I outnumber you 50 to 3! You could barely handle seven of my lovelies, so 50 of my finest creations would be more than you could hope to handle," she said triumphantly. "Speaking of which, you remember Hector, don't you?" The door opened to reveal the same thug who accosted us on the streets in Juarez. This time, he looked better prepared for it. He was dressed in black body armor and carried a pair of batons. He was breathing hard through a gas mask, and glared at us through the visor of his helmet, his glowing blue eyes burning with pure hatred.

"Damn," I said. "Are they all dressed like that?" I asked.

"This armor is just a prototype," she said, as if she were selling it to an investor. "Soon, my entire army will be this well-equipped."

"So it's really just one on three then, seeing how you won't be taking part in the fight," I said. "I assume that dress doesn't hide any secret weapons, and your footwork would be shaky at best in those heels."

"I told you, I have 50 soldiers at my command!" she protested. Dragonman's ears suddenly perked up.

"They're here," he told me. I sighed in relief.

"They took their sweet time," I said.

"Who?" she asked. "You called in reinforcements?"

"Sort of."

"Who would you call to help you? You wouldn't send in your fans to fight for you, would you?"

"No, of course not. We just called in a superhuman fighting expert," I said.

"What?" she asked. "Is Thundergirl out there?"

"Please, we don't rely on her as much as people think," I said. "I called in Task Force 52."

"You…" she said, her jaw dropping open. "You called them!?"

"Yeah," I said. "People don't really understand this, but they are trained to take down threats that fall 'outside' normal investigation. Sure, their job is to arrest us, but we aren't the only super threat out there. Other superheroes less successful than us exist, and the new laws against vigilantism means that there needed to be someone designated to hunt down superheroes and bring them to justice."

"But, they're just normal people!" she said. "My army was meant to surpass human capability! You just sent them in to die."

"Dragonman, cover your eyes," I said. He sighed and moved an arm over his face. One of my shoulder cannons swiveled around to face Hector and fired a blast of white light at him. He screamed in agony and clawed at his eyes, dropping his batons, and writhing in pain.

"See, your army is ferocious, but they have a glaring weakness: their eyes. They are super vulnerable to bright lights. I told 52 to come in with flashbangs and tear gas. They should be taking down your army with ease now," I said.

"We struggled with the seven earlier because I didn't figure it out until recently. See, Professor Magic was using a light spell with great efficiency. I was curious as to how it work so well, so I checked your notes again. Their eyes are sharper, but sensitive. As are their other senses. Tear gas is twice as painful for them, as is pepper spray."

"What!?" Death Doctor said, backing up. "No! This can't be!"

"Face it Doc. You lose," I said. "You are a brilliant woman. You've created something that could really help people. A drug that could cure muscle-related injuries, make the blind see. Hell, it could even be used to treat AIDS and cancer. But this villain thing is so not you."

"You don't know me!" she snarled.

"I know you," I said. "You were a straight-A student from Middleton High School, Prom Queen, and captain of the cheerleading squad. You were one of the brightest students there. You got a full ride to MIT and interned with Alley Cat. You're a scientist with a bright future. Don't throw it away for vengeance."

"You don't know what I went through. Who cares if you looked me up on Google? Those facts mean nothing!" she snarled. "I won't let 52 take me!"

"Alice…" I said gently. "Let it go…"

"Never!" she said. "You gambled with 52, Lab Rat! They're after your blood too!"

"We've been dodging them for years. And this time they're on our terms," I said. "We're ready for them this time."

"Ah, that's because of him!" she said dramatically. "You escape through his portals! I know how you Jesters work. I know your plans!" She reached into the seat behind her and drew a strange-looking gun. "Have fun escaping when your magician is too far gone to reach!"

"No!" I cried. She fired a bluish cloud from the gun. I dove in front of the Professor, who looked up with surprise from his phone. I can hardly blame him. Villain speeches get so droll, and she caught us all unawares. I should've known she would have a weapon. The cloud flowed around me, and Professor Magic caught a full blast of it. Dragonman reacted faster. He grabbed the Wizard by the cape and pulled him close. The massive hunter dove out the window, shattering it. I saw his jacket spread into massive black wings as the two glided down to the field. I saw Alvarez totter out the door, wobbling on her stilt-like heels. I leapt after her. I could hear the FBI clashing with the barbarians, and my suit was picking up on whiffs of tear gas. They were getting closer.

Alice was never good with heels, and I caught up to her in seconds. I grabbed her and slammed her against the wall.

"What did you do to him!?" I demanded. She cackled, her eyes tearing at the encroaching tear gas.

"Little something I whipped up on the side," she said maliciously. "A mix of peyote and psilocybin. You won't be going anywhere while his mind is on Jupiter."

"You bitch…" I snarled.

"If I'm going down, so are you," she said. Her tongue started working something in her molars.

"I'll see you in hell, Lab Rat," she hissed. I ejected my helmet and slammed my lips onto hers. I sucked in, my mouth filling with the bitter almondy taste of cyanide. Once I had it all in my mouth, I spat it out onto the floor. She blinked up at my face in shock.

"You…" she said.

"I'm not gonna let you die, not like that," I said. "You still have a lot to answer for." I gave her a quick jab in the head to knock her out. I didn't want to give her a chance to recognize me. I put my helmet back on and set her down on the ground. I replaced my helmet just in time for an FBI agent to reach me.

"Freeze!" he shouted, his voice muffled by his gas mask. I activated my cloaking device and ran down the stairs. Live ammunition peppered the wall and floor behind me, but I was long gone. I hoped that Alice would survive it.

I really hate losing friends.

Chapter 8: Dude, Where's My Portal?

"Rat!" Dragonman called out. I reappeared next to him.

"How is he?" I asked, checking the Professor. His eyes were wide open, and his pupils dilated to the size of dinner plates.

"Whoa…" he said, looking around. "Is this Hollywood?"

"Oh no," I said.

"Yeah," Dragonman said. "He didn't get that much of it, but he's out of it."

"Down there!" one of the FBI agents yelled. Even muffled by her gas mask, I recognized the voice of Agent Mary Kane. "After them!"

"Shit!" I said. "We need to move!"

"No kidding!" Dragonman said. "They have the place surrounded, and my aura won't keep us hidden."

"We need a diversion," I said. "You take the Professor to the van, I'll handle 52."

"How?"

"Like this," I said. I held out my hand towards the encroaching squad of agents and triggered a hack. 'We like to Party' by the Vengaboys blasted in their earpieces.

"Is that…?" Dragonman asked, his super hearing picking up on the sound.

"Go!" I said, hitting him in the back. We sprinted towards the parking lot. Dragonman charged ahead, crashing through two stunned agents like bowling pins. I sprinted behind him, the servos in my armor wheezing to keep up with him. The agents were recovering, and started after us. Dragonman slowed as we approached the van. I fired it up remotely from my suit. I jumped into the driver seat and floored it. Dragonman jumped in the open door and slammed the van shut. We raced out the parking lot, two FBI vans hot on our tails.

"How long does that hack work?" Dragonman asked.

"Until the song ends," I said. "About three minutes."

"Shit," he said. "Professor, we need a portal now!"

"A what?" Professor Magic asked.

"Come on, man!" I said, looking back at him. "Get us out of here!"

"RAT!" Dragonman exclaimed. I looked up to see massive, armored truck pull into the road ahead of us.

"Shit!" I said. I tried to stop and turn, but I did it too sharply. The van tilted and fell, toppling to the side and rolling. I had forgotten my seatbelt, and apparently so had Dragonman.

"The Mushrooms!" Professor Magic cried with joy. "They're planning something!"

"Shit!" I cried. We slammed into the armored truck. Thankfully, my forcefield was activated. I was dizzy but unharmed.

"You guy okay?" I asked. Dragonman gave a thumbs up and groaned in pain. He had instinctively wrapped himself around the Wizard and kept him safe. I climbed out of the door and onto the street. The van was wrecked, but I could fix it. Probably.

"Jesters!" Agent Kane called. The two vans had caught up to us and agents were filing out, weapons drawn. Agent Kane climbed out and removed her helmet.

"You've got some nerve, calling us to do your dirty work like that," she said.

"Hey, it's the responsible thing to do, right?" I asked. "Call the authorities, right?"

"Yeah, and I fully intend to bring you in!" she said. "Surrender and come quietly."

"I don't think you know us very well," I said. "We don't *do* quietly."

"I'm going to the MOOOOOON!" Professor Magic shouted, and opened a portal. I wasn't going to waste this moment. I grabbed the wizard and dove in. We were barely in when Dragonman yelled.

"Duck!" I looked up to see the van come sailing in after us. I yelped and forced Professor Magic's head down as it sailed over us. Dragonman leapt in after us.

"Get them!" Agent Kane shrieked.

"Bye bye, knights in shining armor!" Professor Magic said, waving goodbye and blowing kisses at the FBI agents. The portal closed, and the last thing I saw there was Agent Kane looking furious, her arm reaching out before the portal slammed shut.

"That was close," I said. "Way too close."

"You're telling me," Dragonman said. "Sorry for throwing the van at you. We couldn't just leave it behind."

"It's fine," I said. "Where are we, anyways?" I looked around. It was some sort of cave.

"I think…" Dragonman said, sniffing around. "I think we're in Nidavellier."

"Where?" I asked.

"The Realm of the Dwarves," he said.

"Dwarves?" I said. "Like in the *Hobbit*?"

"Pretty much, but darker," he said. "No one comes here anymore."

"Why not?"

"This place closed itself off after Ragnarök," Dragonman explained. "Of all the realms, they were the most unaffected by it."

"I thought Ragnarök was the end of the world," I said. Dragonman picked up Professor Magic and gently started leaving him down a tunnel.

"Not exactly. The Norse gods wiped themselves out ages ago," Dragonman said. "By the time the Norsemen discovered their ruins and temples, they had been long dead."

"Wow," I said. "So, the prophecy of Ragnarök…"

"Wasn't a prophecy. It was an account from the survivors," Dragonman said.

"Survivors?"

"Some of the gods made it out. Magni and Modi were two that did, the sons of Thor. I've heard rumors that Odin pulled through as well."

"Anyone else?" I asked.

"I can't remember off the top of my head," Dragonman said. "But we need to find our way out of here."

"So, how similar are the dwarves in modern fantasy to the ones in mythology?"

"Very similar," Dragonman said.

"So, they probably won't like a bunch of outsiders just showing up here, would they?"

"Seeing how they haven't had any contact with the other realms for millennia, no. I don't think they would," Dragonman said. "And of course, our only ticket home is currently high as a kite!"

"Dragonman, this place is dark," Professor Magic said. "Have I ever told you two how much I love you guys?"

"Plenty of times," Dragonman snapped at him. "Lab Rat?"

"Yeah?"

"We don't tell the girls about this."

"Why not?"

"Because Blue Fox won't like that we got the Professor high, and Silverbolt is going to want some for herself."

"What about Thundergirl?" I asked.

"We almost got caught by 52 because he's on drugs," Dragonman said, jerking his head towards the Professor, who was playing with his cape and giggling. "We'll never hear the end of it."

"Yeah, this ain't good," I said. "So, what are the dwarves like?"

"They were master smiths and craftsmen," Dragonman said. "They made the best weapons and armor in Norse mythology. So…" he froze. I frowned and followed his gaze. My jaw dropped as well. The cave opened up to a massive area showing a city straight out of a cyberpunk movie. Neon lights lit up the cavern, and towers reached up to the ceiling, all emitting holographic advertisements in a language I couldn't read.

"Holy shit," I said.

"That's what they've been up to," Dragonman breathed. "Should've guessed it." I stared in awe. It was breathtaking. A race of people with technology thousands of years ahead of us. It was beautiful. Terrifying. Awe-inspiring. I heard a rumbling next to us, and we turned to see the cavern wall collapse next to us. Behind it was a large yellow drill machine, like construction equipment back on Earth. I could barely see who was inside the cockpit, but they didn't look very tall. I heard shouting in some foreign language, and short stocky figures charged past the drill machine. I heard the familiar clicking of guns.

"Oh fuck," I said. The dwarves opened fire and we bolted.

Dragonman and I sprinted down the corridors, the uneven terrain threatening to trip us at every step. One of the bullets whistled past me and shattered part of the wall next to me like a grenade.

"They're using explosive rounds!"

"I noticed!" Dragonman said. "Professor, we need a portal! Now!"

"Your beard is so smooth..." he said, massaging Dragonman's beard.

"Now!" Dragonman said. His foot caught on the rocky ground.

"Dragonman!" I yelped. I slowed to help him up.

"Go!" he said. "Get the Professor out of here!" A bullet hit him in the shoulder. The dragonhide held, but his shoulder broke under the impact.

"Go!" He repeated. Dragonman turned to face the encroaching dwarves and spat a column of fire at them. They slowed, and seemed daunted by the sudden heat and light.

"Professor, we need to get back home," I said. "Come on, man."

"Home?" he asked.

"Yes, home! We can have tea, and watch *Doctor Who*, and… uh… do other British things!"

"I'm British."

"Yes you are," I agreed. "But you're going to be dead soon if we don't leave." I glanced back. Dragonman was holding them off with blasts of dragonfire, but the dwarves were testing themselves against it. I had a feeling their armor could withstand it, somehow.

"The mushrooms!" Professor Magic said, staring back at the dwarves. "They're onto us!"

"Yes!" I said. "We can't let them catch us!"

"Not today, mushrooms!" Professor Magic shouted, then raised his hands.

"Yes!" I said. "That's it!"

"ARBORAS MAXIMA!" he cried. A massive wall of wood formed between his hands.

"No!" I shouted. "Not that!"

"Die, mushrooms!" he shouted, and the wood rocketed towards the dwarves. It landed between Dragonman and the dwarves. We heard saws cutting and drills firing up.

"Shit!" Dragonman said. He blasted it with fire, burning the dwarves who were cutting through it.

"Professor, you jackass!" I shouted. "We need a portal!"

"Of course we do, why didn't you tell me?" Professor Magic said.

"Seriously!?" I demanded. Professor Magic raised his staff and it started to glow like a blue nebula.

"Midgard!" he cried, and a portal opened, showing us our living room.

"Go!" I said, and shoved him through it.

"And that's when you saw us," Lab Rat said. "Smoking and covered in soot."

"Wow," I said. "That's one hell of a story."

"No kidding," Lab Rat said. "It was a hell of a night."

"You're immune to cyanide?" I asked.

"I'm immune to most things, but cyanide does affect me. It's why I had to spit it out so fast."

"Dude, not swallowing cyanide doesn't need an explanation," I said. "It's poison for the rest of us."

"Right," he said. He looked distracted.

"So, about this Alvarez girl," I said. He winced.

"She was a monster. Nothing like the girl I knew," he said.

"I meant her boss," I said. "Did you ever find out who they were?"

"No," Lab Rat said. "But she was willing to die for him."

"That's unsettling," I said. "Do you think he's behind the other attacks?"

"You mean the Ringleader and the Pastor?"

"Yeah."

"I do. 100%," he said. We were quiet for a bit.

"You gonna be okay?" I asked. "It's not every day your first tries to kill you and then herself."

"I'm fine," he said. "I appreciate the concern, but I'm fine." He pulled out his phone and started texting on it.

"Who are you texting?" I asked.

"Maria, that waitress from Juarez," he said. "I told her I'd call her."

"Really?" I said.

"Of course," he said with a small smile.

"Well, don't let Blue find out. She'll start encouraging you to go all the way with her," I warned.

"Honestly, that doesn't sound too bad to me," Lab Rat said. "After all, she has *very* nice legs."

THE END

www.ingramcontent.com/pod-product-compliance
Lightning Source LLC
Chambersburg PA
CBHW060557300726
48975CB00005B/1358